GREY SEER

BLAZING LIGHT SWEPT through Thanquol's vision, banishing the less than magnificent display of his bodyguards as the power of the warpstone surged through his body. The grey seer felt the warlock engineer's body being rolled off of him. The assassin had recovered one of his blades and was struggling to pull the second from the battery lashed across the corpse's back. He turned to snarl at Thanquol, but his expression quickly changed as he saw the glow behind the grey seer's eyes. Like most of his kind, the assassin's glands had been removed so that his scent might not betray him. There was no musk of fear to tease Thanquol's nose, but the grey seer could see the mark of terror in his would-be murderer's eyes. If the power of the warpstone was not intoxicating enough, the fear of his foe was.

By the same author

PALACE OF THE PLAGUE LORD
BLOOD FOR THE BLOOD GOD
MATHIAS THULMANN WITCH HUNTER
RUNEFANG

Also available

GOTREK & FELIX: THE FIRST OMNIBUS
by William King
(Contains books 1-3: *Trollslayer, Skavenslayer* & *Daemonslayer*)

GOTREK & FELIX: THE SECOND OMNIBUS
by William King
(Contains books 4-6: *Dragonslayer, Beastslayer* & *Vampireslayer*)

GOTREK & FELIX: THE THIRD OMNIBUS
by William King and Nathan Long
(Contains books 7-9: *Giantslayer, Orcslayer* & *Manslayer*)

Book 10 – ELFSLAYER
by Nathan Long

A WARHAMMER NOVEL

Thanquol & Boneripper

GREY SEER

C. L. Werner

For Bill King,
who showed the way.

A BLACK LIBRARY PUBLICATION

First published in Great Britain in 2009 by
BL Publishing,
Games Workshop Ltd.,
Willow Road, Nottingham,
NG7 2WS, UK

10 9 8 7 6 5 4 3 2 1

Cover illustration by Ralph Horsley
Map by Nuala Kinrade

A CIP record for this book is available from the British Library.

ISBN 13: 978 1 84416 739 5

Distributed in the US by Simon & Schuster
1230 Avenue of the Americas, New York, NY 10020.

Printed and bound in the US.

THIS IS A DARK age, a bloody age, an age of daemons and of sorcery. It is an age of battle and death, and of the world's ending. Amidst all of the fire, flame and fury it is a time, too, of mighty heroes, of bold deeds and great courage.

AT THE HEART of the Old World sprawls the Empire, the largest and most powerful of the human realms. Known for its engineers, sorcerers, traders and soldiers, it is a land of great mountains, mighty rivers, dark forests and vast cities. And from his throne in Altdorf reigns the Emperor Karl Franz, sacred descendant of the founder of these lands, Sigmar, and wielder of his magical warhammer.

BUT THESE ARE far from civilised times. Across the length and breadth of the Old World, from the knightly palaces of Bretonnia to ice-bound Kislev in the far north, come rumblings of war. In the towering Worlds Edge Mountains, the orc tribes are gathering for another assault. Bandits and renegades harry the wild southern lands of the Border Princes. There are rumours of rat-things, the skaven, emerging from the sewers and swamps across the land. And from the northern wildernesses there is the ever-present threat of Chaos, of daemons and beastmen corrupted by the foul powers of the Dark Gods. As the time of battle draws ever nearer, the Empire needs heroes like never before.

Norsca
Sea of Chaos...
L'Anguille.
Couronne.
The Wasteland.
Marienburg.
Arden forest.
Gisoreux.
Bordeleaux
Bretonnia
Brionne.
Loren forest
Quenelles.

North of Here Lie The
Dreaded Chaos Wastes.

Claws

Erengrad.

Here Be Trolls...

Praag.

middle mountains.

heim.

Kislev

Kislev.

Wolfenburg.

Talabheim

The Empire

dorf.

Karak Kad

Nuln.

The
Moot.

Sylvania.

Dracken
-hof.

Zhufbar.

Averheim.

Black
Water.

Black fire Pass.

k
Norn.

CHAPTER ONE
Something in the Sewers

'FAST-QUICK, FLEA-MAGGOTS!'

The scratchy voice was thin as a whisper, like the rasp of snakeskin against cobblestone, but it carried through the dank, crumbling tunnels like a thunderclap. Scrawny rats with jaundiced eyes and matted fur skittered away, hugging the earthen walls as the fury of the voice moved them to flight.

For others, retreat was an option long ago taken from them. Emaciated creatures nearly as thin as the starveling cave rats, their scarred bodies covered in stringy brown fur, cowered and grovelled but heavy chains of corroded iron forced them to stand their ground. Each of the creatures was a horror of blisters and scabs, their bodies gouged by the violence of whip and fang. Only the most sardonic of observers would liken them to men, though there was a loathsome mockery of man in the shapes they wore. The things that dangled limply from their wasted arms were as much paws as they were hands. Naked tails, scaly and pallid, lashed the floor between their clawed feet. Above the iron collars that circled their necks was a narrow head, pinched and pulled into the rodent-like visage of an enormous rat. Yet even here could be found a gruesome echo of humanity, for it was more than the blind fear of vermin that shone in their beady red eyes, more than the unthinking pain of a simple beast that gave their gaze its stamp of dejected misery.

'Fast-quick!' the voice snarled again. This time the words were punctuated by a loud crack as a scaly whip, like the severed tail of one of the creatures, flashed through the green-shadowed gloom of the tunnel. Something cried out in a wordless shriek that spoke equally of pain and terror. The echoes of the cry had not even started to shudder through the tunnels when the slaves were moving once more, attacking the walls with their clawed hands, slashing and scratching at the earth and rock with frantic desperation.

Kratch coiled the macabre whip around his arm, exulting in the panic of the slaves. Not the slightest twinge of sympathy for the miserable throng moved him; pity was a concept utterly alien to the skaven mind. The slaves existed only to further Kratch's own position and power; beyond that simple fact, Kratch had no concern for them or their suffering. It was the most basic foundation of skaven society: the weak existed to exalt the strong.

Kratch rubbed his white-furred hands together, a pleased gleam in his eyes, as he considered the wisdom of such an arrangement. Perhaps he would have been less pleased had the Horned Rat not smiled so kindly upon Kratch and made him one of the strong. But the skaven god had favoured him, shaping him in the belly of his brood-mother and placing his mark upon Kratch. The ratman lifted a paw to his forehead, stroking the bony nubs protruding through his fur. Horned skaven were the chosen of their god, the voices and instruments of his will. More than the frayed grey robes and warpstone charms he wore, it was his horns that marked Kratch as one of the exalted, one of the grim brotherhood of sorcerer-priests known as the grey seers.

As he stroked his tiny horns, some of the pleasure ceased to sparkle in Kratch's eyes. He had been marked, but he was still far from the magnificence he wanted. Kratch was young, barely eight winters from the whelp-nests, his horns still developing and his magical knowledge small. He was only an adept, an initiate into the secrets of the grey seers, not a grey seer himself. One day he would wield such power, but until then he would be an apprentice, serving those who Kratch knew were his inferiors for all their horns and magic.

Kratch looked away from the frantic slaves, casting an appraising glance over his shoulder at his current 'master'. Grey Seer Skabritt was several times again as old as Kratch, his horns grown into a double-curled knot of bone that encased the sides of the priest's head like a helmet. Skabritt fancied himself a cunning strategist and plotter, weaving a nest of intrigue and deception to cloak his activities from his many rivals and enemies, but Kratch knew he could do so much more with Skabritt's resources and power.

The adept lashed his tail in annoyance. Looking at Skabritt caused Kratch's blood to boil with resentment. The grey seer stood well away from where the slaves were working, surrounded on all sides by his armoured stormvermin. The big black-furred skaven kept an easy grip on their halberds when they weren't scratching fleas from their fur. So very like Skabritt to spare himself any chance of danger. Distance would protect him from any cave-in that might result from the attentions of the work gang on the crumbling walls. The stormvermin would guard him against the unlikely, but possible event of a slave revolt. The armoured ratmen would cut down any berserk slaves long before they could lay a paw on Skabritt.

However, such hazards were perfectly acceptable for Kratch to be exposed to. The skaven gnashed his fangs as he reflected on that fact. Skabritt had insisted it would be a good learning experience for his apprentice, something to bolster his abilities to command and lead the unwashed masses of the Under-Empire. More pragmatically, Skabritt could always get another apprentice if something went wrong.

'Fast-quick!' Kratch growled, spinning back around and striking out with his whip. He wasn't sure if the brown-furred wretch he struck had really been slacking off and didn't really care. Lurking about in this forsaken network of burrows – burrows that had been sealed off since the skaven civil war – was far from Kratch's idea of safety and comfort. The number of stormvermin Grey Seer Skabritt brought along, and the amount of warpstone tokens he had spent in the markets of Under-Altdorf arming them, told Kratch that his mentor expected trouble. That Skabritt had not shared from what quarter he expected that trouble didn't do much to reassure Kratch.

Still, the adept reflected, Skabritt would hardly put himself at risk for some miniscule gain. Whatever he hoped to find in the abandoned burrows the slaves were excavating, it would be something of importance. Perhaps some lost cache of warpstone or a lost trove of

Clan Skryre technology. Kratch began to salivate as he considered the magnitude of such a find. Skabritt would earn the favour of the seerlords and the Council of Thirteen itself presenting them with such a treasure. Or perhaps he would instead choose to deal with a single clan, tempting them with the power his discovery would offer them. Under-Altdorf was a nest of intrigue already, each of its dominant clans striving against the others for control of the city, the largest in the entire Under-Empire with the exception of Skavenblight itself. Clan Skryre would pay well for anything that would tip the balance in their favour, just as the other clans would pay to keep such power from slipping into their paws.

Whatever Skabritt chose to do, Kratch would be there, clinging to his tail every step of the way. Even if only the smallest portion of the wealth and glory Skabritt was after trickled down to his apprentice, Kratch would take it. Unless of course he saw some way to cut his mentor out of the equation. Accidents did sometimes happen, like the time a swamp troll had broken free in the mines beneath Rat Rock and nearly devoured the grey seer. In the right paws, a sharp file and a rusty chain were as deadly as any assassin's poisoned dagger.

A sharp squeal of alarm stirred Kratch from his murderous visions. The adept cracked his whip against one of the slaves, slashing through its mangy hide, then wrinkled his snout in disgust. The workers were venting the musk of fear from their glands. Kratch fought back the instinctive response to do the same, his contempt for the wretches overcoming the tyranny of biology.

The slaves were skulking away from the wall of the tunnel. Kratch could see a dark opening where the bloodied paws of the skaven had broken through into a sealed chamber. A murky, stagnant odour wafted from the opening, overcoming even the pungent musk of the frightened slaves. Kratch felt a tremor of anxiety as his senses drank in the cold, evil smell. He quickly calmed himself. Anything with such an intimidating stench would also be obscenely powerful. His thoughts turned to visions of some lost trove of warpstone quietly festering away in the dark for six centuries and again his jaws became moist with anticipation. There was certainly a suggestion of warpstone about the clammy stench issuing from the darkness.

Kratch started to scramble down from his perch atop a pile of loose earth. Sounds behind him had the adept spinning about in alarm, one paw slipping to the dagger concealed in the sleeve of his robe. A gruff snarl froze Kratch's hand. The adept winced, screwing his eyes shut and lifting his head, exposing his throat in deference and humility to the creature he called master.

Grey Seer Skabritt had been drawn from his cautious observation point well away from the excavation by the clammy smell issuing from the opening. There was a feverish light shining in the priest's eyes as he shuffled forward, his stormvermin flanking him.

'Yes-yes,' Skabritt chortled, clapping his paws together. 'Mine it is! Power-strength! The Wormstone belongs to Skabritt!' The grey seer's eyes narrowed with suspicion, casting a hostile glance at slaves, stormvermin and apprentice alike. In his injudicious enthusiasm he had let too much slip off his tongue. The priest seemed to almost swell with malignity as he drew energy into himself, his eyes glassing over with a greenish film of light. After a moment, he allowed the energy to dissipate, satisfied that none of those around him knew of what he spoke. The ignorance of his minions filled

Skabritt with contempt. There was no danger such wretches could pose to him.

Kratch was careful to maintain his subservient poise, to keep any suggestion of his thoughts away from Skabritt's keen nose and penetrating gaze. The grey seer's scrutiny of his apprentice lasted only a moment, then he was turning his attention back on the tunnel. Skabritt was growing forgetful with his years. He had forgotten the apprentice who had scoured the records of Under-Altdorf for him, sniffing out any mention of the war with the plague priests of Clan Pestilens and the doom of Clan Mawrl. He had forgotten the many weeks Kratch had spent poring over the rat-hide scrolls and their cramped lines of hieroglyphs. Skabritt had forgotten that everything he knew about the Wormstone, his apprentice had learned first.

Stormvermin kicked and bullied their way through the huddled throng of cowering slaves as Skabritt ordered them forward. Warpstone lanterns were pulled down from the crumbling walls, casting the tunnel into blackness. Kratch scurried after the light, not trusting the darkness to guard him against the attentions of a vengeful slave. He crept after the rearmost of the stormvermin as Skabritt entered the exposed chamber.

The light from the lanterns warred against the centuried darkness that filled the burrow, casting green shadows against the dripping walls. The burrow was not large, its other entrances as choked with rubble as the one Skabritt's slaves had broken through. The other clans of Under-Altdorf had been most thorough in their plot to bury Clan Mawrl alive. Evidence of how successful they had been was littered all across the floor. The bones of hundreds, perhaps even thousands of skaven were scattered everywhere. Even a cursory glance told Kratch that something had fed off the dead, the marks of fangs clearly visible on the bones, though whether the damage had been done by common vermin or fellow skaven was impossible to determine.

Kratch quickly dismissed the question, his focus shifting to the object standing almost in the exact centre of the burrow. Here the skeletons were at their thickest, piled about the object as though seeking succour from it in the long hours of their slow deaths. Kratch's fur crawled as he looked at it, as its evil smell hammered at his senses. Yet even in the midst of his fear, he could not deny the fierce desire and awful hunger the thing provoked in him.

A sickly yellow haze surrounded the Wormstone. The artefact was the size of a skaven, the colour of swamp slime laced with veins of pitch-black. Two hundred pounds if it was an ounce, the smell that came off it told Kratch what formed the bulk of its composition. Warpstone, the sorcerous rock that was the very foundation of skaven civilisation. It was food, power, wealth and more to the ratkin, used to power their technology, feed their brood-mothers and fuel their industry. A piece of warpstone the size of the find he now gazed upon was more wealth than any but the strongest clan-leaders and sorcerers could ever expect to possess.

There was something more in the scent of the Wormstone, something that reminded Kratch of what he had read. The warning checked the adept's greed, and he backed away from the glowing rock.

The stormvermin, however, were ignorant of the Wormstone's history. Two of them rushed forwards, snapping and spitting at each other as they rushed for the massive shard of glowing rock. One of the ratmen slashed his paw across the other's face, staggering his rival as black blood spurted down his forehead. For an instant, it seemed that Grey Seer Skabritt might intervene, but then the priest's face pulled back in a gruesome sneer. Skabritt was a big believer in object lessons: the more ghastly the better.

The foremost stormvermin covered the last few yards between him and the Wormstone with a fierce pounce, his teeth bared in challenge to any who would contest his new possession. Skabritt's tail twitched with amusement as the defiant warrior stretched his arm around the massive rock. Instantly he cried out with a pained squeak, leaping away in terror. Kratch could see the same ghoulish light that surrounded the Wormstone now glowing around the stormvermin's arm. Was it a trick of shadow, or were there really gigantic maggots burrowing into the warrior's fur?

The stormvermin was scratching and tearing at himself now, his body twitching in a fit of agony. The ratman whose eyes he had nearly scratched out snickered and drew his sword. No thought of seizing the tainted Wormstone now, but the stormvermin could still glut his need for revenge against his treacherous rival.

As the avenger approached the twitching wretch, the stricken stormvermin reared up, lunging at his rival with paws spread wide. Kratch realised with revulsion that the sick skaven wasn't attacking, he was appealing for succour. The swordsrat backed away in revulsion, horrified by the squirming ripples beneath the sick skaven's fur. He wasn't fast enough; the paw of the maddened wretch struck his foot, leaving a touch of the glowing taint on his clawed toes.

The swordsrat shrieked and brought his blade smashing down. The sick skaven's head burst open like an overripe melon, exploding into greasy quarters. From the grisly mush, fat green worms plopped and slithered.

The watching skaven vented their glands at the sickening sight. Several stormvermin braced their halberds, pointing the blades at the now infected swordsrat, trying to keep both him and the glowing worms in view. Kratch began trolling through his mind for a spell that would guard him against the ghastly magic he had witnessed, prayers to the Horned Rat rasping through his fangs.

Skabritt was unmoved, however. A fiendish, exultant light was in his eyes now. 'This,' the sorcerer hissed, 'this is the weapon that makes Skabritt seerlord!'

His master's words had barely registered with Kratch before the adept's attention was riveted once more upon the Wormstone. The bones piled behind the relic were moving, heaving and undulating like a boiling pool of pitch. A new scent imposed itself upon his snout, a thick beastly reek like an orc abattoir after a hot summer day mixed with the stink of wet rat ogre.

The stormvermin were too preoccupied with fending off their infected comrade, jabbing at him with the points of their halberds, trying to keep him back without puncturing his hide and spilling more glowing worms onto the floor of the burrow. They did not see the pile of bones rise up, did not see the old gnawed skeletons crash back to the floor as something immense and monstrous shook them from its peeling hide.

What it was, Kratch did not know. He suspected such a thing had no name. It was immense, bigger even than the blind burrowers that Clan Moulder used to expand the caverns of the Under-Empire. There was certainly the suggestion of rat in its overall shape, a loathsome bulk that conspired at once to appear both bloated and emaciated. Patches of piebald fur clung to random bits of its anatomy; the rest was leprous and dripping. Its paws were oversized, like those of a snow bear, and tipped with more talons than it had toes. The head was withered to the point of being almost skeletal and the eyes that stared from either side of its peeling snout were swollen and pale. It lashed its tail against the floor and scrabbled forwards, darting to the carcass of the slain ratman.

Now the stormvermin could not fail to notice the monster. They froze, eyes wide with fright as they stared at the imposing beast. The rat-thing ignored the warriors, instead snuffling at the floor, licking green maggots into its maw with its thin slimy tongue. The stormvermin backed away from the feeding monster, nearly trampling Kratch in their slow retreat.

Along with the healthy warriors, the infected swordsrat also withdrew from the monster, visibly shivering as he watched it feed. The sick skaven blundered into one of his former comrades. Instantly the stormvermin cried out, slashing the swordsrat from throat to belly with his halberd. Glowing worms oozed from the wound, slapping against the floor like greasy raindrops.

The sound caused the enormous rat-beast to lift its skeletal head. The monster sniffed at the air, then its jaws opened in a sharp hiss. Before any of the skaven could turn to run, the beast leapt across the burrow and was in their midst. Giant claws ripped and tore the tight knot of warriors, shredding armour like paper. Squeals of terror and agony became deafening as the smell of blood enraged the beast still further, provoking it into a frenzied state.

Kratch didn't wait to see anything else. The adept dived from the burrow, scurrying on all fours in his haste to flee. In the tunnel, the panicked slaves were struggling to rip the iron spikes that anchored their chains to the crumbling walls from their earthen fastenings. When they saw Kratch, some of them abandoned their efforts, turning instead toward the savage taskmaster. Several leapt at him, tearing the empty air with their bloodied paws as they reached the limit of their chains.

Kratch backed away from the maddened slaves, but found his retreat blocked by something warm and furry. Grey Seer Skabritt's scent held an unfamiliar taint of fear, but Kratch still recognised the smell. He lifted his gaze to the sorcerer-priest. Like the stormvermin, Skabritt's eyes were wide with fear. Unlike the warriors, however, fear was not the only thing Kratch saw in his mentor's stare. He saw anger, the smouldering fury of a mad genius who at the moment of triumph sees his prize stolen from him.

Then Skabritt's eyes were changing, glossing over with a greenish luminance as he drew upon the arcane power of the Horned Rat and the warpstone talisman he clutched in his fist. Kratch could feel tendrils of energy oozing into his brain, trying to smother his thoughts. It took all of his own willpower and sorcerous knowledge to drive them back, to free his mind of their numbing touch. The adept slumped to the floor, physically drained by the effort of resisting Skabritt's spell.

The slaves were not so fortunate. From the ground, Kratch could see them grow still. Fear withered from their eyes, dispelled by a green glow that was an eerie echo of Skabritt's own charged gaze. When the grey seer gestured, the mob stirred, pulling once again at their chains and the iron staples anchoring them to the walls. This time, however, they did not attack the task as a disordered rabble but rather as a unified body guided by a single will: that of Skabritt. One after another, the combined strength of the slaves tore the staples from the walls.

The last staple came free just in time for Skabritt. The sounds of carnage and slaughter had faded from the burrow. In the exposed mouth of the chamber, its mangy pelt smeared in the black blood and yellow fat of the stormvermin, the rat-beast snarled and spat. Skabritt spun about, glaring at the loathsome creature and pointed a clawed finger at the monster.

At his command, the ensorcelled slaves surged forward, a chittering mass of claws and fangs. Like a furry tide, they crashed upon the rat-beast, crushing it beneath their sheer weight of numbers, bowling it over and slamming it into the crumbling wall of the tunnel. Earth and rock showered down from the ceiling, throwing dust into the musty air.

The rat-beast fought back, disembowelling slaves with every turn of its massive paws, snapping spines with its iron jaws. For all their numbers, for all the grey seer's magic, the stink of fear began to rise from the tangled knot of skaven sweeping over the monster. Skabritt gave voice to an inarticulate howl in which was both terror and outraged fury. The sorcerer-priest scurried forwards, desperate to reinforce his hypnotic control of the craven slaves.

Kratch watched the grey seer rush closer to the battle and his mouth pulled back in a predatory smile. He pulled a small piece of blackish-green rock from beneath his robes, a tiny sliver of refined warpstone. The adept's teeth gnawed at the rock, letting little bits of stony grit burn their way down his throat and through his body. Now it was Kratch's eyes that began to glow with an unholy light, the apprentice's brain that roared with the mighty power of the Horned Rat. Kratch could feel his body pulse with strength, swell with godlike vitality. He felt the essence of the warpstone flow through his entire being, hearing its seductive whisper crawl through his flesh.

It was almost worse than Skabritt's spell, fighting down the euphoric mania of the warpstone, but Kratch knew if he lost control now, his opportunity would be lost. That cold, ugly fact helped him maintain a grip on his reason. He forced his eyes to focus on the rat-beast and the slaves, on Skabritt now standing so very close to the fray.

On the crumbling walls and weak ceiling of the tunnel.

It seemed so easy. A few words, a few gestures, and the primordial power that raced through his body was reaching out. Like a great hammer, it smashed against the walls, it battered against the ceiling. A deafening roar thundered through the tunnel. In that last instant, Skabritt turned, locking eyes with his apprentice.

Kratch grinned back, baring his fangs in challenge to his hated mentor. Then thousands of tons of earth and rock came crashing down, obliterating Skabritt's expression of disbelief. Grey Seer, slaves and rat-beast, all were buried in the collapse.

Kratch coughed, spitting dirt from his mouth, choking on the dust that filled the tunnel and stifled the warpstone lanterns. He wiped at his almost blind eyes, even as he was pressing a rag to his snout to act as a filter for his nose. Briefly, Kratch considered waiting to see if the entrance to the burrow had remained intact. Skabritt was not the only skaven who could put the Wormstone to good purpose.

It was the memory of the stormvermin who had been infected by the Wormstone's power rather than the dust and dirt that made Kratch decide to flee. He would not brave such a fate as he had seen. He would let others take those risks.

Yes, Kratch decided as he scurried through the raw, desolate tunnels, he would need helpers if he wanted to recover the Wormstone and reap the rewards of such a find. Kratch's muzzle dripped as he salivated in anticipation of those rewards. He knew where to find his allies. He knew where his report about Skabritt's discovery would benefit him the most.

'STOP YOUR WHINING or get an honest job!' growled Hans Dietrich for what felt like the hundredth time since they had set out from the docks. It was a serious threat to make against men like those who lumbered after him through the stinking, dripping corridors. Most of them had been born one kind of thief or another. Compared to their past activities, smuggling was an almost legitimate enterprise, if no less dangerous. There were stiff penalties for bringing contraband into Altdorf. Everyone from the Emperor downwards took a dim view of cheating the excisemen, though nobody really seemed to mind that it was the excisemen who were the biggest thieves. Popular theory on the wharves was that if even half the money the excisemen collected on goods coming into the capital actually were to go where it was supposed to, Karl Franz would be able to buy back Marienburg.

Reviled villains, the excisemen were everywhere on the waterfront, and if they weren't around, then there was always the chance that some wrinkle-faced old charwoman or bleary-eyed stevedore was employed by one, acting as their eyes and ears. The Fish, probably the most notorious of the waterfront gangs, took especial pleasure in floating such toadies in the river. Still, there was always someone desperate enough to take a few coppers from an exciseman, whatever the risks.

Which was why men in Hans's profession avoided the wharfs and the streets. There was another, surer way to navigate the swarming, crowded warren that was Altdorf, and do so completely unseen. The sewers of Altdorf were the biggest in the Empire, if not the entire Old World. Built by the dwarfs so long ago that some said Sigmar's water was the first to christen them, the sewers existed as an unseen underworld, ignored and forgotten by nearly all who prowled the streets above. Sewerjacks and ratcatchers, maybe the odd mutant hiding from the witch hunters, but largely no one bothered the sewers or even thought about doing so. Far from prying eyes and wagging tongues, the sewers were more than a filthy nest of scummy brickwork and walls dripping with slime to Hans: they were his secret road to anywhere in the city.

There were dangers, to be sure. Sewer rats grew to the size of small dogs and were infamous for their ferocity and the filthy diseases they carried. There were the grisly water lizards brought back from the Southlands for Emperor Boris Goldgather, which had escaped the Imperial Menagerie to slink and stalk through the humid damp of the tunnels. Hans himself had seen one of the things once, pale as the belly of a fish and with a tail thick enough to choke an ox.

Then there were the floods, when the reservoir beneath Altdorf would overflow and dump its spillage for the sewers to cast the excess into the Reik. There was little warning when these floods would rush through the tunnels; only by watching the rats could a man find any hint of alarm. If the rats started scrambling for the surface, the smart man was right behind them. Hans cursed the fiendish cunning of the dwarfs; no human would have thought of using the reservoir as a means to clean the tunnels. He cast a nervous look at one of the grimy chutes that yawned in the wall, somewhat reassured to find a big black rat staring back at him from the muck, its whiskers twitching as it gnawed on some nameless filth clutched in its hand-like paws.

'Are we there yet?' the thin, reedy voice of Kempf called out from the rear of the little procession. There were ten men in Hans's little gang, just big enough to keep their cut of the merchandise lucrative, but too small to bounce anyone from the mob. Even an annoying weasel like Kempf.

'You seen the mark?' Hans snarled back, turning around to glare at Kempf. Like the rest of the smugglers, Kempf was dressed in a grimy set of homespun and wool that was only slightly too good to be called rags. Kempf affected a goatskin coat two sizes too big for him, the garment hanging well below his knees while a gaudy scarf circled his throat, hiding an Adam's apple so big the man looked like he'd swallowed a goblin.

Kempf lifted his hands in a placating gesture, causing Hans to roll his eyes. Kempf had an ugly habit of excusing himself from all the heavy work. While the rest of the men laboured under the weight of a half-dozen casks of bootleg Reikland hock from Carroburg, Kempf had conned his comrades into posting him as rearguard to keep a wary eye out for sewerjacks... or worse.

'Maybe we passed it,' Kempf suggested, visibly cringing when he saw the reaction on Hans's face. The reedy smuggler bobbed his head like a punch-drunk stork and started a bout of his braying, nasal laughter. 'I know, I know,' he said. 'You keep a good eye out for the marks. Nobody says you don't. I mean, that's why you're the leader.' Kempf's thin face spread in a toothy smile that was both ingratiating and smarmy. 'But, I mean, everyone makes mistakes.'

Hans scowled at the rearguard, sucking at his teeth as he imagined burying his fist in that smug smile. He counted to ten, then reversed the numbers. His brother was always on him about his temper. They'd lost a few clients and quite a few men because Hans didn't keep a tight leash on his tongue. More than a few of their enemies had started that way by being on the receiving end of Hans's ire. Someday, Johann was always warning him, his temper was going to get all of them into more trouble than they could handle.

Hans looked away from Kempf and gave Johann an exasperated look. His brother was younger but taller and more muscular, his features handsome in a rugged sort of way that had all the girls at Argula Cranach's making cow-eyes at him and offering discounts. His leather tunic, despite years of abuse and crude mending, still managed to constrain his brawny build. Hair the colour of old corn was cropped close to the skull, starkly contrasting eyes as cold and blue as the waters of the Upper Reik.

Johann had inherited all the better qualities. Hans was short, his unimposing build fading to fat, his left ear swollen out of proportion thanks to the impact of a Reiksguard's bludgeon during the Window Tax riots many years ago. His nose was crooked, bent into its current asymmetrical fashion by the fist of a dock-ganger from the Hooks. His hair was a scraggly brown mop, like some disordered bird's nest threatening to burst from beneath his battered felt hat. It wasn't just looks that Johann had won out on. The younger brother was smarter, stronger, more cautious, less emotional and decidedly braver. What Johann lacked, what his older brother provided, was ambition.

Starve or steal was a simple choice to make for the people who inhabited the waterfront. The Dietrich brothers had chosen to steal, at first petty acts of thuggery that yielded petty results. There wasn't much coin to be had rolling drunks as they stumbled out of the Orc and Axe. The real money was to be had by smuggling, sneaking goods from river trader to city merchant without the excisemen interfering.

They'd been profiting well from the venture, too. Even with his hot temper, Hans had a steady cadre of clients quite willing to put up with him for the sake of avoiding usurious duties and customs. Johann had scouted out a large section of the sewer over the course of several months, making marks in chalk and soot where the walls of the stinking tunnels corresponded with some important landmark above. By watching for the marks, the smugglers always knew where they were and where they needed to go.

Only Hans hadn't seen any marks for quite some time now. Far too long, now that he thought about it. He didn't like to give any credence to one of Kempf's slippery suggestions, but the sneak might be right this time. Maybe he had missed something.

Before he could speak, Hans saw Johann's eyes narrow into a suspicious squint. Slowly, the younger Dietrich began to lower his cask of cheap Carroburg booze.

'Something's wrong,' Johann said, his voice low. His hand dropped to a weapon belt that was in far better shape than his tunic, fingers tightening about the grip of his dagger.

'Who...' but Hans had no need to finish his question. Torches blazed into life from the sewer tunnel up ahead. More lights burst into flame from the cross-tunnels to either side. Dark silhouettes moved through the blackness, naked steel reflecting the flickering flames. Hans felt his stomach turn as he decided that the sewerjacks had finally caught them. In the next moment, he found himself wishing they were sewerjacks.

'The Dietrich boys,' a deep voice growled, a voice Hans and any other scoundrel on the waterfront knew only too well. Gustav Volk. In a district infamous for casual violence and brutality, Gustav Volk was a name held in fear. As the speaker stepped out of the shadows, Hans reflected that it wasn't size or strength that made Volk so feared, the man possessed neither in such abundance as to overwhelm the feral courage of rakes and thieves. It was the face – that grizzled scowl with its stubbly hair and heavy brow. Volk carried an expression that could make a wolf pass water. It burned in his eyes, the pitiless rage looking for any excuse to allow the man to do his absolute worst to his victim and enjoy every screaming, bloody minute of it.

Volk oozed out from the darkness, accompanied by a bull-necked bruiser carrying a torch. Other thugs followed close behind. Volk looked the smugglers up and down, his lip curled in scorn. 'Quite an accomplishment,' he snarled. 'Your operation has become big enough to become annoying to Herr Klasst. Bad news for you.' To add emphasis to his statement, Volk slapped the hilt of his sword. For the moment, it was sheathed. Nobody was fool enough to think the moment would last.

Klasst. Vesper Klasst. He was even more of a bogeyman to the inhabitants of the waterfront than Volk. A big-scale racketeer and gang-leader, it was said Klasst controlled criminal bands all across Altdorf, from Little Tilea to the Morrwies. After the Fish and the Hooks had been at least partially broken up by the Altdorf Dock Watch in the weeks after the murderous Beast had finally been brought to ground, it was Vesper Klasst who had become the undisputed power on the waterfront. And Gustav Volk was his enforcer, extorting a percentage from every transaction, criminal or legal, that happened in his territory, brutally coercing many of the district's thieves to join Klasst's 'family'.

Hans had resisted Volk's suggestion that his band of smugglers accept the protection of his gang. That meeting had ended with one of Hans's fingers bent so far backward it wasn't so much broken as snapped. It had also ended with Johann's dagger tickling a piece of anatomy Volk wasn't too keen on losing. The last view the brothers had had of Volk was him screaming for a chirurgeon and clutching his blood-soaked breeches. That had been three months ago. They'd been lucky to avoid him so long. Now Ranald had decided their luck was at an end.

'I want the wine,' Volk stated, his tone broaching no argument. 'Then you're going to show me where you were taking it. I'll make a good example of somebody who thinks they can still use independents without Herr Klasst finding out.'

'How do we know you won't just kill us anyway?' Hans challenged.

Volk's smile was as ugly as an orc in a nursery. 'You can die here, slow, or you can die there. I'll have other things to do there, so I'll make it quick.'

Johann pulled his dagger from its sheath. 'How about I just gut you like the pig you are and leave you floating here with the rest of the...'

Hans stared in horror as his brother lunged at Volk. The entire sewer exploded into madness, armed men charging from the darkness to confront the smugglers. Hans dodged the murderous sweep of a boat-hook, driving his elbow into the thug's belly and knocking the wind out of him.

So much for Johann being the level-headed one, Hans thought as he drew his own dagger and joined the fray in earnest.

Six casks of Reikland hock, three dead and two men missing. Johann knew he should be thankful that any of them were still alive, but he still couldn't help but grumble over their losses. They'd accounted for at least two of Volk's gang, but unfortunately he wasn't one of the casualties. Not bad considering they'd been outnumbered three to one. Still, if Volk's men had known the sewers half as well as the smugglers, there was no chance they'd have given the thugs the slip.

Then again, giving them the slip had also put Johann in a situation he hadn't encountered in quite some time: he had no idea where they were. It was more than Volk's men removing marks from the walls – Johann would swear on the Hammer of Sigmar he'd never seen this stretch of tunnel before. He tried to keep his confusion to himself, not wanting to panic the men. He felt that his brother had some inkling as to what was wrong but trusted him to keep quiet.

When they came upon the breach in the sewer wall, however, even the dullest of the surviving smugglers knew something was wrong. The jagged tear in the brickwork, like the yawning mouth of some immense snake, was certainly something they would remember. Johann edged forwards, peering through the opening. He risked lighting a candle. Beyond the breach was a tunnel, raw earthen walls that looked to have been carved out with bare hands rather than tools. There was a foul smell as well, a thick animal stench that even the reek of the sewers couldn't overwhelm.

Hans appeared at his side, staring into the earthen tunnel. He glanced back, watching the fear grow in his small band of thieves.

'We can hide from Volk's gang in here,' Hans proclaimed boldly, gambling that their fear of the unknown wasn't quite so robust as their fear of Gustav Volk.

The gamble played out and soon the entire band of smugglers was creeping through the narrow, winding tunnel. The unsettling sound of earth shifting overhead and the occasional stream of dust falling from the ceiling did nothing to improve their spirits. But it was when the huge Emil Kleiner, a former stevedore before he decided that even so marginally legitimate a profession wasn't to his taste, found the body that things really took a turn for the worse. His ear-battering shriek was such that if any of Volk's gang were still following the smugglers, they could not fail to find their quarry now.

A snarled reprimand died on Johann's lips as he stared down at the ugly, mangled thing that had so terrified Kleiner. The noxious carcass was almost man-sized, dressed in a crude grey robe even the most pathetic of Altdorf's beggars would have refused to be seen in. It was covered in bloodied fur and its appearance, for all its mutilation, was that of a giant rat: a rat that seemed to have thought it was a man!

Frightened whispers came from the circle of smugglers gazing down on the thing. Half-remembered childhood tales of the verminous underfolk and their kidnapping ways rose to the forefront of each man's mind. Several made the signs of Ranald and Sigmar, praying to their gods for deliverance from such mythic nightmares. Even Johann felt the nervous urge to glance down the tunnel, to discover if the dead thing had any of its living fellows about.

Hans bullied his way through the frightened men, sneering with contempt at both their fear and the unnatural corpse that sprawled at their feet. 'Gunndred's noose!' he swore. 'What is wrong with you slack-jawed curs? Never seen a dead mutant before?' Hans punctuated his outburst with a strong kick to the dead thing's horned skull. The corpse rolled obscenely from the impact.

Their leader's outburst rallied the men and nervous laughter echoed in the crumbling tunnel. Hans was right of course, the smugglers decided. The thing was no more than a mutant wretch. Looking like it did, there was small wonder the scum had chosen to hide itself down in the sewers. The only thing remarkable about it was that it had avoided the witch hunters long enough to even reach the sewers.

Underfolk? Bah! Everyone with half a brain knew there was no such thing as the skaven!

The smugglers began following the tunnel once more. The air was dank and foul, leading Johann to believe it didn't lead anywhere, but Hans was more obstinate. They passed carefully around several places that showed signs of recent collapse. Once, a great pool of black blood rewarded their investigation, seeming to seep from beneath a recent cave-in. The men carefully avoided the ominous sign and pressed on.

Not far from the cave-in, the smugglers found a large chamber. If anything, the air was even fouler here. The floor of the cavern was littered with bones and fresh offal, putrid blood splashed everywhere and gobbets of gnawed meat splattered against the walls. A quick inspection told Johann that whatever the place had been, the other tunnels that opened into it had collapsed a long time ago. He tried not to look too closely at the strange bones and furry meat littering the floor.

'Look at that.' The words left Hans's mouth in an awed whisper. The smuggler was staring in open wonder at a huge chunk of greenish stone resting at the centre of the room, glowing faintly with its own inner light. Johann felt his skin crawl just looking at it. He could tell most of the other men felt the same way.

'Black magic,' hissed old Mueller, the eye that hadn't been pulled from its socket by an over-eager river pirate squinting with a mixture of suspicion and loathing. At his words, other smugglers began making the signs of their gods for protection.

'Maybe,' agreed Kempf, 'but have you ever heard of any kind of magic that wasn't worth a fair number of crowns?' The little thief scrambled forwards and joined Hans beside the weird rock. He grinned as he studied the thing, reaching out a hand and scratching at the rock. Kempf sniffed at his finger and his smile broadened.

'Wyrdstone,' Kempf declared. The eyes of every man present grew wide not from fear, but from greed. Wyrdstone was a valuable commodity, so valuable that even the lowest cutpurse knew its worth. A type of rock soaked in magic that, it was said, could do everything from curing shingles to turning lead into gold. It was said to be able to remove wrinkles from the old and build strength in the young. Pigments mixed with wyrdstone dust could allow even the most talentless artist to create a priceless masterpiece, and a single whiff of a wyrdstone poultice was certain protection from the evils of mutation and madness. Those who lusted after wyrdstone insisted it was a different substance from the abhorred warpstone, the raw stuff of Chaos that brought madness and mutation with its touch. Such connections were the delusions of ignorant, superstitious fools in their minds. There was almost nothing alchemists and wizards wouldn't do to possess even a small measure of wyrdstone. What they were looking at was anything but a small measure.

Still, the avarice of the men was tempered by the grim knowledge that few substances in the Empire were as forbidden as wyrdstone. If there was nothing wizards wouldn't do to get some, there was nothing the witch hunters wouldn't do to anyone caught with any. Even for men who daily risked hanging or an indeterminable stay in Mundsen Keep, the thought of what the witch hunters did to heretics was sobering.

Hans stared at the glowing rock for several minutes, then nodded his head slowly. 'Kempf, do you think you could find us a buyer for that thing?'

'One? Why not a dozen?' Kempf replied enthusiastically.

The answer decided Hans. 'Kleiner, Mueller, fetch that thing down. We'll take it back to the hideout.'

The men hesitated, but a sharp look from their leader had the pair lumbering up to the pile of bones and pulling down the heavy rock. They drew frayed rags from their pockets, wrapping them tightly about their faces to fend off any sorcerous fume, wound ribbons of torn cloth about their hands to defend their skin from the touch of magic. Johann felt a shiver pass through him as he saw the green light stretch and grip the arms of the men, casting a diseased pallor across their skin. The men carrying the rock didn't seem to notice and Hans was already conferring with Kempf in a soft whisper, trying to figure out how they would best bring their strange discovery to market.

As they worked their way back down the crumbling tunnel, Johann could not share the optimism of his brother. He could not shake the impression that far from making their fortune, their troubles had instead only just begun.

CHAPTER TWO

The Maze of Merciless Penance

IN THE FLICKERING dark of the burning city, with the night pierced by the screams of dying men and the air stagnant with the stench of scorched flesh, he could feel power surge through his body. Raw, primal and awesome in its terrible magnificence, it roared through his veins like a living thing, firing every nerve and synapse, awakening them to the eldritch power that soaked his flesh.

Power! The power to rip apart mountains! Power to smash the puny warrens of his enemies and entomb them forever with their treachery! Power to obliterate the stinking hovels of the humans and grind that pathetic, preening breed beneath the clawed feet of the skaven! Power! Power second only to that of the Horned Rat himself, mightiest of gods!

No, he corrected himself. With such power he was no longer a simple thing of flesh and spirit. He was a god himself, ascended like the infamous blasphemer

Kweethul the Vile! His was the power to rend and slay and rip and tear! His was the power to rule, to hold the entire Under-Empire, and the broken rubble of the miserable human surface realm, in a claw of iron. He would squeeze that claw until the world screamed and everything knew that it lived only because he allowed it.

Then the power flickered, cringing from him, retreating from his body like a wisp of ashy smoke from a smith's furnace. His mind railed with horror as he felt his new-found magnificence deserting him. It was unfair, unjust that he should be cheated of his moment of ascendancy!

His eyes were pits of rage as he scoured the darkened streets of the burning city, looking for the traitor who had sabotaged his ultimate triumph. There would be blood and vengeance when he found them. He would bury his muzzle in their breast and gnaw out their beating heart with his fangs!

Then rage shattered in his mind, sent whimpering to some black corner of his being. The last of the divine power that had swept through his body abandoned him as he squirted the musk of fear from his glands.

There were figures moving in the dark street, striding purposefully through the swirling smoke and dancing embers. One was the tall straight figure of a man, his reek foully familiar as it struck the skaven's senses. He felt only contempt for the man, but there was a reason he had vented his glands in terror.

If the man was here...

The second figure emerged from behind the veil of smoke. He was much shorter than the man, but stoutly and broadly built. Thick knots of muscle, like writhing jungle serpents, coiled around the apparition's arms. Crude tattoos in the cut-scrawl of the dwarfs littered the figure's bare chest and the sides of his shaven pate. A massive cock's comb, dyed the same bright orange as the dwarf's thick beard, sprouted from the centre of his otherwise shorn scalp. The dwarf's battered face grinned evilly behind its old scars and bruises. A missing eye was covered by a weathered leather patch. The other eye burned into the skaven's with a stare of murderous malevolence.

'This time, vermin, you taste my axe!'

Huge and cruelly sharp, like the hand of some savage daemon of war, the star-metal blade came hurtling towards the skaven, driven by all the monstrous power in the dwarf's swollen arms...

GREY SEER THANQUOL snapped awake, his entire body twitching in terror at the nightmare that had fallen upon his sleeping mind. Empty glands tried to squirt the fear-scent, but he could tell from the heavy fug that surrounded him that he had already emptied them in his sleep.

More troubling than his undignified display of scent, however, was the fact that he hadn't heard himself cry out. Thanquol tried to open his jaws, finding them thickly tethered by a leather muzzle. Rolling his tongue around inside his mouth, he found that he had been further gagged with an iron bit. Instinctively he raised his hands to remove the vexing intrusion. He found his paws carefully bound by little mittens of iron, his clawed fingers safely locked away inside the cold metal shell.

Panic thundered inside Thanquol's chest, his heart hammering like a crazed goblin against his ribs. Carefully, desperately, Thanquol forced himself to become calm. Turn fear into hate, he told himself. It was the maxim that had built the Under-Empire and given the skaven race dominance of the underworld. Fear wouldn't do anything to help him now. Hate, however, just might. Revenge was a powerful incentive for staying alive.

Thanquol cursed the nightmare memory of that devil-spawned dwarf and the preening human he kept as a pet. All of his misery and misfortune had started the day that whoreson pair intruded into his affairs. He was so close, so tantalisingly close to achieving the grand plot he had proposed to Seerlord Kritislik. The traitorous human dupe he had spent so long training and grooming to become his pawn was finally reaching his potential, finally ready to be put to the purpose Thanquol required of him. Fritz von Halstadt, chief of Nuln's secret police, would have murdered the brother of the human emperor once Thanquol provided him with 'evidence' that the aristocrat was involved in a conspiracy against the countess of Nuln. Thanquol understood enough about the brood loyalty of humans, even if he found it incomprehensible. The Emperor would retaliate, the countess would resist, believing the evidence von Halstadt presented her. War would be the result, war between the Emperor and the wealthy warren-kingdom of Nuln. Favours and loyalties owed to both sides would cause the conflict to spread, and where these were not enough, agents of the skaven would sow further lies and deception. Before long, the humans would be slaughtering one another wholesale. When they were weak enough, the skaven would emerge from their burrows and take their rightful place as inheritors of the surface world.

Such a grand scheme, surely inspired by the Horned Rat himself! Even the seerlords had been impressed, though Kritislik had insisted on tampering with it slightly so that he could claim part of the glory when the humans were brought to ruin. Perhaps that was where things had started to go wrong, when Seerlord Kritislik had started tinkering with Thanquol's brilliant vision. It was a thought that had occurred to Thanquol before, but one he knew it would not take a gag to prevent him from ever speaking aloud.

He doubted if even Seerlord Kritislik could contrive a scheme complicated enough to employ that hell-sent dwarf as a pawn, either willing or unwittingly. Yet who else could have managed such a feat if not Kritislik? Thanquol refused to believe it had been dumb blind randomness that had drawn the dwarf and his pet across his path. Everything would have succeeded but for them! Thanquol would have become the most renowned grey seer since Gnawdoom rescued the Black Ark from the wizard who dared steal it from its sanctuary deep beneath Skavenblight.

It was too much to think that it was circumstance that caused the cursed pair to kill von Halstadt before Thanquol could make use of him. Too much to think that any dwarf, however crazed, could fell a mighty rat ogre like his unfortunate Boneripper with a single blow! Nor was that the end of their meddling. The pair had lingered in the human warren-kingdom of Nuln, interfering in Thanquol's attempts to recover the situation. They had spoiled his efforts to abduct the countess, ruined his attempt to cement an alliance with the warlock engineers of Clan Skryre by stealing a human-built steam-tank, and thwarted his all-out attack against Nuln itself, an attack that by rights should have left the city a smouldering crater.

Oh, to be certain the Lords of Decay had been most lavish in their praise of Thanquol's efforts. They had tactfully ignored the intention of his grand scheme and instead focused upon the damage inflicted on the man-city and the severe losses suffered by the warriors of Clan Skab during the fighting. Clan Skab, they said, had been growing seditious. As a result of the fighting in Nuln, they were now too weak to act on any rebellious thoughts. Seerlord Kritislik himself had rewarded Thanquol, presenting him with a new rat ogre to replace the one he had lost. He was even given freedom and resources to pursue his vendetta against the cursed dwarf and his underling.

Thanquol should have suspected then, but he allowed his own ambition and his deep need for revenge to cloud his judgement. He gathered a new band of minions and pursued the dwarf far into the north. The battle that followed should have been a resounding victory; Thanquol had planned it out to the smallest detail. Instead his wretched minions had allowed themselves to be destroyed and routed by the filthy dwarfs. His second Boneripper performed even more wretchedly than its predecessor, killed by the dwarf's pet before it could even lay a paw on him! Thanquol was right to have been suspicious. Few skaven would have had such sharp instincts. If he'd trusted the miserable wretch to protect him... hadn't it been Kritislik who had suggested he employ the rat ogre as a bodyguard?

Pursuing the dwarf and his allies had led Thanquol even further north, most of his carefully hoarded wealth being spent to gather more warriors and to purchase a proper bodyguard, a hulking beast worthy of the name Boneripper. To remind Seerlord Kritislik of the importance of Thanquol's brilliant and cunning mind, he sent a runner back to Skavenblight telling the Lords of Decay about the airship the dwarfs had built and in which his despised enemy had so cravenly quit the battlefield. Now he was not simply going to accomplish the elimination of a hated foe of the Under-Empire, but also secure a technology that made the loss of the steam-tank in Nuln insignificant.

But things continued to go wrong. His agent, the snivelling and faithless Lurk Snitchtongue, who in his foresight Thanquol had sent to hide in the airship before its escape, returned from his experience mutated and savage, exposed to the raw forces of the blighted Chaos Wastes. His paw-picked warriors, after occupying the airship's staging area in Kislev and imprisoning its human defenders, were too glutted on their recent successes to obey his exacting commands when the airship returned. Had they followed his strict orders, the damnable contraption would have been his and all its miserable occupants at the grey seer's mercy. Instead they had foolishly, treacherously rushed in and gotten themselves slaughtered. Even the wretched dolt of a rat ogre managed to get itself killed. Boneripper! Fah! Thanquol always knew the gruesome things were nothing but bad luck!

Only the grey seer's genius (and a liberal ingestion of warpstone to augment his magical powers) had enabled him to escape the treacherous bungling of his subordinates. His only comrade as he scurried away from the debacle was the grotesque Lurk, now little more than a rat ogre himself, albeit with a troubling knot of hunger in his scent. Even worse, they had been captured by the pickets of a massive horde of deranged humans from the northlands. It had taken a wit as sharp and tricky as Thanquol's to deceive the barbarians into releasing them, and he had made sure to use the escape to put as many of their fellow skaven between the marauders and himself as quickly as possible, seeking out the closest and largest skaven warren in the area.

That led to his entry into Hell Pit, the noxious city of Clan Moulder, breeders of the many beasts and monsters that slaved for the skaven in the dark reaches of their realm. Izak Grottle, the fat worm, had been there, spinning his lies to the elders of his clan, convincing them it had been Thanquol and not his own conniving and perfidy that had resulted in the failure of the attack on Nuln and the loss of many of the clan's beast masters. Instead of welcoming the grey seer, Thanquol found himself a prisoner... and one destined for a very short stay.

Again, destiny and the Horned Rat smiled on him. At any other time, Clan Moulder would have happily disposed of Thanquol, indeed it was a rare thing for a grey seer to fall into any clan's paws in so vulnerable a condition. Working up the nerve to actually do the deed was what was delaying them, Thanquol was certain, for even as a prisoner his reputation was enough to strike terror in such vermin.

The issue never came to open confrontation, however. In their foolishness, the fleshchangers of Hell Pit had taken Lurk away to experiment upon in their laboratories. Instead the mutant had broken free, lost himself in the lower warrens and incited a rebellion among Moulder's skaven slaves! Hopelessly out of their depth, unable to keep even their clanrats from defecting to the insurrection, the High Packmaster had turned to Thanquol to save Hell Pit.

A pettier skaven would have refused, but Thanquol was gracious enough to aid Clan Moulder, despite the indignities they had inflicted upon him. With his brilliant leadership, the revolt was quickly broken. His only regret was that in the confusion Lurk had somehow contrived to lose himself in the tunnels and escape his well-deserved reward for betraying his old master and blasphemy against the Horned Rat.

Still the danger was not past. Lurk had treasonously allowed himself to be used by the sorcerers of the northmen to weaken Hell Pit for their horde to conquer. Selflessly, Thanquol did not depart for Skavenblight and his long-deferred report to the Council of Thirteen, deciding to stay and help Clan Moulder escape complete ruin. After all, had it not been the mighty Grey Seer Thanquol who had led the warriors of Clan Moulder in battle against the northman warlord Alarik Lionmane when he had brought his barbarians against the strongholds scattered beneath the Troll Country? The horde had been broken and all but annihilated as a result of Thanquol's decisive strategy. If Moulder's dull clawleaders had followed the grey seer's intricate battle plan more closely, Moulder's army would have emerged unscathed. But no reasonable mind could hold him to blame for the loss of an army that was too stupid to display a proper understanding of tactics.

Fortunately, the brood-mothers of Hell Pit had used the years since Alarik's horde was routed to birth a new army for Clan Moulder. Thanquol led the solid ranks of armoured stormvermin, fierce clanrats and the many terrible beasts from Moulder's flesh-forges against the brutish northmen, the elite vanguard of Arek Daemonclaw who had entrusted only the best of his warriors with the task of facing the skaven, taking the dregs of his host to attack the humans in Praag.

Thanquol had to admit that Clan Moulder's new army was better than its last one. But then, of course his battle plan was better as well, even with the fat, squealing Izak Grottle trying to take a hand in the strategising. When it was over, Thanquol had the pleasure of watching his second northman horde break and scatter like the skull of a baby dwarf. This time there was none of the awkwardness of being the only skaven alive to enjoy the retreat.

After the battle, Thanquol took his leave of Clan Moulder, Hell Pit and the two-scented Izak Grottle. The grey seer accepted only the smallest measure of reward from the High Packmaster. After all, the flesh-changers were a simple and foolish breed, and it would be unkind to take advantage of them and point out that what they offered him was hardly what a more refined skaven would call generous. Besides, he was eager to make his report to the Council of Thirteen. In Skavenblight he would have friends, ones who would help him settle debts incurred during his stay in the north.

Through the tunnels of the Under-Empire, carried by the sickly skaven slaves given to him by Clan Moulder, Thanquol hurried, his mind afire with future plans and past grudges.

THANQUOL RUBBED ONE of his horns against his shoulder, trying to get at an itch he couldn't reach with his chained paws. No matter which way he twisted his neck or tilted his head, he couldn't quite find the spot. Another indignity unjustly inflicted upon him by those who were jealous of his genius and the favour displayed to him by the Horned Rat!

He'd had a fine taste of how deep the envy of his fellows went upon his return to Skavenblight! Instead of being welcomed back as the loyal and capable servant he was, Thanquol had been seized by the elite white stormvermin who guarded the Lords of Decay and the Shattered Tower. He was dragged before Seerlord Kritislik in chains, presented to them like some seditious heretic! Kritislik informed him that they were displeased by his failure to capture the dwarf airship, disturbed by his inability to inform the Council of Arek Daemonclaw's attack on Kislev in time to allow them to exploit it for their own purposes, and upset by reports that he had engineered a slave revolt in Hell Pit without the seerlord's authorisation.

Despite his best efforts to explain these seeming failures to Kritislik, the seerlord was deaf to his words. He was stripped of his staff and amulet, the talismans of his office as grey seer and agent of the Council, and thrown into some blighted hole deep beneath the streets of Skavenblight.

Thanquol was more certain than ever that Kritislik had been behind his downfall from the start. It was the seerlord who had put that hell-spawned dwarf in his way, probably the treacherous Lurk and all the other enemies who had beset him as well! Envious of Thanquol's brilliance, doubting Thanquol's tireless devotion and loyalty! Thanquol was right to have plotted against the senile old mouse! When he thought of all the times he had squirted the musk of fear just to convey a respectful scent in the fool's presence...

As Thanquol's eyes adjusted to the darkness, he suddenly froze. His surroundings were different; he wasn't in the same dreary little hole anymore. He thought back to the pathetic bones he had been thrown by his guards the night before. They had tasted strange, but he had been too ravenous with hunger to care at the time. Now he knew the marrow had been treated with some kind of drug, a drug that left him insensible long enough for his captors to gag and bind him, to remove him from his prison to this place.

But where was this place? Thanquol's stomach clenched and his empty glands tried to vent. He had a terrible feeling he knew. The Maze of Inescapable Death, the most insidious of the many ways the Council of Thirteen employed to dispose of those who displeased them. The maze was a trap-filled network of tunnels and warrens, a nest of pits and spikes and boiling oil, the walls reinforced with steel rods so that even the most desperate skaven couldn't gnaw his way to freedom. In all the centuries since its construction, no skaven had ever escaped from the maze for one simple reason: there was no way out.

Thanquol stared at the ceiling, feeling his head swim as he saw tiny lights wink into existence, as the comforting closeness of the roof faded away into the vast, horrifying emptiness of the night sky. He knew it was a trick, a dwarf-made illusion plundered from the shattered halls of the City of Pillars. He knew that it was not stars he saw, but simply tiny bits of amber and pearl set into a black-painted ceiling. He recognised the deception for what it was, but he could not stop the instinctual revulsion that crawled through his body. Untold generations of breeding, fighting and dying in the close tunnels and cluttered caverns of the Under-Empire had made the skaven a race of agoraphobics, imprinting a terror of open spaces into the most primal part of their psyche.

The grey seer tried to overcome his fear with his knowledge, to let intellect subdue unruly instinct. It was the fiendish nature of the nameless and accursed ratmen who had constructed the maze that the labyrinth should use a skaven's own natural urges to destroy him.

Instinct versus intellect, an unequal contest in most skaven, who were little cleverer than the common rats who shared their burrows, but in the case of a mind like Thanquol's, genius would prevail. The nameless architects of the maze had not figured upon a brilliance such as that of the grey seer!

Thanquol caught himself as he was edging towards the wall of the tunnel, fighting down the desperate need to feel raw earth against his whiskers, to assure himself he was not falling into the enormous void of the sky above. He ground his fangs against the bit in his mouth, feeling annoyance that he had allowed his body to move at such primitive and petty urgings. The builders of the maze would know that huddling up against the wall would be the natural response of a skaven confronted by the sprawling starfield over him. They might have hidden anything in the wall to settle with such weak minds: spring-loaded spikes treated in warp-venom, jets of immolating warp-flame billowing outwards from projectors buried beneath a thin layer of crust, perhaps even a hidden pivot to allow the wall to spin and crush its victim.

Each image made Thanquol more nervous than the last and he slowly backed away from the offending wall. When he felt raw earth crumble behind his furred back, the skaven leapt ten feet into the centre of the tunnel, wide-eyed with fright, not caring how inappropriate such a display of raw fear was for a grey seer of his status. His retreat from the first wall had backed him into the other side of the tunnel. Only reflexes as honed and precise as his own could have allowed escape from so injudicious a moment. Thanquol watched the wall he had brushed against, waiting anxiously for it to explode in some manner of violence. When it didn't, he felt almost disappointed, but he should have guessed that the speed of his amazing reactions was quicker than whatever device the architects had hidden. Before the death-machine could even be triggered, Thanquol was already gone.

Now, as he stood in the darkness, listening to his own heart pounding in his chest, Thanquol's other senses became more alert. He could discern a faint, bittersweet smell. He could feel the air shifting slightly, betraying the merest suggestion of current and movement. He could hear an indistinct noise, a dim scratching sounding from beneath the rocky floor, giving him the impression of rusty gears grinding together.

There was no escape from the maze, but Thanquol was determined to fight just the same. If he could find something to rid himself of his muzzle and fetters, he would be able to draw upon his magic to tip the balance back in his favour. However fiendish the architects, Thanquol did not think they could have reckoned with the mystic might of a grey seer when they built their traps.

Keeping his eyes averted from the disconcerting illusion of the false sky, Thanquol carefully made his way down the tunnel. He was careful to stay away from the walls and kept a wary watch on the places he set his feet. Ahead, the tunnel split into five separate corridors, like fingers stretching away from a hand. He paused, sniffing at the air, trying to decide which corridor to take. He had a good feeling about the leftmost path. The skaven lashed his tail in annoyance, remembering that this place was designed to goad a victim into destroying himself.

Thanquol turned away from the left path, instead creeping down the centre corridor. He had only taken a dozen paces when instinct took over and he threw himself to the floor. An instant later a great blast of green warpfire whooshed overhead, searing its way down the tunnel. The smell of singed fur told the grey seer how nearly he had been caught, the flames licking at his back even as he crushed himself against the floor.

Thanquol lifted himself from the ground, scowling at the darkness. There was no mistaking the sound of gears grinding together beneath the floor this time. He could feel the tunnel itself rumbling. Quickly he retreated back the way he had come. He just reached the intersection when the trapped tunnel began to rotate, moved by machinery hidden beneath it. Soon, where the corridor had been, Thanquol could see only a bare stone wall.

The grey seer did not spend overlong contemplating the buried machinery or the question of whether it operated automatically or was guided by some malefic intelligence. Having escaped the warpfire, Thanquol was more inclined to trust his initial impression and travel down the leftmost tunnel. Certainly it couldn't be any less hazardous than picking a path at random, as he had done.

That bittersweet scent was stronger as Thanquol entered the left tunnel. Now the grey seer identified the odour, his suspicions of trickery became even more pronounced. It was the smell of refined warpstone, but warpstone that had been allowed to age for an unbelievable amount of time. It was the sort of thing that would pluck at a skaven's mind and guide him on even without his conscious mind being aware of its pull.

Thanquol, however, was aware of what it was that lured him down the tunnel. He knew he walked into a trap, and his every sense was on the alert. He froze when a slight shift in the heavy air suggested movement. When the bright flash of metal in the blackness flickered past his eyes, he arrested his every muscle and waited for the pendulum to withdraw back into its hidden niche. Briefly he toyed with the idea of using the sharp edge of the pendulum to cut his fetters, but quickly disabused himself of the impulse, fearing the blade had been treated with some ghastly poison by his captors.

Scurrying through the dark, Thanquol allowed the scent of warpstone to guide him. He continued to shun the walls, continued to avert his eyes from the disorienting glare of the starfield. It was not escape that goaded him onwards. He knew there was none from the Maze of Inescapable Death. No, it was something more primitive and elemental that motivated him. Food and water were his concerns now, excited by the smell of warpstone. His physical needs must be sated before he attacked the problem of removing his bonds and making a fight of the maze's ordeal.

Down through the murk of the winding tunnel, Thanquol was drawn, even his cunning mind tortured by the effort of keeping track of his trail. The way the tunnel doubled back upon itself, he wondered if perhaps buried machinery wasn't moving the corridors behind him, rotating and turning so that he was caught in an endlessly repeating pattern. The thought chilled him as much as it excited his appreciation for the sadistic minds that had built the maze.

If the winding tunnels were being rotated by machines, at least there was a purpose behind their movements. Turning one last corner, Thanquol was surprised to find himself looking out into a wide cavern. Stalactites dripped from the ceiling, spoiling the effect of the pearly stars and silver moons suspended overhead. The walls were at least partially worked, displaying the marks of tools rather than the scratches of claw and fang. He could not see any other openings into the cavern and very soon lost interest in looking for any, his eyes locked to the object at the centre of the chamber.

It was a black stone marked by veins of green that glowed in the darkness. If Thanquol had any doubts about the bittersweet scent, he could not mistake the colours of warpstone. The rock stood upon a small plinth of copper upon which the grey seer could see scratchy runes and elaborate pictoglyphs. Old writing, very old indeed, possibly even predating the rise of the skaven themselves.

Intrigued now by something more than hunger, Thanquol crept towards the plinth. Curiosity was a vice that had served the skaven race well down through their long history, though given the opportunity any skaven with an ounce of wit preferred to let one of his subordinates take on the inherent risks of exploration and inquiry. Thanquol did not have that luxury, however, a fact that made him curse Kritislik once more. A few skavenslaves, or even a truculent giant rat, would have been reassuring under the circumstances. No skaven felt at ease without the scent of a dozen of its underlings filling its nose.

Thanquol fought down the urgings of both hunger and curiosity, remembering only too well where he was. Instead he kept his distance from the plinth, circling it warily and studying it from afar. Abruptly he stopped, fixing his gaze on the block of warpstone. Now he could see that the rock had been sculpted, carved into a crude likeness in a style as primitive as it was ancient. It was the rough shape of a skaven, paws set upon its knees and with its tail curled about its lap. Great horns, like mighty glaives, rose from the brow of the statue's head. Thanquol prostrated himself on the floor, grovelling in pious fear before this representation of the Horned Rat himself.

Now Thanquol understood where he was. This was not the Maze of Inescapable Death. It was the only slightly less deadly Maze of Merciless Penance, used by the seerlord to test those grey seers whose loyalty and capability had been cast into doubt. This Maze was designed to determine whether a skaven yet retained the good favour of the Horned Rat. Only those who proved themselves were ever seen again. The others became victims of the labyrinth.

Like any skaven, Thanquol feared and envied his god, but now there was a despair-born sincerity in his pleas to the Horned Rat for salvation. If the Horned One would only spare his miserable and unworthy servant, Thanquol would work tirelessly to ensure his domination of the world above. No more would he think of his own ambitions and greed, his secret dream to raise himself as seerlord and see Kritislik's bones gnawed by the whelps of his own brood. He would even forsake his vengeful obsession to destroy the damnable dwarf and his foppish pet, if only the Horned Rat would hear him now.

In the midst of his deal-making prayers, Thanquol suddenly felt the compulsion to lift his head from the floor. He stared at the image of the Horned Rat for only an instant, then his eyes fixed on something above and beyond the statue. Two blue stars shone in the eerie false night, set amidst some of the rocky growths that peppered the ceiling. There was something disquieting about the sapphire-lights and Thanquol started to turn his head when he became aware of something that had him forgetting about mazes and gods, even about warp-stone and hunger.

The blue stars were moving.

Slowly, agonisingly slowly, the sapphire-lights were creeping across the roof. Now Thanquol could see that they weren't merely set amid the rocky growths, they were fixed to a big projection of stone. Only it wasn't stone, just something that blended itself with the stone, the better to hunt prey.

Terrors from whelp-hood rose up fresh in Thanquol's mind. All the bogey stories told by vindictive skavenslaves to frighten their charges. Tales of the Under-Empire and the lightless miles of empty tunnel between burrow and warren. Gruesome fables about what haunted those tunnels, ready to reach out and snatch the unwary skaven who dared the dark alone.

The thing on the ceiling was one such myth. Until this moment, Thanquol had not believed such a thing to be any more than the crazed imagining of the insect-obsessed Clan Verms. Still, there was no mistaking the monster for aught but what it was. Now that he was aware of it, Thanquol could pick out the shape of its many spindly legs, the long abdomen and the armoured thorax. He could see the angular head with its jewel-like eyes of sapphire and its hideous mouth of serrated plates. Two arched shadows dangling down from it were certainly the monster's claws, great ripping things designed to catch and hold prey while the monster's mandibles tore slivers of meat from its screaming victim.

A tregara, the panther of the underworld, a monstrous mantis-like predator that found no prey quite as much to its liking as skaven. Even now, staring back at its sapphire eyes, Thanquol found it difficult to believe the thing was real. He ransacked his mind for every half-remembered story he had been told about the creatures. Above him, slowly and silently, the tregara continued to creep forwards.

Blind! Yes, that was something he remembered. Thanquol prided himself on recalling such an old and seemingly useless bit of memory. There was more, it wasn't able to scent prey any more than a skaven could catch a scent from the insect's own pale, rocky body. How then did it hunt?

The tregara was almost directly above the plinth now. Thanquol shuddered as he saw how immense it was, at least twice his own weight and coated in thick plates of chitin. As he trembled, the insect rotated its head, seeming to fix its blind gaze on the grey seer. Thanquol knew it was not his imagination when the tregara's lethargic stalk across the ceiling quickened.

Movement! That was how the tregara hunted its prey! Even the slightest motion would betray Thanquol to the monster. The skaven struggled to calm himself, to still his lashing tail and quivering limbs. He forced himself to look away from the gigantic insect, only too aware that while he looked at it, any effort to calm himself was doomed.

Long moments passed. Thanquol expected the scythe-like claws to come sweeping down to snatch him at any moment. When nothing happened, he risked raising his face from the floor.

The tregara was almost directly over him. He could see the stone-like markings on its back now, could hear the scrape of its body against the rock as it moved. The sight was too much for Thanquol's self-control. Screaming into his gag, the grey seer scurried across the floor on hands and feet, racing away from the sinister predator with all the grace and terror of some mammoth rat. Dignity and decorum were the furthest things from his mind as the grey seer darted back into the tunnel, like a giant mouse disappearing into its hole.

Down the narrow, winding tunnels Thanquol ran, his replenished glands venting themselves. Only once did he risk a look back. Two sapphire-lights shone from the roof of the tunnel, the tregara's clawed legs stabbing into the black rock as it hurtled after its fleeing prey. The insect's grim silence disturbed Thanquol more than the hiss of a serpent or the snarl of a cat, lending the tregara an unnatural, almost elemental aura of inevitability.

Thanquol was not about to submit to the inevitable, whatever shape it assumed. There was always a way, a deception to work, a minion to blame, a superior to flatter. He had survived many things over his life, from the black arts of the necromancer Vorghun of Praag to the vile poxes of the Plague Lord Skratsquik and the mutated warriors of Arek Daemonclaw. Even that hell-spawned dwarf had proven incapable of besting the mighty Grey Seer Thanquol. To end as fodder for some mindless tunnel-lurker was too much for him to countenance.

Now Thanquol was back at the intersection. Once more there were five tunnels branching away. Close behind him came the tregara. He hesitated for only a moment, then quickly darted into the centre tunnel. Thanquol threw himself against the floor, crushing his body against the earth. For a terrible instant, he wondered if the trap mechanism had reset, or if the tunnel was indeed the right one.

Suddenly, green fire roared overhead. A sickly, satisfying smell of burnt meat struck Thanquol's senses. He looked overhead and watched as a long, scythe-like claw dropped away from the charred husk of the tregara, its sapphire-lights dimmed forever by the scorching blast of warpfire.

The tunnel began to rumble once more. This time Thanquol was too slow to retreat, instead being carried away as the entire corridor rotated. As it finished its cycle, the grey seer found himself blinking in the harsh glare of warpstone lanterns. He could hear the grind of machinery all around him and could dimly perceive a massive treadwheel powered by skavenslaves looming in the distance.

Thanquol's heart hammered against his ribs. He wasn't going to die! He hadn't been cast into the Maze of Inescapable Death, but rather into the Maze of Merciless Penance! The Horned Rat had not abandoned his favoured instrument! He was being given another chance to prove himself. His masters had not consigned him to destruction.

Much closer than the slaves was a large cluster of armoured skaven, their pallid fur taking on a greenish hue in the warplight. They were big, slavering brutes with breastplates of steel and wickedly hooked halberds clutched tightly in their paws. Thanquol knew their scent: albino stormvermin, the elite guards of the Council of Thirteen.

In their midst was another figure, nearly as tall as the hulking stormvermin. His fur was a murky grey that contrasted with the iron hue of his long, flowing robes. Sigils picked out in black rat-hair thread formed intricate patterns on the skaven's garments. Huge horns as black as the thread rose from the skaven's skull, curling into spiral antlers of bone. The face beneath the horns was pinched and drawn and filled with such timeless malice as to make even the fiercest giant seem small and vulnerable.

Thanquol abased himself before Seerlord Kritislik, baring his throat to the elder priest-sorcerer. If there was anything left in his glands, Thanquol would have vented them in deference to his master, but all the musk had already been used during the horrible chase by the tregara.

Kritislik's face pulled back in a fang-ridden smile of challenge, annoyed by the lack of respectful scent from Thanquol. After a moment, however, Kritislik divined the reason for such impropriety. The seerlord chuckled darkly.

'You survive the maze, Grey Seer Thanquol,' Kritislik hissed. 'Good-good. The Horned One still like-favour you.' Kritislik gestured with his paw and two of the stormvermin advanced to the captive. Roughly, but quickly, they removed the muzzle from Thanquol's snout and the fetters from his paws.

Coughing, Thanquol spat the iron bit from his mouth and tried to work feeling back into his jaw. He became aware of Kritislik's impatient gaze upon him, and threw himself back to the floor.

'I serve only the will-desire of the Horned One,' Thanquol whined. 'The word of the most terrifying-magnificent seerlord is my sacred commandment, oh benevolent tyrant,' he added, deciding a display of fawning devotion might keep him from being returned to the maze.

Kritislik seemed to ponder Thanquol's flattery, then a cruel light crept into the ratman's eyes. 'You have been a capable servant, Grey Seer Thanquol,' Kritislik said.

'The Council finds itself in need of a dispo- a competent servant for a matter of the utmost delicacy.'

Kritislik gestured again and the white stormvermin grabbed Thanquol by the shoulders and started to lead him away. The grey seer knew better than to struggle or protest. A less keen mind might have thought there was nothing worse that could be inflicted on him than the ordeal of the maze and that there was nothing to be risked by resisting.

Thanquol knew better. Where the insidious imaginations of the Lords of Decay were concerned, there was always something worse.

CHAPTER THREE
Worms and Rats

THE HIDEOUT, AS Hans Dietrich called it, was nothing more than a disused cellar beneath the *Orc and Axe*. The little gang paid Ulgrin Shatterhand, the proprietor of the tavern, a tidy sum to keep the cellar that way. There was a hidden door in the small foyer between bar and kitchen that allowed the smugglers entry to their secret storehouse. It was a vital element of their operation to have a safe place to store merchandise when immediate delivery proved impractical. The *Orc and Axe*, infamous as one of the most violent dens of vice and drunkenness on all the waterfront, made a perfect disguise for their activities. The place was so notorious there wasn't a watchman in all Altdorf who would look beneath the surface for more crime. The panderers, weirdroot addicts, river pirates, mobsmen, thieves and murderers who patronised the tavern's taproom were more than enough to meet any thief-taker's quota. If there was one thing that had impressed itself upon Hans over the years it was the fact that the only person stupider and lazier than a watchman was the common outlaw.

Staying out of Mundsen Keep or Reiksfang Prison wasn't a question of being a genius, only a matter of being cleverer than the next thief and keeping quiet when he took the fall. It was a philosophy that had kept Hans clean so far as the magistrates were concerned, despite over a decade of larceny. His brother, Johann, had violated the precept of not meddling in somebody else's fight. He'd been tossed into the Reiksfang for three years after getting caught up in the Window Tax riots. Perhaps it would have been better had he spent a few more years in the dungeons of the Reiksfang, the extra time might have knocked a bit more sense into Johann's thick skull. As it was, the younger Dietrich still had disturbing displays of idealism from time to time.

At least he was a dependable lieutenant, a vital asset when the gang included slippery weasels like Kempf among their numbers. Watching the diminished gang move through the narrow, garbage-ridden back-alleys of the waterfront, Hans realised he'd need to recruit some new muscle, sooner rather than later with Gustav Volk on the prowl for them.

Hans slipped in the side door of the tavern after making sure no one was about. He was always cautious about government informants and watchmen keeping a low profile, and tonight he was doubly so. If what they found in the sewers was really what Kempf claimed it to be, they'd make back what they had lost with the wine and then some. He held the rickety door, nothing more than a few planks fitted to a hinge, as the rest of his gang shuffled out of the shadows and darted inside. Johann brought up the rear, his dagger drawn, following close behind Kleiner as the big man shuffled his way down the alley, his arms wrapped about the strange stone. Even with an oilskin draped over it, the rock gave off a faint green glow in the darkness. Hans wrinkled his nose. The last thing they needed was somebody spotting that and getting the witch hunters involved!

The rumble of voices and bawdy songs from the tavern's main room covered the entrance of the smugglers. The only one watching the side door was Greta, a plain-faced serving wench with a body like an over-sexed cow. She had a thing for one of the gang and always hung around the door when she could to watch their comings and goings.

'Evening, Greta,' Hans said as he slipped inside. The girl grinned at him, then craned her head, looking slightly disappointed that only Kleiner and Johann were still outside.

'Is Krebs not with you?' she asked, a dejected note in her voice.

'Sorry, love, the Dockwatch nabbed him. You won't see him until they let him out of Mundsen Keep,' Hans lied. Johann gave his brother a sour look. They had both seen Krebs spitted like a fish on Gustav Volk's sword. The only way Greta would be seeing him again was with the help of a necromancer.

'He was just a bit too slow tonight,' Hans continued, returning his brother's sour look. There was no sense telling the girl the truth and spending half the night trying to console a bawling female. 'Nobody's fault, really. Sometimes the blasted griffons get lucky is all.'

Greta's eyes were starting to turn red and damp, a flush rising in her plump face. Hans patted her shoulder.

'Don't fret none, poppet,' he told her. 'Me and the lads will see the bribe gets doled out. He'll be back knocking at your window in no time.'

Hans didn't have time to wipe the smile off his face before Johann was pushing him into the pantry and down the steps to the hidden cellar.

'Anyone ever tell you that you're a worm?' Johann growled.

'You think telling her that her darling swain is a notch on Volk's sword would make her feel any better?' Hans retorted. 'I have to say, brother, sometimes I think dear old mum did our father wrong when you get all stupid on me.'

Hans ignored the ugly stream of invective his turn of phrase provoked and descended into the cellar. It was a rude, dilapidated affair, plaster walls bulging with the Altdorf damp, a timber ceiling that creaked every time anyone headed out the tavern's back entrance to use the privy, spider webs so thick they could choke an ogre. Still, what it lacked in the niceties, it made up for in discretion. A smuggler had to choose inconspicuous over luxury every time.

The rest of the depleted gang was clustered around the only lantern in the place, a glass-faced storm lantern they'd somehow acquired from the ship of a Marienburg trader. The glass was cracked, throwing weird shadows across the floor, but at least it was better than sitting in the dark and far less stifling than a smoke-belching torch.

Hans did another quick head count. Mueller, Kleiner, that rat Kempf, Wilhelm and Johann. No doubt about it, but Volk's little ambush had cost them a lot of manpower.

'You can set that thing down now,' Hans told Kleiner. The big oaf was still holding the glowing rock against his chest, even with sweat dripping down his forehead and veins bulging from the sides of his neck. He let the rock crash to the floor and crumpled into a gasping wreck. The other smugglers cursed at the loud noise and instantly trained their eyes on the ceiling, trying to decide if they had been heard.

Hans shook his head. With all the racket rising from the taproom, they could be murdering the Emperor's mistress down here and nobody would hear it. He smacked his hands together to draw the men's attention back to him.

'Well boys, we had a bad night of it,' Hans said.

'Bad night?' Wilhelm snarled. He waved his bandaged hand at the gang chief. 'They cut off two of my fingers!'

'Next time you'll get out of the way,' Hans quipped. Johann stepped beside his brother, a menacing reminder to Wilhelm that he would get much worse than a few missing fingers if he started anything.

'Khaine's black hells, Hans!' cursed Kempf. 'That wasn't the Dockwatch or sewerjacks that rumbled onto us, that was Gustav Volk! In case you forgot, he works for Klasst! Those people don't throw you into Mundsen Keep, they bury you under it!'

'And they don't never stop lookin' for you either!' Wilhelm added. 'Never!'

Hans shook his head. 'So you'd prefer that we were working for Volk all this time? Funny, I don't remember anybody complaining about splitting the forty-percent that leech would have taken off every job.'

'Yeah, well now's different,' Kempf spat. 'Now Volk's onto us!'

'So what do you want to do? Everybody wants to quit and bottle out because the big bad Volk is after them?'

Hans was a bit annoyed by all the nodding heads that greeted the suggestion.

'We've enough stashed from the last few jobs to get good and far from Altdorf,' Mueller told him. 'I'm thinking Wurtbad might be far enough to stay out of Volk's grasp.'

'If it's just Volk,' Johann interrupted. 'If it's his boss looking for you, Kislev isn't far enough away.'

His brother's sobering remark brought a decidedly depressing chill to the air, like a schoolroom bully letting all the air out of a pig's bladder. Hans decided to play the card he had been holding back. He fished in his tunic and pulled out a sack of coins. With a flourish he threw the bag onto the floor, making sure everyone could hear the clatter of metal against metal.

'There's all the swag from the last three jobs,' Hans said, smiling as the men pounced on the bag. 'Divide it up any way you like, and may Ranald's favour go with you.' Hans paused, letting a sly twinkle into his eye. 'Of course, if you leave now, you don't get a share.'

That remark made some heads turn. Suspicious eyes fixed on Hans.

'Share in what?' Mueller demanded.

Hans patted the oilskin-draped stone, letting his fingers tap against its sides, letting the drumming noise echo across the cellar. 'If this is wyrdstone, Kempf, how much would it be worth?'

'You wouldn't cut us out of that!' Kempf snarled, more than ever resembling some cornered rodent.

'But you men all want to leave Altdorf,' Hans said. 'Those who stay behind to sell this... commodity... should reap the rewards. What have we always said? An equal share of the risk, an equal share of the swag. That simple rule has kept us honest so far, I see no reason why it shouldn't still apply.'

The men looked at Hans as if he'd spat in their beer. Kleiner rose from the floor, looking for a moment as if he'd like to rip the sneering rogue limb from limb. Wilhelm fingered his knife, a gruesome thing that looked like it was made for gutting sharks. Mueller just stood and glared. Kempf muttered to himself, chewing on his moustache.

'How much do you say it would be worth?' Johann asked, backing his brother's play.

Kempf glared at both of the Dietrichs. 'If, and I say *if* the thing really is wyrdstone, there's no saying how much it is worth.'

'How do we see if it is wyrdstone?' Hans asked.

Kempf looked like he had just swallowed something bitter. 'I know people...' he began.

'Who?' prodded Johann. It would be like the little weasel to keep everything to himself and leave the rest of them hanging in the wind if he got the chance. Even Kleiner wasn't stupid enough to let Kempf keep anything secret.

'I could take it to Doktor Loew, the alchemist,' Kempf said after a moment. 'He'd know.'

Hans nodded. 'A good plan,' he agreed. Then he drew his dagger. Before any of the other smugglers could react, Hans smashed the edge of his blade against the brittle rock, knocking an inch-long sliver from its side. 'But what if we don't take the whole stone to him? I think that would be safer, don't you? We wouldn't like your Dr Loew to get any queer ideas about stealing the whole thing from us. We take him a little piece and maybe we can keep him honest.'

'What about the rest of it?' asked Mueller.

Hans looked around the small cellar for a moment, looking for a place they could hide the bulky rock and its unnatural glow. His gaze finally settled on an old wine cask that had been in the cellar before the building above was even called the *Orc and Axe*. It had been cheap to begin with and over the years it had soured itself into pungent vinegar. Hans pointed to the barrel and all the smugglers smiled at the suggestion.

'I suppose you want me to lug it over there?' grumbled Kleiner.

THE TAPROOM OF the *Orc and Axe* was filled almost to bursting by the time the smugglers emerged from their hasty conference. It was just the way Johann preferred it. Crowded, the sudden arrival of the smugglers would pass largely unnoticed. More tactically minded than his brother, Johann was a good deal more cautious than Hans about the secrecy of their lair. Hans, in his opinion, trusted to luck and the favour of Ranald the Trickster too much and too often. The eyes of the Dockwatch weren't just on the streets. And now there were Gustav Volk's spies to worry about as well.

Johann's steely gaze swept across the taproom, studying the motley gutter-sweepings sitting about the tavern's dilapidated tables and gathered about its knife-scarred bar. Grimy, sour-faced visages sometimes looked up from their tankards of beer and flagons of ale to return his challenging inspection. Waterfront stevedores, back-alley swindlers, leather-faced fishermen, squinty thieves, swaggering sailors, brutish muggers, and foppish panderers all clustered about the cheap booze and scarcely edible fare of Ulgrin Shatterhand's establishment. Johann could see the gaudy fabrics of Marienburg, heavy fur cloaks from Kislev, the stripped homespun of Nuln and Wissenland, the threadbare greens of Wurtbad, even the balloon-like cut of Tilean tunics and trousers. The smuggler laughed grimly. It wasn't in the lofty spires of government and aristocracy where men from foreign places and foreign minds came together as equals with common purpose. It was in the lowest rungs of society that men set aside their differences. It was in the gutter they came together.

Any one of those faces that looked back at him might be one of Volk's spies. Johann shook his head. The organisation Vesper Klasst had put together had its fingers in every district in Altdorf; even if none of Volk's people were in the crowd, some of Klasst's were certain to be. Hans was really testing the limits of Ranald's divine indulgence. It was Johann's experience that the gods seldom favoured fools overlong.

Hans and the others had already sidled over to the bar, pushing a knot of grumbling stevedores to make room for them. The labourers looked ready to make trouble, but proved too sober to pick a fight with any mob that included someone like Kleiner among its number. Hans was barking out orders for Reikland hock when Johann joined them.

'This is stupid, Hans,' Johann hissed from the corner of his mouth. 'Somebody is sure to be looking for us.'

'They won't start anything here,' Hans protested. He smiled as he took the clay tankards from the dumpy woman behind the counter. He pushed drinks down the bar to his men. He rolled his eyes when Johann refused the last tankard.

'You worry too much,' Hans grumbled, pointedly taking a swig from the tankard he had offered to his brother. 'Comes from all that thinking you're doing all the time. A man can't think his way out of whatever the gods have in store for him.'

'It damn sure can't hurt,' Johann retorted. 'You ever stop to think Volk is sure to hear about us being here?'

Hans sighed, looking back down the bar. His annoyance grew when he saw that the rest of his men were watching the two brothers with rapt attention. Wilhelm wasn't even drinking, instead soaking his mangled hand in his tankard. Kempf had a slithery look in his expression and his frequent glances in the direction of the pantry and the cellar beneath it told quite clearly where his thoughts were. Kleiner was scratching at his arm in between trying to stifle a suddenly persistent cough. Old Mueller just looked resigned, like a beetle waiting for the other boot to fall.

Hans leaned into his brother, keeping his voice low, but not so low that the other smugglers couldn't hear him. 'I want Volk to know about this place. If his people are watching it, then there's small chance one of us is going to come sneaking back here on his own and try to make off with the wyrdstone. It'll take all of us to even have a chance of getting something that big out of here.'

Kempf hissed something unrepeatable. Wilhelm slammed his hurt hand against the counter and took a drink from his tankard. Kleiner coughed. Mueller just gave voice to a pained groan. Hans grinned like the face of Khaine, enjoying his brother's look of disbelieving horror.

'That's right,' he said. 'I'd rather put us all on the spot than have somebody getting rich off my sweat.'

Johann decided not to point out that it had been mostly Kleiner's sweat, any more than he was minded to observe that their chances of making off with the wyrdstone even together weren't going to be good. Volk's gang was sure to get some of them. He felt disgusted as he saw the answer reflected in his brother's twinkling eyes. That was part of the plan: fewer shares to go around. Not stupid, just callously reckless and ruthless.

Disgusted, Johann looked away from Hans, staring instead at the massive axe fastened to the wall above the bar. It was a huge weapon, the runes and craftsmanship proclaiming its dwarfish origin. It was a testament to how much the tavern's proprietor was feared and respected on the waterfront that no one had seen fit to try and steal it. Ulgrin Shatterhand was known for his black tempers and a sadistic streak seldom found in a dwarf. Some said the loss of his hand had made him mean enough to choke a giant with the one he still had. Others said it was some secret shame that made him an exile from his own people and which had made him as bitter as the waters of the Sour Sea. Johann had heard a slightly different version from the few dwarfs he'd met in the Orc and Axe. They said Ulgrin Shatterhand was such a miserable *grumbaki* because of that splendid axe above the bar: a cheap human-crafted forgery if they'd ever seen one.

Thinking about the axe made Johann look down the other end of the counter where an enormous glass jar rested. If the axe was a forgery, there was nothing fake about the tavern's other mascot. Pickled and preserved, the jar was filled with the swollen, snarling head of the largest, nastiest orc anyone in Altdorf had ever seen; many fights in the tavern started as arguments about whether the thing had really belonged to a large orc or had instead come from a small troll. Whatever the case, it was generally agreed that Ulgrin had lost his hand to orcs before he settled down to establish his tavern. The standing offer of free drinks to anyone who brought a larger orc head to the dwarf only helped to support such rumours.

As Johann looked at the leathery, green-skinned scowl of the head, his eyes were drawn to movement beyond the trophy. The bat-wing doors at the front of the tavern swung open, admitting a knot of armed men. Instantly the murmur of conversation in the taproom faded away to a whisper of muttered curses and hastily concealed contraband.

The foremost of the men was nearly as tall as Johann, with much broader shoulders. His features were regular, almost aristocratic if they hadn't been spoiled by a jagged knife scar along the left cheek, pulling the corner of the man's mouth into a slight pucker. Dark eyes, like the black pits of Mundsen Keep, fixed Johann with their gaze, then quickly looked past him and focused on his brother. The scarred mouth did its best to spread into a smile. The man dropped his hand casually to the longsword he wore at his side, the leather of his glove creaking as his fingers assumed a deceptively easy grip on the pommel.

'I've paid!' The outburst came from behind the counter. A hinged section of the bar swept upward and the stocky figure of Ulgrin Shatterhand stormed out. The dwarf's long white beard was tucked into the belt of his beer-stained apron, his grubby hand wiping foam across his leather leggings. The steel hook that gleamed from the stump of his other arm was held menacingly at his side. 'You can't go abusing my custom, griffon! I've paid!'

The man with thc scar turned a withering scowl against the dwarf. 'Funny, the captain must have failed to mention it.' He made a gesture with his hand, tapping the bronze pectoral that hung above his hauberk of reinforced leather. A griffon rampant, a halberd clenched in its talons, stood out upon the flat metal plate. It was the same figure that was represented upon the white armbands each of the armed men wore. It was the symbol of the Altdorf city watch. The bronze pectoral denoted the speaker as a sergeant in that stalwart organisation.

'He'll damn sure mention it after I get through talking to him!' Ulgrin snarled. 'And then he'll take that fancy jewellery away from you and kick your arse back down with the sewerjacks!'

The sergeant fixed Ulgrin with his most authoritarian stare. 'He'll be happy to hear you are so vocal about the bribes he accepts, drok,' the soldier said. 'It might make him reconsider the arrangement.'

The words had their intended effect. Sputtering and cursing, Ulgrin Shatterhand retreated back behind the counter, leaving his patrons to the attentions of Theodor Baer and his watchmen.

It wasn't a general raid for outlaws and contraband that interested the sergeant tonight, however. There was a very specific purpose behind his visit and as he turned his attention away from the angry dwarf and back to the men clustered about the bar, he found himself looking at that reason. Nodding to his men, Theodor Baer strolled over to where Hans Dietrich was trying his best to look inconspicuous.

'Heard you had some trouble tonight,' Theodor said by way of greeting.

'Get stuffed, griffon,' Hans spat.

'No thanks,' Theodor replied, pushing the tankard away from Hans's fingers, forcing the man to turn around and face him. 'Though I think Gustav Volk has some idea about doing something of the sort to you.'

'Volk is always talking tough,' Johann interrupted. 'But we're still here.'

Theodor looked down the bar, letting his eyes rest a while on each man. His gaze lingered on Kleiner, watching as the man almost doubled over from a fit of coughing. 'Seems to me there's a lot less of you here than a few nights ago.'

'I think some of the boys might have caught a ship for someplace,' Hans said.

'If they caught a ship, its port of call was the Gardens of Morr,' Theodor retorted. He raised the tankard, sniffed at it and wrinkled his nose at the reek of the cheap beer. 'Though I can't blame them for keeping away if this is the best stuff you can get here.'

'Whatever you are fishing for, griffon, you won't find it here,' Johann said, glowering at the sergeant.

Theodor shook his head. 'I'm not interested in you lot,' he said, though once again his attention was distracted by Kleiner's coughing and scratching. 'You're small fish. I want the big shark. I want Volk.'

'I'd like to give him to you,' Hans smiled. 'But unfortunately that is a commodity that isn't mine to sell.' The elder Dietrich threw down several silver coins onto the bar and shuffled away from the counter. The rest of the smugglers followed him, Kleiner last of all. Theodor watched them leave, but made no move to stop them.

In the doorway, as the small band left the *Orc and Axe,* Johann looked back at the sergeant. Theodor wasn't watching the smugglers anymore. Johann saw him further down the bar, near where Kleiner had been standing.

Across the distance, Johann couldn't see what Theodor found so interesting. He didn't see the strange, fat green worm writhing on the counter as it burrowed its way into the woodwork.

THE CHAMBER OF the Council of Thirteen was deep within the Shattered Tower. An ancient structure, older than even the skaven race, the Shattered Tower loomed above the decaying sprawl of Skavenblight like the warning finger of a malevolent god. Even with its foundations sucked down into the mire of the Blighted Marshes, there was no corner of Skavenblight upon which its shadow did not fall. It was a potent reminder of the authority and reach of the Lords of Decay, a physical tribute to the awful power of the Horned Rat and his domination of his chosen people: the skaven.

Enormous doors, carved from black Southland wood and engraved with the sinister sign of the Horned Rat, guarded the entrance to the council chamber. Before the black doors, the biggest rat ogre Thanquol had ever seen crouched beside the wall. The chain fixing its collar to thick iron staples set into the floor looking to have been stolen from a warship's anchor. The ugly brute rose up as it caught the scent of Thanquol and his escorts. Nearly furless, every inch of the rat ogre's exposed hide had been branded with the mark of the Horned Rat. It snuffled grotesquely at the air, like some great hound, then slowly lurched away from its post beside the doorway.

Thanquol controlled a quiver of fear as he felt the flagstones beneath his paws tremble from the huge monster's plodding steps. The albino stormvermin who flanked him, the guards who had led him through the streets of Skavenblight to ensure he kept his meeting with the Council, gave the faintest hint of musk as the brute's muscular bulk thundered past. Thanquol did not find the subdued fear of his grim escorts comforting. He wondered how many of those summoned to the chambers of the Council ended up in the monster's craw.

The rat ogre's immense paw closed around an enormous club with a head of grotesquely carved warpstone. To Thanquol's awed gaze, it looked as if the brute held an entire tree in its claws. He could imagine the weapon smashing down, pulverising whatever it struck into a gooey smear on the floor. The grey seer took a few nervous steps back, ensuring at least a few of the stormvermin were closer to the beast than he was.

The rat ogre, however, seemed to take no further notice of Thanquol and his entourage. Turning, the brute ambled over to a gigantic brass gong. With one swift motion, the monster brought its club smashing into the suspended metal disc, the violence of the impact sending a puff of green dust rising from the warpstone head.

A sound, low and sinister and evil, droned through the black corridors of the Shattered Tower, vibrating through the stones with malefic purpose. Thanquol could feel the sound pulse through his bones and ground his fangs against the terrifying sensation.

The single, throbbing note faded away, seeming to devour its own echoes. As it passed into nothingness, a new sound scratched at Thanquol's senses. Slowly, with eerie precision, the great doors of the Chamber of Thirteen were swinging open, moved by some force even Thanquol's sorcerous gaze could not discern. Smells, ancient and evil, billowed out from the room beyond the doors. Thanquol fought to keep his heart from racing. There would be time enough for terror after he crossed the threshold.

White paws closed about the grey seer's shoulders, giving him an encouraging shove towards the doorway when he hesitated. Thanquol scowled at the mute armoured ratmen. Obviously the cowardly wretches had no intention of accompanying him further. He wished the shrivelling of their rathoods and a thousand other curses upon them as he carefully crept across the threshold, watching every step with a caution that made his experience in the Maze of Merciless Penance seem overbold.

No sooner had Thanquol stepped inside the chamber than the great black doors slammed shut behind him with a resounding boom. The grey seer sprang forward ten feet, his pulse racing. Anxious paws flew to his long, hairless tail, stroking it like a brood-mother with a favourite whelp. Thanquol let out a long gasp of relief. It was all there. Somehow his tail had managed to avoid being caught in the slamming doors.

A low, bubbling chuckle took Thanquol's thoughts from his near-escape to the greater peril that still menaced him. It was a deep, throaty laugh, sickening and rotten, Thanquol was reminded of gas escaping from beneath a bog. It was a cruel, savage sort of humour that brooked no good will towards whatever it was directed against. He knew such a voice could belong to only one creature: Arch-Plaguelord Nurglitch, the foul master of the disgusting plague monks of Clan Pestilens.

The grey seer peered across the chamber. It was a great, round hall, its ceiling lost in the darkness far above. Braziers of glowing warpstone cast flickering shadows across the room, somehow managing to further obscure the far end of the hall even as they illuminated the centre. Even Thanquol's keen gaze could scarcely make out the other side of the chamber. He had the impression of a rounded dais and a circular podium draped in red cloth. Behind the podium were chairs, but whatever sat upon them was nothing more than an indistinct shape, a blotch of blackness that might hide anything or nothing.

Thanquol did not need to count the chairs to know that there were thirteen. Their occupants, if any, would be the Lords of Decay, the warlords and masters of the most powerful clans in the Under-Empire. He could barely make out the banners that stood behind each chair, casting a darker shadow upon its occupant. Each banner depicted the sign of the great clan or warlord clan the Lord of Decay ruled over and represented. The assassins of Clan Eshin, the fanatics of Clan Pestilens, the brutal warriors of Clan Mors and Clan Skab, all had their representative upon the Council of Thirteen.

Two of the seats bore no banner, however. Instead there was a metal icon, the crooked crossbars that represented the Horned Rat. One of the seats would be occupied by the seerlord, the voice of the skaven god and his chosen prophet. The other stood above the centremost seat, a seat that was always kept vacant, kept waiting for the presence of the Horned Rat himself. The seerlord would interpret the will of the Horned Rat whenever the Council was called upon to vote upon some matter of policy. In effect, the tradition gave the seerlord a double vote, but no skaven was bold enough to challenge the connection between Kritislik and their merciless god.

'Grey Seer Thanquol,' a growling voice echoed from the shadowy podium. Some trick of acoustics made it impossible to pinpoint from which seat the voice emanated, magnifying and distorting it beyond any semblance of mortal speech. Thanquol tried to identify the voice, unable to decide if it belonged to General Paskrit or Warlord Gnawdwell. 'The stink of fear is in your fur.'

Thanquol lowered his head and exposed his throat in abasement, trying to leave no question about his humility before the forbidding masters of his race. The warpstone braziers made it impossible for him to catch the scent of the seated warlords, but clearly the same disadvantage was not shared by the ratmen upon the dais. 'Only a fool does not cower-grovel before the magnificent terror of the Council, oh mighty tyrant.'

Scratchy laughter chittered from the darkness. 'Save your flattery and your lies for those witless enough to listen, mouse-bellied offal,' a knife-thin voice, possibly that of Nightlord Sneek, snickered.

'Come forward, wretched one,' the voice of Nurglitch, stagnant and slobbering, oozed from the shadows. Thanquol's glands clenched. 'Stand where the Council can see you.'

Thanquol quivered. Even the trickery of the chamber could not disguise that voice. Nurglitch, the decayed master of Clan Pestilens and its plague priests. One of Thanquol's earliest successes had been at the expense of the plague priests, orchestrating the assassination of Plague Lord Skratsquik before the disease-worshipping ratman could finish his improved strain of Yellow Pox. Nurglitch had been forced to decry Skratsquik as a renegade after the fact to save face with his fellow Lords of Decay, but it was convenience more than belief that moved his fellow skaven to accept the story. The bloated old plague rat was not one to forget any slight against his clan.

'Come forward,' the command came again, this time from a voice fairly creaking with age and brittle with wickedness. Thanquol had no difficulty identifying his own master, the Seerlord Kritislik. 'The Council does not ask twice,' Kritislik added with both menace and irony.

Thanquol forced himself upright and timidly approached the dais. His heart was hammering in his chest now, only a supreme effort kept his scent glands clenched. What game was Kritislik playing with him? Had the seerlord released him from the maze simply to destroy him before the entire Council? It was just the sort of grandiose display that would appeal to Kritislik. The horrible thought came to him: maybe the seerlord was looking to earn some good will with Clan Pestilens! Killing Thanquol in some gruesome manner before the eyes of Nurglitch would certainly accomplish that. The grey seer's eyes narrowed, darting from side to side, looking for some route of escape. Nurglitch wasn't the only member of the Council who might welcome his death. Clan Moulder was among the more recent enemies he had unjustly acquired, blaming him for their own incompetence and inadequacy.

Now Thanquol stood within a little ring of light, the exact centre of the warpstone braziers. The smell of the smoke was intoxicating, almost euphoric. He could feel the fumes dulling his senses, clouding his wit. He tried to shake off the effect, trying to claw his way free of the pleasant sensation. He needed every speck of his brilliance and cunning if he was going to leave the chamber alive. However seductive, the numbing draw of the smoke was threatening his chances to escape this audience alive.

'That is far enough, grey seer,' a scornful voice wheezed from the darkness. Even this close, Thanquol could not see a shape upon any of the seats, nor pick out the chair from which the speaker spoke. The grey seer's fur stood on end, knowing the eerie absence to be a display of Nightlord Sneek's terrible skill.

Through the fog of warpstone smoke, Thanquol could pick out other smells now. Faint, distant, but reeking of horror. He detected the faint tang of stagnant water and the thick musk of reptiles. He shifted his feet and felt the floor beneath him creak ever so slightly. Thanquol struggled to keep from bruxing his teeth together in an overt display of terror. No skaven in Skavenblight had failed to hear the stories of the execution pit, the long, cold drop into an unclimbable well, its depths filled with the most horrid of Clan Moulder's creations. Things, it was said, that swallowed their victims whole and alive, that left their prey breathing and screaming even as they were dissolved in their bellies.

'You have failed the Council, Grey Seer Thanquol,' the grating voice of Kritislik spoke. There was no room for question or argument in the tone, only accusation and condemnation.

Thanquol abased himself upon the floor, grovelling against the symbol of the Horned Rat picked out upon the tiled mosaic in luminous green stones. 'I was betrayed by my most worthless and cowardly minions,' he said. 'If they had followed-obeyed my plans...'

'Your plans!' snarled one of the voices. 'Then you admit it was your strategy that cheated Clan Skryre of the airship!'

Thanquol shivered before the voice. Distorted, almost fleshless, like the tones were drawn from a steel pipe instead of a living throat. The grey seer could easily suspect which of the Lords of Decay it was who spoke: Lord Morskittar, master of the warlock engineers of Clan Skryre. He could readily guess how eagerly the scientist-sorcerers of the clan had been waiting to study the dwarf airship and learn its secrets. Such a weapon would have been a potent addition to the arsenal of the Under-Empire and a monstrous boost to the prestige and power of Clan Skryre.

'We are not here to whine about the past,' a shrill, sharp voice interrupted. Thanquol tried to identify the voice, shuddering as he decided it might be that of Packlord Verminkin, overlord of Clan Moulder and its obscene science. 'The failures of the past do not concern this Council. It is the promise of the future that is our focus.'

A faint tremor of hope whispered through Thanquol's mind. He dared to lift his face from the floor. 'How may this most unworthy one serve the great and mighty Council of Thirteen, oh ravenous despots?'

'Still your tongue and you shall hear, Thanquol,' Verminkin snapped. Thanquol abased himself once more and the packlord continued. 'It has been brought to the Council's attention that a potent artefact long thought lost has been discovered in our settlement of Under-Altdorf.'

'You will recover this artefact,' the growling Paskrit/Gnawdwell continued. 'You will recover it and you will bring it back here, to the Council of Thirteen.'

'You will act as our agent,' Kritislik said. 'You will have the full authority of this Council behind you. The council of Under-Altdorf will submit to that authority in every way.'

Something came hurtling out of the shadows, clattering against the flagstones near Thanquol's bowed head.

The grey seer shifted his gaze, observing that it was a thick black pendant upon which the symbol of the Horned Rat was picked out in crushed ruby. It was a talisman of the Lords of Decay, entrusted only to those they sent upon the most vital of missions. Suddenly the thrill of hope shrivelled inside him. Anything vital to the Council was also bound to be grotesquely dangerous, dangerous enough that none of the clans felt safe pursuing it on their own.

'If... if this wretched one might speak...' Thanquol asked, lifting his head ever so slightly, careful to keep his lips over his fangs lest anything he do be interpreted as a challenge. When no voice snarled from the shadows to silence him, the grey seer proceeded. 'Just one small question, oh virile sires of stormvermin. This artefact which you would have this most unworthy of servants retrieve for you...'

Nurglitch's oozing voice rose from the darkness. 'It is the Wormstone,' the plaguelord declared. 'Lost for a thousand breedings in the collapsed burrows beneath the man-nest of Altdorf. A potent weapon crafted by Clan Pestilens for the greater glory of the Horned Rat and the skaven race. Stolen before it could be presented as a gift to the Council.'

It didn't take a faint hint of Nurglitch's putrid breath to smell his words, but Thanquol knew better than to challenge the lie. Skaven politics was built upon letting adversaries and rivals spew whatever inanity they liked and pretending to accept it as something more than rubbish. If the Council saw fit to accept Nurglitch's story for the time being, Thanquol wasn't about to stick his own neck out.

'The Wormstone is a masterpiece of alchemical creation,' this time it was the metallic voice of Morskittar that spoke. 'A block of pure warpstone endowed with new properties through a process now lost and forgotten.'

'The Wormstone is the key to tearing down the decaying kingdoms of men and dwarfs,' said Nightlord Sneek. 'With it, we can unleash such plagues as the soft races have never imagined even in their darkest nightmares!' The statement ended with another peal of chittering laughter.

'Your colleague, Grey Seer Skabritt discovered the location of the Wormstone,' said Kritislik. 'He was killed in the attempt to recover it, but his apprentice, Kratch, escaped to bring word of his find to us.

'You will succeed where Skabritt failed, Grey Seer Thanquol. You will return to Under-Altdorf with Kratch. You will recover the Wormstone and you will bring it back.'

Thanquol nearly leapt out of his fur as a pair of armoured white stormvermin appeared silently beside him. One of the stormvermin held a tall wooden staff in its paw, a staff tipped with a bronze icon of the Horned Rat. The other held an ornate amulet, a solid piece of pure warpstone engraved with the symbol of Thanquol's god. The Staff and Amulet of the Horned One, the potent magic devices that had been confiscated from Thanquol upon his return to Skavenblight. The grey seer lashed his tail in delight just seeing them again.

'These two will accompany you,' General Paskrit said. It took Thanquol a moment to understand that he meant the two stormvermin, not the objects they held. 'They will be another reminder to the leaders of Under-Altdorf that you are the representative of this Council.'

Thanquol nodded his head in agreement, though he easily saw through the deception. The warriors wouldn't be simply protecting him, they would be the eyes and ears of the Lords of Decay, watching and waiting for any sign of treachery or duplicity on Thanquol's part. It was another example of how much importance they placed on the recovery of the Wormstone.

'I will leave at once, most grim and terrible of potentates,' Thanquol said, abasing himself before the dais once more. He could hear a murmur of conversation in the shadows.

'One last thing,' Kritislik said. 'Do not divulge anything of your mission to any within Under-Altdorf. This Council has been aware of a growing trend of independence and wilfulness among the faithless tail-lickers of that city. Under no circumstance are they to be made aware of the Wormstone.'

'Fail us in this, Thanquol,' came the bubbling voice of Nurglitch, 'at your most dreadful peril.'

Thanquol tried to keep a trace of dignity in his speedy withdrawal from the chamber as the black doors creaked open once more. After standing before the Lords of Decay, even the giant rat ogre in the corridor outside was a friendly sight.

KLEINER WAS HOLDING his sides, trying to push his ribs together, trying to squeeze out the pain. His insides felt as if they were on fire, as though little flickers of flame were dancing beneath his skin. The scratching had become maddening, his fingers were caked in blood. The coughing had become even worse, filth bubbling up from his throat that was too greasy to be blood and phlegm.

After retiring from the *Orc and Axe*, Kleiner had withdrawn to his lodgings, an attic apartment in a rundown hovel overlooking the Imperial shipyards. He was certain he had become the victim of some ill humour he had been exposed to in the sewers. He could feel it gnawing at his body. Kleiner had seldom prayed to any of the gods, even Ranald the patron of thieves, but now he found himself begging Shallya the goddess of mercy to make the pain go away. If only she would show him that small grace, he would abandon his wicked ways. This time he wouldn't let Hans talk him back into a life of crime either.

Kleiner stuffed a rag into his mouth as another burst of violent coughing seized him. He couldn't let his landlady discover that he was sick. The best he could expect would be to be thrown into the street. He could also imagine the paranoid old bat killing him in his sleep and dumping him in the Reik to keep any rumour of plague away from her boarding house.

The big smuggler rose from the straw-covered pallet that served as his bed, kicking old bottles from his path as he hobbled across the dingy room. He picked a few stained rags from the floor, feeling his stomach churn as he saw ugly green worms slither away when he moved them. For hours now, he'd been picking the loathsome things from his skin, dumping them in a copper slop-bucket. Kleiner almost gagged at the smell rising from the bucket, then dropped the bundle of rags into it. A vicious attack of coughing seized him and the big man fell to his knees beside the reeking can.

Lifting himself from the floor, Kleiner found the strength to carry the nauseating bucket to the tiny window that was the only ventilation in his room. He brushed aside the strip of canvas acting as a curtain. A blast of cold early morning air struck him and he blinked in the starlight. The city lay still and silent below. Summoning another reserve of strength, Kleiner dumped the bucket's contents out the window. He watched as the rags and waste splashed into the gutter far below, then felt his gorge rise again. A pack of scrawny mongrels darted from the nearest alley, enthusiastically lapping up the filth he had cast below.

Kleiner lurched away from the disquieting sight, letting the bucket drop to the floor. Another attack of coughing seized him. As he reached up to stifle the sound, he plucked something fat and squirming from his cheek. The worm resisted his effort to pull it free, its slimy dampness twisting away from his touch.

The horror taxed the last reserves of the smuggler's strength. He tried to make it back to his pallet before he collapsed.

Kleiner didn't make it.

THE AGONISED SCREAM echoed from the alleyway, ripping Theodor Baer from his sombre thoughts. Immediately the sergeant was dashing down the lonely, darkened street, two of his soldiers close behind him. It was simple circumstance that caused the men to be patrolling such a lonely stretch of street. Theodor had been hoping to locate members of Gustav Volk's gang out hunting for Hans Dietrich and his smugglers. When he heard the cry, his first reaction was to connect it to the brutal gang leader's vendetta.

The scream, however, had not come from an adult. It was the shrill voice of a child. Rounding the darkened corner at a run, trying to avoid the muck and garbage heaped in the gutters, Theodor saw that the victim of the outrage was no cocksure smuggler getting more than he bargained for. Nor was the perpetrator some wharf rat ruffian out for revenge.

Instead the watchmen found a little girl, probably a bonepicker or dung gatherer judging by the smelly goatskin bag slung over her back, crouched in a corner trying to defend herself with a broken chair leg. Her attacker was a large mangy dog, so thin Theodor could count every rib, its hackles raised and its jaws foaming. Theodor shouted at the cur, thinking to scare the maddened beast. The shout didn't frighten the mongrel. With lightning speed, the dog spun about, snapping and snarling at the would-be rescuers.

That was when things took a strange turn. In the dim starlight, Theodor could see the dog's eyes glowing with a weird green luminance. The cur's tan pelt was thin and rubbed raw, but Theodor could see things moving across it, like ripples in the river. It was with horror that the sergeant realised the effect of motion was caused by hundreds of wriggling worms burrowing up from beneath the dog's skin.

The slavering mongrel did not wait for the watchmen to recover from their disgust. Snarling, it leapt at them, snapping its foam-flecked fangs at each of them in turn. One of the watchmen stabbed the animal with his sword, gouging a grisly wound in its flank. What bubbled up from the injury was too putrid to be called blood and the man recoiled from the rancid stench. As the dog turned to focus on the man who had struck it, Theodor's own blade licked out, slashing it across the back, severing its spine. The brute flopped to the street, twitching, trying to pull itself upright with only its front paws. Even half-paralysed, the dog's instinct was to kill, its jaws snapping at Theodor as the sergeant moved towards it.

Theodor's second blow finished the animal, a quick sharp thrust through one of the weirdly glowing eyes and into the stricken mongrel's brain. A stench, even fouler than before, erupted from the dog as it slumped across the sergeant's steel. The soldier drew a kerchief from his tunic to wipe the blood from his sword, then cast the rag from him when he was finished.

'Check the girl,' Theodor told his men. The two soldiers had been staring in amazement at the gruesome carcass of the dog. Now they remembered the little girl whose screams had drawn them into an encounter with the strange beast. She was still pressed into the corner of the alley, seeming as though she was trying to push herself through the plaster wall. As the watchmen came for her, in her terror, the girl struck at them with the chair leg. One of the soldiers took a blow against his forearm, then relieved the child of the crude weapon.

'I don't think she's been bitten,' one of the watchmen called to his sergeant after a cursory examination of the frightened waif.

'Take her to the hospice just to be sure,' Theodor said. With something as unclean as the dog he had killed, it wouldn't do to take any chances. The gods only knew what evil might arise from even a small cut delivered by such a wretched beast. The Shallyan sisters would know what to look for better than some overworked, underpaid Altdorf watchmen.

As his men carried the child away, Theodor lingered behind, continuing to study the gruesome cur. The worms weren't moving now; as the dog had died, they had grown still. At least most of them had. Several had dropped away from the body and wriggled away, burrowing into the muck of the gutters.

Theodor knew there was some foulness beyond his understanding at work here. He knew this was more than just a matter of thieves and murderers. Just as he didn't know what to look for in the way of infection or injury on the little girl's body, he also accepted that he didn't know what to look for here. There was a connection, he was sure, between the horrible green worms here and the one he had seen in the *Orc and Axe*, the one he was certain had dropped off the smuggler's arm while he was scratching it. Something unclean, unholy, was at large in the waterfront. It would take a different sort of man to root it out and bring it to ground.

There was no pleasant way to do what Theodor knew he had to do next. When his men led away the little girl, they left behind her goatskin bag. Theodor walked over to it, upending it and spilling its contents of rubbish and rags into the street. He needed it to carry a different kind of garbage.

Using the chair leg, Theodor poked and prodded the carcass of the dog until it rolled into the open bag. Tying the loathsome burden into a bundle, dragging it behind him, he made his way through the deserted streets. It wasn't the hospice or even the watchhouse that was his destination. He knew where he must take the wretched carcass. He knew where to take it if there were to be any chance of solving the strange enigma of the worms.

Through the early morning chill, Theodor made his way, picking a circuitous path through back streets and alleyways. Peeling plaster walls gave way to splintered timber frames as his journey took him into the oldest, most neglected section of the district, a place so forgotten that it was ignored even by the lamplighters. He found himself trudging down muddy lanes surrounded by sagging structures that might have stood in the days when the city had still been called Reikdorf. Shingled eaves frowned down at him, shuttered windows stared at him through lidded eyes. Somewhere a cat yowled and a night bird made its raucous call. Theodor felt his skin crawl, and a cold shiver ran up his back. However many times he followed the path, followed the secret marks visible only to those who knew how to look, he could not shake the eerie impression that now gripped him.

This part of the city was more than simply forgotten.

It was forsaken.

Forbidden.

Theodor stopped outside a dilapidated storefront. A pane of frosted glass set into the timber wall bore gilded letters in antiquated script, though Theodor could not make them out. There was no hint of the room behind the glass, so frosted with age and neglect was the window. Only those who had been inside could tell what the place housed. The curious would have been disappointed. Theodor was when he had first opened the heavy oak door set in the wall beside the window.

He pulled an iron key from his belt and fitted it into the door's lock. There was a trick to working the key, a system of half-turns that had to be precisely worked to open the door. As it creaked inward on its hinges, Theodor found his nose filled with the musty smell of the building. The room beyond was just as it had been when he had first laid eyes on it many years ago: empty save for a thick layer of dust upon the floor.

Theodor dumped the goatskin bag and its grisly contents upon the floor. As he had done every time he'd visited the derelict building, he studied its walls, scrutinised the crumbling stairway that led up into the structure's upper levels. As he had found every time before, there was nothing to be seen. No hint of secret doors and hidden watchers, no clue to anything that suggested the place was more than an abandoned ruin on an abandoned street.

It was more, however. Theodor retraced his steps and locked the door again behind him. Even if he had never been able to puzzle it out for himself, there was much more to the building than met the eye. Somehow, in some way, whatever was left in that room did not stay there.

Somehow, it would be retrieved, taken by the one man in Altdorf who would know how to unlock its secrets.

The man Theodor Baer called 'master'.

CHAPTER FOUR
The City Below

DARKNESS FILLED THE windowless room. A hissed command whispered through the blackness and a ghostly glow began to slowly form in the empty air. The weird grey light threw rays of illumination upon the polished surface of a long steel table, and upon the table alone. The unseen walls, the ceiling and floor, these remained untouched by the spectral orb, lost within the thick shadows of perpetual gloom.

Upon the table, a goatskin bag was spread, its tattered edge held open by heavy weights. The centre of the bag had been cut open and peeled back, leaving its gruesome contents exposed beneath the sinister light.

For an instant, the light flickered. A stretch of shadow seemed to detach itself from the surrounding gloom. The strange apparition advanced upon the table, leaning above the objects spread across it. Pale, slender hands emerged from the dark shape. Powerful, claw-like fingers gripped steel instruments, pressing them into the corrupt husk of the creature on the table. A pincer-like device gripped one of the long, fat-bodied worms and pulled it free from the scrawny carcass.

Long moments passed as the hand turned the gruesome object around in its grip. Burning eyes studied the worm, committing its every contour and wrinkle to memory. Suddenly, the pincers were laid down upon the table beside the carcass. The pale hands retreated back into the formless shape, which withdrew in turn back into the lurking gloom.

Another hiss crawled through the empty room. As eerily as it had formed, the ghost light faded away, consigning the carcass of the dog Theodor Baer had killed once more to the darkness.

THE DANK DARKNESS of the river had a soothing effect on Grey Seer Thanquol as he stood upon the deck of the flat-bottomed barge. He could feel the wood creaking and rolling ever so slightly beneath his feet, swaying in time to the current of the underground channel and the skaven bargerats poling their vessel through the black deeps of the world. He could hear sleepy riverbats croaking and chittering to each other from their perches on the ceiling high above the water, he could see the faint splashes in the stream as pallid cave-fish burst the surface to slurp great gulps of air into their slimy bodies. He could smell the thousand odours sweeping down the channel: the stink of wet fur, the decaying reek of rotting wood, the pungent tang of rat roasting over an open fire, the sharp suggestion of rusting metal, the seductive scent of warpstone smouldering in a metal brazier. They were the smells of civilisation and after a week upon the sunken rivers of the Under-Empire, they were a welcome sensation.

Thanquol straightened his body and muttered a hiss of satisfaction. Soon, soon he would be in Under-Altdorf, second greatest city in all skavendom! Nor would he be a non-entity in that city! Far from it! He would be the chosen representative of the Lords of Decay, their trusted agent, their invaluable proxy. Even the leaders of Under-Altdorf would be forced to bow their knee to him and wait upon his every whim. Such was the importance the Council placed upon Thanquol and his mission.

The grey seer felt a twitter of fear pass through him as he thought about that mission. The Lords of Decay had been somewhat evasive in their description of the artefact he was to retrieve. He knew it was some potent weapon crafted by Clan Pestilens, and had his suspicions that its intended use had not been confined to the furless humans and their decadent society. Anything developed by Clan Pestilens was apt to be monstrously dangerous, this was an accepted fact, but Thanquol was no simpering whelp. He would meet such danger boldly and headfirst. He wondered how many clanrat warriors it would be prudent to commandeer from Under-Altdorf to help him retrieve the Wormstone. Too many might make him seem cowardly, but too few would be imprudent. After all, there was no glory in confronting danger if he was to be one of its victims.

Thanquol cast a suspicious glance across the flat deck of the barge. The bargerats, all wearing leather jerkins stained in the colours of Clan Sleekit, were mostly clustered about the sides of the vessel, working their metal-tipped poles through the black water of the river, prodding the unseen bottom to push the ship forwards. The grey seer gave the skaven sailors only glancing notice. He continued his scrutiny of the barge, looking across at the piled sacks of grain and metal slag that formed the bulk of the barge's cargo, even a small barrel of the black corn grown in the Blighted Marshes. A little taste of Skavenblight's only crop was a mark of status anywhere else in the Under-Empire, and many a warlord and clanmaster paid many warpstone tokens to boast that he dined upon such fare. Thanquol little understood the practice: black corn was all but inedible, even for a skaven. It was the staple of Skavenblight's diet out of necessity rather than choice. Having survived on such fare too often in the past, he felt his stomach clench every time the scent from the barrel struck his snout.

Chained to the deck, just out of reach of the cargo, was a line of scrawny skavenslaves, their pelts branded with the mark of Clan Sleekit. The bargerats didn't trust their slaves with the delicate task of navigating the ship, however rough and demanding the work might become. They would leave the slaves in their fetters throughout the voyage, sometimes lashing the huddled wretches out of spite. When the barge reached its port of call, things would change. Then the slaves would be pressed into action, unloading the cargo their masters had brought so very far.

The grey seer turned his gaze away from the huddled mass of skavenslaves. Away from them, looming near the prow of the barge, were his 'bodyguards', a pair of hulking white ratmen in red steel armour. Garrisoned within the Shattered Tower itself, the white stormvermin were an enigma even Thanquol's keen, perceptive mind had failed to penetrate. Mute, gigantic in proportions and possessed of a distinctly unskavenlike incorruptibility, Thanquol wondered about their origins. The two that had been sent along with him as overseers and spies – for he did not believe for an instant the Council's claim they were really his protectors – were so alike they could only be from the same litter. Was that possibly the secret, some hidden clutch of brood-mothers kept by the Council that only produced these hulking, white-furred specimens? It would not be the first instance of skaven using warpstone and other substances to influence the ratlings forming in the bellies of the brood-mothers. Clan Skaul in particular was known for the high numbers of horned skaven born to its litters, while Clan Skab's ratmothers produced inordinate numbers of ferocious black skaven. If that were the case, Thanquol would give much to learn the Council's secret of instilling such incorruptible loyalty in their warriors.

Thoughts of loyalty shifted Thanquol's attention away from the white ratkin to a grey one. As he glanced in the direction of Adept Kratch, the apprentice grey seer quickly turned his head. Thanquol's lip curled in a fang-ridden sneer. Kratch knew a good deal more about the Wormstone than he had told the Council. Certainly more than he had told Thanquol! The grey seer lashed his tail in annoyance. What plot was the young seer hatching within that scheming little brain? Thanquol had studiously avoided taking on any apprentices; the fate of his own mentor, that trusting old fool Sleekit, was a bit too vivid for him to have any ambitious young whelps nipping at his tail.

An ugly idea occurred to Thanquol, and not for the first time. He wasn't the first master Kratch had served. It was rather convenient for the apprentice that he alone had escaped the death that had overtaken Grey Seer Skabritt and his entourage. Already raised far beyond his station by the Council, made apprentice to the famous, renowned Grey Seer Thanquol, allowed the fabulous opportunity to learn from the most brilliant mind in all skavendom, Thanquol suspected that Kratch was still not content. The adept would require some careful watching... or perhaps a convenient accident when the time was right.

'Grey Seer Thanquol.'

Thanquol turned about as he heard himself addressed, his name spoken with the right mixture of fear and respect his position warranted. The bargemaster, a pot-bellied, one-eyed ratman with piebald fur and oversized incisors, bowed on the deck before him, head tilted to the side to expose his throat. Thanquol flicked his claw, motioning for the skaven to speak.

'Under-Altdorf, merciless and beneficent master,' the bargerat said. 'City scent is strong-strong, close-near.'

A clawed foot kicked out, striking the bargerat's head. The skaven reared away from the blow, flattening its muzzle against the deck.

'Fat-tongue flea!' Thanquol snapped, annoyed by the grovelling bargemaster. He slapped a claw against his own muzzle. 'Think-think I did not smell city-scent?' The grey seer's foot kicked out again, but this time the bargerat was quick enough to duck. 'Sail this flotsam, leave thinking to those with wits.'

The bargemaster scurried away on all fours, waiting until he was well out of kicking distance before straightening. He turned, prowling over to the nearest knot of bargerats, swatting and swiping at them with his claws, allegations of slothfulness and other misdeeds flying from his tongue like little daggers. He threw one of the bargerats from the pole and assumed the duty for himself. The displaced bargerat skulked across the deck, stopping when he reached the shackled slaves. He didn't bother concocting an excuse as he drew the ratgut whip from his belt and began to lash the skavenslaves.

Thanquol licked his fangs hungrily as the smell of fresh blood rose from the slaves. He was rather tired of cave fish and grain after so many days trapped on the rickety barge. A flank of fresh slave would do wonders relieving the tedium of the voyage.

Culinary considerations quickly faded as Thanquol's sharp eyes detected the glow of torches in the distance. Rounding a bend in the underground river, the channel widened, opening into a cavernous expanse. The expanse slowly sloped upward from one side of the cave wall. It was from here that the flickering glow of torches shone. As they came nearer, the city-scent increased. Thanquol could see ramshackle wharfs projecting out into the water, crudely cobbled together from splintered planks and lumber stolen from the surface. The wharfs were swarming with ratmen of many sizes and colours, hurrying to unload sacks of grain, coffles of skavenslaves, boxes of warpstone and other cargo from a small flotilla of Clan Sleekit barges. Others were busy loading cargo onto empty barges: blocks of masonry, cords of lumber, baskets of steel, bundles of cloth, the plunder and loot from hundreds of midnight forays into the nest of humans above Under-Altdorf. Thanquol snickered as he saw coffles of pale, shivering humans being led onto some of the barges. After his recent misfortunes, his contempt for the furless breed had only grown. He wished the humans ill fortune in their new lives as slaves. Perhaps they would find themselves being sold to Clan Moulder to use in their ghastly experiments. With the recent slave revolt in Hell Pit, the master moulders would be needing a new supply of subjects for their studies.

The barge slowly manoeuvred through the press of ships clustered about the wharfs. The bargemaster snapped orders to his crew and the boat shifted about, making for an empty dock that had just been vacated by a ship loaded with bolts of brightly dyed cloth. Another ship tried to slip into the position, nearly colliding with the barge. Angry squeaks of accusation from the other ship quickly died when the bargerats saw Thanquol's imposing figure standing upon the deck. With indecent haste, the other ship pulled away, not caring how many other barges it jostled as it made its retreat.

Thanquol straightened his posture, tightening his grip on the staff clutched in his claws, as the barge slid into place beside the ramshackle dock. Activity around the wharf came to a standstill as skaven paused in their tracks to stare at the sinister grey-clad priest. The scent of fear-musk rose from the most timid, others hurriedly averted their eyes and quickly remembered reasons why they should be elsewhere. An unnatural hush fell across the waterfront, and for the first time the sloshing rush of the river was not drowned out by the squabbling squeaks of the ratkin.

A big brown skaven, its scarred body pressed into a tattered collection of rags bearing the sign of Clan Skab, emerged from the awe that suppressed the rest of the waterfront. Brandishing a thick iron rod, he savagely struck at a huddle of emaciated humans, their bodies even more scarred than that of the ratman. The wasted slaves shuffled to the wharf, casting ropes to the bargerats on Thanquol's ship. The skaven snatched the ropes from the cowed humans, swiftly tying off their vessel to the rickety dock.

Thanquol waited until the brown slavemaster encouraged his charges to place a gangplank between the deck and the dock before thinking about disembarking. He was relishing the respect and fear he smelled rising from the ratmen all around him. News of his coming had preceded him. Despite the Council's unjust blaming of him for his recent setbacks, the numberless masses of the Under-Empire remembered him as the great and mighty Grey Seer Thanquol. They remembered, and they shivered in his presence.

The bargerats started to release their own skavenslaves to unload the cargo. Thanquol shot a malicious glare at the bargemaster as he noticed the activity. The ratman wilted before the grey seer's fiery gaze. Did the idiot really intend to put his petty business before Thanquol's disembarking? The wretch should be praising the Horned Rat with his every breath that he'd been allowed the unrivalled honour of conveying a personage so esteemed upon his dilapidated scow! Thanquol stalked towards the cringing bargemaster, whose terror only swelled when the red-armoured stormvermin fell in to either side of the grey seer, murderous smiles on their muzzles. Thanquol raised his staff, gripping it close beneath the metal icon. It hung poised above the bargemaster's head like the iron bludgeon of the waterfront slavemaster.

Instead of dashing in the bargerat's skull, Thanquol brought the staff crashing down into an iron-banded barrel, splintering its lid. The grey seer sneered at the bargemaster and dug a paw into the barrel. He made a point of popping a few kernels of black corn into his mouth as he strode away. The vile taste still made his stomach clench, but there was a deep satisfaction in the humiliation of the thoughtless bargemaster.

Thanquol clambered down the gangplank, his head raised imperiously as he strode past the awed throng of slaves and wharf-rats around him. He could see the great tunnels that stabbed through the earth away from the docks, thrusting down into the twisting burrows of Under-Altdorf proper. A few structures, gouged into the sides of the tunnels and supported with lumber and stonework stolen from the humans above, stood illuminated by torches and warpstone braziers. Vaults for cargo unloaded at the docks, slavepens, even the workshops of Clan Sleekit's shipwrights loomed against the walls of the cavern. Thanquol could see a battered sign, probably stolen from a human tavern, hanging from a rusty chain above what could only be a garrison of the settlement's warriors.

It was from the garrison that an armed body of skaven emerged, marching quickly across the waterfront, kicking and biting any ratmen too slow or slack-witted to make way for them. Thanquol was not surprised to find that they were stormvermin, of the more usual black-furred kind. Their steel armour and weapons were better than most settlements in the Under-Empire could boast, but then few places had the rich opportunities to bloat their armouries through theft and bribery the way Under-Altdorf could. The black stormvermin looked puny beside the albinos the Council had sent along with him, but there were at least a score of the fang-faced brutes. Any lingering confidence Thanquol had in his bodyguards suffered when he noticed that counting was not one of their deficiencies and the two warriors began to slowly back away from the grey seer.

The company of stormvermin came to a ragged stop before the dock. If they had been a less menacing sight, Thanquol might have snickered at the foolish attempt at aping the drill and precision of a human regiment. Most skaven were content to leave such pompous nonsense to the humans, but then there were many strange ideas among the inhabitants of Under-Altdorf. The Council saw rebellion and treachery everywhere they looked, but perhaps their paranoia about this city was not misplaced.

A crook-backed skaven bulled his way through the armoured ranks of the stormvermin. He wore the symbol of Clan Skryre upon his leather robes, a thick tool-belt straddling his waist. There was a chemical stink to his fur, and a metallic tinge to his overall scent. The ratman's eyes were hidden behind a set of iron goggles, pitted with tiny openings so that the skaven resembled a fly as much as he did a rodent. The creature raised his head high, striving to stare down at Thanquol despite his malformed back.

'I am name-call Vermisch of Clan Skryre, honoured emissary of their great and terrible lordships, the Grand High Supreme Council of Under-Altdorf, Festereach and Gnawhome. I am delegated to meet-speak with Thanquol…'

'Grey Seer Thanquol,' Thanquol corrected Vermisch, putting his most menacing hiss into every syllable. The little warlock engineer was like his stormvermin, pompous and preening. Far too recently, Thanquol had trembled before the Lords of Decay, before the Council of Thirteen itself. Moles would chew his bones before he would cower before this self-important functionary of a ten-flea circus with delusions of grandeur.

Vermisch was still blinking in nervous confusion as Thanquol took a pull of warpstone snuff to fortify himself. The grey seer closed the little ratskull box with a loud snap and glared at the befuddled emissary. 'I am Grey Seer Thanquol,' he said needlessly. As much as the snuff helped pour fire into his veins, it had a disconcerting habit of dulling the wit. 'I am the chosen representative of their malevolent majesties, the Lords of Decay, the Council of Thirteen of holy Skavenblight and the living claws of his most vengeful divinity the Horned Rat. I am the eyes, nose and ears of Skavenblight. I am their judge and their dagger! Know me and tremble, spleenless-mouse, and beg my indulgence for your impiety!'

There was no confusion in Vermisch now. His head lowered and turned, exposing his throat in the traditional display of subjugation. Several of the stormvermin had likewise dropped down, lowering themselves before the formidable figure who had so thoroughly cowed the sinister Vermisch.

Thanquol's tail twitched in satisfaction as he saw the display his fierce words had provoked. For an instant he considered drawing upon his sacred powers and immolating a few of the cowering ratmen as a reminder to the rest of the finality of the Horned Rat's holy wrath. He quickly relented, understanding it was the warpstone inciting him to such recklessness. Scolded, the Under-Altdorf warriors might prove tractable. Attacked, they might respond in kind. Thanquol still didn't like the way the numbers favoured Vermisch.

'Forgive-forget this unworthy flea, most awful of dooms, Grey Seer Thanquol,' Vermisch stammered, a suggestion of musk in his scent now. 'My masters bid-ordered me wait-seek you. They wish-want to speak with your terrible eminence at once... if it pleases you, most dreaded of sorcerers.'

Thanquol stared down his snout at the contrite Vermisch, giving him only a slightly menacing display of fang to keep him in his place. 'It pleases me to see your chieftains,' Thanquol told him. 'You may lead the way to their chambers.'

Bowing and grovelling, Vermisch hurried to reform the stormvermin into two columns, then waited for Thanquol to join him at the centre of the protective formation. With a measured, unhurried and unworried pace, Thanquol slowly strolled towards the armoured warriors. He snapped a few whispered commands to his bodyguards, promising unspeakable things if they should leave his side again. Even the elite white stormvermin seemed disturbed by some of the sadistic images he conjured.

'A masterful display, grey seer.'

The fawning words were like a weasel's whisper against Thanquol's ear. The fur on his back crawled as though feeling the bite of a knife, but Thanquol forced himself not to break stride. In his preoccupation with Vermisch, he'd forgotten about Kratch. He blamed the oversight on the warpstone dulling his mind.

'Adept Kratch,' Thanquol snarled. 'An apprentice's place is before his master... where his mentor can watch-see and point out his pupil's... missteps.'

Kratch hurried forwards, bowing his head in deference to Thanquol's reprimand. 'Forgive me, master,' Kratch said. 'I did not want any enemies to sneak up behind you.'

Thanquol gave his apprentice a blank, dumbfounded look, then blinked away his disbelief. Either the ratling thought himself incredibly clever or else he was the most painfully obvious backstabber ever suckled by a broodmother!

As he continued to stare at the simpering apprentice, Thanquol noticed that Kratch was furtively snacking on something clenched in his left paw. The grey seer gestured at his apprentice with a claw.

'What are you eating?' he demanded.

Kratch's eyes became downcast, his body posture wilting like a flower beneath the Lustrian sun. Guiltily, he opened his paw, revealing a few kernels of black corn.

Thanquol snickered, understanding now why his apprentice had such a sickly scent. He realised that he still held a few kernels himself. With a broad gesture, one that could not fail to be noticed by Vermisch and his warriors, Thanquol placed the rest of the kernels in Kratch's paw.

'A reward-gift for your tireless loyalty,' Thanquol told his apprentice. The display of black corn, such a valued commodity in Under-Altdorf, given so liberally to a mere underling would go far to impress upon Vermisch that Thanquol was above the thieving, cringing inhabitants of this city. He was reinforcing his fierce words, reminding Vermisch of where he was from and who he represented.

Stalking onward to join the functionary, Thanquol watched Kratch from the corner of his eye. There was, of course, another, purely selfish reason for the display, and each time he saw Kratch's face twist with revulsion Thanquol felt a little shiver of amusement tingle down his tail.

THE SHOP OF Dr Lucas Phillip Loew was an old half-timbered building that looked old enough to have been the birthplace of Magnus the Pious. A balustrade of brickwork seemed to be all that was keeping its eastern wall from collapsing into an alleyway, while the roof was missing so many tiles that the support beams stood naked and exposed to the elements. It didn't matter overmuch. None of the upper three floors of the structure were inhabited; if it were not for Dr Loew's shop, the entire building would have been abandoned.

The glassblower that had once operated the store next to Dr Loew was long gone, a faded playbill still pasted to the window advertised a Detlef Sierck tragedy that had stopped being performed twenty years ago.

Even if the building was not threatening to collapse into ruin every time a stork landed on its chimney, the landlords would have been hard-pressed to find tenants after Dr Loew moved in. In the wealthier and more educated districts of Altdorf shops like that of Dr Loew, an alchemist by profession, were shunned because of foul odours and the very real threat of dramatic explosions. In a superstitious, backwards slum like the waterfront, the situation was worse. The denizens of such places had little tolerance for magic of any sort, having listened only too intently to the fiery sermons of zealous Sigmarites. To their minds, there was no separating an alchemist from a wizard and a wizard from a sorcerer.

Still, a shop like that of Dr Loew did not depend upon local custom for its business. His patrons were scattered all across Altdorf, in every district and at every level of society. He did not need to seek out his customers, they would seek him out. And, because of the isolated, lonely situation of his shop, they would feel even more comfortable about patronising the alchemist.

At present however, the men moving about the wooden racks of powders and pastes, peering into the jars of dried spider legs and pickled salamander eyes, were sellers, not buyers. Dr Loew, seated at a long table at the rear of his shop, watched the men through the jungle of alembics and jars scattered across his workspace. Scruffy, caked in the grime and poverty of the waterfront, they were the sort of unpleasant creatures circumstances often forced the alchemist to deal with.

Such creatures had low morals and few scruples when it came to gathering the morbid, often illegal substances desired by his patrons.

Hans Dietrich and his little band of smugglers were men Dr Loew had only dealt with rarely in the past, far less than the weirdroot growers and graverobbers who were his usual sources of supply. Dietrich didn't seem to have the spine for engaging in activities that might earn him the attentions of the witch hunters, and generally gave the alchemist a wide berth. This time, however, he'd found something valuable enough to overcome those concerns.

Dr Loew looked away from the smugglers, returning his attention to the little bronze firepot and the iron bowl resting above it. He studied the way the heat played across the strange rock the criminals had brought him. The stone was like a sponge, absorbing whatever was inflicted upon it. That was in keeping with wyrdstone; the substance was notoriously hard to refine and smelt. Part mineral, part something else entirely, the weird rock had defied the best scholars of ten centuries to accurately classify. Of course, being unknown rather than understood, wyrdstone was condemned as tainted with Chaos by the short-sighted officials of temple and state. Mere possession of even the smallest fragment was grounds for torture and public execution... and there was no court of appeal when the prosecutors belonged to the Order of Sigmar.

Still, there were uses to which wyrdstone could be put that made knowledgeable men seek it out and pay small fortunes to possess it, whatever the risks. It could be used to heal the most terrible of illnesses, elixirs derived from its pulverised dust could cure fevers of the mind, pastes made from its ground powder could reverse the ravages of age and leave the skin as fresh and smooth as a baby's bottom. Of course its most prized ability was its most elusive. Wyrdstone was held as the true alchemists' stone, that fabulous substance that would be the catalyst for transforming lead into gold!

Dr Loew watched the thin stream of green smoke rising from the smouldering rock. It had an unusual smell to it. Not something he would associate immediately with wyrdstone, but still somehow making him think of the outlawed mineral just the same. Perhaps this was some exotic ore, some incredibly rare variant of the wyrdstone more commonly known to scholars and wizards. If that was true, there was no telling what price the substance might command.

'Well, Herr Doktor?' a gruff voice intruded upon the alchemist's thoughts. Looking up, Dr Loew found himself staring into the hard features of Johann Dietrich, the larger and more imposing brother of the crafty Hans. Johann had a shrewd look about him, one that set Dr Loew on his guard. Smugglers were, after all, thieves, and it wouldn't do well to let them know just how valuable their find was.

'I can't be sure,' Dr Loew said, pulling off the copper-scaled gloves he had donned to protect himself while handling the stone. 'I think perhaps I need to run more tests.'

Johann smiled and shook his head. 'I think you recognised that rock as soon as we set it down,' he said. 'Play your games on your own time, frogcatcher, we don't have any to spare.'

Dr Loew leaned back in his chair, crossing his arms defiantly. He wasn't about to be lectured by some illiterate slob from the gutter, certainly not in his own shop. He sniffed at the silver pomander dangling from his neck, letting its medicinal fumes ward off any tainted dust that might have dispersed into the air from his handling of the specimen. 'You tell me what it is, then,' he snapped.

'I think it's wyrdstone,' Johann told him.

The alchemist laughed. 'And what do you base that on?' he scoffed. 'The word of some hop-headed cut-purse?' Dr Loew pointed a finger at the lurking figure of Kempf. The weasel-faced thief grinned back, making no secret of his eavesdropping.

'No,' conceded Johann, 'I base that on the smile you keep trying to hide. Greed doesn't become you, doktor.'

The alchemist scowled, making a show of prodding and poking the sliver of stone in the bowl with a copper rod. 'It might be wyrdstone,' he admitted reluctantly. 'If it is, I might be able to find a buyer for you.'

'How soon?' Kempf interjected, his voice eager and hungry. Johann glared at the small thief, only relenting when he backed away from the table.

'It would take awhile,' Dr Loew said after a moment of thought. He tapped the table as he considered his answer. 'One has to be careful making inquiries of this sort, you understand.'

'If you have a buyer, we might have more to sell him,' Johann said in a low voice.

Dr Loew's eyes narrowed and he directed a cautious stare at the big smuggler. 'How much more?'

'More.'

'A lot more?'

Johann gave him a slow, knowing nod. 'A lot more,' he said.

Dr Loew didn't try to hide his smile now. 'It looks like this may very well prove to be wyrdstone. If you have much more, it will take some time to find enough buyers to move it.'

Johann shook his head. 'We'd prefer to dispose of it all at once.'

'Very dangerous to try and sell a large quantity of wyrdstone,' Dr Loew told him. 'The authorities aren't very understanding.'

'But it could be done?' Johann asked.

'It could be done,' Dr Loew said, rubbing his fat, warty nose. 'I could find a buyer outside Altdorf, that would be safer than selling it to someone inside the city. There's a man I know in Nuln who might be interested – if it proves to be wyrdstone.'

'If it proves to be wyrdstone,' Johann repeated, turning away. He grabbed Kempf's shoulder and prodded the small thief towards the door. Hans and the others saw Johann moving to the exit and started to follow.

'Where can I contact you?' Dr Loew called after the departing men.

Hans turned around and smiled at the alchemist. 'You don't,' he told Dr Loew. 'We'll contact you.' The smuggler gave a last look at the shelves of dried herbs, crushed powders and pickled reptiles. 'Interesting stuff you have here, doktor. Disgusting, but very interesting.'

Dr Loew scowled as he watched Hans amble out his door. Ignorant peasants! What did they know of scholarship and learning! The fools had no idea what they had found, no idea at all. The specimen they had left with him was worth a small ransom on its own. Certainly more than the thugs would earn in a month sneaking wine past the excisemen.

The alchemist sucked his teeth and leaned over the iron bowl again. It was wyrdstone, every passing moment made him more certain of the fact. He had several contacts in the Colleges of Magic who would jump at the chance to buy such a fine specimen. Briefly, he considered informing them of the find that had fallen into his hands, but Johann's claim that the smugglers had more gave him pause. It might be the bold promise of clever criminals trying to ensure a square deal from the alchemist, but Dr Loew was reluctant to dismiss the possibility out of hand.

He thought of his contact in Nuln. Dr Drexler had been obsessed with the study of wyrdstone since the Nuln riots several years ago. The physician would pay handsomely if Loew could provide him with a significant supply of the mineral. It was said he was supported in his experiments by no less than the Countess von Liebowitz of Nuln.

The image of the bulging coffers of Nuln settled Dr Loew's dilemma. He rose and retrieved quill and parchment from his desk. Sitting back at the table, he began to compose a letter to his colleague in Nuln.

As he started to write, Loew's left hand absently scratched at his forearm, trying to stifle the sudden irritation of his skin.

'YOUR NOTORIETY PRECEDES you, Grey Seer Thanquol.'

The speaker was Grey Seer Thratquee, the highest ranking representative of the Horned Rat's priesthood in Under-Altdorf and the occupant of the centremost seat on its ruling council. An aged, white-furred skaven with mismatched horns, Thratquee had the smug scent of a cunning politician, well-versed in the arts of corruption and cronyism. Thanquol took an instant dislike of the elder grey seer, not least because without the talisman he had been given by the Lords of Decay, it would be Thratquee, not Thanquol enjoying the dominant position.

The council of Under-Altdorf met in a large hall called the Supreme High Leader Nest. It was extravagantly ornamented with a motley collection of marble blocks and granite columns stolen from the human city above. A riotous array of colourful tapestries drooped from the walls, some of their human subjects crudely disfigured to resemble triumphant skaven warriors. The floor was a tiled mosaic of different coloured bricks while a crystal chandelier swung from the roof overhead. Thanquol was reminded of the pretentious opulence of the palace of Nuln's breeder-queen, only on a shabbier scale. Perhaps the self-important lords of Under-Altdorf might intimidate some witless ratling from the hinterwarrens of skavendom with such a crude display, but for one who had walked the tunnels of Skavenblight, Thanquol saw it for the pathetic excess it was. The skaven of Under-Altdorf had perhaps spent too much time around humans; they were starting to adopt some of their habits.

Like the true ruling council of the Under-Empire, that of Under-Altdorf boasted thirteen seats. In a touch Thanquol found impious and possibly sacrilegious, no seat had been reserved for the Horned Rat. Instead the positions of authority had been shared out between the city's most important clans, with the exception of Grey Seer Thratquee's own seat. One chair was held by Skrattch Skarpaw, the Shadowstalker of Clan Eshin, with a further two seats held by his subordinates. Another chair was held by Fleshtearer Rusk of Clan Moulder. Pontifex Poxtix was the Clan Pestilens representative on the council. Other seats were held by the warlords of Clans Skab, Skaul and Mors.

The remaining seats were held by Clan Skryre, a potent display of their influence and power in the city.

Warplord Quilisk was the highest ranking of the warlock engineers, a sinister figure with a lower jaw sheathed in metal and a riot of tubes and pipes running from a complex iron pump into his chest. The other Clan Skryre representatives were clustered around him and in obvious fear of the local clan-leader.

A final, non-voting seat, was reserved for a Clan Sleekit fleetmaster, a fat, sleepy-eyed ratman with thinning fur and the smell of weirdroot about him. He affected the frilly cuffs and sleeves of some effete human and wore gaudy rings on his fat little paws. If the decadence of the meeting hall itself were not evidence enough of Under-Altdorf's corruption, a single sniff of Shipgnawer Nikkitt would be.

Thanquol ignored the offensive fleetmaster and tried to focus his attention on Thratquee on his overstuffed chair. Thratquee's seat, indeed those of all the council members, appeared to have been purloined from an opera house, still carrying a lingering stink of the human about them.

'Honoured clan-lords of Under-Altdorf,' Thanquol began, careful to keep one paw stroking the black talisman around his neck. He could feel the eyes of every skaven fixed on the amulet, burning with envy and fear in equal measure. 'I have come to you as the chosen representative of…'

'We know all that,' snapped Viskitt Burnfang, one of Warplord Quilisk's underlings. Burnfang was an emaciated warlock engineer with a distinct patch of black fur running across one side of his face, jarringly offsetting his otherwise light brown pelt. Burnfang had a complex network of pipes and pistons running down his arms, some arcane supplement to offset his withered muscles. 'Why do the Lords of Decay send you to spy on us?'

'Because of your reckless experiments and blasphemous speak-talk!' snarled Poxtix. Bundled in his ragged green robe, only the pontifex's decayed snout projected into the murky light, though even so reduced a sight of the plague priest's face was revolting enough. 'Repent-revile the abominations of your technomancy and embrace the festering gifts of the Horned One's true face!'

'It is your blasphemies that bring the suspicions of Skavenblight upon us, tick-licking toad-mouse!' The vicious snarl this time belonged to Warlord Gashslik of Clan Mors, a hulking black-furred brute clad in the steely skin of a human knight. 'Pushing your pestilential faith into excesses no skaven of conscience can tolerate!'

Thanquol blinked at the quarrelling clan leaders and tried to inject a greater volume and authority into his voice. 'Masters of Under-Altdorf, I come here in the name of...'

'You should snarl!' roared Warlord Staabnash of Clan Skab. Shorter by a head than his rival from Clan Mors, he was if anything twice as broad, so swollen with muscle that his bronze armour seemed ready to burst every time he moved his massive frame. 'You and your toe-stabbing runt-stickers have been sucking up to Poxtix and his fanatics like they were your mother's teats! How convenient that your warriors should happen to save this maggot-eater's pelt last Vermintide when he dared preach his heresies in the scrawl and the clanrats rose up in pious indignation!'

'I come to Under-Altdorf...'

'Muscle-brained orc-fondler!' spat one of the Clan Skryre leaders, a twitchy creature in red robes who had somehow managed to burn off his ears as well as all the fur on top of his head. 'We know who was behind that riot! I am sure Clan Skab did not shed any tears when our warpfire thrower workshops were burn-wrecked! Not after you were told your bid for our weapons was low-low!'

'The Lords of Decay have sent me...'

'My clan knows those weapons well, death-peddling grub-biter!' Skrattch Skarpaw rose from his chair, menacingly fingering the array of knives he wore across his chest. 'They ended up in the paws of Clan Skaul so they could attack the dojo of my night runners!'

There was silence a moment, then the eyes of the council of Under-Altdorf shifted to Naktwitch Nosetaker, the local head of Clan Skaul. The scrawny ratman with the reddish-hued fur puffed idly at a ratskull pipe and blinked at his scowling contemporaries.

'It seemed like a good idea at the time,' Naktwitch said with a purely human shrug of his shoulders.

The comment caused the council chamber to erupt into a dozen arguments, each voice trying to hiss down the other. Thanquol ground his teeth together, then settled back while he waited for the bickering leaders to quiet down. This was the hierarchy of Under-Altdorf? These were the skaven who thought they could make their city the new Skavenblight?

A cunning gleam entered Thanquol's eyes as he leaned against one of the columns and crossed his paws. Such enmity between the clans could serve him even better than any unity of purpose. He could play each rivalry for all it was worth. He wouldn't seek to curry favour with any of the clan leaders. Let them seek to earn his favour! Each would seek to outdo the other trying to support Thanquol, giving the grey seer far more resources than he could draw from any single clan. It was a prime situation to exploit, and if some small part of what was generously donated by the clans went to rebuild Thanquol's diminished personal fortune rather than achieving the Council's mission, well that was simply something the Lords of Decay didn't need to know about.

Thanquol was just beginning to feel quite pleased with himself as the hissing, snarling music of the clan leaders swirled around him when he happened to glance at old Thratquee. The elder grey seer wasn't participating in the bickering of his fellows. No, he was instead being quite silent. Just sitting back in his chair, his gaze fixed on Thanquol, watching every breath the younger seer took, observing every twitch of his tail and flicker of his whiskers.

Thanquol couldn't hold that stare. It felt too much like Thratquee was trying to look inside him, to let those old eyes burn a hole right down into his soul.

THE BRIGHT GLOW of kerosene lamps shone down upon a long, marble-topped table. Fluted columns flanked a circular chamber, supporting the domed ceiling high above. Tiered seats formed a semi-circle around a sunken pit, making it seem almost like the stage of a small amphitheatre. It was upon this stage that the marble table reposed, and around it, two figures moved with all the care and precision of the most rehearsed thespian.

One of the figures was old, a full white beard compensating for his bald, liver-spotted head. He carried himself with a pronounced stoop, but with the dignity of a man of position and authority. His rich clothes were obscured by a crude smock of white that covered him from neck to knee, providing only the most scant glimpse of the finery beneath.

His companion was also in white, but her garments were of the softest fabrics, flowing robes that might have been spun from snow. The image of a heart dripping a single bead of blood was embroidered upon the breast of her robe, picked out in yellow thread. About her neck, she wore a silver pendant displaying a dove. She was not so old as her associate, but the stamp of time had already seeded silver in her long, dark hair, and little wrinkles spread away from her deep, sombre eyes.

The object of their attention was spread out across the table. It had been the carcass of a mid-sized dog, though now it had been dissected into its component parts. Standing in a surgical theatre in Altdorf's prestigious university, it would have been strange for the two examiners to know that their subject had only the night before been killed while menacing a little girl deep in the city's worst slum.

The old man stepped away from the table, wiping his hands on his smock. He shook his head in consternation. 'I am at a loss,' he finally confessed, throwing up his gloved hands. 'I can't say how this cur died, nor what horrible disease so thoroughly ravaged its body.' He gestured at the hound's skull and the marks left by Theodor Baer when he brought down the animal. 'These injuries for instance,' he said. 'I cannot decide if they were made ante-mortem or post-mortem. Everything about this creature is simply wrong, Leni!'

Leni Kleifoth, the woman in white, nodded her head sympathetically. 'I share your confusion, Professor Adelstein. The affliction this poor animal suffered is nothing known to the Temple of Shallya. I thought at first,' thc priestess suppressed a shudder and a haunted look crept into her eyes. 'I thought at first it might...

might be the work of... of the Fly Lord, loathed be his name.'

Professor Adelstein's head bobbed up and down in agreement. 'You had every reason to believe such. The ways of the Ruinous Powers are infinite and horrible.' He stepped back to the table and removed a glass jar from the marble top. Inside was one of the hideous worms that had infested the carcass. 'I've examined this thoroughly. Whatever it looks like, it isn't a worm! I don't think it was ever even alive, not as we understand life. It isn't a thing of flesh and ichor. Do you know what it is composed of?' The professor paused for emphasis before speaking his discovery.

'Dust,' he said. 'That's all it is: dust!'

Leni stared intently at the strange thing that looked like a worm. Dust! But how could it be simple dust? How could dust corrupt an animal in such a gruesome fashion! Why would dust mould itself into a semblance of life! She felt a chill pass through her. The temple of Shallya was devoted to combating the myriad diseases and afflictions that plagued mankind, even the daemonic fevers sent by the Fly Lord. This was something else entirely, something beyond her experience, perhaps even beyond the experience of her entire order.

'No common dust,' the professor continued, pacing behind the table as though conducting one of his lectures. 'I'll grant you that. It is a strange, weird sort of dust, like nothing I have seen before. But it is dust.'

'What does it mean?' Leni asked, her voice a grim whisper.

Professor Adelstein's look became as sombre as that of the priestess. 'You know who wanted us to examine this carcass,' he said. 'That alone should tell you what it means. Something dark and terrible is at work in this city.'

SKRATTCH SKARPAW CREPT through the gloom and murk of the old burrow system. Abandoned generations ago when the underground river had flooded and drowned its inhabitants, the tunnels still carried a musky reek of death. The assassin kept to the thickest shadows as he made his way through the dripping corridors and half-flooded chambers. He was careful to keep his feet beneath the water, trying to offset any betraying splash that might carry through the darkness. The assassin paused many times, feeling the current of the air with his whiskers. He stifled the impulse to twitch his tail in amusement. The current was blowing towards him, carrying his scent back into the sprawling network of Under-Altdorf and away from the one he had come here to find.

Arrogant and insulting, the message Skarpaw had received evoked the ratman's deepest ire. Only a fool would provoke one of Clan Eshin's most savage killers to such anger, and Skarpaw was not one to suffer fools. He would add the insulter's pelt to that of the skavenslave who had acted as his messenger, a vivid reminder to any others who thought to dishonour Skarpaw and his clan.

The assassin's whiskers twitched as he caught a new smell beneath the musky death-stink. It was the scent of mangy fur and festering sores, the smell of mouldy rags and rusty metal. Clan Pestilens! He should have expected some fanatic from the disease-worshipping cult to be behind such madness. Pontifex Poxtix would be short a few followers after this night's work. Maybe Skarpaw would send the plague priest the heads of his deranged followers as an example of Clan Eshin's prowess.

Skarpaw lifted his head. Even to his keen eyes, even knowing what he was looking for, he couldn't see the slightest sign of the menace prowling above him on the roof of the tunnel. Trained in the arts of stealth and murder by the hidden masters of Cathay, the team of black-clad killers who formed the triad were Skarpaw's most potent warriors, living weapons that struck from darkness and melted back into the shadows before the most wary skaven could draw a breath. Steel climbing claws were fitted about their paws, allowing them to find purchase even in the slippery rock of the abandoned tunnels. Even if some quick-eared sentinel did detect Skarpaw's approach, his foes would expect the assassin's guards to be around him, not above him.

A sickly light glimmered in the darkness ahead. Skarpaw's lips pulled back in a feral smile. This would be easier than he thought. He drew the weeping blade from its scabbard, a sweat of poison dripping from its serrated edge. One cut from such a blade would finish even a plague monk, however many contagions the fanatic had invited into his flesh.

The musky smell intensified as Skarpaw crept forwards. Above him, he could smell the eagerness of the triad as they hurried along the roof, eager to begin the killing. Briefly, Skarpaw entertained the notion of allowing his minions to settle the affair for him, then he remembered the condescending lines he had read upon the ratskin parchment and his rancour rose once more. He'd cut the flea's tongue from his mouth and feed it to him!

The greenish light now revealed a small chamber. Skarpaw could see a clutch of plague monks gathered about the far end of the chamber, their robes frayed and decaying. At the centre of the chamber, upon a crude dais that helped it rise above the level of the water, a throne-like seat of old bones had been set. Upon that seat rested a figure as abhorrent as anything Skarpaw had ever seen. Even the assassin was repulsed by the swollen boils that disfigured the seated ratman's face, by the sickly green taint to his flesh and the thin patches of fur that yet sprouted from his diseased hide. The tattered robes the ratman wore were heavier and thicker than those of his minions, ugly symbols stitched across the border of the long cowl that framed his face. A heavy book bound in skavenhide rested in the monster's lap while his claws played absently with the tiny copper bells that dangled from a long wooden staff.

Skarpaw's eyes were drawn to that staff, widening as he saw the spiked metal globe that topped it. The green light was coming from openings in that globe, forming a pungent fog as it billowed away from the throne, caught by the current in the air. The assassin had seen the plague censers of Clan Pestilens before and knew their potency on the battlefield. The biggest troll, the most stubborn dwarf, none were immune to the toxic fumes of the plague monks. He started to back away, deciding that perhaps it would be best to allow the triad to do the job for him after all.

Then Skarpaw felt something slide against his leg. The assassin's head snapped around, staring at the dimly seen object bobbing on top of the water. It was the bloated carcass of a rat, and it was far from alone. Having spotted one, now Skarpaw's keen eyes could pick out dozens. The assassin realised with horror something he had observed but failed to appreciate during his vengeful passage through the tunnels. Every corner of Under-Altdorf was swarming with rats of every size and shape. They formed an important part of the skaven diet. But the old, flooded tunnels had been devoid of them. Now Skarpaw understood why.

Before the assassin could retreat, he heard a moaning gargle drip down from the ceiling of the chamber. He watched in horror as first one, then another of the triad killers plummeted from the roof, their bodies swollen with corruption. The musky death stink! It wasn't some lingering stench left by the drowned skaven, it was the pestilential fumes rising from the seated plague priest's staff!

As the last of the triad splashed to the chamber floor, Skarpaw felt his chest starting to burn from the inside. Whatever had struck down his killers, he had been exposed to it just as much. Realising he was already dying, the assassin lunged forwards, snarling his defiance. If he could not escape, then neither would his murderer!

Skarpaw's feet drove through the flooded chamber, a savage hiss pushing through his clenched jaws. The assassin raised the weeping blade clutched in his paw, intent upon burying it in the sneering, diseased face beneath the priest's cowl.

The assassin's strength deserted him before he covered half the distance. Skarpaw sank to his knees, his sword slipping through claws too weak to grip it. Spots danced before his eyes and the chamber refused to stay in focus. His head sagged against his chest, bloody foam flecking his mouth.

Suddenly a fierce grip closed about the back of his neck and raised his head. Skarpaw felt something slimy and cold pressed against his lips, felt something like molten ice race down his throat. Slowly his bleary vision began to clear. He found himself staring into the warpstone eyes of the disfigured plague priest. The sneer was still curling the monster's face as he backed away from the recovering assassin and resumed his seat upon the morbid throne.

Skarpaw could feel the burning sensation leaving his chest, but his limbs still felt like granite weights. The assassin glared murderously at the seated plague priest. 'Tell-speak Pontifex Poxtix he will suffer-suffer for this!'

The seated plague priest laughed, a bubbling chortle that made Skarpaw cringe. 'I shall tell-speak nothing to Poxtix,' the skaven pronounced. 'That is why I need-take you, Skrattch. You serve-obey me and speak-tell nothing to Poxtix.' The decayed lips pulled back, displaying the ratman's blackened teeth in a broken snarl. The plague priest pulled the chain of one of the tiny bells dangling from the head of his staff. Metal plates slid down, cutting off the glowing green light of the censer ball and its infectious fumes. The plague priest's eyes shone in the darkness and Skarpaw could hear the other plague monks shuffling forwards through the water now that the dangerous fog was cut off.

'I am Lord Skrolk,' the skaven on the throne said in a guttural hiss. 'You will be my sniffer-spotter, my knife-fang. Otherwise I will not give-gift you more of my antidote. Think-ponder, Skrattch, then give-gift me your allegiance.'

CHAPTER FIVE
Knives in the Dark

THE LAIR OF Grey Seer Thratquee was a resplendent, vault-like hall buried deep beneath Under-Altdorf's temple of the Horned Rat. Thick walls of stone reinforced with bars of steel ensured that even the largest burrower bred by the diseased flesh-shapers of Clan Moulder would not be able to penetrate the skaven priest's sanctuary. The flagstones upon the floor were massive blocks of granite plundered from the sewers and cellars of the human city above. Green light flickered from warpstone lanterns set high into the ceiling, crafted from the mangled remains of chandeliers and candelabra. Mouldering rugs and tapestries, their colours faded by skaven excretions, their finery frayed and tattered by the gnawing of rats, covered much of the floor. At the centre of the hall, a monstrous heap of soiled pillows rose, heavy with the stink of ratkin musk. In a shocking display of wealth, decadence and power, the heap of pillows was occupied by a pair of immense, bloated masses of fur and fat, the swollen bulks of a pair of skaven females, the nearly mindless brood-mothers of the ratkin. Steel collars circled their swollen necks, thick chains fixing the huge creatures to metal rings set into the floor.

Thanquol was unable to decide what he should feel as he stalked into the hall; envy, fear or disgust. He settled on a mix of the three. Thratquee was clearly trying to impress his guest with this show of opulence and power, yet Thanquol could not help but see in the elder grey seer's lair a vivid display of the priest's own decadence and corruption. Like the rest of Under-Altdorf, Thratquee had pretensions of grandeur, imagining himself some manner of petty seerlord. For someone who had only recently grovelled before Kritislik, there was something shabby, laughable, in such a display.

An emasculated human slave rose from a small kennel at the side of the hall and approached as Thanquol entered the chamber. The temple guards who had conducted him through the temple into Thratquee's sanctum withdrew, casting a few jealous looks over their shoulders as they stalked back up the stairs. His own stormvermin, the matched set of albino mutes from Skavenblight, had been left in the temple, but Thanquol's persistence had forced the temple adepts to allow him to bring Kratch with him to this private audience with Thratquee. It was comforting to know he had at least one underling to throw between himself and any treachery Thratquee might be plotting.

The slave bowed before Thanquol, making the gesture a strange hybrid of human and skaven by twisting his head to expose his throat to the grey seer. Thanquol paid scant notice to the wretch, instead sniffing at the platter of delicacies he carried. An array of cheeses and sweetmeats teased his senses, setting his stomach growling. Whatever his other faults, Thratquee had certainly cultivated an expensive taste for human cuisine.

Thanquol started to reach for the platter, then his paw froze, thoughts of treachery reasserting themselves. He glowered at Kratch, nudging the apprentice forwards. The young adept hesitated, twitching nervously as he felt Thanquol's impatience grow. With a shivering paw, Kratch timidly retrieved a wedge of cheese from the platter. Thanquol continued to watch him as the apprentice took slight, dainty nibbles of the food.

'Grey Seer Thanquol,' the voice of Thratquee rose from the midst of the pillow nest. The elder grey seer peered from the mess of feathers and lace, eyes glazed with the effects of warpdust and human liquors. Thratquee had made no effort to disguise the smell of his vices, something that made Thanquol decide the old villain was far less impaired by them than he would like his guest to believe. 'I am humble-honoured that so terrible and magnificent a visitor should grace my meagre nest.'

Thanquol's tail twitched with annoyance. After visiting the other members of Under-Altdorf's ruling council for private audiences, even his ego had grown weary of empty flattery and hollow praise. Again, the grey seer's eyes prowled across the walls, looking for any sign of secret doors or hidden guards.

The old skaven nestled among the pillows chittered a peal of manic laughter. 'No-no, my friend, there is no-no trick-trap. I have all the protection I need right here.' Thratquee's paws reached out to either side of him, patting the furry flanks of the brood-mothers. At his touch, the swollen females reared up, like living pillars, their whiskers brushing the ceiling. Thanquol could see that what he had mistaken for layers of fat were in fact knots of muscle. Thratquee's consorts were built more like rat ogres than proper females. Some sick adjustment to their diet, perhaps, or some perverse misuse of his magic, but whatever the cause, the feral ferocity smouldering in the eyes of the breeders was enough to chill any would-be assassin.

After a moment, the brood-mothers subsided, flopping lazily down beside their master once more. Thanquol calmed his pulse and recovered the paces he had retreated when the females had reared. He could appreciate what fine guardians such monsters would make. No skaven would find anything menacing in the scent of a female. The worst traps were those that did not need to be hidden. But why had Thratquee deigned to disclose this secret?

'A gesture of trust,' Thratquee answered the unspoken question. 'We are both disciples of the Horned Rat. We must have faith-trust in ourselves.'

Thanquol looked aside at Kratch. The apprentice was showing no sign of poisoning and was attacking a second wedge of cheese with anything but his earlier timidity. Thanquol brought the edge of his staff smacking into Kratch's snout, knocking the young adept back. Seizing one of the sweetmeats for himself, the grey seer made a bold spectacle of himself as he approached the nest of Thratquee.

'There are suspicion-stories in Skavenblight,' Thanquol said between mouthfuls of food. The human slave struggled to keep pace with the advancing grey seer. 'The Lords of Decay question-doubt the loyalty of Under-Altdorf.'

'Some would say-squeak that the Lords of Decay lack vision,' Thratquee replied in a scratchy whisper. It was a shockingly rebellious comment to make, especially to one who had been sent as a representative of the Council. Was the remark a sign of Thratquee's opinion of his own power and position, or was it a mark of the old skaven's madness?

'Perhaps Skavenblight should step aside and allow those with vision to guide our people,' Thratquee continued, his words whispering into the stunned silence. 'They talk of destroying the humans, endless plots to conquer and despoil! Why? Why bother to seize with fang and claw what can so easily be taken with craft and cunning? Why conquer when we can rule from the shadows? The humans make so much for us already, never bothering to discover what happens to all that we steal and seize. Why would we wish to jeopardise everything they give us without even knowing?'

'Some would say-squeak that such words are heresy,' Thanquol warned, his claws tightening about the heft of his staff. 'It is the destiny of the skaven to inherit the world of men. This is the sacred promise of the Horned Rat.'

Thratquee chittered his laughter once more. 'The best slaves are those who do not know they are slaves. Look at Under-Altdorf. This city has grown to be the most powerful in all the Under-Empire… except for Skavenblight itself, of course. It has prospered so not by fighting the humans, but by using them, growing fat off their labour and industry. The Horned Rat favours cunning, favours those with vision. Skaven such as me, and you, Grey Seer Thanquol.'

Thanquol bruxed his teeth together, hearing his name associated with the deranged 'vision' of Thratquee. If the Council had any spies listening, his life would not be worth a waterlogged mouse when he returned to

Skavenblight. The grey seer lifted his snout, trying to assert his lack of subservience to the corrupt heretic lounging on the pillows.

'I am a loyal servant of the Council and the Horned Rat...' he began, his words sharp as knives. If the Council did have any spies listening, such a display might save his skin when he returned to Skavenblight.

'Do you understand what it is they have sent you to find, grey seer?' Thratquee interrupted. The question took Thanquol off his guard. He blinked at the old priest, waiting for him to continue. Instead, Thratquee pointed a shrivelled claw at Kratch. 'Tell him what it is Skabritt thought to find,' Thratquee ordered. 'Tell him more than you told those fools in Skavenblight,' he added with a display of his fangs.

Kratch's body was trembling as he felt the eyes of both grey seers fasten upon him. He scratched anxiously at his pelt, his glands dripping scent into the rug beneath his feet. It was almost on his tongue to deny Thratquee's assertion, but a look at the massive shapes of the grey seer's consorts and their immense fangs made the adept reconsider.

'I would have told-told when it was safe-alone,' Kratch began, apologising to Thanquol. His tone became more wheedling and his posture lower to the floor when he saw the disbelief in Thanquol's eyes. 'I did not want anyone to cheat-steal from your glory, most omnipotent of despots, most ravenous of killers, most...'

Thanquol swatted Kratch's muzzle with the end of his staff, almost knocking the fawning apprentice from his feet. 'Say-squeak something interesting,' he warned.

'Skabritt... the Wormstone...' Kratch winced as he saw Thanquol start to raise his staff again. 'It is a weapon!'

Thanquol bared his fangs in a threatening smile. 'I already know that,' he snapped.

'You don't know-think what kind-type weapon!' protested Kratch, holding up his paws to protect his snout. 'Clan Pestilens make-bring to use against Under-Altdorf not manling Altdorf!'

Thanquol looked from Kratch to the seated Thratquee. The old skaven was almost smirking among his nest of pillows.

'Skabritt tunnelled deep in the archives of Under-Altdorf to learn of the Wormstone, and I follow-find his trail,' Thratquee explained. 'He learned of Clan Mawrl and its fate. How Clan Mawrl entered into alliance with Clan Pestilens during the Second Plague War and was given the Wormstone as tribute for their loyalty to the plague lords.'

'But it was not a gift,' Kratch said. 'It was death that Nurglitch gave to Clan Mawrl. The Wormstone's power infected the clan, destroying it from the lowliest whelp to the most powerful warlord. Before the infection could spread to the rest of Under-Altdorf, the other clans banded together and collapsed all the entrances to Mawrl burrows before any of them could escape.'

Thanquol leaned against his staff, digesting the account. He could well understand why the Council had kept this from him. It was one thing to send him after a weapon that would be used against the humans, it was quite another to trust him with a weapon that could decimate an entire clan.

'You understand-see the possibilities?' Thratquee asked. 'The power of the Wormstone can makes us masters of skavendom! Every stronghold in the Under-Empire will tremble before the one who holds the Wormstone! Even the Council will bow to such a menace. We shall cast down the Lords of Decay, replace them with the sort of easily-manipulated fools I have contrived to seat upon the council of Under-Altdorf. With the power of the Wormstone, I can make myself seerlord, and you, Grey Seer Thanquol, shall be my most exalted and trusted lieutenant, the claw of a new Council of Thirteen!'

Thanquol's tail twitched as he listened to the old skaven spout his mad ambitions, the insane scheming of a mind grown foul with corruption and intrigue. The hidden lord of Under-Altdorf, now Thratquee dared to reach even higher. Thanquol wondered just how deeply Skabritt had been entangled in the old rat's plotting. Clearly Thratquee expected to use Thanquol to succeed where his predecessor had failed.

The thought brought a flash of scorn rushing through Thanquol's brain. Perhaps Thratquee was right, perhaps the Wormstone was powerful enough to do everything he said. But as he looked at the bleary-eyed skaven nestled among his pillows, Thanquol knew that if there was a new seerlord it would not be the high priest of Under-Altdorf.

PROFESSOR ADELSTEIN SAT at his desk, a black-feathered quill fairly racing across a browned piece of parchment. This part of the university was deserted at this hour and only the scratching of his pen against the sheet disturbed the eerie silence that filled the darkened building. Beads of sweat dripped from the professor's brow, his breathing short and sharp. It was not merely the grisly nature of what he was committing to the parchment that caused him such distress, though the ghastly carcass of the hound had been horrible enough.

It was the strange quill and the thin, smelly ink he employed to write his report that preyed upon Professor Adelstein's mind. No clean thing, this pen and ink, but the stuff of sorcery and darkness. He lifted his eyes from the page to stare again at the macabre inkpot, a thing seemingly crafted from a piece of frozen fire, glowing with an unclean light in the black of his office. However many reports he was called upon to write with the strange ink contained in the weird vessel, the pot never went dry. The fact was the least of its unearthly qualities, however. Looking back at the page, he could see the words he had written writhing and slithering like a nest of serpents, rearranging themselves into new and unfathomable designs. They would remain that way, Adelstein knew, until a certain word was spoken above the parchment and the words reformed from the squirming mess of lines and splotches.

Adelstein had received the quill and inkpot long ago, under circumstances he did not care to ponder in the dark hours of the night. He had received many messages written by another who possessed the same sinister ink. A word, a whispered sibilant that was more like the rasp of a jungle snake than anything related to a human tongue; this would unlock the orders that came to Adelstein from his hidden master. Such a message had led to his examination of the dog carcass. Leni Kleifoth, he knew, had received a similar message. Neither knew what they were expected to find, or what the importance of their examination was. They did not need to understand. It was enough that they obeyed.

The quill stopped moving as Adelstein hastily completed his report. He watched as the last words he had written slithered into a meaningless jumble, then tightly rolled the pages together, tying a string about the bundle.

The professor was breathing even more heavily as he walked across his darkened office, navigating between tables strewn with books and shelves groaning beneath the weight of pickled specimens in glass jars. He pushed a chair against the wall, climbing up onto its seat. Adelstein stretched his hand above him, pushing open the window set high in the wall. He stretched his other hand to the opening, holding the roll of parchment through the open window.

Since the message had reached him, Adelstein knew his office was being watched. Somewhere in the darkness, something was waiting for his report. The distinct, pungent smell of the ink would reach out to it, carrying to it even through the fog of Altdorf's night.

Adelstein felt something cold briefly brush against his hand, scales brushing against his flesh. The parchment was tugged from his fingers by a firm, powerful grip. Faintly, Adelstein could hear something flutter into the night. He hurriedly closed the window again and dropped down from the chair. Adelstein stepped to one of the specimen shelves and reached behind a pickled pig foetus to retrieve a hidden bottle of schnapps. The professor took a quick pull from the bottle, feeling a warm flush pulse through his quivering body.

He'd contrived to see what retrieved his reports once, when he had not known better. Scaly and hideous, he had been careful never to look at the strange courier again. There were books in the university with illustrations of the fauna of distant Lustria. What he had seen was not unlike the Lustrian lizard-bat, but there was none of the scholarly detachment of looking at an illustration in an old book when one saw such a thing fluttering outside his window in the dead of night.

The professor shuddered and took another drink. The creature was frightening enough, but his memory was clear enough to know it was nothing beside the master it served. The same whom Adelstein himself obeyed.

GREY SEER THANQUOL took up the position of honour well to the rear of the mass of skaven who stalked through the dripping sewers of Altdorf. It was a motley gathering of warriors and specialists bestowed upon him by the clans of Under-Altdorf; swordrats from the warlord clans, scouts from Clan Eshin and Clan Skaul, sharpshooters and globadiers from Clan Skryre, and green-garbed monks from Clan Pestilens. At the head of the procession, flanked by hulking warriors twisted by unnameable experiments, one of Clan Moulder's beast-masters led the way, a pale, twisted thing hopping through the sludge ahead of him. The beastmaster's charge was a warp bat, weird denizen of the under-world's deepest caverns and tunnels, a massive flightless bat with an uncanny facility for sniffing out concentra-tions of warpstone. The creatures were the most prized possessions of skaven miners and convincing Clan Moulder to lend the animal to Thanquol's expedition had involved making promises even the grey seer's lying tongue hesitated to agree to.

The alternative, of course, would have been to trust Kratch to lead the way, but Thanquol's distrust of his apprentice had grown by leaps and bounds following his meeting with Thratquee. It was better to limit his dependence on the adept as much as possible. The fate of Skabritt remained foremost in Thanquol's mind as they navigated the network of brick-walled tunnels and slimy canals. He tried to watch Kratch from the corner of his eye and made certain that his white stormvermin were positioned securely behind him. Their presence would discourage any thoughts of putting a knife in his back.

Kratch, of course, wasn't the only enemy he had to worry about. It had taken a fair degree of coercion and manipulation of Under-Altdorf's ruling clans to gain the support he needed for his expedition. Any one of the city's scheming councillors might be plotting treachery, to seize the prize Thanquol was looking for. If Thratquee felt safe enough to be so indiscreet about his loyalty to Skavenblight, strange ideas might have sifted down to the clan leaders themselves. Warplord Quilisk in particular was being quite heavy-pawed in his dealings with the grey seer. He had sent one of his subordinate councillors, Viskitt Burnfang, to 'assist' Thanquol. The number of representatives Clan Skryre sent along was also a bit more than Thanquol had asked for. Somehow, he doubted the fact was intended to benefit him. At least it set the representatives and warriors of the other clans on their guard. They would be too busy watching the Skryre ratkin for the first sniff of betrayal to think about moving against Thanquol himself.

Down through the murk of the sewers, the pack of skaven plodded. The stink of human filth was everywhere, the sounds of their feet and wagons filtering down from the streets above. Thanquol felt his contempt for the surface dwellers swell. Furless, undisciplined vermin, arrogantly thinking themselves masters of the earth! They would be forced to remember who the real masters were! Too many times had their kind stood between the skaven race and its destiny, too many times had they defied the prophecy of the Horned Rat! Too many times had they thwarted the ambitions of Thanquol the mighty! Thratquee was wrong... destruction of the humans was the most sacred duty any skaven could aspire to. And Thanquol would be that skaven!

The beastmaster at the head of the pack cried out, a sharp squeak of warning and excitement. Thanquol snapped orders to the stormvermin behind him, inciting them to lift him above the throng. Planting his feet in their strong paws, Thanquol peered over the heads of his minions. He could see a jagged patch of raw earth where the human brickwork had been pulled away. The tell-tale marks of skaven claws and fangs pitted the damp earth, vanishing into the blackness of a tunnel. The beastmaster stood before the opening, the pallid warp bat straining at its leash in its eagerness to dash into the gloom.

'Find-search, quick-quick!' Thanquol snapped, slapping the muzzles of the stormvermin to encourage them to lower him. The motley pack of skaven milled about uncertainly for a moment, but then their own leaders began to echo Thanquol's order. Cautiously, but with speed, the skaven began to converge on the earthen tunnel. Thanquol let the mass of ratkin plunge ahead, lingering behind as was the right of any wise leader. He waited until only himself and his immediate entourage were still standing in the sewer, then turned on Kratch.

'Tell me again how Skabritt died,' Thanquol hissed. His claws slowly tapped on the sword dangling from his ratgut belt. 'In case you forgot anything the first time you told it.'

Kratch ground his teeth together nervously, only managing to make eye contact with Thanquol by the most severe of efforts. 'Great and terrible scourge of the man-spawn, I have told-said all. Unlucky Skabritt was crushed when the cave collapsed upon him.'

'But Kratch was luckier,' Thanquol stated, displaying his fangs. He gestured with the head of his staff, pointing at the tunnel. 'You first, most loyal and eager apprentice. That way if anything happens to me, it happens to you first.'

Kratch gave a backward look at the sewer behind them, looking for a moment as though he might flee. Wiser impulses prevailed however. Still grinding his teeth nervously, Kratch slowly made his way into the tunnel, feeling Thanquol's eyes glued to his every step.

The grey seer took no reassurance from Kratch's reluctance. He hesitated as he watched Kratch vanish into the darkness, then gestured to his stormvermin.

'Follow him,' Thanquol told the albinos. 'Watch him. Watch everything.' He dug the little box of warpstone snuff from his robes and inhaled a pinch of the gritty dust, feeling its sorcerous energy sear through his body, firing his senses and steeling his courage.

'I'll be right behind you,' he said, pushing his bodyguards forwards. Thanquol gave a last anxious look at the dripping sewers. Briefly he considered the thought that had occurred to Kratch, but decided against such ignoble retreat. His decision was helped somewhat by the way the shadows seemed to coil about the brickwork support pillars in menacing patches of darkness. They might hide almost anything. At least whatever the dark tunnel might be hiding would have plenty of other skaven to distract it from himself.

Thanquol turned and scurried after his stormvermin with just enough haste to not undermine his carefully woven air of authority.

After the grey seer vanished down the tunnel, one patch of shadow detached itself from a nearby pillar. Sheathing his sword, Skarpaw gave a disappointed cough. He should have realised that killing Thanquol would not be so easy.

'I'M STILL WORRIED about him,' Johann told his brother. The two smugglers were prowling the narrow streets of the waterfront, trying to keep to the back alleys and seldom-travelled lanes that twisted their way between a festering array of hostels and tenements.

'You worry too much,' Hans chided him. The older Dietrich kicked a broken jar lying in the muddy lane. He grimaced as something that smelled of old cabbages splattered across his boot. He motioned for Johann to wait while he tried to wipe the muck off by rubbing his shoe against the plaster wall beside him.

'Gustav Volk is still looking for us,' Johann said. 'What if he found Kleiner?'

Hans abandoned his effort to clean himself. He wrinkled his nose at the revolting brown smear he had made on the wall, then shrugged and jogged up to catch his brother. 'If Volk's mob found Kleiner, then they're the ones you should be worrying about.'

Johann shook his head as they started down another nameless alley. This time Hans was careful to step around a splintered tankard that was in his path.

'You saw Kleiner when we were in Loew's,' Johann objected. 'The man could barely stand. I've seen beggars who looked healthier.'

'Most beggars are healthy,' Hans scolded. 'Best racket in the city, as long as you pay your tithe to the priests of Ranald.' He saw the irritation on Johann's face and changed his attitude. 'Kleiner probably just drank too much,' he assured. 'You know him, probably celebrating selling the wyrdstone before we've even got a single copper from it.'

'We didn't know it was wyrdstone before we went to Loew's.'

Hans let out a disgusted sigh. 'Mother hen, that's you, dear brother! I didn't see Kempf around this morning, but I don't see you worrying about him.'

'Kempf is so slippery a rat couldn't keep up with him,' said Johann. 'He can take care of himself.'

'And Kleiner can't!' Hans protested, his voice incredulous. 'I've seen the man outdrink a kossar and outfight a Norscan!'

'He wasn't sick then,' Johann said. He hurried to the other side of the alley as a window opened in the wall above and someone emptied a slop bucket into the street. Hans didn't match his brother's agility and soon had a cloak to match his boot.

'So what if Volk gets him?' Hans growled, wringing filth from his clothes. 'One more share for the rest of us.'

Johann gave his brother a withering smile. 'Not if Volk makes him talk first.'

Hans's face went pale, his eyes going wide with alarm. He grabbed his brother's arm, fairly pulling the big man down the alley. 'What are we standing around talking for? Let's go check on my friend Kleiner!'

'I WANT HIM out!' The old woman's shrill voice was as piercing as a lance this close to his ear. Theodor Baer glared at the crone, but if her vision was still clear enough to note the expression, she took no notice of it.

'Into the street!' she shrieked. 'I'll not have some pox-ridden vagabond giving my house a poor reputation!'

The old hag stomped one of her feet against the wormy floorboards of the landing, the thick leather clogs she wore threatening to punch through the dilapidated wood. 'I'll not have people driven away because they hear I'm harbouring disease in my house!'

'Then maybe you should keep your voice down, grey mother,' Theodor hissed. 'The way you're shrieking, they can probably hear you at the Emperor's Palace.'

The landlady's face grew flush with indignation. A little, withered specimen of waterfront wretchedness, the crone retreated down the rickety stairs with all the grace of a one-legged cat. Somehow she remained upright throughout her stumbling withdrawal. She turned at the foot of the stairs, pointing a crooked finger at Theodor Baer and the two watchmen with him.

'Not another night under this roof!' she said, her tone as imperious as anything spoken by the Emperor. 'You put him out, or I'll speak to your captain!' Her threat made, the old woman scrambled back behind the door of her own rooms and slammed it behind her.

'What a charming lady,' one of the watchmen commented. 'Is it wrong to hope the goblins come for her?'

'You were the one who heard her screaming for the watch,' the other soldier said. 'If it was left to me, I would have ignored her and kept right on walking.'

Theodor was still staring down the stairs at the old woman's refuge, only absently listening to the conversation of his subordinates. They had spent a long night prowling this district, searching for anything out of the ordinary, and the tempers of all three men were growing short. The tempers of his subordinates would be even shorter if they learned their orders had not come from the captain, but from a strange slip of parchment only Theodor himself had seen. That was something

Theodor did not intend to ever share with his men. There were some things it was better for them not to know about.

Still, there was no denying that their long night vigil had failed to produce any results. Whatever had caused the grisly affliction of the dog the night before, they had seen no further evidence of it. Theodor would have dismissed the incident as some one-off monstrosity, some vile mutant that had somehow eluded the attentions of the witch hunters, if it had not been for the orders he had received from his hidden master. As long as he had served that unseen hand, Theodor had never known the master to be wrong. If the message said the dog was not a lone aberration, then Theodor knew enough not to question.

Something one of his men said began to nag at Theodor. He looked back at the soldiers, then at the door behind them on the landing. 'We might not have ignored the old hag, but somebody is ignoring us,' he said, walking quickly to the door. The sergeant brought his hand smacking against the panels in his most demanding and official knock. Still there was no sign of acknowledgement. He waited a moment, pressing his ear to the door, listening for any sound in the room beyond.

An uneasy feeling crawled up Theodor's spine. Stepping away from the door, he motioned to his men. 'Kick it in,' he told them. The two watchmen were quick to comply, hobnailed boots making short work of the worm-eaten panels. Theodor squirmed his hand through the splintered wood and threw back the bolt.

The smell was the first thing that struck the soldiers as they opened the ruined door, a greasy stench of sickness mixed with a vilely sweet scent. The squalor of the room was made still more foul by the brown, greasy rags strewn about the floor and lying thick upon the straw-covered pallet that had served the occupant as a bed. Pots and buckets of filth were piled all around the bed, abandoned when the inmate had become too weak to tip them out the room's little window. Despite the reek, Theodor was struck by the absence of flies. At this time of year, they should be thick as lice in such surroundings. The sergeant felt the hairs on his arm prickle with uneasiness. There was something wrong, unholy about this place, something more terrible than disease and plague, something that offended even the most base of insects.

Theodor Baer was a brave man, he had patrolled these same dark streets alone during the height of the Beast murders without a thought to his own safety. Yet it took every effort of will for him to approach the pallet. His men lingered behind, steadfastly holding position in the doorway. After taking only a few steps towards the pallet, Theodor quickly rejoined them, pushing both soldiers back onto the landing and slamming the door behind them.

'Fritz,' Theodor pointed to one of his men. 'You will stay here. No one enters this room. Not the old lady, not other watchmen, not even the Grand Theogonist!' Theodor stared into the soldier's eyes until he was certain he had impressed upon the man the seriousness of his orders. It was the pale, frightened glaze over the sergeant's features more than his tone of voice that drove home the gravity of the situation.

Theodor started down the stairs, taking the other watchman with him. 'I am going to make my report to the captain. I will send a relief for you as quickly as possible,' he called up to the man on the landing as he made a swift exit from the crumbling boarding house. Already Theodor was pushing the ghastly thing he had seen in the hovel from his mind, concentrating instead upon his next move. He thought about what he would write in his report, considering each word with the utmost care, words intended for someone much more important and powerful than his captain.

JOHANN AND HANS watched from the blackened mouth of an alleyway as Theodor Baer and one of his soldiers exited the house. There was no mistaking the intense look on the sergeant's face, nor the haste in his step.

'Looks like Baer found something to nab Kleiner with,' Johann commented, smacking fist into palm in a gesture of impotent frustration.

Hans sidled nonchalantly against the peeling plaster of the timber-framed wall behind them. 'Better Baer than Volk,' the smuggler observed with a shrug.

'Kleiner can't spend any time in Mundsen Keep,' Johann growled back. 'Not sick as he was. It would finish him.' The filthy conditions and abysmal deprivations of the prison were infamous among the denizens of Altdorf. For all but the strongest condemned to the dungeons of the keep, a sentence of more than a few weeks was as good as a trip to the hangman.

'We'll get him out,' Hans promised. He noted the doubt in his brother's expression. 'No, seriously, we'll set aside some of the profit from the wyrdstone to bribe the jailors. The way Loew was preening over the little slice we gave him, there should be more than enough to buy Kleiner's way out.'

'That almost sounds like charity, Hans,' Johann said. 'I guess that's why I don't exactly trust it.'

Hans spread his hands in a gesture of hurt offence. 'You wound me, Johann. Of course I'm not going to leave Kleiner in Mundsen. What kind of man do you take me for?' Hans hastily continued before his brother could answer that question. 'Look, it's like this. If Volk had grabbed Kleiner, he might have spilled what he knew to try and swing some sort of deal. But we all know there's no deal you can offer Baer. Damn griffon thinks he's in the Reiksguard. Pure as the winter snow, that one! He'd break Kleiner's jaw just for suggesting a pay-out, and Kleiner knows it. That means he'll keep mum and wait for us to sell the wyrdstone and spring him.'

'You cover all the angles, don't you?' Johann scowled.

'One of us has to,' Hans replied with a smile. 'We can't both of us wear our heart on our sleeve.'

Johann shook his head and started back down the alleyway. Hans watched his brother for a moment, then cast a lingering stare at the decaying boarding house. Kleiner, in Baer's hands, would play for time and wait for the other smugglers to spring him. Of course, by that stage of the game they would already have sold the wyrdstone. Hans knew his brother wouldn't approve, but Kleiner's capture was something of a windfall. One less share to dole out when the time came to make the split.

The smuggler turned and laughed softly as he followed after his brother. He wondered how many weeks it would take Kleiner to realise that nobody was going to bribe the guards at Mundsen Keep. Hans felt little pity for his unfortunate associate. A man who let himself get caught had to look after his own luck.

Hans looked back at the house one last time. The smuggler scratched at his neck as he turned away. His skin had been itching all day, growing more persistent and vexing. He'd have to speak with Argula at the Crown and Two Chairmen. He suspected that some of the girls' rooms had bedbugs.

THE ROUGH, EARTHEN tunnels had a fug about them, a thick stink of rotting meat and decaying flesh that set Thanquol's stomach growling and his nerves on edge. The keen nose of a skaven could easily decipher the smell of their own kind, even in death. There was no horror in the demise of a fellow ratman, of course. Rare indeed was the skaven who had not turned to 'burrow pork' as a way of staving off starvation at some stage in his life. Death was death and meat was meat. What troubled the grey seer was not the presence of corpses, but anxious doubts about how they had died and a nagging suspicion that Kratch was being less than forthcoming about the details of his previous excursion to this forgotten sub-warren of Under-Altdorf.

Ahead of him, Thanquol could see the shapes of his entourage scurrying down the tunnel, rapidly pursuing Clan Moulder's warp bat. The Clan Skryre element, probably at Viskitt Burnfang's command, had produced warpstone lanterns, casting an eerie electrical glow about the throng of ratmen. It was on Thanquol's tongue to reprimand Burnfang for overstepping his authority and not begging permission of the grey seer before illuminating the tunnel, but a sly twitch of his whiskers indicated that Thanquol dismissed the thought as soon as it came to him. Let Burnfang light himself up like a Karak Azgal lava pit, it would make him the most visible and most logical target for anything lurking in the abandoned burrow.

The same thought occurred to Kratch. The young adept hesitated in his quick approach to the mob of skaven, instead creeping back to rejoin Thanquol and his stormvermin. Kratch kept his head low in deference to his master. 'Grim tormentor of the unworthy,' the apprentice squeaked, 'should you not stop the Skryre heretics from displaying their perverse science?' Kratch glanced nervously at the gloom around them, his head cocked in a peculiar listening gesture. 'Something might see them and do them harm.'

Thanquol snickered at Kratch's feigned concern. If the apprentice was ever going to amount to more than a snack for the bone chewers, he would need to learn how to lie better. 'If Burnfang selflessly offers to present us with warning of any lurking danger, it would be inconsiderate to question his generosity.' Thanquol interrupted Kratch's raspy laughter with a cuff across his snout. 'Now why not tell your gracious and beneficent mentor what kind of danger you think will spring from the darkness to seize our friend Burnfang?' The grey seer's lips pulled back, his fangs gleaming from the darkness. 'It wouldn't be the same thing that happened to Skabritt, would it?'

Kratch backed away, grinding his fangs together nervously. 'Most mighty of magicians, dread sire of warlords and chieftains, it was a simple collapse of these miserable and neglected tunnels that crushed the life from my poor old master.' Kratch's nervousness abated and he warmed to the subject Thanquol had forced from him. 'The same fate was almost mine as I tried to save Grey Seer Skabritt from the falling earth. Only by the grace of the Horned Rat was this humble servant spared to bring word of Skabritt's discovery to you, great and terrible liege.'

Thanquol considered cracking Kratch's skull with his staff to stifle the stream of ingratiating flattery and calculated self-abasement, but decided he could make better use of his apprentice. Kratch was the only one who had escaped this place the last time. That made him someone worth keeping around and keeping close.

The musky scent of fear rose from the throng ahead, a scratchy chorus of frightened voices drifting down the tunnel from some point ahead of Burnfang and the glow of his lanterns. Thanquol waited, his ears pricked to detect any sound of battle, one eye watching Kratch. After a moment, without hearing screams or the crash of steel, Thanquol decided that whatever had frightened the scouts wasn't fighting back. He motioned to his bodyguards and straightened his posture as he marched down the tunnel to take direct command of his minions and discover for himself what they had found. Stalking past Viskitt Burnfang and his warlock engineers, Thanquol relieved the Clan Skryre leader of one of his lanterns, glaring at Burnfang, daring him to challenge the grey seer's confiscation of the apparatus.

Instead of defiance, Burnfang sketched an insincere bow. Thanquol decided to ignore the insubordination, at least until a more opportune time. He discovered the source of Burnfang's smirking humour a moment later as he continued down the tunnel and the lantern was nearly pulled from his paw. Stumbling and tripping after him, dragged by the thick wires that connected the lantern to a bulky contrivance lashed across its back, one of the warlock engineers was pulled along behind the grey seer. Thanquol scowled, glaring at the smirking Clan Skryre contingent, daring any of them to find humour in what was, after all, a slight oversight.

Still dragging the warlock engineer and his battery after him, Thanquol found himself approaching a section of tunnel that broadened into a wide opening. Warriors from Clan Mors and Clan Skab stood around the opening, sniffing at the air, staring suspiciously at the walls. One side of the tunnel was choked by a mass of freshly collapsed earth, from which the stink of decaying skaven rose. The same smell was even more potent ahead, however, but Thanquol hesitated to press past his warriors.

It was only when one of the Clan Eshin gutter runners, the slithery scouts supplied to the expedition by Skrattch Skarpaw, crept back down the passage to report to the grey seer that Thanquol felt the imperative to advance.

'Tunnel-burrow go into chamber-cave ahead, dread master,' the gutter runner wheezed, his breath as stagnant and foul as the linen rags he wore around his snout and across his face. Dyed black like the rest of the scout's ragged raiment, the skaven was almost invisible in the gloom of the passage, only his distinct scent picking him out from the darkness. 'Chantor Pusskab find-snatch something,' the scout added in a subdued whisper, nervously looking over his shoulder.

Thanquol bristled at the words. Clan Pestilens! The diseased plague monks and their heretical perversion of the Horned Rat's religion! Too many times had those vile abominations stood between him and the glory that was his right! Nurglitch probably knew full well what sort of artefact the Wormstone was, and had sent word ahead to Under-Altdorf and his followers in the city to keep the device from Thanquol and the Council of Thirteen.

'We'll see about this!' Thanquol hissed through clenched fangs. 'Follow me,' he snapped, pushing his stormvermin into the passageway ahead of him. He'd feel a bit more confident confronting the plague monks with the two albinos between his own pelt and the diseased curses of the chantor. Noting that the clanrat warriors of Mors and Skab weren't displaying any initiative to join him, Thanquol scowled. He'd remember such faithlessness!

The tunnel opened into a larger cavern. Instantly, Thanquol was impressed by the carrion stink. The glow from his warp-lantern disturbed a swarm of starveling vermin gnawing at bones that still bore scraps of flesh. The rats chittered angrily, but refused to abandon their meal. Across the floor of the cave was a litter of other bones, much older bones, which converged into a great heap at the centre of the chamber. Thanquol was quick to notice the way Kratch's attention instantly flashed to the heap and the sharp disappointment that flickered through his posture.

'Something wrong?' Thanquol hissed in his most menacing whisper, low enough that only Kratch and the unfortunate warlock engineer he continued to drag behind him could hear.

'The Wormstone...' Kratch whined. 'It is gone, master!'

Thanquol's fangs ground together, his fur standing straight on his arms as he heard the adept speak. If his hands weren't filled with his staff and the warp-lantern, he probably would have strangled the whining apprentice. What did he mean it was gone! Thanquol shuffled the staff into the crook of his other arm and locked a paw about Kratch's throat anyway.

'What do you mean "it's gone"?' the grey seer demanded. 'Are you telling me that I came all the way up here, to this miserable pit, this human-reeking backwater, for nothing!' Thanquol's clutch tightened. Kratch clawed feebly at the choking hand, even as he tried to gasp out apologetic protests. 'Am I supposed to go back to Skavenblight and tell the seerlord that the weapon he wanted is just gone?' A feral fire burned in Thanquol's eyes now. Even the warlock engineer was spurting musk when the grey seer snarled at his apprentice. 'Gone! You slack-witted, turd-sniffing tick! How am I supposed to tell the Lords of Decay their weapon is gone!'

Kratch's eyes were starting to roll into the back of his skull, his tongue lolling from his jaws. Suddenly, Thanquol relented, letting the adept slump to the earth at his feet. The grey seer turned, remembering what the gutter runner had told him. There were others here more deserving of his wrath than the snivelling Kratch!

There were several distinct groups of skaven in the chamber, an old warren-nest of the vanquished Clan Mawrl. Thanquol could see the Clan Skaul scouts, a dishevelled gang of scrawny runts sniffing about the old collapsed exits to the cavern, pawing about the rubble for any trace of plunder. He could see the Clan Moulder contingent, warriors in vivid yellow and blue cloaks following the erratic movements of the beastmaster and his warp bat as they prowled about the cavern. There were the Clan Eshin gutter runners, sinister in their blackened rags, doing their best to fade into the gloom of the cavern walls.

Thanquol paid scant attention to any of these. His ire was directed against the last group occupying the chamber; the green-clad plague monks of Clan Pestilens and their crook-backed leader, Chantor Pusskab. The plague monks were pawing about among the bones, picking through them with exaggerated care. Thanquol was not tricked by the pretended search. He knew Pusskab had already found what he was looking for. Clan Pestilens had already swiped the Wormstone.

'Looking for something?' Thanquol challenged, his words slashing through the darkness. Every skaven in the cavern turned when he heard the grey seer speak, hoping the fierce snarl wasn't directed at him. Chantor Pusskab's first instinct was to cower, but the plague priest quickly composed himself. The green-clad ratman snuffled and coughed, spitting a blob of phlegm into the bone field.

'Look-seek?' Pusskab's dripping voice oozed. 'No-no, find-find, yes-yes.' The plague priest opened his paw, displaying for Thanquol's eyes something that looked like a fat green-black worm.

Before Pusskab could explain the importance of what he had found, another voice echoed through the cave. Sharp and shrill, the voice resounded from the walls, its frantic cry sending a thrill of fear down the spine of every ratman who heard it.

'Die-die, traitor-meat!'

The gutter runners who had so carefully manoeuvred to positions in the shadows against the walls now sprang from the darkness in a concentrated mass of violence and savagery. Thanquol saw green-clad plague monks dragged down beneath the stabbing, clawing bodies of the black-clad scouts, crushed against the floor until flashing daggers did their gruesome work.

Only for an instant was Thanquol able to watch the havoc the gutter runners made of Pusskab's minions. Even as the grey seer's heart swelled with pride at this display of loyalty and appreciation for his leadership, he saw something leap towards him from the corner of his eye. A gutter runner, its fur showing black beneath its leather rags and linen wrappings, sprang towards him, a wicked-looking knife gripped in both its paws. Thanquol could smell the burning taint of poison rising from the blades.

No mere gutter runner; the skaven leaping for him was one of Clan Eshin's expert killers! The war cry, the attack on the plague monks, these were a distraction to cover the activities of an assassin!

Thanquol's reaction was instant, instinctual. He spun about, diving away from the leaping killer. Still holding the warp-lantern, Thanquol's dive was spoiled by the weight of the warlock engineer on the other end. Stumbling, struggling to maintain his balance, the warlock engineer toppled after the reeling grey seer. Thanquol heard the murderous snicker of the assassin as the black-cloaked skaven struck at him with envenomed blades.

Thanquol felt a heavy weight smash into him, crushing him into the ground. For an instant, he thought the assassin's blow had landed, that some insidious Clan Eshin poison was even now pumping through his body. An agonised squeal in his ear, magnified by a mask of metal, told the grey seer what had happened. The warlock engineer, hurtling after Thanquol, had blundered into the path of the leaping assassin. Instead of striking the grey seer, the killer's blades had stabbed into the body of the unfortunate engineer!

Thanquol's fingers scurried into the folds of his grey robes, pulling a small piece of warpstone from a hidden pocket. Without hesitating to consider consequences, Thanquol popped the nugget between his fangs and bit down on it, grinding the little rock into powder with the frenzied action of his teeth.

Screams of battle raged all through the cavern. From the floor, Thanquol could see other assassins rushing to support the first killer. The albino stormvermin intercepted one of them, slashing at him with their halberds. The pouncing killer dived under the blade of one stormvermin, then leapt high over the blade of the second, slashing an ear from the bodyguard's head as he passed him. The injured stormvermin spun about to confront his attacker, but the assassin was already darting away. While the two bodyguards fretted over the one assassin, the second raced unimpeded towards his target.

Blazing light swept through Thanquol's vision, banishing the less than magnificent display of his bodyguards as the power of the warpstone surged through his body. The grey seer felt the warlock engineer's body being rolled off of him. The assassin had recovered one of his blades and was struggling to pull the second from the battery lashed across the corpse's back. He turned his face to snarl at Thanquol, but his expression quickly changed as he saw the glow behind the grey seer's eyes. Like most of his kind, the assassin's glands had been removed so that his scent might not betray him. There was no musk of fear to tease Thanquol's nose, but the grey seer could see the mark of terror in his would-be murderer's eyes. If the power of the warpstone was not intoxicating enough, the fear of his foe was.

Crackling yellow fire seared from the blazing head of Thanquol's staff as he pulled himself from the floor. The assassin's amazing reflexes allowed him to drop beneath the blast of arcane power with only a scorched cowl to speak of the nearness of his escape. In dodging the attack, however, the assassin was not prepared for a simultaneous strike. Swinging the warp-lantern about with his other hand, Thanquol brought the heavy metal instrument cracking into the assassin's skull. The killer was thrown back, black blood and broken fangs spraying from the side of his mouth. Thanquol sneered at the stricken killer as he rolled through the dirt.

The grey seer's sorcerously enhanced senses did not allow him to savour the wounding of his enemy, however. Even as the first assassin's body came to rest, Thanquol was turning away from him, turning upon the killer springing at him from behind. In mid-air, the assassin was unable to twist his body completely away from the crackling fire Thanquol sent searing at him from the head of his staff. The magical fire bit through the ratman's side like a red-hot sword, adding the reek of burnt entrails to the foulness of the cavern. The assassin flopped against the wall, his paws caked in his sizzling blood as he tried to push his belly back into his body.

There was an adage among the skaven: a dying enemy has the worst bite. It was a proverb that Thanquol had seen to be true far too many times. A dying enemy had nothing left to fear. Before the maimed assassin could make that realisation, Thanquol sent a second bolt of arcane power blasting into his head, leaving only a dripping mass of charred gristle above his shoulders.

To his credit, the third assassin showed an almost unskaven degree of determination and courage. Bolstered by some strange combat-brew that increased his cunning and ferocity, the assassin used the gory demise of his brother as an opening to exploit. Eschewing the pouncing charge of his unfortunate comrade, the killer struck low, seeking to gut Thanquol with a wickedly curved short sword. The blade's serrated edge slashed through the grey seer's robe and shredded several scrolls tucked beneath Thanquol's belt. By only a breath did the poisoned metal miss the flesh beneath Thanquol's fur. The assassin twisted away, spinning his entire body around as though to retreat. Instead of running, however, he turned the motion into a reverse dive, thrusting his sword once more at his target.

If the grey seer's senses were not aflame with the power of the warpstone, the assassin's attack would have been a blinding blur, like a flash of lightning allowing no chance of escape. But Thanquol's body did pulse with that sorcerous power, the corrupting foulness that only the skaven were daring enough to draw into themselves. Everything around him seemed to move as though mired in the bogs of the Blighted Marshes. The assassin was like a ratling whelp, blind and naked, pathetic in its efforts to crawl upon its little pink nubs! Thanquol's sharpened mind had the leisure to consider a dozen ways to destroy this maggot, this faithless flea who had the temerity to dare strike the mighty Grey Seer Thanquol! He bared his fangs in sadistic appreciation for what he would do to this filth.

The blast of fire that lashed out from Thanquol's staff struck the assassin's arm, tearing it from his body at the shoulder, sending the severed limb dancing off in the gloom. The assassin shrieked and crumpled, then struggled to rise, the instinct to escape overcoming the agony of his mutilation. A second blast of crackling flame severed the ratman's leg, spilling him back to the floor. Thanquol turned his back on the squirming wretch, leaving him to the vengeful blades of the stormvermin. It was the ultimate sign of contempt, ignoring the oldest of skaven adages, the sort of recklessness that only the most powerful skaven – or those lost in the grip of warpstone – indulged in.

Thanquol's eyes stared back towards the entrance of the chamber, looking for the first assassin. When he did not immediately see the black-clad killer, he brought the butt of his staff crashing against the floor in annoyance. A brilliant, blinding burst of light filled the cavern, washing out every shadow in a glowing haze. Only Thanquol, his eyes already aglow in the ecstasy of warpsight, was not stricken by the magical brilliance. He savoured the frightened squeals of the skaven around him, giving little care to the fact that the terror was given voice by friend as well as foe. He was much too busy sneering at the figure revealed by the light, the slithery shape that had tried to creep up on the grey seer to make another attack. Slinking along on his belly, the first assassin had come within a foot of Thanquol before being struck blind by the grey seer's sorcery.

The assassin covered his eyes with one paw, hurling his dagger at Thanquol with the other. The spinning blade seemed to move in slow motion as it flew towards the grey seer. Thanquol contemptuously shifted away from its path, only dimly registering an agonised squeal rise from behind him. He had no time for other distractions. He had a killer to deal with first.

The warp-lantern came cracking down into the blinded assassin with the same brutality and strength as before. The ratman was sent tumbling by the impact against his skull. Even as he rolled back down the entranceway, the assassin hurled his other dagger at Thanquol. The Staff of the Horned Rat burned with power once more, sending a spectral green light to surround the flying blade. The weapon darkened within that light, withering with each instant. It splashed against the breast of Thanquol's robe, reduced to nothing more than a greasy smudge by the grey seer's magic.

'You would kill-kill me!' Thanquol hissed, his voice booming with magical energy. Flickers of green light danced from his fangs as he spoke like fiery sparks from the mouth of a furnace. 'Scat-licking frog-nibbler! Curse-curse the moment you were plop-dripped from your breeder's belly!' The grey seer unleashed a burst of power from his staff with each snarl, a burst of pummelling force that smashed into the assassin, throwing him yards at a time through the tunnels. Now the sorcerous glow was gone, Thanquol's wrath and pursuit having taken them back into the passageway. The warriors of Clan Mors and Skab, resolutely refusing to enter the cavern and take part in the violence they had heard, now huddled against the walls, horrified by the awful power the grey seer was unleashing.

'Grovel-beg, worm-feeder!' Thanquol growled at the battered assassin. The wretched ratman bled from every corner of his body, limbs hanging from him in tangles of twisted wreckage. It was all the creature could do to look at Thanquol, much less try to shape words to his broken mouth.

It was not enough. The invigorating, fiery power of the warpstone had magnified Thanquol's arcane power, enhanced his senses, swollen the speed of his devious mind, but one thing had shrivelled beneath its influence: patience.

Thanquol sent another burst of power smashing into the assassin, flinging his shattered wreckage into the mass of broken earth that marked the collapsed tomb of Skabritt. The assassin's impact brought a burst of bloody froth from his muzzle, sent ribs skewering through his pelt. Thanquol favoured the watching clan-rat warriors with a menacing snarl, reminding them to pay particular attention to this example of the grey seer's power, lest they be his next victims.

Grey Seer Thanquol stalked towards the shattered assassin, his steps filled with power and malignity. However, even as his rage swelled, his might began to ebb. The warpsight faded slowly from his eyes, the fire slowly seeped out of his veins. For the first time Thanquol felt the drag of the warlock engineer's body, causing him to drop the dented warp-lantern he had been carrying. Strength deserted his excited muscles and he was forced to lean on his staff for support. Thanquol's breathing became short, his heart pounding erratically against his chest. Panicked thoughts raced through his brain, urging him to consume another warpstone nugget before the power faded from him entirely. Thanquol shivered as he fought to keep his paw away from another hidden pocket, exerting all his willpower to keep the compulsion at bay. Addiction to warpstone was the curse of every grey seer if he was not prudent, an addiction that would end when the terrible powers of the warpstone became too much for any sorcerer to control and the grey seer's body was ripped apart from within.

A bloody smile came to the assassin's face as he saw Thanquol's power desert him. The grey seer simply scowled down at the killer, then crushed what was left of his face with his staff. After all, one did not need magic to settle with vermin.

'Let this be an example!' Thanquol snarled as he turned away from the carcass. His gaze, even without the fire of warpstone behind it, was fierce enough to command the rapt attention of every skaven in the passage. There were many more of them than there had been. Viskitt Burnfang and the rest of his warlock engineers had come forward to join the warriors while Kratch and several survivors from the treacherous attack in the cavern had come back to see for themselves the outcome of Thanquol's fight.

'Smell-see this,' Thanquol ordered, pointing a talon at the bleeding ruin of the assassin. 'Remember-learn! This is what happens to all who betray Thanquol!' The grey seer fixed his fury on Kratch. The apprentice cringed at the attention, seeming to curl up into his own fur.

'Go!' Thanquol growled, now pointing to the cavern. 'Someone has taken what I came here to find! Search-find it, before I think about all those who did not guard the safety of one who serves the Council!' For emphasis, Thanquol fingered the talisman from the Shattered Tower. The reminder was enough. Clanrats and warlock engineers, Clan Skaul scouts and Clan Moulder beast-handlers, an eager, frightened throng, scurried up the passage and into the cavern, almost tripping over themselves in their haste to appease the grey seer's anger.

Thanquol took a moment to enjoy the terror of his minions. The first rule of command for any skaven was to ensure his followers feared nothing more than their leader. The ill-fated attempt on his life had gone far to instil that kind of respect in the ad-hoc entourage he had been provided with by the council of Under-Altdorf. He would need that kind of power base now that the hunt for the Wormstone was proving more difficult than he had anticipated. That was something he would need to discuss with Kratch, preferably while tugging fangs from the lying maggot's mouth.

As Thanquol followed after his underlings, the grey seer gave no notice to the body of the assassin he had killed. So it was that his eyes failed to see a slight trickle of earth drip from the collapsed heap of dirt and rubble and his ears failed to hear a faint, but persistent, scratching sound rising from beyond the cave-in.

Jakob Helmer stamped his feet against the splintered floorboards and clapped his hands together, trying to keep warm. The night chill that rose with the fog from the River Reik seeped through the shabby walls of the boarding house as though they weren't even there, soaking into the watchman's bones with a wintry clutch. Not for the first time, Jakob cursed his sergeant, his job and the thin cloth of his tunic. What was so important about some room in a flytrap flophouse that Baer wanted a man posted on guard all night? He suspected it was the sergeant's idea of a punishment duty after catching Jakob playing dice in the backroom of the Drunken Bastard the previous week. The suspicion, combined with the dampness of the fog and the chill of the night, might have been enough to convince him to abandon his thankless post for a few hours if Baer's despicable penchant for checking up on his men wasn't still so fresh in the soldier's mind. If he was discharged from the watch, the best Jakob could expect from his wife was a cracked skull when she bounced a skillet off his head.

The watchman blinked his eyes, staring into the creeping blackness that filled the stairway and the lower landing. He could only dimly make out the outline of the building's main door below, illuminated by the dim light of a streetlamp outside. For an instant, it had seemed to him that the outline had flickered, vanished for the briefest of moments. Jakob scowled and blew another hot breath against his hands. As cold as it had grown, even his eyes were starting to go numb. He rubbed his fingers together, watching as a little of the blue tinge faded from them. Perhaps he should pay a quick visit to the Street of 100 Taverns and secure something more substantial to fortify himself against the cold of night.

Jakob blinked as he looked up from his hands. The darkness of the stairway seemed to have grown even more pronounced, thicker and blacker than it had been. He was just about to dismiss the impression as some trick of light when a sound arrested his attention. The watchman spun about, his frozen hand dropping to his sword. He could not say what exactly the noise had been, but he was certain of where it had come from; only a few feet away from him on the upper landing.

The watchman felt his blood chill even more as his staring eyes picked out a figure among the shadows that filled the landing. Someone was standing there in the darkness, watching him. He could distinctly make out the silhouette of a tall man, shoulders and head just barely perceptible against the dark background.

'Who is there?' Jakob challenged, his voice low and filled with threat. He allowed only a single breath to pass for an answer to come, then drew his sword. The rasp of metal against leather sounded loud as lightning in the silence of the hallway. The watchman took a step towards the dark figure in the shadows and repeated his challenge. Still there was no reply.

Licking his lips, Jakob raised his sword and took another step. If the stranger in the shadows thought to make sport of the watchman, he would soon discover that Jakob was in no mind to play games. The soldier took another step, his arm tense, ready to thrust two feet of sharpened steel into the body of the intruder.

The last step brought a nervous laugh to Jakob's lips. As he drew closer, the sinister figure he thought he saw vanished. Another trick of his tired eyes, the shadow against which he had imagined he saw some lurking presence proved to be the outer wall of the house. There was nowhere any intruder could have escaped to even if there had been one there. Jakob sheathed his sword and returned to his post, still chuckling over his fanciful fright. He looked back down the stairwell, smiling as he saw the outer door illuminated by the streetlamp. Even the splotch of blackness he had been convinced lay upon the stairs was gone, another phantom of his fatigue and tedium.

It never occurred to the watchman that he had seen something upon the stairway, something that wrapped itself in the blackness of the darkened building, something that had silently and swiftly raced up to the landing when Jakob turned to investigate the noise he had heard. He would not have believed that both the sound and the sinister silhouette were illusory suggestions that had been planted in his brain by an outside will. He did not know that as he had been threatening shadows, something had come up behind him, stealthily opened the smashed door and slipped inside the room he had been set to guard.

Despite the pitch dark of the squalid room, the intruder picked his way with practised ease, only the faint swish of a cloak betraying his presence. Eyes, fiery and piercing like ruddy garnets, penetrated the darkness, dissecting at a glance the place where Kleiner had spent his terrible ordeal. Carefully the invader stalked towards the reeking pallet, like a panther on the prowl. A dark heap, indistinct and almost formless in the gloom, sprawled across the rag-strewn mess of soiled hay and greasy brown stains.

The vile reek was familiar to the strange visitor, just as it had been to Theodor Baer when he had made out his report. It was the same smell of death and corruption that had pervaded the carcass of the dog. But it was not the wreckage of a dog that dripped from the rags and hay. The few bones, the few scraps of flesh and organ that had not ruptured and corroded told the observer that what he gazed upon had lately been a man.

Gloved hands whispered in the darkness, reaching beneath heavy folds of grey cloth to produce two objects. The first was a small glass vial with a topper of cold-wrought iron. The second was a thin copper device, like a knitting pin but hinged at its tip to form something resembling the bill of a gull. Holding the vial firmly in one hand, the intruder leaned above the pallet and prodded among the grisly ruin of what had once been the smuggler Kleiner. After a few seconds of picking about the slimy mush, the hooked bill closed about something fat and elongated, almost resembling one of the dead man's fingers but for its ghastly green-black colour and bloated, wormy shape.

The grisly maggot hung lifelessly from the pincers as the intruder lifted it to the neck of the vial and quickly nudged it inside. The thing had never truly been alive, but there was a chance that its motive power had not yet been entirely spent, a chance that the man in the darkened room did not want to risk. He knew what manner of death had struck here, what terrible corruption had been passed on into the dog Theodor had killed.

It was not that mystery that caused the visitor to linger in the squalid hovel, his penetrating gaze inspecting every nook and crack in walls and floor. He knew what kind of death stalked the streets of Altdorf. What he did not know was why and how it had been brought into the city.

Those questions remained a puzzle to the intruder when, just before the morning sun began to rise, he made his silent departure. There was no need to again ensorcel the senses of Jakob Helmer when he made his exit; the watchman had been asleep at his post for some hours when the intruder left.

In that respect, Jakob was much like the city at large; asleep and unaware of the horror that threatened them all.

It was as well that the city was unaware. Knowledge would bring panic, panic would bring confusion and confusion would bring disorder. Altdorf could not afford such unrest, not when her enemies were so many and so near.

Now that his master had examined what he had found, Theodor Baer would be free to destroy the evidence of how Kleiner had died. The secret would be kept and the ignorance of Altdorf's teeming masses would be maintained.

For how long it could be maintained was a question for which the cloaked figure that vanished in the predawn streets had no answer.

CHAPTER SIX

The Wizard and the Monster

GREY SEER THANQUOL stood within the cavernous warren, perched atop a lump of stone, overseeing the frantic efforts of his underlings as they scoured the floor of the abandoned cave. Their objective was to gather small slivers of blackish green stone, the tiniest of fragments of the missing Wormstone. These toxic flakes were scattered throughout the warren, forcing the skaven to scour every nook, dig under every bone, in their search. The effort was made all the more complicated by the warp bat's refusal to have anything to do with the unnatural debris, anxiously cringing beneath the legs of its beastmaster every time an effort was made to include it in the hunt. After a time, even Thanquol gave up trying to induce the animal to cooperate. If it wasn't so valuable and if he didn't need the goodwill of Clan Moulder, he would have ordered his stormvermin to gut the rebellious vermin.

None of the scouts sent by Clan Eshin had survived the skirmish and assassination attempt, though they had taken most of the Clan Pestilens contingent with them. Chantor Pusskab was among the casualties, a skaven dagger nestled in his chest, whatever strange revelation he had wanted to impart to the grey seer locked on dead lips. The knife in Pusskab's chest looked terribly familiar to Thanquol and he felt uncomfortable when he recalled the throwing knife that had missed him and the death squeak that had followed when the weapon struck a very different target.

Pusskab and several of the other plague monks had been gathering strange wormy growths from the floor of the cavern. The things had a weird, pungent smell that reminded Thanquol equally of warpstone and sewage. Even so, the plague monks had thought the things important enough to collect, so Thanquol bit down on his squeamishness and ordered Kratch to gather them together. Kratch wasn't overly pleased by the task, quickly bullying some Clan Skaul clanrats into doing the work. The studious way Kratch avoided touching any of the dried, crumbly worms was not lost on Thanquol. Anything his apprentice avoided coming into contact with was worth keeping in mind. Later, when there were not so many listening ears, he'd have some questions to put to Kratch about the Wormstone and Skabritt's ill-fated expedition.

The fate of the Wormstone itself was soon explained. Some of the Clan Skaul contingent found faint prints in the dust of the floor; the marks of boots. Humans had been here and, judging by the depth of some of the tracks when they had departed, they had taken something very heavy away with them. Of all the clans, Skaul and Eshin had the greatest contact with the human nest above Under-Altdorf. Knowing the disfavour and distrust with which Thanquol now regarded Clan Eshin, Clan Skaul was quick to offer its services tracking down the errant humans. Their spokesman, an old crook-backed spy named Skrim Gnawtail, promised that Skaul's network of informants, partners and pets among the humans of Altdorf would quickly locate the men the grey seer needed to find. With Thanquol's blessing, Skrim Gnawtail sent one of his younger, spryer subordinates to make contact with Skaul's agents on the surface. Thanquol watched the wiry skaven scurry from the warren, rushing down the black passageway beyond.

'These shards,' Viskitt Burnfang was saying, one of the flakes of stone gripped in his iron-sheathed hand. 'They are strange. I should like to examine them further.'

Thanquol looked at the warlock engineer, studying his posture and scent for any mark of deceit. He was perfectly willing to allow the warlock engineer to suffer the hazards and labour of experimenting with the Wormstone residue. He was less than willing to let such discoveries slip into the paws of Clan Skryre. He gave Burnfang a threatening smile of fangs. 'Perhaps we could study it together,' he told the warlock engineer, lifting his head to remind Burnfang of his superior authority. There was no reason not to allow Burnfang to do all the work. He could always suffer an accident before any report could find its way back to Warplord Quilisk.

Before Thanquol could make more detailed ideas about how to exploit Burnfang's skills without risk, a sharp squeal of terror rose from the passageway behind him. The grey seer spun about, his eyes going wide as he saw an enormous creature waddling out of the darkness. Its scent was sickly, a foul mixture of decay and disease laced with, yes, a suggestion of warpstone. The reek of fresh blood – skaven blood – was heavy about the monster, stemming from the ugly smear splashed across its massive jaws.

Gigantic, rat-like, its foul eyes gleaming with hunger and madness, the rat-beast crept slowly forwards, a rope of bloody drool spilling from its fanged mouth.

'Rat-beast still live-live!' Kratch's panicked shriek echoed through the cavern. The adept dived behind a pile of bones, spurting the musk of fear. Thanquol watched the display of terror. The private discussion about what exactly had happened to Skabritt was going to be very interesting.

The rat-beast growled in response to Kratch's scream. It shook dirt from its mangy pelt and loudly sniffed at the air. Its claws crunched against the floor as it continued to creep forward.

Thanquol hopped down from his perch and started to back away. He smelled the horror in the scent of his underlings, disturbed to see them retreating even more rapidly. The grey seer forced himself to stand his ground, straightening his posture and raising his head. He glared at his minions, showing his fangs. Angrily he pointed at the slowly advancing monster. 'Kill-kill!' he snarled.

The command didn't seem to impress his underlings. When the rat-beast suddenly swung its huge head around and bit through a Clan Skaul ratman trying to sneak past it, many of them began to squirt their own fear-smell. Thanquol ground his fangs together. The craven filth! Their cowardice was threatening his own welfare! He closed his eyes, drawing upon some of the divine power of the Horned Rat. A leprous glow began to gather around the metal head of his staff.

The display of Thanquol's sorcery turned the crisis. His underlings had seen a recent and dramatic display of the grey seer's awful power. They knew the havoc and carnage he could visit upon them with his magic. Thanquol gloated as the warriors of Clan Mors and Clan Skab began to form up into ragged ranks, as the armed clanrats of Skryre began to scurry and creep into positions from which they could employ their ghastly weapons. It did not matter if they feared the rat-beast. All that mattered was they feared Thanquol more!

The muster of the ratkin was not lost upon the rat-beast's feral brain. The monster roared as it saw the warriors form into ranks, then it was charging across the cavern, a pounding surging mass of crushing bestial fury. The beast smashed into the warriors of Clan Mors, battering them with the violence of an earthquake. Broken bodies were flung into the air as the beast ravaged the ranks of the warriors, oblivious to the swords and spears stabbing into its polluted flesh. Squeaks of terror and cries of mortal agony rose from the brutalised ratmen, filling the abandoned warren with a fearful clamour. The stink of fear was drowned out by the reek of spilled blood and ruptured bodies.

Thanquol swung about. The rat-beast's charge had moved it away from the passage; the one exit from the cavern. Snapping quick orders to those around him, Thanquol led a quick retreat, careful to keep his white-furred bodyguards between himself and the rampaging beast. Other skaven were quick to join the exodus, abundantly content to leave the warriors of Clan Mors to distract the monster.

Thanquol led his minions across the cavern, the crunching of bones and the shredding of flesh echoing behind them. It was wisdom, not cowardice, to avoid a senseless fight with a mindless monster. It was more important that he bring his discoveries back to Under-Altdorf than risk himself destroying some brainless brute lurking in a forgotten warren that had been abandoned generations ago. His subordinates would support his position. At least those who made it out would.

Thanquol looked back to see the rat-beast feasting on the fallen warriors. It was a gruesome, hideous sight that made the grey seer's glands clench.

While he watched the monster feed, Thanquol saw something leap up from the floor and begin a mad dash for the tunnel. It was Kratch, abandoning his improvised refuge, scent dripping down his legs. The rat-beast noticed the adept's sudden movement. With live prey to pursue, the monster ignored the carrion crushed beneath its paws. Growling, the brute lunged after the scurrying Kratch.

A timely tumble spared Kratch from the beast's lunge. Sprawled across the floor, Kratch cowered as the monster's bulk swept through the air above him. Thanquol snickered when he saw his apprentice's dilemma, but his amusement quickly died when the rat-beast's pounce carried it past the prone adept. Landing past its intended prey, the beast did not bother to look around for Kratch. Instead its beady eyes focused on the skaven fleeing into the tunnel.

It was just like Kratch to treacherously refuse to allow himself to be eaten so his betters could escape.

Thanquol shoved Burnfang out of his way as he resumed his headlong flight down the passage. The white stormvermin kept pace with him, using their halberds to batter and smash any skaven in their way. Behind him, Thanquol could hear the shrieks of ratmen as the beast ploughed into them, crunching their bodies against the earthen walls. The grey seer risked a look back, horrified to see the rat-beast rushing down the passage only a few yards away. He fumbled at his robe, paws closing around another piece of warpstone. Despite the immense danger of drawing upon such power again so soon, Thanquol was determined it was better than being chewed by a giant monster.

Burnfang's shrill voice squeaked above the roar of the monster and the screams of mangled skaven. Thanquol did not catch the warlock engineer's words, but one of his guards did. Seizing the grey seer by the waist, the stormvermin crushed their charge to the floor. Thanquol spit dirt from his mouth, about to snarl an outraged protest when a chemical smell filled the tunnel. With a whoosh, the gloom of the passage was annihilated by a surge of dripping flame; the liquid fire of a warpfire thrower. Skaven shrieked as the flame licked at their bodies, searing through flesh and fur to gnaw the bone beneath. At the front of the tunnel, a Clan Skryre weapon team stood its ground, their slick oiled smocks resisting the back-spray from their weapon. They played the flame across the tunnel, heedless of whether the fire struck skaven or beast, their sadistic laughter ringing out.

Laughter turned to screams as the monster came racing down the tunnel, its side engulfed in flame. Agonised, maddened, the rat-beast charged the source of the fire rather than fleeing it. The brute's mass smashed into the weapon team, dashing both of the ratmen against the walls. The burning monster did not pause to finish its foes but continued on, rushing down the winding tunnels. Moments later, Thanquol could hear a faint splash as the scorched creature dived into the stagnant muck of the human sewer system beyond the skaven tunnels.

The grey seer pushed the clinging arms of his bodyguards from him and lifted himself to his feet. Brushing dust from his robes, Thanquol dispassionately surveyed the carnage in the tunnel, mangled and broken skaven picking themselves from the smoking wreckage of their fellows. He ground his fangs together as he saw Kratch stepping gingerly through the gory mess.

'I think you forgot to tell me a few things,' Thanquol hissed as his apprentice came closer. Kratch started to stammer out some sort of excuse, but Thanquol was in no mind to hear his lies. A quick smash of his staff into the adept's gut crumpled Kratch in a gasping heap on the ground.

Feeling much better, Thanquol started to see what was still alive enough to be salvaged from the ruins.

'You can trust me, Maus, no less an authority than Dr Loew confirmed it's wyrdstone.'

Kempf stood within a cluttered curio shop, surrounded by shelves bulging with pieces of rusty armour, notched blades, mouldy garments decades out of fashion, cracked pots, dented tankards and the leering bosom of an old ship's figurehead. The building was less store than it was rat run, narrow little aisles winding their way through heaps of old junk and almost-trash. One glance at the motley collection, the gathered hoard of a pack rat rather than the wares of a merchant, the observer might be forgiven for cultivating a belief that the proprietor would buy nearly anything brought into his shop.

It was a calculated deception, for the owner of the shop was notorious for his shrewd business sense and miserly soul. Bitter and sharp, Hopfoot the Maus was far from the happy, hedonistic halflings of the Moot. Frugal to the point of deprivation, as judgemental as the warden of the Reiksfang, as vicious-minded as a goblin warchief, many stories and rumours circulated about the waterfront regarding Hopfoot's past. The halfling's twisted leg was blamed on everything from an extreme case of orcish shingles to a bad fall when he pulled himself out of a giant's cook-pot. The reasons for his exile from Mootland were even more speculative. Some said he'd murdered his father to claim an inheritance and had been forced to flee with the field-wardens hot on his hairy heels. Others said he'd committed the unforgivable crime of stealing recipes from the Baker's Guild and had been tarred and feathered before being run out of the Moot on a rail. Whatever the true stories, Hopfoot kept them as close to his chest as the tiered ring of money belts that hugged his plump frame.

The halfling was fingering one of those belts as he eyed the green-black shard the smuggler had placed on the teakwood counter. There was a foxy, suspicious gleam in his eyes as he lifted his head and squinted at Kempf. 'If Loew thinks this stuff is wyrdstone, why don't you sell it to him?'

Kempf chuckled. 'He's an alchemist, you're a fence. You have more ready money than he does.'

Hopfoot patted the steel barrel of an enormous blunderbuss, its mouth looking wide enough to swallow the Emperor's Palace. It was one of many such weapons secreted about the confusing jumble of the curio shop. In the past, enterprising burglars had thought the diminutive fence would make an easy mark. It was said the halfling had sold their bodies to the medical catechists at the university. Their clothes would be some of those quietly decaying on the dusty shelves.

'I have more money because I am careful with it,' Hopfoot warned. 'Not all thieves use their hands. The clever ones try to use their tongues.' The fence's voice dropped to a sinister snarl. 'You aren't clever, now, are you?'

'Don't threaten me, Maus!' Kempf snapped, reaching out to retrieve the stone shard. The halfling's nimble hands quickly pulled it from the man's reach. 'I can just as easily sell it to Loew.'

Hopfoot grinned, fingering his jewelled money belts again. 'You are a terrible liar, Kempf. If you were going to sell to Loew, you wouldn't have come here. Besides, as you so eloquently observed, I have more money at hand for such expenditures.' The halfling stared at the greenish rock again. 'Tell me, why don't you want to sell to Loew? Worried that he might have spoken with Gustav Volk?'

'Volk doesn't concern you, Maus,' Kempf stated, reaching for the shard again. The halfling leaned away from his clutching hand.

'He's looking for you, you know,' Hopfoot said. 'You and all your friends. Offering a tidy sum too.' The fence made a placating gesture with his hand. 'I buy and sell goods, not information. Ask around, anyone will tell you that Hopfoot's memory is absolutely awful.' The halfling's smile broadened. 'But maybe it isn't Volk who you are hoping to avoid. Does Hans know you're making a side deal?'

'For a fellow with a bad memory, you've got an ugly tongue,' Kempf growled. Before he could move, Hopfoot had his arms around the blunderbuss, raising it menacingly above the counter.

'Let's keep things professional, shall we? Any transaction we agree to stays between the two of us. Discretion is, after all, the heart of good business.' The halfling set down the wide-mouthed gun and picked up a stick of lead from the counter. Writing on a strip of water-stained parchment, he began to make calculations. After a few moments, he set down the lead and pushed what he had written towards Kempf. 'I trust you can read numbers if not letters.'

Kempf's face grew flush, his fingers crumpling the parchment. 'What are you playing at, Maus? This isn't even half what Dr Loew would pay for a good piece of wyrdstone like that!'

'Then see Dr Loew. Or maybe talk to the Dietrichs about your little side-deals. How much of the stuff have you skimmed already, I wonder? Enough to make Volk the least of your problems?'

'Stop baiting me, you poisonous little toad!'

Hopfoot's smile dropped into a thin, friendless sneer. 'I'm just making certain we understand one another. Discretion, after all, doesn't come cheap. Think of it as an added custom or duty. A bit less profit for you, and Hopfoot's memory remains as bad as the roads in Stirland. Nobody needs to know you ever came here... or why.'

Glowering at the fence, Kempf gave a reluctant nod. Hopfoot opened one of the pouches on a money belt and began counting out silver coins. The smuggler watched the little stack of silver rise, all but drooling over the piled money. Absently, he began to scratch at his arms, twitching as he did so. The fence noticed the motion and he gave Kempf a knowing look.

'How long has it been since you visited Otto Ali?' Hopfoot's smile grew back into its former broadness when he saw the alarm seize Kempf's features. 'Don't worry. If I can't remember where you were, I can't very well know where you are going if anyone asks.'

The halfling laughed as Kempf quickly grabbed the fistful of coins and darted down the cramped aisles of his shop. 'Come again,' Hopfoot called after the smuggler. He heard the little bell fastened to the door jingle as the man retreated into the street. He stared back at the green stone in his hand, laughing to himself as he considered how much he could sell it for.

'Always a pleasure to help those in need of discretion.'

GREY SEER THANQUOL stalked through the cramped streets of Under-Altdorf, his albino stormvermin clearing a path for him through the press of mangy, furry bodies. The streets of Under-Altdorf, like those of any skaven warren, were narrow and winding, designed so that those who scurried along them could feel the reassuring presence of solid earth against their whiskers. Stenches and smells inundated the priest-sorcerer, an almost overwhelming stink of musks and scents. Here in the market skrawl of Under-Altdorf, every few feet of tunnel bore the musk of a different individual as merchants and tradesrats marked their shops and stalls. Dingy signs, often no more than a rag drenched in the odour of the proprietor's wares, stabbed out from the tunnel walls, denoting some little wooden stall or the sunken entrance to a more permanent establishment. Large banners hung over the entrances to side-tunnels and connecting passageways proclaiming the clan affiliations of those merchants to be found in that stretch of the market. Sometimes, though rarely, Thanquol even saw signs bearing the scratch-marks of written Queekish, though literacy was considered something of an unattainable extravagance by much of the teeming masses that scurried through the marketplace.

Thanquol patted the heavy bag he bore and his tail twitched in satisfaction. He had turned the fiasco in the old warren of Clan Mawrl into a victory, one that only a skaven of his keen and discerning intellect could have achieved. Playing one clan against the other, he had been quick to accuse each of being behind the plot to assassinate him. Thanquol was not sure he believed Skrattch Skarpaw's insistence that if Clan Eshin had wanted the grey seer dead they would never have been foolish enough to use their own ratmen to accomplish the deed, but it made for a most effective argument to keep the other clans nervous and jumping at shadows. Each had been most eager to show their loyalty to Thanquol and, more importantly, the Lords of Decay in Skavenblight, by lavishing the grey seer in gifts and promises.

They could keep the promises. Thanquol might not be convinced of Skarpaw's innocence, but he was far from satisfied that none of the others were guilty. He included Grey Seer Thratquee in that suspect group. The old villain was probably just impatient enough to try and kill Thanquol even before the Wormstone was in their paws! Thanquol wasn't about to accept further reinforcements from the clan leaders. The remains of his first retinue, those who had survived the attacks of the assassins and the rat-beast, were enough for his purposes, and more importantly could be reasonably assumed not to have been involved in the plot to kill him. They didn't smell of treachery, or at least Thanquol could try to convince himself they didn't. If they thought he trusted them, they'd let their guard down and be easier to watch.

Gifts, however, had been much more welcome. Each of the clans had tried to outdo the others in financing Thanquol's changed mission. A small fortune in warpstone tokens now rattled in the dwarfskin bag slung over his shoulder, enough to rebuild the fortune he had lost trying to pursue his foolish vendetta against that damnable slayer and his manling pet. There was even enough that he could spend part of it on what it was intended for without feeling the bite too keenly. It would certainly help him keep up appearances as far as the council was concerned.

'Most merciful and wise master,' Kratch's whining voice sounded from beside Thanquol. The grey seer turned to see his apprentice's head bobbing submissively at his elbow. 'Allow this wretched underling to relieve-carry your onerous burden.'

Thanquol gave the adept an incredulous stare and clutched the bag tight against his chest.

'When orcs fly,' the grey seer answered. Ever since they had left the council chambers, Kratch had been grovelling and snivelling, trying to get his paws on the swag Thanquol's craft had won. The adept's manipulations might be as transparent as a broken window, but his tenacity was becoming tedious. Of all the skaven the rat-beast had gulped down, how was it possible the nasty thing had missed Kratch? Surely it was some trial sent by the Horned Rat to test Thanquol. The only thing that gave him pause was the nagging doubt that he might still need his apprentice to identify the Wormstone when it was found.

That and concocting an elaborate enough lie about Kratch's future accident that the Council of Thirteen would accept.

Thanquol was pulled from the happy thought of several inventive and torturous ends for his apprentice by one of his albino guards. The hulking armoured skaven bowed before the grey seer, his posture bespeaking the new respect and fear both stormvermin had been displaying ever since his brutal destruction of the assassins. If Thanquol had even considered intimidation would work on the elite warriors, he'd have tried it long ago instead of bribery and deception.

The white-furred stormvermin waited until Thanquol acknowledged him, then lifted a paw and pointed at the bright yellow and blue banner stretched across a nearby tunnel entrance. The rune scratched across its surface in what smelled like a particularly septic sort of blood proclaimed it as the demarcation for Clan Moulder's section of Under-Altdorf's skrawl market.

Thanquol's tail twitched and a feral gleam came to his eye. When he had told the council he did not need more ratmen to serve him, he had, of course, meant minions provided by the clans. If he was to master the Wormstone, he would need to experiment with the pitiful remnants recovered from Clan Mawrl's abandoned warren. For that, he would need test subjects... many test subjects. The slavemasters of Clan Moulder and Clan Skaul had ample stocks of shackled wretches to be had for a few warpstone tokens. Clan Skaul specialised in human slaves, starveling drug-fiends abducted from the nest of humans above Under-Altdorf, the dregs and detritus of the largest concentration of humans in the Old World, the nameless and faceless who were barely missed by their fellows. Thanquol had already negotiated the purchase of a few score of these manlings to test the effects of the Wormstone upon. Before he returned to Skavenblight and presented a weapon before the Lords of Decay, it would be advisable to make sure it worked first.

Clan Moulder, however, specialised in skavenslaves, miserable ratmen whose clans had been conquered and vanquished, the survivors becoming a commodity to be traded and abused by the victors. In his audience with the council, Thanquol had explained he would need a control group of skaven to test the Wormstone on and to see what safeguards would be required to make it safe for the ratmen to handle. Skavenslaves represented the cheapest and most expendable way to conduct controlled exposures and develop countermeasures. Viskitt Burnfang was even now ransacking the shops of Clan Skryre's engineers for the equipment Thanquol would need to make his experiments. He knew he would not need to fear any subterfuge from Burnfang: the warlock engineer would be heading the experiments himself and any sabotage would strike down him before the grey seer. No skaven, however large the bribe or threat, could be bullied into sacrificing himself.

Of course, Thanquol's real motive in testing the skavenslaves was not to find a way to protect against the Wormstone, but to see how potent it was against his own kind. Some of Thratquee's grandiose scheming hadn't sounded completely insane to Thanquol. As a weapon against the humans, the Wormstone would represent power for the Council of Thirteen. As a weapon against skaven, the Wormstone would represent the might of Grey Seer Thanquol.

The tunnels of Clan Moulder's section of the skrawl were wider than those elsewhere, the ceilings stretching higher than the comforting closeness of the other trader districts. Thanquol knew it was practicality rather than aesthetics that had caused such a divergence in construction. Many of the strange beasts bred by the master moulders were much larger than even the biggest skaven and such lumbering brutes needed the extra space if they were not to become lodged in the passages.

A thousand new smells assaulted Thanquol's senses, odours of corruption and suffering, bestial stenches and the reek of raw meat. The shops that loomed from the walls of the tunnel were larger than elsewhere, expanded to accommodate the living wares of the merchants. Iron cages and wattle pens were everywhere, smashed into each nook and cranny, wherever a beastmaster or slaver could squeeze his property and set up an auction block. The gloating, bullying voices of the merchants chittered through the passages, alternately whining and threatening, using a bizarre combination of enticement and intimidation to draw custom their way.

The throng that packed the tunnel was a motley array from all across Under-Altdorf. Clan Sleekit bargemasters scurried through the press, eagerly negotiating for more slaves. Fat hedonists of Clan Skaul bartered in the shadows for weird, mind-warping elixirs and powders from garishly robed beast-breakers. warlock engineers prowled through the crowds, their bodies bent beneath masses of strange machinery, little strings of servants scurrying after them with baskets bulging with recently purchased rats. Towering above the mob, immense rat ogres stalked along the passages like walking mounds of muscle and claw, doggedly following in the tracks of their colourfully cloaked masters.

Sight of the huge monsters brought a new thought to Thanquol. His eyes narrowed as he looked at his white-furred guards. Their performance against the assassins had been less than zealous and he could not forget that however much they might fear him now, their loyalties still ultimately rested with the Lords of Decay. He needed protection of a more dependable sort, the kind that didn't scheme behind its master's back or plot intrigue with his enemies. He turned his eyes away from the tunnel ahead, instead training his attention on the shops and pens they were passing, sniffing at the air and trying to pick from it the scent he was looking for. After a dozen twists and turns of the tunnel, a feral smile came to the grey seer as he found what he was seeking.

Raising his staff, Thanquol motioned to his underlings to precede him into a cave-like shop that gaped in the wall of the passage. The reek of beasts and meat was overpowering as the skaven stepped from the corridor and into the dimly-lit shop. Metal cages hung from the ceiling, displaying a variety of oversized rats with an outrageous array of mutations twisting their verminous bodies. A big wooden mew stretched across one of the shop's walls, its cramped interior filled with a colourful collection of bats, a popular pet and status symbol for affluent skaven.

Thanquol ignored the bats and rats, turning instead to the far side of the store. Here a deep pit had been excavated, lined with wickedly barbed iron spikes. A thick, brutish smell rose from the hole and he could hear the rumbling breath of some gigantic creature.

'Greetings-greetings, holy one,' the proprietor of the shop chittered as he crept towards Thanquol. He was a small, large-fanged ratman with strange streaks of red in his fur. A variety of whips and leashes dangled from the copper belt that straddled the merchant's paunch, clattering against his belly with each waddling step. 'How may humble-honoured Schafwitt be of service to terrible Grey Seer Thanquol?'

The stormvermin bared their fangs when they heard Schafwitt address the grey seer, lowering their blades menacingly. Thanquol waved them back. As much as he approved of this display of paranoid caution, it was not surprising that the merchant should recognise him. Word of the presence of so renowned and respected a personage as himself would have spread to even the lowest levels of Under-Altdorf by this time. Moreover, the frightened scent and submissive posture of Schafwitt was too compelling to be trickery. An old hand at deceit, Thanquol knew an amateur's smell.

Thanquol did not answer the merchant, instead pushing past the runtish ratman, stalking towards the pit. He peered over the side, his beady eyes narrowing with greed as he saw the thing below. A thrill of fear rushed through the grey seer's body, teasing at his glands. His muzzle spread in a fierce smile. The fear he felt would be nothing beside that which would grip the craven hearts of his enemies.

Kratch slithered up beside his master, his conniving curiosity pulling him after Thanquol. The adept peered down into the pit, cringing back as the thing below looked back. The apprentice's feeble valour abandoned him and he began to creep away. 'Perhaps, grim and horrible biter of throats, this one should scurry-seek the slave-meat for your studies. If great master Thanquol will allow-favour poor Kratch with a few hundred warpstone tokens to make-take from the slavers...'

'Still your tongue and your feet, Kratch,' Thanquol snarled. 'Or I will nail both to the floor.' He gave his apprentice a glower that ensured there was no doubting the sincerity of his threat. Turning away from the subdued apprentice, Thanquol rested his paws against the fence of metal spikes and grinned down at the occupant of the pit.

It was a colossus of bone and muscle, every inch of its massive frame boiling with barely restrained violence and bloodlust. Taller than three skaven, six feet across at its broad shoulders, weighing as much as the barge he had travelled to Under-Altdorf on, the thing in the pit seemed more like some elemental force than a beast of flesh and blood. Its leathery flesh was pale and pitted with vicious scars, the visible heritage of a brutal and savage life. Patches of stringy black hair dripped from the huge body, its scaly tail dangling behind it, as thick around as one of Thanquol's legs. A massive head filled with yellowed fangs the size of daggers sprouted from the broad shoulders, bestial and rat-like with a dull, murderous intelligence shining in its bloodshot eyes. The beast's arms were enormous concentrations of knotted muscle and thick bone, each ending in a fist bigger than a skaven's head, each fat finger tipped with a sword-like claw. The imposing limbs were made even more menacing by their disparity: a mutant, the thing sported a third arm, its right shoulder splitting to accommodate the extra extremity.

It was, quite simply, the most monstrous rat ogre Thanquol had ever seen and when he saw the giant, spear-like horn growing between the brute's eyes, he knew the creature was meant to be his. It was a sign, an omen from the Horned Rat. A sacred protector to guard the god of vermin's favourite and most devout servant. Thanquol had used rat ogres to protect him from his enemies in the past, the first having loyally and fearlessly sacrificed itself upon the axe of that thrice-damned slayer in order that its master might escape. In need of a dependable guardian, Thanquol had come to the skrawl foremost to procure a rat ogre bodyguard. After one look at the hulk in the pit, he knew no other beast would do.

'What price for the beast?' Thanquol asked, his eyes locked on those of the monster in the pit.

'Dread-mighty Thanquol,' Schafwitt whined, '…expensive-expensive. Much-much cost to unlucky Schafwitt to feed and keep such fearsome stock.'

Thanquol's eyes narrowed, his fangs gleamed in a challenging smile. 'How much?'

'It kill-eat Schafwitt's other rat ogres,' the merchant explained, spreading his paws in a helpless gesture.

The irritating habit of Under-Altdorf skaven to adopt human mannerisms set Thanquol's fur bristling, darkening his mood and collapsing his already fragile patience. 'Name a price while there is still a tongue inside your snout,' he warned in a low snarl.

'F… four-hun… hundred warp-t… t… tokens, merciful and fearsome Thanquol,' Schafwitt stammered.

Thanquol turned his head away from the merchant, looking instead at the white stormvermin. He gave a twist of his horned head and the two warriors seized Schafwitt, pushing the merchant to the lip of the pit, pressing his body over the spikes. Below, the mutant rat ogre watched the spectacle with rapt – and hungry – attention.

'Th… three… three-hundred seventy warpstone tokens,' Schafwitt pleaded. A flick of Thanquol's claw had the stormvermin push the merchant a little farther over the edge. 'Three… three-hundred fifty four warpstone tokens… three-hundred thirty three… three-hundred twenty!'

Grey Seer Thanquol listened to the merchant rattle off prices. Eventually he would reach a fee that reflected the proper amount of respect and admiration for Thanquol's position and prestige. Until then, Thanquol returned his attention to the pit. The rat ogre looked back at him, the smell of Schafwitt's fear provoking a rope of drool to fall from its immense mouth.

'Twenty! Twenty warpstone tokens!' Schafwitt shrieked.

Thanquol chuckled, motioning for his mute stormvermin to pull the merchant up from the pit. It was a miserable-looking Schafwitt that grovelled and fawned before the grey seer.

'Pay the wretch!' Thanquol barked at Kratch.

Looking almost as miserable as Schafwitt, Kratch dug a pawful of coins from his ratskin purse. Scowling at his miserly master, Kratch threw the coins at Schafwitt, the little discs of warpstone scattering across the floor. The merchant dived after them, scrambling about on all fours to recover his money.

The albino stormvermin used their wiry strength to drag a heavy beam from one corner of the shop and tip it over the side of the pit. They glanced down into the depression, then hurriedly retreated, scurrying after the halberds they had set leaning against the wall with almost as much indecent haste as Schafwitt scrabbled after his coins. Behind them, the beam groaned and shook as something immense clawed its way up from the darkness.

The horned rat ogre's head just peeked above the lip of the pit, all three of its immense claws dug into the wood of the beam, streamers of drool dangling from its fangs. Thanquol felt a tremor of fear as he felt the rat ogre's beady eyes stare at him, but the monster had small interest in his new owner. It was the sight of Schafwitt, still scurrying about the floor for his fee, that seemed to incense the monster. With a tremendous bellow, it exerted the massive strength of its powerful frame. The beam splintered and cracked as the rat ogre lunged from its perch, clearing the pit and crashing to the floor of the shop. Schafwitt had just enough time to recognise the vengeful paw that came smashing down to grind his skull into the ground.

The other skaven backed away from the monster as it continued to pull slivers of meat from the merchant's corpse, flinging them from its claws with an almost noble contempt as it continued its bestial retribution. Thanquol saw the indecision in the eyes of his bodyguards, their halberds shaking in their paws. The longing look they gave to the doorway was eloquent in its expression of cowardly treachery. Thanquol lashed his tail in spiteful annoyance, his anger only swelling when he heard Kratch yelp as his master slapped him across the snout. Thanquol turned a baleful eye on his apprentice, furious at the temerity of any minion to cower behind his master in a crisis.

Anger (and a good pinch of warpstone snuff) fuelled the grey seer's contempt for all and everything around him. He straightened his back and stormed across the shambles of Schafwitt's shop, being careful to step over the spreading pools of the merchant's blood. Thanquol stalked directly towards the raging rat ogre. Angrily, he brought the head of his staff smacking into the monster's snout.

The brute reared back, a deafening roar rumbling from its lungs, all three arms raised over its head in readiness to crush and maim. Thanquol just glared back at the beast, no suggestion of fear seeping into his scent. The monster stared into Thanquol's glowing eyes. The arms drooped slowly to its sides, jaws snapped close as the rat ogre's expression faded from one of exultant rage to cowed timidity. A subservient scent poured from the beast's glands.

Thanquol turned from the subdued rat ogre and snarled at his own cowering minions. Let them fear, he was better than them. That was why he was destined to be the greatest skaven who ever lived. Even a dumb brute like a rat ogre recognised the might of Grey Seer Thanquol!

With their own heads lowered in humility, the stormvermin crept forwards. Kratch, with one eye still fixed on the rat ogre, began to paw among the mangled meat that was the remains of Schafwitt looking for warpstone tokens. Thanquol drank in their fear as though it were a sweet perfume. It was not the rat ogre they feared, but the skaven who was able to command such a beast's loyalty through force of will alone.

He would name his new property Boneripper, Thanquol decided. No matter how many times he used it, the grey seer felt there was an appealing menace to the name, a promise of the horrific savagery his guard would unleash on his command.

THE BLACK BAT was one of the many establishments on Altdorf's notorious Street of 100 Taverns. It was well outside of Theodor Baer's normal hunting grounds, being close to the university and well away from the docks. However, swathed in a heavy leather coat and with his pectoral stuffed inside an inner pocket, Theodor wasn't on official business and didn't need to worry about stepping on the pride of the local watch house responsible for this stretch of the capital. He was not visiting the Black Bat in his capacity as a sergeant of the city watch.

His visit here was more important than his normal duties, orders not from his captain but from the invisible being to whom he owed his ultimate loyalty.

The tavern was crowded, even at midday. The long beer hall that was the Black Bat's common room was bisected by a rectangular counter of sombre Drakwald timber polished to a remarkable shine. The counter formed a little island amid a sea of oak tables and beech wood benches from which the barmen could minister spirits and beer to the thirsty throngs who rolled around them like crashing waves. A trapdoor behind the beer barrels led to the cellar beneath the tavern, allowing the workers to replenish supplies without pushing their way through the masses of patrons.

Most of the clientele of the Black Bat were labourers; teamsters and muleskinners, stonemasons and carpenters, roofers and plasterers. Odd pockets of students from the university, slumming from their usual haunts, were scattered among the tables, keeping as much to themselves as was possible in such crowded conditions. At a glance, Theodor could see the styles of Marienburg and Nuln, the rich fabrics of Estalian pantaloons and the frilly extravagance of Tilean shirts, threadbare wool tunics from Wissenland and wolfskin boots from Middenland. Long Kislevite beards mingled with swarthy Miragelan complexions. At one table, Theodor could see a dusky Arabyan horse trader boisterously arguing with a Bretonnian sea captain. All roads lead to Altdorf was a common saying in the Empire, and nowhere could the truth of such an assertion be better displayed than in the city's taverns.

Theodor turned away from the noise of the hall, looking instead to the stairs that rose from the tiled floor. These led up to a wooden deck that circled and overlooked the hall below. Climbing the stairs, he found the upper floor divided into small booths separated by partitions, affording each occupant a level of privacy impossible in the room below. Each of the niches held a table and several straight-backed chairs. A candle provided each alcove with illumination, dispelling the shadows that threatened to consume them. Theodor marched past the alcoves, studying each face he passed. The occupants, mostly wealthy businessmen and buxom wenches too young to be their wives, ignored the sergeant as he stalked along the walkway.

At the end of the walkway, just as the raised floor made a turn to the right, Theodor noticed an anomaly, an alcove that seemed somehow out of place. Appointed just as the others, the light of the candle was somehow weaker than those elsewhere. Where the other private booths had been bathed in light, this one was lost in shadow. The sergeant felt the hairs on his neck prickle as he stepped towards the niche, his mind suddenly gripped by a thrill of alarm and uneasiness. The air felt colder as he leaned into the alcove, his breath misting before his face.

'Be seated,' a low, whispering voice spoke from the gloom of the apparently empty alcove.

Startled, Theodor could do nothing except obey the commanding tone. As he started to settle in one of the chairs, a long-fingered hand swathed in charcoal-grey gloves emerged from the shadows, gesturing for him to take the chair to his left. Theodor turned and sat where the pointing finger indicated. He glanced at the hall below, noticing that his original position would have obscured the speaker's view of the Black Bat's main entryway.

The gloved hand vanished back into darkness. Straining his eyes, Theodor could not make out so much as a silhouette amid the patch of shadowy blackness. An instant later, the hand reappeared, tossing a token down on the table before him. Theodor heard the clank of metal against wood, looking down to find that the token was a coin-like square of metal, its face engraved with strange, squirming characters and a device he could liken only to a snake skull wearing a feathered headdress. His eyes had only a moment to register the weird talisman before the gloved hand dragged it back into the shadows. Even so, he knew it to be the sign he had been instructed to look for.

'Report,' the chilling voice in the darkness told him.

Theodor licked his lips nervously, knowing now that he sat in the presence of his master rather than another minion such as himself. 'The dead man was Emil Kleiner, a small time smuggler, part of Hans Dietrich's gang. The body was burned, the tenement where it was found quarantined, as per instructions.'

'Dietrich's gang. Progress in finding them.'

Theodor found himself glancing away from the darkened corner even though he could not see the face of his interrogator. 'No progress. There was a fight between Hans Dietrich's men and those of Gustav Volk five nights ago. Dietrich has been lying low ever since. Many in the gang may have been killed by Volk's men.'

'Known survivors,' the chill voice's clipped words hissed from the gloom.

'Dietrich and some of his gang were seen in the *Orc and Axe* the same night as their fight with Gustav Volk. Poorly treated wounds on several of the men make it likely this occurred after their encounter with Volk. In addition to Dietrich and Kleiner, the others present were Dietrich's brother Johann, Bogdan Kempf, Max Wilhelm and Niklos Mueller. I have issued orders to the soldiers in my district to look for these men and detain them on sight.'

'Countermand those orders. The men are not to be detained or followed. Sightings of any of them are to be reported. Take no further action until otherwise instructed.'

Theodor sat in silence, considering the strange commands he had been issued. The importance of finding the smugglers was something that he could not doubt and which he had been certain he had impressed upon his master. The new instructions seemed to betray that urgency.

A rasping sound, like the rustle of scales against cloth, hissed from the darkness. 'More importance must be placed on following and observing these men than catching them. At least for the moment. Nothing must be done to put them even more on their guard than they already are. Other operatives will take up the vigil. You will stand by with your men and be ready to act when indicated.'

'I obey,' Theodor said, relieved by his master's explanation but now more perplexed than before. He knew, of course, that there were other operatives in service to the master, but he wondered who could be better qualified to watch the waterfront than the men who patrolled it day in and day out.

'Dismissed,' the voice hissed from the shadows.

Theodor rose from his seat and bowed. Turning away from the table, he started to walk back across the platform. As the sensation of unnatural cold passed from him, he looked back at the alcove where he had sat in conference with his mysterious master. The sergeant stared in dumbfounded wonder. Where the alcove had been, there was now only the outer wall of the Black Bat, a single window looking out over the street behind the building! By some sinister art, the little alcove had been conjured into existence in a place where it could not exist!

As many times as he had experienced the abrupt vanishment of his master, the watchman could not keep his skin from crawling and his blood from turning cold in his veins. Theodor backed away from this evidence of dark powers, turning his thoughts to more clean subjects such as murderers and smugglers as he quickly descended to the main floor of the Black Bat. Even in the light of day, there were some things a man feared to dwell upon.

KEMPF STUMBLED ON the stairs as he exited the little tea shop and descended into the building's cellar. He always stumbled, his excitement overwhelming his coordination, overwhelming everything in fact. Hans, Volk, the watch, nobody and nothing existed as far as Kempf was concerned. All that mattered was now, was his descent into the cellar, the magical place hidden beneath the shop. His eyes barely registered the growing gloom of the poorly-lit landing at the base of the steps, his nose didn't even notice the musky, cloying stink that rose to meet it, his ears didn't trouble themselves about trying to make sense of the muffled voices that could be faintly heard. What little concentration Kempf was able to drag away from the excruciating anticipation that gripped his mind was focused upon the steps beneath his feet.

A hulking man with arms thick enough to strangle an ox greeted Kempf at the bottom of the stairs.

'Back for more, eh scum? Didn't take you long, did it?'

Kempf had to crane his neck to look into the guard's scarred visage. 'I want to see Otto Ali,' he said, licking his lips as he spoke.

The guard poked a finger into Kempf's chest, pushing the weasel-like man back onto the stairs. 'I don't think the boss wants to see you,' he grunted.

'Please!' Kempf whined, stepping down to regain the ground he had lost. 'I must see Otto Ali!'

A massive hand slapped against the sheathed length of a thick-bladed broadsword. 'Go drown yourself, rat,' the guard growled. 'No layabouts and no charity. Beat it before you start to annoy me.'

Kempf dug frantically into his tunic, dragging out the little leather pouch Hopfoot had given him. He opened it, displaying the coins for the guard. The thug grunted appreciatively and thumbed a few coins from the purse.

'Why didn't you say you could pay?' the guard muttered, stepping aside and allowing Kempf to scramble past him.

Beyond the guard was a thick oak door. Kempf gave a practised knock against the wooden panel, a series of raps and taps that would allow him entrance to the lair of Otto Ali. The door opened and a glowering brute, every bit as large and imposing as the outer guard, looked Kempf over from head to foot before motioning the little man inside.

Within was a brick-lined grotto, its exact dimensions hidden by shadow and the litter of wooden bunks crammed into every inch of the main floor. The smell of human sweat and urine was too strong for even Kempf's distracted senses to ignore, the delirious moans and mumbled words rising from the bodies sprawled on the bunks too persistent to escape his ears. A few old lanterns, their glass cracked and caked in grime, flickered from rusty chains set in the ceiling, casting a feeble glow upon the drug den.

'You come to visit us again, my friend,' a thickly accented voice beamed. Kempf's heart fluttered like that of a young lover in the presence of his paramour. He turned quickly to face the speaker. The man who had addressed him was swarthy, his complexion darker even than that of a Tilean. Oily black locks, their lengths curled and stringy, draped down across his thick brow. A smarmy smile split his broad face, displaying teeth that matched the thick gold rings piercing his ears. The man's attire was like his lineage; a curious mixture of the Empire and far distant Araby. A wide sash circled his heavy gut while foreign slippers with curled toes covered his feet. The mixed-blood Arabyan laid a heavily jewelled hand on Kempf's shoulder, like an old friend rather than a man who had used violence to eject the man from this very cellar only the night before.

'More gold, and so soon?' Otto Ali laughed, knowing that the smuggler would never have penetrated this far into his establishment if he were still as destitute as when he had left it. Kempf handed him the pouch Hopfoot had given him for the shard of wyrdstone. Otto Ali poured the contents into his hand and tutted. 'Only silver,' he sighed.

Kempf's shoulders sagged, his face falling into a mask of despair.

'Still,' Otto Ali mused, 'this should be enough to buy a few dreams... small dreams,' he added when he noticed the joyous relief that seized the smuggler. It would not do to raise the man's hopes too high. That might lead to another ugly scene such as the previous night.

Otto Ali clapped his hands together and a thin servant joined the two men. A long-stemmed pipe was in the servant's hand and Kempf could barely contain himself as the minion led him away towards one of the bunks. Otto Ali started to follow, but a sharp voice demanded the Arabyan's attention, pulling him into one of the drug den's many dark corners.

Kempf dismissed the proprietor from his thoughts. Dismissed everything in fact as the servant poured a pinch of shiny black powder into the bowl of the pipe, then pressed the stem to the smuggler's lips. Another servant, one of the few trusted to carry an open flame in the den, manifested beside the bunk and placed a candle beneath the bowl. After a moment of smouldering against the river-clay bowl, the contents of the pipe began to vaporise. Greedily, Kempf drew the fumes up through the pipe and into his body.

Dreams gripped Kempf, dreams such as the smuggler preferred to his bleak reality. There was only one distraction as he slipped into the visions filling his mind. Something was snuffling close beside his bunk, something like a big stinky dog. It was too much effort to turn his head and see what it was, so he drew another lungful of vapour into his body.

Voices came to him. One was thin and scratchy, the other was Otto Ali's.

'Take-watch human-meat,' the thin voice chittered. 'Smell-scent like warpstone. No-no warpstone, maybe-might.'

'This man is a good customer,' Otto Ali objected. 'If I keep him I can't get more of his silver.'

'Take-watch!' growled the voice. 'Take-watch or no-no black dust for Ali-man! We pay-pay shiny ore to Ali-man.'

'I can give him more black dust,' Otto Ali mused. 'He will dream for days. But why do you want him?'

The scratchy voice laughed, a weird trilling sound that was ugly enough to almost pull Kempf from his drugged indolence. 'Not want-find. Thanquol want-find! Thanquol Grey Seer! Reward much-much! Use human-meat find-take maybe-warpstone! Thanquol reward much-much!'

A SHABBY-LOOKING GUTTER snipe in tattered coat and scuffed boots, there was nothing in the appearance of Ludwig Rothfels that made him stand out among the shambling crowds that filled the streets of Altdorf, pushing and squirming their way through narrow streets choked with unwashed masses of humanity. There were hundreds of his ilk creeping through the busy market squares and thoroughfares of the capital, waterfront vagabonds stealing forth from their habitual squalor to rub elbows with their betters. Beggars and thieves, cutpurses and muggers, only when the crowds thinned as the sun began to set would the city watch be able to separate them from their marks and drive them back into the lawless slums.

Ludwig ducked the sweep of a chicken farmer as he gawped and gaped at the sights of the city, forgetting the long pole slung over his back, squawking poultry dangling from it by their tethers. He dodged the carriage of a nobleman as the dignitary rushed through the street, allowing no delay as the traffic parted before his horses. The wheels of the carriage threw up great sheets of muck and mud as they ploughed down the lane. Curses and garbage pelted after the noble as he vanished down the avenue.

Ludwig wiped mud from the coat he had used to shield himself, spitting against the cobblestones as he added his own curses to the chorus. The miserable toffs!

One day they'd answer for their pomposity and arrogance! The red hand of revolution would rise again and the great palaces in the Imperial Quarter would burn! Then the streets would run with blue blood and the roar of the oppressed would be heard!

The little, scrawny man's face grew crimson as emotion welled up inside him and his hand clenched itself into a fist at his side. Then reason reasserted itself and Ludwig gave a nervous, hunted look up and down the street, fearful of who might have noticed his momentary loss of control. Paranoia had quietened his revolutionary spirit, deadening his ideals beneath a shroud of fear. Not fear of the politicians or the nobles, not even the witch hunters and their brutal ways. Ludwig was a man who had defied all of them to do their worst and never backed down before their threats and violence. His right hand was missing two fingers from the time he had been rounded up by the Reiksguard and encouraged to betray his fellow revolutionaries. All they had wrested from his tongue was the same spittle he'd given the street.

It was later, much later, that he'd discovered true fear. It was when he'd first set eyes on the sinister being he would call master that Ludwig had learned the nature of terror. The cell of conspirators, a revolutionary group calling itself the Red Talon, had gathered in the old abandoned manor house of Prince Steffan, planning their own addition to the festivities being arranged to celebrate the birthday of the Emperor. The plotting had not gotten far when the meeting was disturbed, disturbed by a spectral apparition that seemed to grow out of the darkness. Ludwig was a man of words and ideas, not a fighter, but many within the Red Talon were seasoned warriors, veterans of military campaigns, naval engagements and underworld skirmishes.

Ludwig was to learn much that night, as the violence of that tremendous battle stripped away the mask that had cloaked the true nature of the Red Talon. Many of his fellow revolutionaries were exposed as twisted mutants, hiding their corruption beneath a veneer of normalcy. Their leader, Ulrich Schildenhof, proved to be a disciple of the Ruinous Powers, a sorcerous agent of the Purple Hand.

Lofty principles and fiery rhetoric crumbled beneath the horror and shame of the moment, Ludwig's mind numbed by the guilt of being used as a pawn by such unholy things. Then his horror was magnified when he saw the lone, shadowy intruder spring into battle with Schildenhof and his inner circle. One man against the awful mutations of a dozen degenerate horrors and the infernal sorcerer whom they served. It should have been a slaughter. It was, but not the way Schildenhof expected. Ludwig could still remember the look of absolute disbelief on the black magister's face as his head rolled across the manor's ceramic floor.

The former agitator and rabble-rouser shuddered at the image and hurried on his way. Ludwig had preached to any who would listen about the Emperor's spies and how they were steadily attacking the privacy and dignity of every soul in Altdorf. He had believed his words. Now he knew them for the exaggerated lies that they were. Now he knew what it was like to be watched by a being who *did* have eyes everywhere.

He did not know why he had been spared that night. Perhaps it was because he had been an innocent dupe of the ring's cultist leadership. Perhaps it was because in him Jeremias Scrivner found skills that would be useful to his own organisation. Whatever the reason, Ludwig knew it would have been a death sentence to refuse the offer that spectral shadow spoke to him amid the gory shambles of the Red Talon's ruin.

The agitator shook his head, trying to dislodge the terrifying memory. He was still not sure if what he had been granted was reprieve or simply deferment. What he was certain of was the folly of delay. His new master did not have much patience for folly.

Ludwig saw the darkened doorway of a cellar, its iron-fenced steps climbing to join the level of the street. He fumbled at the pocket of his coat, producing a strange gilded key. His father had been a locksmith, among a dozen other professions as his family had quietly starved in the squalor of Altdorf's waterfront, but Ludwig had never seen the likes of the key before. He would almost swear that it changed each time he placed it into a lock, an impression that was always as hard to shake as it was to accept.

With one last glance over his shoulder, Ludwig darted down the cobblestone steps and pressed his body against the iron-banded cellar door. The key slithered into the bronze lock like a hand into a glove, producing a scratching, clicking sound as it turned the mechanism. He pulled the key out quickly and stuffed it back into his pocket, not daring to look at it, fearful he might notice some change in its shape. Muttering a prayer to Verena, goddess of wisdom and light, Ludwig pulled the door open and ducked inside.

His prayer was not answered. Ludwig could tell at once. The cellar was as black as the belly of a daemon, not even the feeblest light trickling through its glazed window, as though the day feared to trespass upon this lingering patch of midnight beneath the streets of

Altdorf. A cold iciness crawled through his flesh, seeping into his body and numbing his soul. His breath became a frosty whisper as he forced himself to step deeper into the darkness. Somewhere in the gloom, he knew, was a little metal box painted to look like one of the flagstones. Perhaps he would still be allowed to place his message there and withdraw.

'Report,' came the hissed command, at once both distant and near.

Ludwig shivered as he heard the voice of his master. He fumbled again in the pockets of his coat, drawing the letter he had written with the master's crawling ink. There was no sound, no sense of anyone moving towards him, not even the slightest brush against his hand, yet somehow the sheaf of parchment was plucked from his fingers just the same.

Ludwig could hear the parchment crinkle somewhere in the darkness. He could imagine grey eyes of smoke gazing upon those pages as the mind behind them willed the ink to form itself into letters once more. Somehow, he knew that the written words would not be enough.

'Johann Dietrich spotted,' Ludwig said, forcing the quiver from his voice. 'I followed him to the shop of Dr Lucas Phillip Loew the alchemist. Dietrich remained there for some time. Upon leaving, he pursued an indirect route to the *Crown and Two Chairmen*. I waited for three bells, but he did not emerge from the tavern. At that point I decided that he was not coming out again and hurried here to make my report.'

There was silence in the darkness, silence as thick and menacing as anything Ludwig had experienced in the dungeons of the Emperor. Ludwig knew that a tremendous intellect was digesting his words, twisting and turning them, viewing his account from angles Ludwig could neither understand nor fathom. There were some things it was best not to understand... or question.

'Assume position outside Dr Loew's. Observe any visitors. Await further instructions.'

Ludwig sketched a deep bow, putting far more sincerity into the gesture than he had ever showed the Emperor or the Grand Theogonist. 'I obey,' the scrawny man whispered. He reached behind him, feeling for the door, his hand closing desperately about the handle. Lingering only a moment to hear his master's cold voice, Ludwig pulled open the door and rushed back into the fading daylight.

Behind him, in the perpetual shadow of the cellar, a figure stirred, its footsteps echoing as it too deserted the room, vanishing into the deeper darkness beyond.

GREY SEER THANQUOL found that his progress through Clan Moulder's stretch of the skrawl was much easier with Boneripper's enormity looming beside him. The mutant rat ogre was a creature of some notoriety among the merchants and beastmasters of Clan Moulder. Few of them had failed to see the brute in the clan's fighting pits, tearing through every beast, slave and captive he was pitted against. Beside such gruesome memories, even the fearsome reputation of Skavenblight's elite stormvermin was insignificant.

He'd given Kratch the unenviable job of holding onto Boneripper's leash. It would take time for the rat ogre to accept his new master, though feeding him the best part of his previous owner had certainly helped improve the monster's attitude. If Boneripper was still hungry, Thanquol felt better with Kratch being the closest thing to him. Being eaten by one's own bodyguard was a terribly silly way for someone of his fame to end his brilliant career. With that in mind, Thanquol glanced at his apprentice. The wretch was once again treacherously lingering behind, stretching Boneripper's chain to its full extent. Thanquol snarled a few threats and brought his apprentice sullenly back into place. Selfless, loyal underlings were so very hard to find.

Up ahead, Thanquol saw his stormvermin suddenly grow tense. Squeals and frightened squeaks rose from the crowd filling the passageway, the musk of fear rising prominently among the fug of the streets. Skaven scurried and scrambled into shops and dived into slave pens in a maddened, frightened dash for safety. Low chittering howls told the reason for their flight. Thanquol snarled at his stormvermin as the two albinos shared an anxious glance, then retreated behind the bulk of Boneripper. As an afterthought, he grabbed Kratch by the shoulders. He wasn't forgetting that the rat ogre might still be hungry.

A heavy, stagnant smell assaulted Thanquol's nose, a reek of beasts and blood, ratlike yet lacking the pleasantness of a purely rodent scent. Loping into view a few moments later was the source of the scent. A thrill of terror ran through Thanquol's glands as he saw the crouched shape, thinking for a moment that the rat-beast had somehow returned to hunt him down. It took only an instant to realise that the creature he gazed upon was much smaller, only about twice the size of a skaven. It was more doglike than ratlike, with a broad build and powerful, square-set jaws. The hand-like paws and long scaly tail were distinctly ratlike, however, and when it sniffed the air, it lifted its body in the fashion of a rat rather than sniffing the ground like a dog.

It was a wolf-rat, one of Clan Moulder's loathsome creations, a fearsome, barely tractable beast bred for those warlords and degenerates for whom the usual strains of giant rat and mole were not large enough. Thanquol grinned savagely, pushing Kratch away and cuffing the apprentice for observing his moment of fear. Formidable as a wolf-rat might be for a lone skaven, Thanquol was anything but alone.

Then the wolf-rat caught his scent. It stared straight at him, singling the grey seer from among his guards. It was an unsettling moment, made worse when the animal uttered another of its chittering howls. Instantly other shapes loped into view, first one, then another. Before Thanquol could even twitch a whisker, a half dozen of the mutant beasts filled the tunnel ahead.

'Stand-fight!' Thanquol snarled as his stormvermin started to back away. They looked at him, eyes wide with alarm. Thanquol raised his staff threateningly. 'Stand-fight or burn-burn!'

Then there was no more time for threats and commands. Howling, the wolf-rats bounded down the tunnel, foam dripping from their jaws, their eyes still locked on the robed figure of the grey seer. Thanquol forced his eyes shut, focusing his mind on the power of the Horned Rat. A green glow gathered about his staff. Opening his eyes again, he sent a bolt of shimmering energy crashing into the oncoming pack. One of the wolf-rats yelped, crumpling as the bolt struck it. Smoke rose from its singed fur, blood dripping from its mangled body as it dragged itself away across the floor of the tunnel.

The other wolf-rats kept coming. They struck the position of the stormvermin like a furry avalanche. Each of the white-furred warriors lashed out, their halberds flashing like scythes through the beasts, slashing their flesh and splitting their bones. Any lesser skaven would have been overwhelmed on the instant by such adversaries. The elite warriors from Skavenblight managed the impossible: they managed to hold their ground long enough for Thanquol to draw upon his powers once more.

The temptation to nibble a piece of warpstone flashed through Thanquol's mind, but the hazard, the way he had lost control, was too fresh in his memory for him to weaken to it. Instead he concentrated and evoked the might of the Horned Rat once more. Another bolt of energy, this time smashing into a pair of wolf-rats as they swarmed over one of his stormvermin. The blast incinerated all three, engulfing them in burning, roaring malignance that scorched the fur from their flesh and melted the marrow in their bones. Thanquol was certain the beleaguered warrior died happy knowing his sacrifice had destroyed two of the grey seer's enemies.

The other stormvermin was not so diligent about delaying the grey seer's foes. Occupied with one wolf-rat, the warrior allowed the other two to get past him, the beasts heading straight for Thanquol. No time for concentration now. Thanquol grabbed one of the warpstone tokens, raising it to his muzzle. He was suddenly struck violently from behind, the nugget of warpstone flying from his paw. Thanquol dived after it, scrambling to recover it.

Too late he realised the mistake of his instinctive dive for the errant warpstone. Thanquol lifted his horned head to see both of the wolf-rats driving down upon him. Their dripping jaws flashed, their clawed paws slashed at the earthen floor. As one, the beasts leapt, pouncing upon their prey. Thanquol covered his head and cursed anything and everything he could think of.

Stabbing teeth and slashing paws never touched Thanquol's fur. The grey seer uncovered his head and looked up in disbelief. Towering above him was Boneripper, and in two of the rat ogre's immense paws he held a struggling wolf-rat. The brute seemed oblivious to the jaws that snapped at his fingers, at the paws that slashed at his chest. With a dull, disinterested look, he simply stared at the animals, almost as though trying to figure out what they were.

Thanquol understood now. In his diatribe against all skavendom, he must have squealed Boneripper's name. The rat ogre had reacted with admirable speed, rallying to his master's defence. Even in so short a time, he had accepted both his new name and his new master. Surely another sign that the beast had been gifted to Thanquol by the Horned Rat himself.

The grey seer looked up at his bodyguard and the struggling wolf-rats in his paws. He looked down the tunnel to where the last stormvermin was just finishing off his opponent with a stab of his halberd into its throat. Thanquol looked back at Boneripper, determined the rat ogre could do better. 'Boneripper!' he called, pleased when the brute fixed his dull gaze on the grey seer. Thanquol made a snapping motion with his paw. 'Rip-tear!' he snarled. 'Rip-tear!'

Boneripper nodded, a loathsome human gesture he must have been taught by Schafwitt's decadent human mannerisms, but instead of ripping apart the wolf-rats, the rat ogre began to squeeze. Tighter and tighter his paws closed, ignoring the desperate spasms of terror from his captives. Thanquol could hear bones crack beneath the pressure, then a hideous squish as the heads of both animals popped from their necks. It wasn't what he'd had in mind, but he was reasonably satisfied with the results. As a reward, Thanquol allowed Boneripper to settle down onto his haunches and start to feed off the carrion.

'Master-master! You are safe-well! No-no pain-hurt?'

Thanquol's claws tapped the hilt of his sword, then he reminded himself that he might still need Kratch. For prudence, he'd have to dismiss that treacherous shove from behind as an innocent accident. 'Be more careful fool-flesh!' Thanquol snapped, contenting himself with swatting Kratch's snout with his staff.

A quick investigation further up the tunnel found a dead Clan Moulder merchant inside a shop with an empty kennel. A scrap of the grey seer's old robe, the one soiled during the fight in Clan Mawrl's warren, was clutched in the dead traitor's paw. Having failed with Clan Eshin's gutter runners, Thanquol's enemies in Under-Altdorf had turned to Clan Moulder's beasts. He didn't like to think what their next trick might be.

Perhaps he would spend a few more of the council's warpstone tokens after all. Thanquol snapped a curt order to Kratch and the last of his stormvermin. They would head for the armour shops of Clan Mors. Thanquol would feel a bit better with something heavier than his fur standing between himself and a stab in the dark. Then perhaps they would visit the temple again and collect some protective charms and amulets, just in case his enemies decided to use something less physical than a knife or a wolf-rat.

Dr Loew descended the stairs that connected his living quarters with his shop, taking extra care to step only upon the thickly carpeted centre of the stairway so that his footfalls might be muffled. One of the alchemist's hands was wrapped about the handle of a heavy ceramic pestle, holding the tool after the fashion of a horseman's mace, while the other hand clutched the glass neck of a more grisly weapon; a powerful acid derived from vitriol and troll vomit. He paused in his descent, cocking his head in a wary, watchful manner, his senses trained on the gloom of his darkened shop, waiting for any betraying sound to again reach his ears. It had been many years since any of the scum of the waterfront had been bold enough to try and rob him. Loew was determined to make an example of this clumsy burglar.

The sound came again, a scratching rattle from the direction of his workroom. The alchemist's expression grew vicious. It was trespass enough to try and steal his wares, but to disturb his experiments was a violation he would not forgive. As the sounds continued, Loew's pace quickened, caution cast aside in his anger. He pushed through the darkness, rushing past the shadowy shelves of bottles and potions, towards the curtain that separated workroom from shop. Abruptly, the alchemist froze, every sense afire with alarm.

Before him, the shadows seemed to reach out, to assume a solidity of shape and form. Something was standing between him and the curtain, something that seemed to mock his efforts to see it. Loew started to lift the bottle of acid, but a frightened chill that had nothing to do with the sudden coldness of the room arrested the motion. From the darkness, a voice hissed at him.

'Return to your bed,' the whisper warned him. 'There is nothing to find here except death.'

There was a fearful menace in that voice, a nightmarish air of unreality that made even the alchemist pale as he heard it. Loew took a few stumbling steps back almost before he was aware of his own retreat. Remembering the sounds that had drawn him downstairs, remembering what it was he had left in his workroom, the alchemist drew upon his own miserly greed to put steel in his spine.

'Who are you to order me around in my own home?' Loew snarled indignantly. 'I'll settle with you, be you ghost or phantom!' He started to raise the heavy pestle for a strike at the patch of thick darkness where he judged the whisper to have emanated. Suddenly, the darkness lessened, fading away and exposing what it had concealed. The pestle dropped from nerveless fingers.

Tall, swathed in the heavy folds of a charcoal-grey cloak, his head hidden beneath the shadow of a deep hood, his face muffled beneath a thick grey scarf, all that Loew could see was a sharp hawklike nose and a pair of smoky grey eyes. The alchemist's willpower was trapped by the intense stare of those eyes, swirling pools of darkness that drew him into their formless depths. There was power in that chill gaze, power beyond that of hypnotist and street-corner mystic, Loew could feel the icy touch of the arcane world in those eyes.

The sinister apparition raised a hand swathed in black, motioning for silence from the stunned alchemist. 'Preserve your life, forget what was brought to you,' the shade's hissing voice told Loew.

A sound from beyond the curtain, louder than anything Loew had heard before, broke the hypnotic spell that had started to numb his mind. The alchemist tore his eyes away from the smoky pits of the apparition's hidden face, rushing past the menacing darkness and seizing the curtain in a trembling hand. With a snarl of defiance, Loew ripped the curtain away, ready to confront the burglar who had violated his workroom.

For the second time, Dr Loew was confronted by a sight that drained the strength from his spine. The alchemist's retreat was more rapid than before, his terror impossibly even greater than when he had been confronted by the cloaked wraith in his shop.

What was rummaging about his workroom was no burglar, at least no human burglar. It was a gigantic, feral thing, its general shape that of some enormous vermin. A great swathe of scorched, crusty hide stretched along its side from the edge of its snout to the tip of its tail, the ugly wound still dripping a filthy blue treacle that sizzled as it struck the floor. As Loew gasped in horror, the rat-beast swung its head around, fixing the alchemist with its beady red eyes.

With a low chittering growl, the monster began to stalk after the terrified man, its fangs gleaming like daggers in the gloom.

CHAPTER SEVEN
Black Dust, Black Death

IRON FINGERS GRIPPED Dr Loew's shoulder, pulling him back, throwing him to the floor. The alchemist could only gape in astonishment as the spectral figure of the intruder stepped between himself and the ghastly monster stealing slowly from the workroom. Even in the clutch of terror, Loew was horrified by the madness of such an act. Phantom or thief, it was suicide to stand before such a monstrous abomination.

'Do not move,' the hissing whisper commanded, the force of the voice brooking no dissent. The grey-shrouded figure threw his arms wide, his splayed fingers pointing to the ceiling. Strange, rasping words crawled through the air and Loew felt the coldness of his shop become steadily more pronounced, little beads of ice beginning to form on the floor.

More remarkable than the falling temperature, however, was the way the darkness seemed to swell and thicken. Shadows crawled from every corner and crack, swirling about the cloaked man, clinging to him like a second skin. In less time than it took for Loew's mind to register the fact, the man was gone, veiled in a patch of solid blackness that all but filled the doorway to the workroom.

Loew's breath came in a ragged gasp. A dabbler in the arcane, the alchemist knew a master of the black arts working his craft when he saw – or failed to see – one. The intruder, the strange apparition who had warned him away from the workroom, was a magister, though whether one of the sanctioned wizards of the Colleges or some renegade warlock, he could not say.

Loew quickly forgot his concerns over the wizard's identity and purpose. More important to him, at the moment, was the effect his magic had upon the rat-beast. As soon as the wizard bound that wall of darkness about himself, the monster stopped its slow, steady creep into the shop. Its beady eyes blinked, its head swung about in confusion. It reared up, sniffing at the air, trying to pick up the scent of the prey it could no longer see. Even this sense was foiled by the wizard's spell.

Rendered invisible to both sight and scent, the rat-beast lost interest in Dr Loew and his mysterious benefactor. Almost absently, it swung back around, pawing its way across the floor, its claws scraping deep furrows in the wood. Loew could just see its verminous bulk as it sniffed and snuffled about his workspace. Sometimes a decayed tongue would flick from its mouth to lick at his tools and instruments. There was more than randomness in what the creature chose to study and what it ignored. With horror, Loew realised what had drawn the monster to his shop!

The alchemist could not restrain himself when he saw the rat-beast lurch up, setting its paws on a table so that it could sniff at a cupboard set into the wall. It was here that he had secreted the metal box in which he kept the wyrdstone Dietrich had left with him! When the rat-beast's dagger-like fangs began to gnaw at the wood, any last trace of question about its intentions were gone.

The monster was after the wyrdstone!

Avarice overcame terror. A shriek of protest burst from Loew's lungs as he lunged past the blurred form of the wizard, plunging through the chill darkness and into the workroom beyond. With a roar that would not have shamed a Norscan berserker, the alchemist dashed the vial of acid full into the face of the rat-beast as it spun about to snarl at him. The hulking monster recoiled, its fur and flesh sizzling beneath the clinging, burning fluid. Its bulk lurched backward, crushing the cabinet into splinters. The metal box with the stone shard clattered to the floor, little tinny protests rising from it as it rolled away.

Instinctively, Loew started to dive for the box, but once again he felt a clutch of iron close about his shoulder. The wizard's touch snapped the alchemist back to his senses. Terror resumed its dominance of the man's mind. Loew's eyes bulged as he saw the stricken rat-beast rise from the floor, the flesh of its face still steaming, patches of bone gleaming through the corroded skin, its giant fangs made all the more enormous without lips to cover them. It chittered madly, then sprang like a raging mammoth.

Loew was flung to the floor by the powerful thrust of the wizard's steely arm. At the same instant, the magister was fading, his body twisting and shifting as though possessing all the formlessness of water. The lunging monster charged into the space between alchemist and wizard, the place where only a breath before, both men had been standing. The rat-beast's pounce had it crashing against the wall, its head smashing through the partition that separated shop from workroom. Growling with the fury of a tempest, the monster tugged and tore, seeking to rip itself free of the obstruction.

Now the wizard's form became more distinct, as solid and real as anything else in the nightmarish scene unfolding before Loew's eyes. Hissing words slithered from behind the heavy scarf wrapped about the magister's face, seeming to burn with a dark malignance as they escaped from his hidden lips. Again, Loew could feel the atmosphere grow icy. Shadows crawled across the floor like living things, answering the sorcerous call of their mysterious master. Like jungle pythons, thick ropes of darkness converged upon the rat-beast, wrapping about its struggling frame, dragging it down with spectral strength.

'The box,' the wizard's voice cut through the eerie scene.

A long-fingered hand shrouded in black was stabbing across the room, pointing at the metal casket. But the smouldering eyes of the wizard were fixed upon Loew, burning into his own. The alchemist knew he could not defy the commanding presence.

However, as he picked up the casket, Loew's old greed returned. The wizard had returned his attention to the rat-beast, using his arcane might to bind the creature even tighter in coils of shadow. For the moment, Loew was unobserved, an opportunity he knew might not arise again. Quickly his fingers worked the hidden latch on the box, his hand plunging inside to close about the treasure he now knew both monster and magister coveted.

The instant the box was opened, the scent of what it contained was released into the air of the workroom. No longer the faint, old odour the stone had left behind on table and scale, but the fresh smell of its own substance. The scent burst through the rat-beast's primitive brain like an explosion, sending shockwaves rippling into every muscle and tendon. Even the shadowy coils wrapped about it were not enough to bind its frenzied might. Roaring, shrieking, the rat-beast ripped itself free from all fetters, physical and magical. The partition was torn apart by its fury, splinters sent hurtling through the room like gnarled skewers. The shadowy tendrils snapped, seeping into the floorboards as they lost their phantom substance.

Quickly the wizard's dark hands were in motion, fingers splayed and curled into arcane gestures, arms crossed before his cloaked body. A wave of freezing shadow swept before him, smashing into the rat-beast with a pulse of withering force. The monster was bowled over by the mystic energy, thrown across the workroom as though it were a child's doll. Furniture shattered beneath its weight, floorboards cracked and splintered. A dozen new wounds opened across the monster's vile shape as the wizard's spell drove it smashing through everything and anything in its way. Its bestial bulk slammed into the far wall, crumpled beneath a heap of debris.

Even for the sombre emissary of darkness, the magic of his last spell had been taxing. Cloaked shoulders sagged, the hooded head nodded weakly against a chest shrouded in grey. For the first time since setting eyes upon the magister, Loew's stunned awe of him was disrupted. The alchemist was reminded that for all his spells and sorcery, the wizard was nothing more than a man. A man who would rob him of the precious wyrdstone.

Loew turned his head, snatching a heavy iron flask from the floor beside him. A murderous grin spread over the alchemist's face as he unfastened the stopper and spun back towards the recovering wizard. The Colleges of Magic had many arcane spells and rituals that could visit horrific death upon their enemies, but so too did the ancient and eldritch Alchemists' Guild. Among the oldest and most closely guarded of their secrets was that of nafaalm, the terrible mixture known as Nehekharan Fire.

As Loew turned to deal death to his rescuer, the wizard's face turned towards him. Grim and judgemental was the grey gaze of the magister, his strange eyes biting into Loew like knives of hoarfrost. The alchemist almost faltered, but the realisation that he had already removed the flask's stopper decided him. The muscles in his arm tensed as he prepared to dash the nafaalm against the wizard's body.

Before Loew could move, the wizard's hand shot forward. Something dark and sharp and thin shot from the black-swathed hand. Loew felt a blade of icy pain flash through his gut, spilling him to the floor. Too late he realised that what covered the magister's hands were not gloves but an arcane skin of shadow, enslaved darkness that only awaited the merest gesture from the wizard to do his bidding. Faced with Loew's treachery, the wizard had sent a portion of that darkness speeding into the alchemist's body with the precision and deadliness of a throwing knife.

Crumpling to the floor, Loew could only groan in horror as the iron flask rolled from his fingers. The gooey, syrup-like nafaalm was already eating away at its iron prison now that it had been exposed to the open air. Weakened to the point of brittleness, the flask shattered as it struck the floor.

Instantly the back corner of the workroom exploded into flame. Loew shrieked as he was immolated by the blast. The entire building shook like a rowboat in a gale, plaster and dust raining from the ceiling. A roar like that of some caged beast swept through the alchemist's shop, bringing with it a withering burst of heat that banished even the wizard's unnatural aura of cold.

The grey-cloaked magister was sent reeling by the explosion, knocked from his feet, thrown out the alcove and dashed against one of the heavy shelves in the shop beyond with bone-jarring force. The wizard braced himself for the crushing impact, coiling like a serpent within his sombre robes, gathering the darkness around him to cushion his body. Knocking the shelf down with the force of his velocity, sending clouds of powder and dust billowing into the gloom as hundreds of vials and bottles shattered, the wizard rose from the tangled debris. His stern gaze pierced the smoky shadow of the shop, watching as flames greedily devoured Loew's workroom. Before the room was lost within a wall of fire, he could see the immense shape of the rat-beast, risen from its own jumble of wreckage, madly forcing its way through the smoke and fire, its dull mind still fixated upon the alchemist's box and what it contained.

From behind him, a dull crash sounded. The wizard faded into the darkness of the shop, blending his substance into that of the shadows. Another crash and the front door of the shop burst inwards. Men rushed inside, men wearing the livery of the Altdorf city watch. In command of them was Theodor Baer. Contacted by the agitator Ludwig Rothfels, who had lingered outside the shop, Theodor had employed his own initiative rushing to his master's aid when the same shop had been rocked by an explosion. Now he raged through the smoke-filled shop, trying to fight his way into the flames beyond.

'Instructions,' a low voice hissed from the smoke. Theodor spun about, trying vainly to find the source of words only he could hear.

'Have your men withdraw,' the voice continued. 'Evacuate surrounding buildings. Contain the fire. Allow Loew's shop to burn. Be watchful for anything trying to escape the flames.'

Theodor could see several of his men already trying to fight the spreading fire with blankets and tools hastily salvaged from the shelves of the shop. The sharp, shrieking cries of someone trapped in the fire rang out, agony twisting them into something bestial and inhuman. It sickened Theodor to abandon someone to such a fate. All the same, he knew what duty demanded of him. 'I obey,' the sergeant said, almost choking on the words.

'Search the ashes of this building,' the master's voice whispered. 'Recover a small metal casket. Do not open it. Do not touch what is inside.'

Theodor was calling back his men from their futile efforts against the fire, using every bit of his authority to compel them away from the source of such miserable screams. Only dimly was he aware of a lightening of the darkness around him, as though the smoke and shadow had withdrawn from the shop, drawn elsewhere by the presence they shrouded.

What was asked of him, he knew. What was expected of him, he knew. The why behind his orders, however, was something Theodor could not fathom. Another in an endless chain of riddles and mysteries he knew were beyond his ability to resolve. Like so many times before, he had to trust the wisdom and intentions of the man who he knew as Jeremias Scrivner.

THE SHARP SQUEALS rising from the sunken pit were ghastly, so eloquent in their suggestion of unspeakable pain and terror that even Grey Seer Thanquol felt a thrill of fear race along his spine. It was like a choir of damned souls as the flames of Chaos licked their naked flesh. For all the horror in the screams, Thanquol felt a sense of immense power. The knowledge that he and he alone was able to induce such a hideous fate upon other creatures made him feel bigger than Boneripper, more powerful than the Lords of Decay. Stronger than the Horned Rat!

Thanquol quickly glanced about the cavern-like chamber, guilty eyes staring at each of his minions in their turn, grinding his teeth as he wondered if any of the spying sneaks had guessed the impious turn his thoughts had taken. He fingered the amulet he wore, muttering apologies and renewed oaths of loyalty and service to his god. He had enemies enough to go around, he did not need to add the Horned Rat's wrath to his worries.

The incident in the skrawl was foremost among Thanquol's concerns. First Clan Eshin, then Clan Moulder had made an attempt against him. Who would be next? Which of Under-Altdorf's clans was after his blood, or perhaps it was all of them working together? Grey Seer Thratquee had certainly woven a web of intrigue around the other council members long enough to draw upon the resources of each in turn.

Perhaps the senile old priest-sorcerer had sense enough to regret the injudicious discussion he had shared with Thanquol beneath the temple of the Horned Rat.

Thanquol did not like being thrust into a situation he could not dominate. The schemers and manipulators of Under-Altdorf were better at their game than some rustic warlord clan-hold in some forgotten hinterland of skavendom. He did not have the time or effort to spend trying to ferret out their secret alliances and rivalries to gain the leverage he needed to truly control them. His only hold over them was the talisman he had been given by the Council of Thirteen, and that wasn't enough to dissuade whichever of the clan leaders had decided they wanted Thanquol dead.

Or was it Thanquol they wanted? The grey seer's pride was such that he didn't like to consider the possibility, but perhaps it was the Wormstone the killers were after. He cast a suspicious look at Viskitt Burnfang as the warlock engineer and his technicians scurried about the work tables, studying a bewildering array of rusty machinery and grimy alembics as they experimented upon the slivers of Wormstone that had been recovered from the warren of Clan Mawrl. The warlock engineer was attacking the task Thanquol had set him with a good deal too much enthusiasm as far as the grey seer was concerned. Not the enthusiasm of a dutiful servant doing his master's bidding. No, it was more the enthusiasm of someone intending to keep his discoveries for himself. Thanquol had seen such base treachery many times. He would keep Burnfang only as long as the Clan Skryre engineer was useful, then it would be time for a little accident. He'd let Kratch handle that when the time came.

The grey seer shifted his attention to his apprentice. The young adept was trudging through the chamber, buckets of slop and offal swinging from his shoulders. Thanquol had given his apprentice the humiliating duty of feeding the dozens of slaves he had purchased. It would keep Kratch too busy to concoct any new half-witted schemes to usurp his mentor's position and authority. Thanquol hadn't forgotten the 'accidental' shove from Kratch that had knocked the warpstone from his paws just as the wolf-rats were nearly upon him.

Thanquol smiled evilly. A little while longer, just long enough to be certain his usefulness was at an end and it would be Kratch's turn to suffer an 'accidental' push. Straight into Boneripper's mouth. The rat ogre would probably appreciate the light snack.

Looking away from Kratch, Thanquol turned his attention instead to the nearest test-pit. He stalked towards the depression like a hungry jackal, rubbing his paws together in greedy anticipation. The immense Boneripper lumbered beside him, his massive weight causing the earthen floor to shiver. Thanquol had been right to secure such a brute for his bodyguard. No skaven in his right mind would dare try anything if it meant confronting such a monster. During his spending frenzy in the skrawl, Thanquol had lavished his new pet with armour and weapons from the forges of Clan Mors. A thick skin of chainmail protected the monster's head, sheets of the metal falling about his neck and cheeks. Boneripper's huge horn had been sheathed with steel to improve both its impressiveness and lethality. A huge bronze shoulder guard was strapped to Boneripper's left shoulder, protecting its solitary arm. On a whim, Thanquol had fitted the shoulder guard with a steel spike bigger than his own leg. Woe-betide any slinking enemy who was charged by his bodyguard now! Finally a glove of mail covered Boneripper's extra hand, the tightly-woven links of metal in turn fitted with fist-spikes fashioned from sword blades. It pleased Thanquol to picture what would happen to anything Boneripper punched with that paw!

Thanquol had not been lax in seeing to his own protection, however. As impressive and fearsome as his new Boneripper was, he could not shake the nightmare image of that vile dwarf dropping the first Boneripper with a single blow to the head. He could not depend upon a bodyguard alone to preserve himself against his enemies. Thanquol had purchased an elaborate bronze helmet from a Clan Skab armourer, arranging with the artisan to alter the helm to accommodate the grey seer's curling horns. From a Clan Sleekit trader, Thanquol had secured a warpsteel blade, its blackened edge engraved with deathly runes that glowed faintly with arcane energies. A collar of boiled leather reinforced with iron studs and a lining of chain nestled between layers of fur had been provided by a one-pawed Clan Skaul merchant. To protect against more magical threats, Thanquol had secured a riotous array of charms and talismans. Little shards of warpstone engraved with protective sigils, rat skulls taken from the sacred vermin of the temple, little bronze icons of the Horned Rat, an elfskin mojo bag filled with sacred powders and bones – all of these dangled from Thanquol's belt and the head of his staff.

A pair of scrolls, written upon the flayed skin of slaves and marked with the scratch-script of the Queekish language, marked the most expensive of Thanquol's protective measures. Each scroll bore the secret words of a mighty spell: bound into the simple markings and skaven-skin vellum was an awful magic. Only the wealthiest and most powerful of ratmen could afford such potent artefacts, but Thanquol had found a few disreputable dealers in the alleyways of the skrawl who had been able to provide what he needed. The white stormvermin from Skavenblight had seen to it that neither of the dealers would tell anyone what they had sold and to whom. Altogether, Thanquol felt much more secure in his security. Though it would still be prudent to keep some lack-wit lackeys close at hand to put between himself and any sniff of danger.

There was danger enough to go around, and the most potent of them all was the one Thanquol could not afford to spare himself from: the Wormstone. For days now, the grey seer had been experimenting on the subjects he had secured in the slave markets of Under-Altdorf. The results had been as terrifying as they were enticing. To think that Clan Pestilens could have developed such a powerful weapon was unsettling. If the diseased plague lords who ruled the heretical sect had pursued their experiments, they might easily have conquered the entire Under-Empire. It was fortunate that their decayed brains had not seized upon the promise of their creation, leaving it abandoned and forgotten until a skaven of Thanquol's vision and genius should find it.

Down in the pit, Thanquol watched the results of his latest test. A half-dozen skavenslaves and a few humans had been dropped into the smooth-walled pit, then exposed to slivers of the Wormstone. It had been Burnfang's fiendish idea on how to effect the exposure, securing the shards to thick ropes and then swinging them through the pit like pendulums. It was entertaining to watch the wretches try to escape the swinging ropes. Once a few of them had been hit by the blackish-green rock, there was no need to strike the others. The exposed victims would see to the infection of the rest.

It was remarkable, the way the infection worked. Once exposed to the Wormstone, a skaven's fur began to become mangy, filthy wormlike growths sprouting from his skin. In a matter of minutes, the skaven would become insensible from the pain, a twitching, grovelling thing. Fat green worms would begin to drop away from the ratman's body, slithering across the pit, drawn to other skaven like iron to a magnet. A single worm would be enough to infect a ratman, the filthy things burning their way into the fur of their victims. Most dramatic of all was the final stage of the infection, when the skull and organs of the skaven would burst into a writhing mass of worms. This could take anywhere from minutes to hours, a process Burnfang had not yet been able to fully understand.

Humans were not immune to the infection, though they were much more resistant to it. Where a skaven would show signs of his corruption in a matter of minutes, a human might endure for days before becoming sick from his exposure. The end was, if anything, even more loathsome than the fate of the ratmen as the human's body corroded into a syrupy mush. It was a curious fact that the body of a human did not yield nearly so many of the fat green worms as that of a skaven; another puzzle Burnfang had not yet solved.

The implication was not lost upon Thanquol, that the Wormstone would make a much more efficient weapon against his fellow skaven than it would the furless hordes of mankind. It gave the grey seer pause, exciting both his paranoia and his ambition. What did the Lords of Decay want with such a horrible thing and could he trust their gratitude that he was the agent of its delivery to them? At the other end of the spectrum, Thanquol saw himself stalking through the streets of a humbled Skavenblight, supreme among the ratkin, power such as no lone skaven had ever held clenched tightly in his iron paw. It was a vision that made him almost forget his fears.

'Most gracious-kind despot,' a snivelling voice squeaked nearby. Thanquol did not need to turn to recognise the decrepit scent of Skrim Gnawtail, the Clan Skaul sneak. He waved his paw, motioning for Bonerip-per to allow the aged ratman to approach. Even so, Skrim kept his eyes fixed upon the hulking rat ogre as he scurried around the imposing monster.

'Speak-squeak, underling,' Thanquol commanded. Whatever Skrim was peddling, it was interrupting the grey seer's observation of the slave-subjects. One of the ratmen was about to burst and Thanquol didn't want to miss the grisly sight. 'Quick-quick!' he snapped, dis-playing his fangs.

'Mighty claw of the Horned One,' Skrim whined, 'this loyal-true servant has found one of the man-things that took-stole the Wormstone!'

Thanquol spun about, giving Skrim his full attention, slaves and infections forgotten. A greedy gleam shone from Thanquol's eyes. From habit, he drew the little ratskull box from his robe, tapping a bit of warpstone snuff into his paw. 'Speak-squeak!' he repeated impa-tiently.

'One of Clan Skaul's business ventures is selling Black Dust to the foolish man-things in the over-city,' Skrim told the grey seer. 'Our agent among the humans is name-scent Otto Ali. The man-thing runs a dust-den where other man-things come to breathe the poison.'

'They pay to be sick?' Thanquol asked, incredulously. He knew that the humans were insane, from their concepts of 'self-sacrifice' to their unintelligent devotion to offspring and birthkin. They even treated their breeders as something more than brutish property to be used and forgotten. But to deliberately inhale Black Dust, the poisonous residue of warpstone refinement, was such an excessive display of stupidity that he had a hard time believing it.

'Yes-yes,' insisted Skrim, bobbing his head up and down. 'They pay much-much! Do anything to breathe the dust again!' The crook-backed ratman's voice faded into chittering laughter. 'Clan Skaul use dust-addicts much-much!'

Thanquol took a pinch of snuff and drew it into his nostrils. Such contemptible weakness was only to be expected from the man-things, further proof, if any was needed, that the skaven were the only fit rulers of the world. Clan Skaul had used the weak nature of the man-things to swell their own power, gaining a clawhold in Under-Altdorf that was almost the equal of the greater clans through their network of drug addict dupes and tools. It was such a sneaky ploy, Thanquol was tempted to admire it. At the moment, however, he only wanted to know how it helped him find the Wormstone.

'A man-thing addicted to dust came into the warren of Otto Ali,' explained Skrim. The ratman tapped his snout. 'He smell-scent of Clan Mawrl warpstone.'

Thanquol clapped his paws together, tail twitching in excitement. 'The man-thing is being held-kept?'

'No-no, great and terrible priest-master,' Skrim said. 'The man-thing was allowed to leave.' He saw the fury start to rise in Thanquol's eyes and hurried to elaborate.

'The man-thing might be suspicious-wary if he was kept longer. His dust-hunger is much-much. He will be back. Soon-soon.'

'Good,' Thanquol snarled. 'When the man-thing comes back, I will see-smell him for myself. If he leads me to the Wormstone, you will be rewarded. If not...'

Thanquol didn't describe what would happen if Skrim's discovery didn't pan out. Sometimes it was enough to let an underling imagine his own punishment.

'STOP FUSSING OVER me, Johann,' Hans growled for what seemed the hundredth time. This time a fit of coughing didn't spoil his insistence that he was alright.

Ensconced within one of the finest rooms in the *Crown and Two Chairmen*, the smuggler had spent the last two days virtually bedridden, plagued by fits of coughing and the interminable scratching. He made for an amusing sight; the hardened dockland rogue who had boldly defied Gustav Volk and the Vesper Klasst organisation, now partially sunken into an overstuffed mattress of dainty pastels and frilly lace. At least Hans would have made for an amusing sight if it weren't for his deathly pallor and the hollowness of his cheeks.

The remaining members of his band, minus the still missing Kempf, were gathered around the bed like mourners at a wake, their expressions as grave as that of a dwarf told the beer had run out. His brother's expression was the dourest of them all. Johann had heard rumours about Kleiner being very ill before the watch had come for him. The big man might have caught nearly anything down in the sewers. And he might have shared his affliction with Hans before Baer came calling on him.

Hans seemed to read his brother's thoughts. He gave Johann what was supposed to be a cheery smile. The effect was rather spoiled by the anaemic condition of his face. 'I'm fine,' he insisted. 'Just a bit tired is all. Too many late nights,' he added with a lascivious wink.

The woman perched at the end of the bed made a loud harrumph at the comment and rolled her eyes. Argula Cranach was blonde, buxom and built like an Amazon. Her looks were on the harsh side, not quite manly but neither the appearance of a Detlef Sierck heroine. She reminded Johann of statues he had seen of the warrior goddess Myrmidia. Her cheeks were brightly painted, her face thickly powdered as she tried to hide too many years of hard living and ill repute. Even so, as Johann considered it, she was a damn sight too decent to be entangled with his manipulative sibling. As part owner of the *Crown and Two Chairmen*, and sole proprietor of the tavern's upstairs brothel, she was a damn sight closer to being legitimate than Hans. And for all her shrewdness in business, she was as naïve and helpless as a Shallyan nun when it came to matters of the heart.

Argula and Hans enjoyed an on-again, off-again relationship. That is, Hans enjoyed it while Argula simply suffered through the storm. When Hans was flush, when his luck was high and his pockets full, Argula and her tavern were the last places he wanted to see. When things were bad, when the watch was hounding him or the loan sharks looking to break his legs, Hans always turned to Argula for help. Like an idiot, she always took him in, hiding him until things cooled down. Then Hans would be off again, leaving a mouthful of empty promises and false hopes behind. Johann always felt the woman would be better off taking in some back-alley cur.

Of course, under the current circumstances, Johann had to admit the masochistic relationship was like a gift from Ranald. In need of a new hideout, the *Crown and Two Chairmen* was about the best the smugglers could ask for, even if the girls were remaining staunch in their policy of not extending further credit to the men. Argula tended Hans with the doting affection of a mother hen, worrying about his health even more than Johann. It had been by her suggestion that Johann and the others had come into the madam's boudoir to see for themselves their leader's condition.

It was anything but reassuring.

'Late nights!' she scoffed, adjusting her bodice. The garment clung to her ample frame so tightly, Johann wondered if she knew some trick to keep from breathing. 'For which of us, Hans? You coughing your lungs into my hair or me trying to sleep through the racket?'

'Now don't be coy, my love,' Hans scolded her. His lewd smirk vanished in a fit of coughing. Argula rushed to coddle the smuggler, crushing him to her breast and trying to massage his back at the same time.

'I understand you have a surgeon on the premises?' Johann said, intruding upon the scene. 'Perhaps it is time we sent for him?'

Argula turned her head, her eyes wide with disbelief. 'Gustaf? That swine? The only thing Gustaf Schlecht is able to handle is sewing up holes in the bouncers after a rowdy night and helping the girls with... indelicate problems! I won't have that butcher touching my sweet Hansel!'

Hans grimaced as Argula used the diminutive name, but soon he was more concerned with an even worse fit of coughing. The liquid that spilled from his mouth was green and bilious, smelling like raw sewage that had sat out in the sun for a week. Mueller grabbed at his nose and hurried to open the room's window.

'Argula, we can't help him,' insisted Johann. 'Much as we'd like to, we just don't know how.'

Argula closed her eyes, rocking Hans slowly back and forth in her arms. A hard woman, she was trying her best to fight back a show of feminine weakness. Johann saw the tears anyway. He turned away from the woman, joining the other smugglers beside the open window. Next to the stench of whatever Hans had coughed up, even the smell of the streets was refreshing. Johann tapped his fingers against the window sill, his mind lost in thought. From below the racket of drunken university students, the clatter of carts, and the shrill voice of a street-corner activist declaiming the evils of Bretonnian brandy rose to invade the room. Trust the crack-pot agitator to choose the corner outside the tavern for his soapbox!

'He needs a physician,' Johann told his comrades.

'You heard Argula,' Wilhelm said. 'She won't let this man Schlecht anywhere near Hans.'

Johann clenched his fist. 'Then we'll need to get someone else is all,' he growled.

'Someone else?' Mueller scoffed. 'You expect doctors to just come dropping out of every harlot's bed in the place?'

'I'll have to go out and fetch one,' Johann said.

Mueller shook his head, his one good eye narrowing into a squint. 'Look, I know he's your brother and all, but use your head man! Where do you think Kempf is? The watch might have done for Kleiner, but I'd wager my bottom teeth Kempf is spilling his guts to Volk as we speak. Anybody sees you on the street, it's all of our necks!'

Johann glowered at Mueller, then favoured Wilhelm with the same challenging look. 'Try to stop me, and you won't have to worry about Volk.' The two men backed away. They knew only too well Johann's skill with the blade. Together they might be able to take him at such close quarters, but one of them wouldn't walk away to brag about it. Neither of the smugglers wanted to chance being the unlucky one.

Johann marched to the door. He paused on the threshold. 'Keep an eye on things, Argula,' he said, giving a meaningful look to his skulking companions by the window. 'I'll be back soon with a real physician for Hans.'

There was nothing else to be said and Johann wasn't of a mind to waste more time questioning the wisdom of what he was doing. Rapidly, before common sense could really start to nag at his conscience, Johann descended the carpeted stairway that connected brothel and bar, navigating his way through perfumed whores and eager university students. He was through the tavern almost as soon as his feet left the bottom step, pushing his way out the bat-wing doors and into the foggy streets of Altdorf.

He paused for only an instant outside the tavern, trying to get his bearings. A soft voice beside him brought Johann spinning around, his sword in his hand. A small, shivering man backed away, pamphlets falling from his hands as he tried to display his lack of weaponry and malice.

'Peace, good sir,' the little man said. Johann recognised the voice as that of the agitator who had been making speeches outside the tavern. 'I mean no offence. I am quite harmless, I assure you.'

'Then what do you want?' Johann demanded, his sword remaining poised to run the agitator through.

'I am Ludwig Rothfels,' the agitator introduced himself, 'a prophet of the streets, wise in the ways of...'

'Cut to the chase before something else gets cut.'

Rothfels smiled nervously. 'Quite so, quite so. I understand your brother is sick and you are in need of a physician.'

Johann took a step towards Rothfels, ready to run the man through right then and there. Then he remembered the open window. It was possible the little sneak had heard the smugglers' discussion by mere chance. It was, of course, equally possible he was one of Volk's informants.

Sweating, Rothfels seized Johann's moment of delay. 'For a small gratuity, good sir, say three pieces of silver, I could bring a healer back to this... establishment. I could do this far more quickly than you could, for, you see, I happen to know of a healer who will come here like that,' Rothfels paused and snapped his fingers, 'should I ask her to.'

'Her?' Johann asked, suspicion in his voice.

'Er... yes, good sir,' Rothfels stammered. 'You see, I don't know any physicians, but there is a priestess of Shallya who shares a... mutual acquaintance. The ties that bind us are quite strong, I assure you. If I ask a favour of her, she will feel honour bound to come.'

'A Shallyan priestess?' Johann scoffed.

'Do not mock the powers of the gods!' Rothfels replied, deliberately mistaking the reason for Johann's doubt. 'Shallya has been ministering to the sick and wounded long before these book-smart quacks started meddling with things!'

Something about the agitator's tone made Johann decide the man was on the level, or at least running an honest hustle. 'All right, little man,' he said, fishing a pair of silver coins from his pocket. 'I'll play your game. Bring your priestess. If you can have her here before I find a physician, I might even give you the other coin you asked for.'

Ludwig snatched the coins from Johann's open hand. Sketching a hasty bow, he hurried off through the fog. He had to make a report to the master and pass word to Sister Kliefoth. Ludwig was quite pleased with himself. He had not only verified that the Dietrich brothers had returned to their old haunt, but had also arranged matters so that another of the master's servants would be able to keep tabs on the smugglers from within their own hideout!

KEMPF WAS SPRAWLED in one of Otto Ali's rickety bunks, a clay pipe dangling from his numbed lips. The smuggler had lasted only a few days before he started to feel the urge to return to the drug parlour. He'd been forced to return to the cellar of the *Orc and Axe*, using care and caution to elude any watchers Gustav Volk might have posted around the tavern. Another shard of wyrdstone broken off from the rock hidden in the barrel of vinegar, another visit to Hopfoot the Maus, and Kempf was ready to 'chase the dragon' once more.

Otto Ali had been more friendly than the last time Kempf had come to him, even going so far as to admit him into one of the small private alcoves normally reserved for guild masters and aristocrats, the prestigious patrons of the den who could not afford to be seen in such places.

The black dust tasted as sweet as before, filling every pore of Kempf's body as he drew it into his lungs. The dingy surroundings, the tattered curtain that separated the alcove from the main room of the parlour, all these faded into a soft blur as the smuggler's senses were drowned beneath a tide of intoxicating warmth and kaleidoscopic swirls. Kempf's squalid reality vanished as his mind was sent soaring. When the curtain was pulled aside and Otto Ali crept into the alcove, it was more unreal to Kempf than a dream.

'He has taken the dust,' Otto Ali said, his voice shaking with nervousness, sweat beading his swarthy brow.

Another figure stalked into the room, something so wild and weird that even in the midst of his dust-dream, Kempf managed a laugh of disbelief. It was a big rat dressed in a ragged grey robe, a bogey from nursery rhymes, one of the underfolk. To add to the unreality, the ratman sported immense curling horns and a long staff tipped with a strange metal icon. Kempf began to giggle, wondering if the thing had come for him because he had sucked his fingers as a boy. Then he lost interest in the weird figure, abandoning himself to the colours of dream.

Thanquol leered at the sprawled figure of the addict, sniffing at the man's hands and hair. A cruel smile spread on the grey seer's face. Skrim was right, this wretch did smell of Wormstone. The question was, where had the filthy man-thing hidden it! Thanquol was tempted to claw the information out of the maggot, but he knew that in his present condition the man wouldn't feel even the most vicious torture.

'How long?' Thanquol snarled at the anxious operator of the drug den.

'S... several hours,' Otto Ali answered, being careful not to smile or make eye contact with the horned ratman. In all his long years of dealing with the skaven, he had never encountered one that filled him with such terror as the imposing grey seer. Otto Ali knew the dangerous temper of the underfolk and wasn't about to take any chances with a creature even Skrim Gnawtail feared.

Thanquol bared his fangs, staring down at the smuggler. 'Good-good,' he decided. 'When the man-thing awakes, we will begin.'

Otto Ali raised a hand to his throat, horrified by the menacing suggestiveness of Thanquol's words.

Suddenly, one of the addicts in the main parlour cried out. The scream was not unusual; many times the dreams of the pipe smokers were not pleasant. What was unusual were the shouts of Otto Ali's guards that followed the outburst. Man and skaven tore aside the curtain and stormed into the drug den. At the same time, the crash of steel against steel reached their ears.

Thanquol's eyes narrowed with suspicion even as his glands clenched in alarm. A dark figure was in the far corner of the room, fending off a half-dozen burly humans with a pair of notched black blades. The grey seer could smell the odour of skaven fur, but could not detect an individual scent. His alarm grew. Only one clan of skaven descented themselves: the assassins of Clan Eshin.

Outnumbered, the assassin was still a blur of steel and black fur. His dark swords struck sparks from the blades of the guards when they didn't slash into the flesh behind them. In the first instants of conflict, two of the humans were down, the others backing away in fear. As they withdrew, Thanquol was afforded a clear look at their attacker. The grey seer felt another spasm of fright. No simple assassin, but Skrattch Skarpaw himself! His very position as clan leader of Under-Altdorf's branch of Clan Eshin made him the deadliest killer in the entire city!

Thanquol grabbed a fistful of white fur, pulling the albino stormvermin he had left to watch the entrance of the alcove closer to himself. He would have liked to have brought Boneripper into the lair, but the rat ogre was simply too massive to fit. Certainly the absence of Boneripper had factored into Skarpaw's decision to attack now.

'Get the others! Quick-quick!' Thanquol snarled at Kratch. The apprentice nodded, but made no move to leave the cover he had found behind a wooden bunk. Thanquol ground his teeth at his minion's cowardice, but soon had bigger problems to concern him. Skarpaw had heard the grey seer's voice. The assassin spun, plunging one sword into a human's gut, leaving the weapon sheathed in the dying man's flesh. With his now empty paw, he drew three sharp metal disks from his ratskin tunic.

Instinctively, Thanquol dragged the white stormvermin into the path of the assassin's throwing stars. The skaven warrior's body shivered and shook as the weapons slammed into him, their envenomed tips sending poison rushing through his veins. Thanquol tightened his hold on the living shield as he felt the body shiver and go limp. He snarled again for his minions to stop cowering behind cover and help him.

Relief came from the timely action of Skrim Gnawtail and his underlings. The Clan Skaul skaven flooded into the drug den, tipping bunks and addicts to the floor as they rushed the lone assassin. Willing to risk being outnumbered by the comparatively slow and ungainly human guards, Skarpaw was less inclined to take his chances with a score of vengeful ratmen. Another pawful of throwing stars downed the foremost of the snarling clanrats, then Skarpaw was dashing through the drug den, leaping over toppled bunks and slashing at intervening foes. The assassin seemed intent on gaining the hidden tunnel that would lead him back into the maze of passageways beneath Altdorf. He abandoned his purpose, however, when the entrance to the tunnel exploded in a shower of brick and earth.

Looming within the entrance, his body almost bent double to accommodate the low ceiling, Boneripper glared death at the would-be murderer of his master. The rat ogre's armoured fist swung for Skarpaw, narrowly missing the assassin as he dodged away. The monster's fist smashed into the wall with the force of a steam-hammer, cracking bricks into powder. Boneripper swung his head around, ropes of saliva dripping from his immense fangs as he growled at Skarpaw.

Boneripper before him, Skrim Gnawtail's clanrats coming up behind him, and ever mindful of Thanquol's magic, Skarpaw realised his escape rested upon a matter of instants. The assassin danced away as the rat ogre lurched after him, gutting a clanrat with his sword and pushing the maimed ratman into the monster's path. Spinning away from the chittering ratkin squeaking for his blood, Skarpaw lunged for the locked doorway that led into the cellar of the tea shop. A glass orb drawn from a pouch on the assassin's belt made explosively short work of the portal and the human guard beyond it. Before any of his enemies could recover from the roaring explosion, Skarpaw was darting through the debris, scrambling up the stairs to the streets above.

'No-no!' squealed Skrim Gnawtail as the clanrats started to pursue. 'Man-things must not see-see skaven!' The decrepit old ratman was shoving one of Otto Ali's men after the fleeing assassin. 'Find-find!' he snarled. 'Kill-kill!'

Reluctantly, fearfully, the men hurried to carry out the orders of their inhuman patrons. They knew what happened to those who defied the underfolk.

As silence slowly regained its hold over the drug den, Clan Skaul skaven began to seize those addicts who had been shaken from their stupor by the violence swirling around them. These wretches would be destined for the slave market of Under-Altdorf now that they had seen the skaven. The others, still lost in their dust-fuelled dreams, would be allowed to stay.

Grey Seer Thanquol let the limp body of the albino slump to the floor, its white fur now tinged with green from the poison of the assassin's throwing stars. He strode through the wreckage, the butt of his staff tapping menacingly against the floor. Kratch hid his head as his mentor stalked past him, the adept trying to press himself into the frame of the bunk. Thanquol gave the apprentice a spiteful swat of his claw, licking Kratch's blood from his fingers and snickering as he heard the flea yelp in pain. If he wanted to last long enough to have an accident, Kratch would need to grow a spine, and quickly.

Just now, however, Thanquol had a more important victim of his wrath. As Skrim snapped quick orders to his clanrats, Thanquol approached the sneaky ratman from behind. A blow of his staff sprawled Skrim Gnawtail on the floor. The old skaven snarled, reaching for his dagger, but quickly thought better of the suicidal action when Boneripper loomed behind the grey seer.

'Safe-secure?' Thanquol snarled through clenched fangs. 'Brainless tick-feeder! Where did the assassin come from?' He punctuated his words by driving the butt of his staff against the ratman's skull, drawing blood from his temple.

'Please, forgive-forget miserable Skrim,' the stricken ratman whined. 'Not-not Skrim's fault. Skrim would not-not betray great and terrible Thanquol! Clan Eshin, Skarpaw, they are traitor-meat worthy of Thanquol's most holy vengeance!'

Thanquol struck the grovelling ratman again. He had a point, unfortunately. Skrim would hardly have put himself in the front lines if he was aware of the attempt to kill Thanquol. Of course, that didn't mean someone higher in the ranks of Clan Skaul might not be in collusion with the assassin. Moreover, Skrim had not fabricated the human who smelled of Wormstone.

'Off the floor, flea-biter!' Thanquol spat. He pointed a claw to the alcove where the drug-addled Kempf had slept through the entire incident. 'We must take away the man-thing and torture the hiding place of the Wormstone from it before Skarpaw returns.'

Skrim Gnawtail wiped at his bleeding head, bowing in deference to Thanquol's imperious authority. 'Wise and holy despot, would it not be smart-smart to leave the man-thing alone? It is selling bits of the stone to pay for its addiction. If we wait-watch, it will lead us to the Wormstone on its own.'

Thanquol pondered the suggestion. It wasn't a bad idea and would save them the risk of breaking the human. Their minds were so fragile and if the human lost his senses under Thanquol's persuasive techniques, they would lose the trail to the Wormstone almost as soon as they had discovered it.

The grey seer irritably struck Skrim's snout. 'Fool-fool!' he snapped. 'What we will do is allow the human to leave. He will come back to buy more dust. Before he does, his metal-tokens will be stolen from him. To get more, he will have to return to where he has hidden the Wormstone.'

Thanquol's tail twitched in satisfaction as he considered the brilliance of his plan. Skrim rubbed at his snout, trying to hide his confusion over how the grey seer's idea was any different from his own.

SKARPAW BURST THROUGH the front door of the tea shop, the slashed body of the thug who guarded it pitching headlong into the street. A thick fog swirled about the bleak streets of Altdorf, rendering even the nearest pedestrians into indistinct shadows. The sound of violence sent them scurrying for cover like a nest of frightened mice. The only one near enough to observe the assassin's inhuman shape was an old toothless beggar crouched upon the stoop of the tea shop. Skarpaw slashed his dripping sword at the old man, shocked when the blow somehow failed to strike the withered human, scraping against the plaster wall instead of through his scrawny neck.

There was no time to correct the amateurish mistake, however. Already Skarpaw could hear Otto Ali's men rushing through the shop he had just vacated. The assassin snarled defiantly at his pursuers, spinning around and launching himself in a full-bodied spring at the building on the opposite side of the street.

The assassin's leap brought Skarpaw six feet off the ground and the skaven plunged his still-gory blade into the wall above his head. Even as the guards scrambled to attack him the ratman pulled himself from their reach, using his sword to hoist himself still further up the wall and from there to the roof of the building. He paused at the peak of his ascent to leer at the men who clamoured for his blood and spit in the face of the foremost of them. Chittering laughter erupted and the assassin disappeared beyond the edge of the roof.

'After him!' one of Otto Ali's thugs shouted. Already, several of his companions had started running in the direction of a low overhang. Behind them, the dishevelled old beggar who had nearly been bowled over when the thugs burst from the tea shop rose to his feet, all suggestion of infirmity and age vanishing as he straightened his body.

The old beggar mirrored the renegade ratman's actions, launching himself at the wall Skarpaw had impaled his sword upon. But where inhuman strength and agility had enabled Skarpaw to perform his incredible escape, it was a darker power that enabled the beggar to match the ratman's feat. The man's outstretched hands closed about the plaster of the wall, little tendrils of darkness clinging to his fingers and stabbing into the structure beneath. Like a jungle lizard, the man used claws of enslaved shadow to rapidly scramble up the roof in pursuit of the vanished skaven.

The wizard's eyes studied the expanse of tiled, shingled and thatched roofs that filled the foggy sprawl of the waterfront. Leaping from rooftop to rooftop, like some enormous and loathsome toad, Skarpaw's fleeing figure could be seen. An unnatural sense of grace and balance served the magister well in this new facet of the chase. Where the skaven had paused to judge distances before jumping from one roof to another, the wizard automatically calculated the speed and velocity needed to carry him across the emptiness between one structure and another and to accomplish it as easily as taking a step. Where the assassin had scrabbled to regain his balance when his foot had encountered a broken tile or his weight had broken through a rotten shingle, the wizard's arcane powers sensed such hazards and avoided them without slackening his pace.

The pursuit was swift and soon the wizard was near enough to his prey that he could hear the skaven's heavy breathing as the beast launched himself across the yawning chasm of a street. Skarpaw crashed against the side of the far building, his clawed hands fastening themselves about the edge of the roof and labouring to pull the assassin's mass onto the tiled surface. The magister employed the ratman's distress to execute his own passage across the street. The wizard twisted his body in mid-air as he leapt between the buildings, lending him greater momentum and carrying him beyond the skaven to land in a crouch atop the tiled roof.

Skarpaw pulled himself onto the roof just as the wizard rose from his crouch. The magister fastened his dark eyes upon the skaven's beady red orbs. The wizard made a sweeping gesture with his hand, banishing the aspect of age and poverty he had worn, revealing himself as a grey-cloaked figure with smoky eyes that matched the fog swirling about the roofs. The assassin cringed as he saw the display of sorcery, noting with something approaching horror the colour of the wizard's raiment. The magister hissed a warning to the creature, stunning him by forming his threat in Queekish rather than any human tongue.

Skarpaw answered the wizard's challenge with a bestial snarl. The skaven tore a tile from the roof and flung the ceramic at the human's head. Moving only his right arm, flicking a sliver of shadow from his darkened fingers, the wizard cut the projectile in two. Skarpaw blinked in astonishment and horror at his opponent's speed and spellcraft.

'Talk-speak or die-die,' the wizard's hissing voice warned.

Skarpaw growled, flinging a tile at the wizard with either hand. Again the magister struck at the projectiles, shattering both of the missiles, but the skaven had already exploited the distraction. Lunging to the right, the ratman rolled down the steep incline of the roof, launching his body at the roof of the next building to the south. Like a giant spider, Skarpaw scrambled up the incline of the opposing roof.

The wizard was quick to match his enemy's manoeuvre and jumped to the flat peak of the roof just as the ratman reached the level surface. The skaven grinned with ferocity as he saw that he and the wizard still shared the same relative positions.

The skaven reached down to the rooftop and again removed a tile, this time with both hands. Hidden from the magister's eyes was the substance the skaven smeared about the back of the tile as he gripped it, the tar-like paste the assassin had removed from one of his many hidden pouches during his graceless ascent of the incline.

Again the wizard's shadow magic licked out, a dark, formless blur. The darkness of the sorcery was as nothing compared to the blinding radiance as it struck the tile. The tile exploded when the shadowy bolt cleft its ceramic surface and struck the black paste smeared upon its underside. Shards of ceramic shrapnel ricocheted off the roof as the force of the explosion threw the wizard into the street below. Trying to grip the close-set walls of the buildings around him, the wizard crashed through a heavy fabric awning and into the wares of a potter's shop.

Skarpaw snarled at the magister as he pulled himself from the pile of shattered pottery. The skaven would be off the roofs and into a sewer before the wizard could regain the rooftop. He would have liked to spare the time to settle with the meddling sorcerer, but he quailed at the prospect of facing him alone.

Even Clan Eshin knew of Jeremias Scrivner, and what they knew was enough to make even the boldest assassin afraid. Skarpaw would almost rather cross Thanquol's immense bodyguard again than risk a second encounter with the shadowmancer.

CHAPTER EIGHT
Hunters, Scavengers and Prey

'I AM VERY sorry, Herr Kempf,' Otto Ali said. The Arabyan wore a broad smile that was as genuine as a Kislevite teetotaller. In the gloom of the drug den, however, Kempf couldn't see the nervous tremor in the man's face or the anxiety in his eyes. 'As you can see, the Hooks raided my establishment while you were enjoying the dust-dreams.' Otto Ali spread his hands in a gesture of helplessness, indicating the smashed bunks and general disorder of the dust parlour's main room. He didn't explain that the damage had been caused by feuding ratmen, the same ratmen who supplied him with the black dust.

'But my purse is gone!' Kempf protested. 'I had ten... er... twenty shimmies in there!'

'They must have stolen it while you were dreaming,' apologised Otto Ali. 'I am afraid they robbed most of my customers when they burst through the door.' Kempf glanced in the direction of the door in question. The

Arabyan hoped the smuggler didn't look too closely at it and notice that it was broken *out* rather than *in*.

Kempf scratched at his neck, feeling sick and disgusted by what he was hearing. His face wrinkled in disgust, as his arm rose. 'What did they do? Piss on me while they were at it?'

'Some men have strange ideas of amusement,' Otto Ali said. He saw anger flare up in Kempf's eyes. 'When someone has a knife pressing against my belly, I don't tell him what he can and can't do,' the dust dealer explained.

Robbed, humiliated, his stomach turning with sickness and his skin feeling like ants were crawling beneath it, Kempf wanted to scream, to let all the pent-up outrage loose in one furious howl. Instead, the fire in his eyes faded into glassy hunger and when he spoke, it was with a shallow whisper.

'But I needed that silver,' Kempf muttered, more to himself than the Arabyan. He lifted his now pitiful face to stare at Otto Ali. 'You will make good my loss? I don't mean in money, but rather... in kind?'

Otto Ali's smile became a great deal colder, but far more genuine. 'I have misfortune enough already, Herr Kempf. I cannot compound my own losses by assuming those of my patrons.'

'But I need... I mean... I was robbed here!'

'Here or in the street, I cannot afford to make it my concern,' said the dust dealer. 'If you seek charity, I suggest the Shallyan hospice.' A shrewd gleam came into Otto Ali's eye. 'The Hooks left little enough dust for those who can pay.'

Kempf clutched at the Arabyan's arm, his face turning a sickly shade of green. 'You mustn't!' the smuggler pleaded.

'First come, first served,' Otto Ali said. 'Those with coin to pay, that is.'

'I can get the money!' Kempf swore, his voice cracking with emotion. 'Please, just give me a few hours!'

'Don't be too long,' warned Otto Ali, but the smuggler had already released him and was dashing through the hastily-repaired door of the drug den. The Arabyan watched the little man run off, his contempt for the man's pathetic addiction twisting his face into a sneer.

'Does it dare-dare bare its teeth-fangs!' a shrill voice snarled from nearby.

Otto Ali quickly threw himself to the floor, abasing himself as Grey Seer Thanquol and his apprentice Kratch emerged from one of the curtained alcoves. Despite his many years as a pawn of the skaven, he still sometimes forgot that the ratmen regarded a smile as a threatening display. With the sneaks and spies of Clan Skaul, such an oversight was dangerous. Around a creature as vicious and megalomaniacal as Thanquol, it could quickly prove lethal.

'He goes to get more of the stone,' Otto Ali said, his face still turned to the floor.

Thanquol pressed his clawed foot on the man's neck. 'Skrim, remind your pet that it does not speak-squeak to me. The ears of a grey seer are not for the chitter-chatter of man-things.'

The crook-backed Clan Skaul spy and several of his underlings cowered around the grey seer, looking almost as miserable as the Arabyan dust-dealer. Their scent was heavy with the odour of submission, their snouts held much lower than that of Thanquol. No danger of any of the ratmen forgetting about keeping their teeth hidden behind their lips.

'Great and malicious potentate,' Skrim whined, 'my... your brilliant plan-plot proceeds...'

'Enough whining,' Thanquol snapped. 'Set your trackers after the thief-meat!'

Skrim hastened to chastise and bully his cadre of skaven sneaks. The wiry ratmen pulled coarse brown cloaks and hoods tight about themselves and rushed after the departed Kempf.

'They will find-seek him soon-soon, master-teacher,' Kratch's weasely rasp sounded in Thanquol's ear.

Of course they would, Thanquol thought. Even the mongrel, degenerate skaven of Under-Altdorf couldn't fail to follow such an easy trail. It had been a stroke of genius to spray the sleeping thief-man with his own musk. The lowest skavenslave could not fail to follow a fleeing human smelling of a grey seer's scent!

'Kratch,' Thanquol said, turning his head ever so slightly to regard his apprentice. 'Gather Burnfang's warriors and my other minions. Have them ready for when Skrim's sniffers run this thief-meat to ground.'

Kratch's face grew pinched, his whiskers twitching. 'You anticipate trouble-danger, wise-brave overlord?'

Thanquol brought his staff smacking down against Kratch's snout. 'Don't ask-ask! Just do what I tell-say!'

Rubbing his injured snout, the rebuked Kratch loped away, scurrying down the crude tunnel that connected Otto Ali's lair to the sewer-runs of the skaven. Thanquol felt better sending the adept to bring the rest of his underlings where he needed them. If Skarpaw had any back-up assassins waiting in the sewers, there was always a chance they might mistake the apprentice for the master.

That happy thought set Thanquol's tail twitching. Kratch was the last possible informant for the Council of Thirteen that remained among his followers since Skarpaw had obligingly removed the last of the white stormvermin. If the traitor could be convinced to do the same to Kratch, things would be much simpler for Thanquol's plans. The closer he came to the Wormstone, the more he wondered if he really wanted to deliver it to the Lords of Decay. Wouldn't such a weapon be of more benefit to skavendom in the paws of one who had the will and vision to use it properly? Wouldn't that be following the true wishes of the Horned Rat?

Thanquol turned to inspect some of the dead addicts who had been left in the lair. He wanted to see what effect long-term abuse of Black Dust had had on them. It might help him judge better what effect the Wormstone might be expected to have on humans who had not been broken by the whips and claws of Clan Moulder.

As he moved, Thanquol absently noticed that the thing beneath his foot was now a corpse. In his angry outburst against Kratch's insolent stupidity, he must have put too much pressure on the Arabyan's neck. Irritably, Thanquol kicked the lifeless thing and continued on his way to inspect more interesting carcasses.

'...ACCORDING TO GALEN...'

Johann held up his hand, motioning the rotund apothecary to silence. 'If Galen is mentioned one more time, I will send you to consult him directly,' he warned. It had been difficult to find a physician anywhere near the *Crown and Two Chairmen*, the closest he had come was a drunken barber-surgeon in the *Pink Rat* and a bleary-eyed horse doctor cheating at cards in the *Wayfarer's Rest*. The most professional prospect he had discovered was an apothecary at the *Mathias II* tavern who had only just started unwinding after closing up shop. Not too deep in his cups, and quite amenable to earning a few gold crowns for his medical knowledge, Sergei Kawolski agreed to postpone his bottle of Reikland hock to accompany Johann back to examine his brother.

The results weren't exactly what Johann had hoped for. The apothecary had puttered around, poking and prodding Hans for the better part of an hour, sometimes pausing to make dour observations or scratch his chin in befuddlement, always reciting the journals of the long-dead founder of modern medicine to lend some manner of veracity to his confusion.

Hans, at least, was oblivious to the apothecary's dubious expertise. The smuggler chief was sleeping, his skin more pallid and drawn than before, ugly tumour-like growths visible beneath his flesh. A little trickle of noxious-smelling slime oozed from the corners of his mouth, every bit as vile as the spittle expelled by his frequent coughing.

Wilhelm and Mueller had abandoned the room and its stench, pushed to their limits. The two outlaws were downstairs, lingering in the barroom, ostensibly keeping an eye out for Volk or the watch. Johann wondered how long it would be before the two rogues decided to desert entirely. Only the promise of selling the wyrdstone had kept them loyal this long. Any hint that they might catch whatever was wrong with Hans and they'd be gone faster than a side of beef at an ogre wedding.

Argula was curled in a chair, the limit of her endurance reached, sleeping even more deeply than Hans, so tired she hadn't even the strength to replace her soiled blouse, just discarding the stained garment in a corner. Sergei had trouble keeping his eyes from straying back to the woman's buxom undress. Johann wondered what Galen would have to say about the apothecary's distraction.

'So what's wrong with him?' Johann asked.

Sergei slid his spectacles down his broad nose and peered above the thick lenses to stare at the smuggler. 'I can't be sure. It might be Reikworms or possibly Crowpox.'

'Crowpox only strikes ravens, falcons and hawks,' a stern voice corrected the apothecary. Both men turned to see a white-clad figure standing in the doorway of the room. Johann's mouth dropped open in disbelief as his mind understood exactly what he was looking at. Rothfels had been on the level after all. The woman standing in the doorway was a priestess of Shallya, the goddess of healing and mercy.

Leni Kleifoth stepped into the room, her movements self-assured. 'And I should think even the lowest medical man in Altdorf would have seen Reikworms often enough to realise that brown sputum is not one of that affliction's symptoms.' The priestess crouched beside the bed, placing her hand against Hans's forehead, smelling his breath and listening to his breathing.

Johann turned on the dumbfounded apothecary. 'Get out.'

'You... you aren't falling for a bunch of religious mummery!' protested Sergei.

'Call me strange, but I think she knows what she's talking about, unlike some people,' Johann answered, shoving the apothecary towards the door.

'But... but my fee!'

Johann gave the bespectacled man a none too gentle push out of the room. 'A man gets what he earns,'

Johann said, his voice low and menacing. 'Right now I'm tempted to throw you down those stairs.'

Sergei needed no further encouragement. With a last lustful look at Argula, the apothecary fled down the hallway. Johann turned back to his brother and the priestess. Kliefoth had his shirt open, her ear pressed against his chest. It had been many years since Johann had given serious consideration to the gods, except of course to call upon Ranald to keep the watch away, but even he felt reassured just seeing the priestess ministering to his brother.

'Can you tell what ails him?' Johann dared to ask.

The priestess looked up at the smuggler, feeling a little knife of guilt stab at her as she saw the hope and faith in his face. She was tempted to tell him the truth. Instead, she told him what she had been told to tell him.

'He has been exposed to something that has corrupted his humours,' the priestess said. 'Has he come into contact with anything... unnatural?' Kliefoth studied Johann's face intently, watching for the slight flicker of suspicion that told her the smuggler had an idea of what might be responsible. 'If I am to treat this man, I must know what has brought this ailment upon him. Even better, if I should be able to examine it for myself.'

Kliefoth did not press the suggestion further. She was silent as Johann made his own calculations. He was wondering about the supposed wyrdstone, wondering if it could have been the source of the disease. He was weighing the reported value of the stone against his brother's life. At length, he reached the decision the priestess knew he would make.

'I think I know what might have done this,' Johann said, already moving towards the door. 'Stay with him, and I will bring a sample of it back to you.'

Kliefoth nodded her agreement and Johann was gone. The priestess shook her head, asking Shallya for forgiveness for her deception of the man. At least, she reflected, her part in it was over. Ludwig Rothfels would take up Johann's trail when he left the tavern, following him to whatever hiding spot the smugglers had secreted their find. Ludwig would be the one to make the final report to the master and bring him to his objective.

Looking at Hans and noting his suffering, Kliefoth only hoped that the source of this terrible corruption could be found in time, could be stopped before the infection spread.

KEMPF CAREFULLY MADE his way through the alleyways and side-streets of Altdorf's waterfront, a slinking shadow veiled by the thick fog rolling off the River Reik. He was careful to keep his body pressed close to the plaster and timber walls of the district's rundown buildings, darting across muddy lanes quickly only when absolutely necessary. He felt like a fish out of water during these brief moments of exposure, imagining hostile eyes watching him with grim fixation. He saw in every stumbling drunk, in every grumbling stevedore or swaggering sailor, one of Gustav Volk's murderous crew. He knew the thugs had been keeping a watch over the *Orc and Axe*, waiting for their chance to nab any of Dietrich's gang.

He had slipped past the roguish watchers before, with contemptuous ease, but Kempf's paranoia was feeding off his desperate need. Fear that Otto Ali would sell the last of his diminished supply of black dust had become frantic imaginings that this time he would be caught by Volk's skulking killers.

Kempf was so worried about watchers between himself and the tavern, he was blind to any threat from behind. He was unaware that he had been followed from Otto Ali's, followed by spotters far more capable than any of Altdorf's criminal scum. Skrim Gnawtail and his cloaked brethren kept their distance from their quarry, never giving him the chance to discover their presence. The skaven did not need to keep their eyes on the smuggler, instead using their keen noses to follow the pungent scent Thanquol had sprayed on the man's clothes.

Every few blocks, Skrim would detach one of his little mob of trackers, sending a ratman scurrying for a sewer opening. The messenger would squirm down the narrow holes with a sickeningly boneless motion, wriggling his body like an eel to slip into the reeking blackness beneath the streets. The messengers would report to the grey seer and his entourage, following Skrim's progress from the tunnels under the city. When Kempf got wherever he was going, Thanquol's troops would be ready to act swiftly and brutally.

JOHANN DIETRICH OPENED the door to the disused cellar and began to carefully make his way down the rickety set of steps, never letting too much of his weight rest on any one foot. It had been a test of his skills at silence and caution to slip past the cordon of thugs watching the *Orc and Axe*. Many times Johann had been certain he would be discovered despite the grey veil of fog that assisted his efforts. Twice he had been almost under the very nose of one of the racketeers before he realised they were even there. Both times he had been spared discovery by the grace of Ranald, the lurking watchers distracted at the last instant by some sound or shift in the fog.

Now close to his goal, Johann was even more cautious. If Volk had discovered the wyrdstone, then he would have his best men guarding the cellar, certain that the smugglers would return for their plunder. His senses keyed to even the slightest disturbance, as he descended the steps Johann became aware of a slight tapping. Muffled, only a faint murmur in the air, but persistent and hurried. It was a strange sort of sound, one Johann had a difficult time connecting with lurking guards. He slowly drew his knife, a fat-bladed scrapmonger's knock-off of the infamous Magnin throwing dagger. Its balance was off, making it useless for anything approaching accuracy, but its broad edge and spear-like tip made it perfect for gutting unsuspecting thugs.

Tightening his grip about the handle of his knife, Johann quietly set his foot on the cellar floor. The gloom of the dusty basement was almost as thick as that of a coal mine, but even so, Johann could pick out the faint suggestion of movement coming from one corner; the same corner the muffled tapping sounds were coming from. Johann started to creep towards the noise, then decided he still could not reconcile the sound with any waiting killer. The smuggler turned, navigating through the darkness by memory rather than sight. He found the little table and its half-used candles. Scratching a match against the splintered wood, he brought the candle sputtering into life.

The light from even so feeble a source was like the brilliance of a small sun compared to the darkness that had preceded its advent. The tapping noise came to an abrupt halt. Johann saw a man scramble away from the barrel of vinegar, a hammer wrapped in goatskin falling from his fingers, his other hand closing tightly around an iron chisel. Propped against the rim of the barrel, its surface still dripping with vinegar, was the wyrdstone.

'I was wondering where you'd gone to,' Johann snarled. 'Taking your cut a little early, aren't you, Kempf?'

'Stay back!' the little man growled back, gripping the chisel like it was a Tilean stiletto.

'You stay back,' Johann said, striding forward, contemptuous of the thief's threat. 'Hans is sick, Kleiner too.' He pointed the tip of his knife at the wyrdstone. 'I think that is what made them that way.'

Kempf's face twisted into an ugly smile. 'Don't try to spread dragon dung over my pasture, Johann. I'm a better liar than you'll ever be.'

'It's not a lie,' Johann said. He took another step forwards, forcing the cringing thief back a space. 'Now back off. I need a piece of that thing for Hans. You can have the whole damn thing after that.'

Kempf's eyes narrowed, his expression became even more weasel-like. He uttered a short bark of laughter. 'Oh, sure, you take a little sliver and leave the rest to me. Leave me to rake in all the Karls and Clanks while you just go on your merry way to fix your dear brother. What do you take me for? Stupid?'

'Yes,' Johann growled. The blade of his knife flickered menacingly in the candlelight, catching Kempf's nervous gaze.

Suddenly, the thief's face broke into a malicious smile. 'You can't kill me,' he said, his voice shrewd. Kempf pointed at the ceiling. 'Volk's men are right up there. Any noise down here and they might investigate. Then where will you be?'

'Your head's in the same noose,' Johann said.

Kempf nodded in agreement, but his expression lost none of its cunning. 'True, but I'm willing to gamble that you have more to lose than me.' The smuggler licked his lips hungrily, casting a covetous glance at the wyrdstone, seeing not the rock itself but what it represented to him. He scratched at his neck, stifling a cough as he considered his next move. Johann watched his every move with intense study.

'I'll take the wyrdstone with me,' Kempf decided at last. 'Not just a little of it. All of it. In return, you don't get killed by Volk.'

'It's a fool's bargain, Kempf,' Johann said, still watching the thief scratch at his skin. There was an ugly pallor to the ferret-faced man, a sickly thinness to him that made Johann think of Hans. The priestess was right; the stone was the source of the poison. 'You'll be the fool if you take that thing. Look at yourself, Kempf. You have only to do that to know I'm telling the truth about Hans and Kleiner. The stone made them sick... the same as you.'

A snicker of scorn passed through Kempf's lips. 'Nice try, Johann,' he said, 'but I know what's wrong with me.' Kempf looked longingly at the wyrdstone again. 'And I know how to make it all better.'

Johann braced himself, watching as Kempf circled back around towards the barrel. The thief was no fighter, there was no question that his wiry frame was no match for Johann's brawn. But it would have to be a quick fight, one or two stabs of his knife. Any more than that and Johann knew Kempf would shout to bring Volk's men running. He watched the thief's movements, waiting for the opening that would allow him to bring quick death to the traitorous cur.

Any plans that Johann made were exploded along with the back wall and part of the floor. A cloud of brick-dust washed over both smugglers as they were thrown against the far wall by the violent discharge, their heads ringing with the deafening roar. For an instant, Johann could smell some sort of explosive powder, then the scent was burned away by the rancid stench that rushed into the ruptured cellar; the stink of sewers and beasts.

Johann heard Kempf scream, a lingering wail that threatened to break his voice. The big smuggler shook his head, trying to force some kind of focus to his eyes. The blast had extinguished the candle, but weird green fire clung to the shattered brickwork scattered throughout the cellar, casting an unreal light across his surroundings. He saw the black cavity of the basement's broken wall. Pouring through it were things even more unreal than the light that illuminated them. Slinking, verminous shapes moving with what was at once half scurry and half sprint, their heads leering from beneath ragged hoods and rusty helmets, beady eyes gleaming as they reflected the eerie green glow. They were things from nightmare and childhood fear, half-believed myths that refused to be purged from the unconscious. The ratkin, the loathsome underfolk! Ghastly legend transformed into hideous, chittering flesh!

As the swarm of ratmen poured into the cellar, Johann saw one swagger through the pack, a tall horned figure clad in mangy grey robes.

'Take-snatch the stone!' Grey Seer Thanquol snarled to his underlings. The skaven's beady eyes caught those of Johann and his lips pulled back in a fang-ridden smile. 'Kill-slay the meat!'

As THE SLINKING ratmen began to converge upon their prey, a hissing peal of laughter brought them up short.

A strange, trilling sound that came from everywhere and nowhere, the laughter seemed to be more like a chorus of serpents than anything rising from a human throat. Thanquol felt his hackles rise, instinctive terror clenching his glands. The lesser skaven around him cringed and cowered. The air grew cold, warmth draining from it like blood from a severed vein. Thanquol gripped the shoulder of Kratch, pulling the apprentice in front of him as the dark shadows clinging to the walls of the cellar seemed to swell, to take on depth and substance.

Ratmen whined and muttered in fear as their sharp eyes detected motion within the shadows. Warriors backed away, the fur on their backs standing on end. Skrim's sneaks slithered between the bigger ratmen, trying to squirm their way back into the sewers. warlock engineers nervously began drawing strange weapons and sinister glass spheres from beneath their tattered robes, ignorant or uncaring of how many of their own kind they should kill using such terrible devices within the closed confines of the basement.

The air became foul with the musk of fear as the nebulous shadows assumed shape and form; great pantherish figures that prowled menacingly towards the ratkin. Rat-soldiers, unable to retreat from the shadows because of the press of bodies behind them, lashed at the dark shapes with their swords and spears, desperately trying to fend off their approach.

Thanquol fought against his instinctive horror of the immense, catlike shadows, his lust for power warring against his compulsion towards self-preservation. The grey seer's scheming mind rose through the fog of terror, denied the weakness of glands and flesh. The Wormstone was near, absolute power was within his grasp! He would not be cheated of his triumph by shadows and the treacherous cowardice of his underlings!

The grey seer's eyes told him the feline horrors were real, his ears could hear their stealthy feet padding across the floor. But there was something wrong, something missing. The panthers carried no scent. Ghost or illusion, it was enough to decide Thanquol's mind. He threw Kratch's cringing form from him and lifted his staff high. 'No-no fear-fright!' his scratchy voice bellowed, rippling with rage. 'This is trick-lie! It is false-scent, nothing but shadow burned away by the light-wrath of the Horned One!'

As he raged, Thanquol brought the butt of his staff crashing against the floor. The metal icon at its head blazed into brilliance, the white-hot explosion of a star. Creeping shadows were thrown back, ripped to shreds of blackness by the light. They slithered and wormed their way across the floor like living things, converging at the foot of the stairs. There they gathered, like frightened curs, about the feet of a sinister figure cloaked in grey. Thanquol blinked nervously as he met a pair of dark, stormy eyes that seemed to burn into his own.

'Kill-kill!' the grey seer roared, jabbing a claw in the direction of the now-visible wizard. Even as he roared, however, Thanquol was flinging himself to the floor. Only the speed of the skaven's instincts saved him as shadowy blades of sorcery swept through the air above him, skewering a warlock engineer that had been standing behind him. By burning away the shadow-shapes, Thanquol had exposed the real enemy, but in doing so he had made himself the target of choice for that enemy's retaliation.

The grey seer's distress, however, was not noticed by the chittering horde of ratmen. With vengeful snarls, the skaven rushed for the lone wizard, their feral minds gripped by indignant fury. The terror of the cat-phantoms had touched upon their most primordial fears. That was an outrage even the lowest ratman would not forgive.

The magister held his ground, hissing his contempt for the massed attack. His hand swept before him in an arcane gesture. The shadows gathered about his feet rushed forwards, crashing down about the ratmen like an icy wave. Instantly they were plunged into darkness, the brilliant glow of Thanquol's magic cut off from them. Panicked by their blindness, the skaven began to cut and stab at one another, fearfully trying to fight off imagined attackers.

It was only a momentary confusion, however. The skaven had other senses, sharper even than their sight. Soon, despite their fear, they would remember them and rise once more to the attack. The wizard was not going to give them that chance.

'Up the stairs,' the magister ordered the two smugglers cowering against the wall as he drew a slender sword from his belt. As the wizard's hand closed about the grip, crawling tendrils of blackness coiled from his fingers, rushing up the length of the blade, turning it from a thing of metal into a thing of shadow.

Only for an instant did the wizard's smoky eyes linger on the two criminals, then he was gone, merging into the darkness he had sent to engulf the ratkin. Sounds of battle rose from the blackness, the terrified screams of ratmen as their bodies were slashed by ensorcelled steel. Johann picked himself from the floor, risking a look at Kempf cowering nearby. The thief was huddled into a trembling ball, muttering to himself in a child-like voice over and again 'the dreams are true.' Johann's skin crawled just hearing the madman, his mind broken by the advent of the ratkin, horror heaped atop horror.

Johann turned to race up the stairs, but the sounds of battle stayed him, stabbing at the core of his rough pride. He did not know why the sinister wizard had appeared to save them from the fangs of the underfolk. He did not know if his rescuer was mortal man or slinking night fiend, witch or sorcerer. All that mattered was that he was human enough to oppose the verminous ratkin. No man could abandon a fighter to such foes and still call himself a man.

Tightening his grip on his knife, Johann prowled at the periphery of the roiling mass of darkness, stabbing and slashing those ratmen who emerged from the wall of shadow. For all their horror, for all the mythical dread they filled his mind with, the things bled when Johann cut them, filthy black blood that sizzled as it erupted from their wounds. Confused, disoriented by the change from darkness to light, the ratmen escaping the wall of shadow made poor opponents for all their inhuman quickness. Johann cut them down with butchering strokes that tore throats and gashed faces, as pitiless as Sigmar's vengeance. Johann was remembering all the fright tales he had heard as a child, about the underfolk and their hideous habits, about their fondness for the soft flesh of babies and children. Such things were not deserving of mercy.

GREY SEER THANQUOL waited for the sounds of battle to reach him before rising from the floor. The priest-sorcerer ground his fangs together in a mix of fear and fury. It was outrageous that some miserable man-thing playing at magic should try to stand between him and ultimate glory! Thanquol would sweep the filthy warlock from his path like a flea from his backside! There was no chance the petty spells of a human could stand against the primordial might of skaven sorcery!

Thanquol started to move towards the wall of shadow, the icon on his staff crackling with energy. Beyond that wall of darkness was the Wormstone, he could smell its sickly odour. He salivated at the thought of the awesomely powerful artefact in his paws, then reminded himself about the lethal consequences of handling it. A particularly high-pitched wail from one of the skaven fighting the wizard reminded him of the lethal consequences of entering that unnatural darkness as well. With all of his might and power, Thanquol knew there was only one thing to do.

All around him, Thanquol was surrounded by ratmen who were less than eager to join their embattled kin. warlock engineers, Clan Skaul lurkers, a few survivors of Thanquol's contingent from Clan Moulder. The grey seer ignored all of these, his teeth gleaming in a savage grin as he spotted the skulking ratman he wanted.

'Kratch,' Thanquol snarled, 'fetch-steal the stone!'

The apprentice cringed as he heard his master's command. His mouth dropped open to squeak a protest, but the fire in Thanquol's eyes made him close it again. Instead he snapped at some of the Clan Skryre ratmen around him. If he was going to risk his pelt bravely covering for his mentor's cowardice, he was determined not to share the danger alone.

Thanquol watched his apprentice scurry into the clinging darkness, flanked by several warlock engineers and Clan Skaul sneaks. With them they bore the huge iron box Viskitt Burnfang had prepared to convey the Wormstone safely.

'Do you-you think-believe Kratch can get past-through the wizard-thing?' Burnfang's voice growled in Thanquol's ear.

A petty tinge of amusement crawled into the grey seer's voice. 'If not, at least I am rid of him.'

Then there was no more time for amusement. The wall of darkness collapsed suddenly, revealing a tangle of stabbing, clawing ratmen and their fallen brethren. Thanquol's stomach turned as he saw the litter of bodies strewn around the fighting skaven. Confused by the darkness and the presence of an elusive enemy who weaved a path through their swarming ranks, the ratmen had turned their swords against whatever was close to them. They had done an excellent job butchering their comrades.

It wasn't the confused infighting and resulting carnage that disturbed Thanquol. He didn't care a pellet for the dead and maimed warriors. What concerned him was the grim apparition their stupid frenzy had allowed to stalk right through their ranks. The grey seer felt a tremor of fear as he once again found himself locking eyes with the wizard's stormy gaze. He reached for Burnfang to pull the warlock engineer in front of him, but the coward cravenly slipped away from Thanquol's grasping paw.

Fortunately, Burnfang's underlings had stronger spleens. A few broke and scurried back into the sewer, but others raised a riotous array of heavy pistols, warplock weapons fitted with scopes and strange mechanised loading clips. The ratmen snarled their hate at their sinister foe.

Thanquol managed to squeak a hurried 'Fire-kill!' as the warlock engineers pulled the triggers of their weird weapons, allowing him to maintain an illusion of command. Thick black smoke billowed from the volley, bringing tears to the eyes of the ratmen. One warlock engineer shrieked as his overly complicated pistol exploded in his face. But the rest of the volley smashed into the grey-cloaked phantom, warpstone bullets capable of exploding steel plate slashing through the unarmoured wizard. Thanquol chittered in victory; nothing could survive such a point-blank assault.

The grey seer's laughter was drowned out by the shrieks and wails of skaven warriors. As the smoke cleared, Thanquol saw many of the clanrat fighters in the centre of the cellar topple and fall, writhing in pained heaps. The wizard stood, seemingly unharmed, glowering at the skaven shooters. Then, as though built of smoke himself, the motionless form of the magister disintegrated, shattering into shreds of darkness. An illusion! Another of the human's insufferable tricks!

Mocking laughter rose from the wall, once again wrapped in shadow and blackness. From that darkness, like a cave-shark rising from the pitch depths of a subterranean pool, the wizard stepped forwards, his icy blade held menacingly before him. warlock engineers squeaked in terror, fumbling and pawing at ammunition belts as they tried to reload their pistols. Those few with mechanical loading devices fired at the magister, but their shots were hurried and ill-aimed, the closest whizzing over the wizard's hood.

None of the Clan Skryre ratmen had a chance to recover. The wizard was among them, stabbing and slashing, spilling maimed skaven in whimpering heaps. Many of the ratmen broke, fleeing down the sewer, Viskitt Burnfang and Skrim Gnawtail leading the way.

Abandoned, feeling the full measure of his predicament, Thanquol drew upon his magic for desperate and brutal salvation. Lightning crackled about the head of his staff as he used the metal icon to channel his sorcery. Snarling, Thanquol pointed the staff at the lone human slaughtering his minions. Searing green tendrils of malevolence burned and seared through the bodies of intervening ratmen, but the wizard himself faded from the magical assault, seeming to melt back into the clinging darkness. Thanquol ground his teeth, ripping at one of the ratskin scrolls at his belt.

The spells he had bought, the power contained in the scrolls, would obliterate the annoying human! Thanquol tore the little rat-gut string sealing the rolled parchment, his lips already parted to begin squeaking the incantation. He stared in disbelief at the scratch-slash symbols that greeted his gaze. The scroll wasn't the same one he had purchased! The snivelling black marketer had pulled a switch! Instead of a spell to draw magical energy from the aethyr and weave it into a ball of annihilating fire, what Thanquol was looking at was some kitchen-rat's recipe for goblin goulash!

A blast of gathered shadow smashed into Thanquol with the force of a hammer, throwing him to the ground. His staff leapt from his fingers, clattering against the floor. Little fingers of darkness wrapped about it, dragging it away from his grasping fingers. Frantic, Thanquol pulled a nugget of warpstone from beneath his robe, but before he could stuff it into his mouth, a stabbing knife of blackness tore it from his paw. Snarling in fearful rage, Thanquol lifted his eyes to see the grey-cloaked magister looming above him, his ensorcelled sword poised for a final, downward thrust.

Thanquol cringed, bracing himself for an ignoble end. Then a cruel smile spread across his face. Just as the wizard loomed above the prone grey seer, a hulking shape loomed above the wizard.

Thanquol's chittering laughter scratched at the wizard's ears in the same instant as Boneripper's huge fist slammed into his body.

JOHANN SLASHED AT a final ratman, his big knife almost severing its spine. The mangled thing flopped to the floor, crawling in a pathetic pile to die in a corner. The numbers of ratmen breaking from the conflict raging amid the wizard's veil of shadow had thinned. After an initial surge of three, they had continued in their ones and twos until Johann had accounted for eight of the vermin. The smuggler was breathing hard, sweat dripping from every pore, his arms feeling like numb lumps of lead hanging from his shoulders. He wondered if there was an inch of skin on his body that hadn't been cut or scratched by the blades and claws of the ratkin. He was only thankful that none of their snapping fangs had managed to sink into the meat of his flesh.

The smuggler hoped the wizard was holding his own, because Johann doubted he had the strength left to even muster the most feeble of assistance. Then again, for all he knew, the wizard could just snap his fingers and vanish any time he wanted, leaving Johann alone to face the vengeful horde.

Alone save for a whimpering madman, Johann corrected himself. He turned his face to look at Kempf curled up against the wall. What he saw sent a thrill of horror down his spine. Five ratmen had gotten through the wall of shadow without his notice. The slinking vermin had circled around the conflict as best they could, intent not upon adding their numbers to the combat but upon some other purpose. Johann felt he knew what the monsters were after.

'Ho! Monsters!' the smuggler shouted, forcing himself to lift his knife once more. Johann's thoughts were of his brother, lying sick and dying in the bed of a whore. The one chance he had might lie in bringing some piece of the wyrdstone back to the priestess. Johann had been ready to kill Kempf, to risk certain death from Volk's thugs, to secure the sample he needed. He would be damned if he was going to abandon his brother because of some slinking fairytale monsters!

The ratmen spun about, snarling at the smuggler. One of them, a wiry creature with little stubby horns, chittered a command to the others. Two of the ratkin drew long rusty swords and began to creep towards Johann. These weren't confused, half-blind refugees fleeing from a fight. Johann could see their scorn for any threat he posed to them shining in their beady eyes. Their fangs gleamed in the weird green light, pink tongues licking hungrily at their furry snouts.

Johann's earlier combat against the ratkin had been butchery. This, he knew, would be a fight. A fight it was unlikely he would walk away from.

KRATCH SNICKERED AS he watched the foolish human try to stand its ground. The Clan Skaul sneaks would make short work of the stupid animal; unless of course they chose to take their time with it. He dismissed the killers and their quarry from his mind. He had bigger concerns to occupy him. Kratch turned and snapped commands to the two warlock engineers who had managed to keep up with the adept as he slipped through the veil of shadows. The two skaven scurried forwards, setting their heavy iron box down on the floor.

Beside the box, glowing with the same eerie light he had seen before, the Wormstone seemed to welcome Kratch as he stretched his paw to seize it. The adept managed to resist the self-destructive urge. He knew exactly what the properties of the Wormstone were, and what it would do to any skaven stupid enough to touch it. It was a little detail he had kept from Skabritt, something he had tried to keep from Thanquol, though his new master had managed to discover it for himself through Burnfang's experiments.

'Take-fetch, quick-quick!' Kratch snarled at the warlock engineers. The masked ratmen stared at each other through their bug-eyed goggles, then back to the mass of darkness behind them. Their job had been to carry the box, another pair of engineers had been tasked with carrying the metal tongs to transfer the Wormstone into the box. They knew only too well the horrific effects of being exposed to the stone. 'Quick-quick!' Kratch repeated, a greenish glow burning behind his eyes as the adept summoned his sorcerous powers.

The display was enough to overcome the hesitancy of the engineers. Using their thick leather gauntlets and praying to the Horned Rat that it would be enough protection, the two ratmen converged on the Wormstone. With indecent haste, they seized the thing and dropped it into the waiting casket. One of the warlock engineers slammed the lid home while the other threw his tainted gloves away with a frightened squeak.

Kratch patted the box affectionately. He looked back at the melee between the Clan Skaul lurkers and the human. The man was somehow holding them back, but Kratch could tell they would soon break through its fatigued defences. The apprentice wasn't of a mind to wait for them to finish playing with the animal. He had bigger fleas to scratch.

'Back to the tunnel,' Kratch growled. The warlock engineers hefted the iron box from the floor, once again chittering little prayers to the Horned Rat that Burnfang's precautions would actually work. They nearly dropped their heavy burden when the wall of shadows suddenly collapsed upon itself. Kratch leapt backwards, landing on all fours, his eyes wide with alarm. But when he saw the grey-cloaked figure confronting Thanquol beyond where the magical darkness had been, the apprentice's lips pulled back in a predatory smile.

'To the tunnel!' he repeated. Kratch let the warlock engineers lead the way, carefully picking a path through the crazed skaven warriors ripping and tearing at each other. There was a hideous instant when the warlock engineers who had remained with the grey seer fired at the human wizard, their bullets passing through the apparition to strike the ratmen beyond, but the shots were wide of Kratch and his crew. Besides, the follow-up to the wasted fusillade played right into the adept's paws. His image broken, the wizard himself emerged from the darkness to confront Thanquol, slashing his way through the Clan Skryre shooters. Most of the skaven broke and ran, abandoning Thanquol to his enemy.

Kratch seized the opening, urging his underlings down the tunnel. Kratch hurried after, dodging aside as the immense bulk of Boneripper charged up the passageway, rushing to his master's aid. The rat ogre had been left behind in the sewer, the warlock engineers protesting that it would take too much explosive to widen the opening to allow the monster to enter the cellar. Reluctantly, Thanquol agreed to their incessant whining.

Kratch ground his fangs together. The rat ogre smashed into the man-thing wizard just as the human was about to put an end to the thieving career of Thanquol! The brute tore his own opening into the cellar while his third hand formed a bludgeoning fist that smashed into the human and sent him flying across the basement. Kratch saw tentacles of shadow wrap about the cloaked figure, deadening the violence of his impact against the far wall as completely as one of Thratquee's over-stuffed pillows. Kratch cursed as he saw Thanquol start to rise from the floor.

The trickle of dust falling from Boneripper's impromptu widening of the tunnel gave Kratch an idea. Most of the spells Skabritt had seen fit to teach his apprentice were minor incantations of no great consequence, but there was one his late teacher had foolishly taught him that held real power. Grinning, Kratch called upon that power now, weaving his paws before him in a complex pattern, syllables rasping off his tongue with rapid-fire quickness.

The roof of the tunnel groaned, dirt trickled down in a steady stream. Kratch locked eyes with Thanquol, then spun about and hurried down the tunnel, pursuing the warlock engineers and their burden. Behind him, the adept heard a terrible roar. He coughed as a cloud of dust washed over him, propelled by the fury of the collapse.

Kratch was almost disappointed. He had thought he would need to come up with something new to get rid of Thanquol. Instead, the same trick that had caught Skabritt had been good enough.

The apprentice grey seer scurried down the tunnel, chittering his wicked glee at the destruction of his hated master, his slippery mind already pawing over his next move. He would seize the Wormstone, take it to some secure place and then ransom the deadly weapon to one of the Lords of Decay. The hoary old rats would pay anything to keep such a fearsome artefact from their rivals on the Council, enough to give Kratch wealth and position beyond his wildest imaginings. Indeed, the thought occurred to Kratch, why should he limit himself to ransoming the Wormstone back to only one of the Lords? He could contact any number of them, then choose whichever one seemed most likely to afford him protection before closing the deal.

Kratch rubbed his paws together in the greedy human gesture of an Altdorf moneylender. With Thanquol gone, the only perceivable obstacle to his ambitions might be Viskitt Burnfang, but he had some ideas about how to deal with the warlock engineer. Strike him down, and the other Clan Skryre metal-mongers would quickly submit to Kratch's authority.

Yes, Kratch thought as his scampering steps brought him into the moist muck of the sewer. Once Burnfang was out of the way, there would be no one to stop him.

The adept blinked in confusion when he found himself snout-to-snout with the warlock engineer. Burnfang's eyes were wide with fear, his paws raised in a helpless gesture of surrender. All around him, the sneaks of Clan Skaul and the survivors of Clan Skryre likewise lifted their hands in defeat. Kratch was about to snarl at the ratmen when he became aware of shapes surrounding them in the reeking corridor of brick and filth.

'Adept Kratch, how kind-easy you to join-find us.' The voice was that of Skrattch Skarpaw, but the cunning assassin was too wise to emerge from the ranks of his followers and expose himself. Instead the black-clad killer simply laughed, a long murderous giggle.

'Take-snatch the stone!' Skarpaw snarled to his minions. 'Kill-slay the meat!'

CHAPTER NINE

A Rat's Revenge

Tons of earth and rock came smashing down into the cellar, bringing with it most of the kitchen up above. Fleeing ratmen were smashed into paste by the deluge of stone or skewered by great splinters of wood from the upper floor. Stairs, smugglers and shadow-wrapped wizard all vanished in a gritty cloud of darkness that rushed down Thanquol's lungs with a smothering embrace.

The grey seer coughed and hacked, fighting for every breath of air, flinching at every fresh clatter of rock against stone. The smell of skaven blood filled his nose, the cries of maimed and mangled ratmen scratched at his ears. Thanquol ignored them all, instead turning his beady eyes to a more vexing question: why had he not been crushed by the collapse?

The answer towered over Thanquol, his huge back arched above the grey seer like a bridge of flesh and bone. By sheer brute strength alone, Boneripper defied the pressure of tons of earth, preventing it from smashing downwards and obliterating his master. The rat ogre's head was crooked in an awkward position, his dull eyes staring plaintively at Thanquol, waiting for his master's approval.

Let the beast wait, Thanquol decided. Of primary importance was making sure the damnable human sorcerer wasn't in any condition to renew his attack on the grey seer. Crawling on all four paws, he squirmed his body around in the small space beneath Boneripper's arched body. He ignored the moans of half-crushed ratmen, slithering away from their groping paws, his sharp eyes fixated only upon one purpose. A cunning smile spread across Thanquol's face. The collapse had been total and complete. Wherever the wizard was, the vermin had been buried.

Thanquol didn't know if his enemy could dig himself out or not, nor did the grey seer intend to wait around and find out. His inspection complete, he crawled back beneath Boneripper's enormous chest. The rat ogre's lungs were rumbling like a bellows, sucking in what little air had been trapped with them in the pocket. Already there was a stagnant smell to it. Thanquol licked his fangs. There were spells he knew that could whisk him out of his predicament as quickly as a filthy human could snap its wormy fingers, but Thanquol did not dare cast them without knowing how far the cave-in had filled the tunnel. It would do him no good to disappear in a puff of black smoke only to rematerialise in solid stone. Fortunately, there were other options available.

'Dig,' Thanquol told the hulking brute looming above him. 'Dig-dig, fool-beast!' he repeated when Boneripper simply gazed at him with dull, vacant eyes.

Boneripper groaned as he shifted his body, trying to adjust his position to both support the ceiling and obey his master's shrill commands. Streams of earth and rock trickled down as the burden rumbled in protest, sending Thanquol scurrying deeper into the shadow cast by the monster's enormity. Boneripper took no notice of the grey seer's fright, however. One arm and one shoulder twisted up above his head, Boneripper began clawing at the rock and dirt choking the mouth of the tunnel with his other arms.

Thanquol watched the excavation with a vengeful gaze, each armload of rock Boneripper clawed away bringing the grey seer's fangs grinding together. He'd seen the look Kratch had given him just before the collapse. The treacherous apprentice was going to be sorry he hadn't finished the job.

Red thoughts of violence and pain clouded Thanquol's vision. His tail lashed angrily against the floor, his fur bristling. So Kratch had thought to get rid of him the way he had Grey Seer Skabritt, had he? Kratch thought to steal the power of the Wormstone for himself, to use it as a weapon against its rightful owners, the Lords of Decay? Thanquol would make him suffer for such callous treason against the Horned Rat and indeed, all of skavendom.

Even if he were not lost in bloody imaginings, Thanquol would have given no notice to the squeals and cries of the trapped ratmen who were crushed by the shifting weight of the collapsed earth, the piteous sounds growing fewer and fewer with each armful of rubble Boneripper clawed away. It was, after all, the duty of such lesser creatures to give their miserable lives that the genius of Thanquol should endure.

* * *

THE FORCE OF the collapse knocked Johann from his feet. A thick cloud of dust enveloped him, coating him from head to toe in a gritty skin of dirt. He scrambled to find his knife, blinking debris from his tearing eyes. All around him he could hear the piteous wails of mangled skaven caught in the collapse, their rodent howls gnawing at his ears with their deafening discord. Johann was bleeding from dozens of small, vicious cuts, his cruel foes taking sadistic delight in playing with their prey. With every motion, Johann could feel his strength ebb.

Strength, a man's only advantage against the abominable ratkin. The loathsome walking rodents were faster than any man, primal reflexes and instincts allowing them to twist and writhe away from the slow, comparatively clumsy strokes of a human blade. They were fiercer too, their savage minds gripped by a vile verminous malignity only the most desperate and degenerate breeds of men might ever sink to. They were monsters, in every sense of the word, but monsters built for murder and ambush, not a straight fight against a man's superior strength. So long as that strength remained.

Johann's foes had not been caught in the collapse. One of the ratmen was clawing at its face, trying to wipe dirt and dust from its sensitive nose with the same sort of frantic frenzy as a courtesan might attack a dress upon which she had felt an insect's crawling legs. The other ratman, however, was not so distracted by the brown coating that covered its fur and face. Its feral gaze was fixed entirely upon Johann, and its lips spread in a fang-filled grin when it saw the man's knife lying on the floor.

With a savage squeal of murder and brutality, the ratman leapt towards Johann, a leap that should have seen the smuggler impaled upon the monster's blade of rusty iron. The blow never fell, however. Sounding from the wall came a wailing echo of the ratkin's cry, a mournful shriek of madness and unimaginable horror. A crazed blur exploded across the space between Johann and the ratman, smashing into the monster while it was in mid-leap.

Only by the shape's clothes could Johann tell the strange vision was Kempf, his erstwhile comrade and fellow criminal. Pushed to madness by the advent of the skaven into the cellar, driven to the limits of despair by his need for black dust, Kempf's face was as pallid as the belly of a fish, his eyes gaping orbs of mindless terror. Seeing the skaven in the flesh, Kempf's mind recalled dreams and visions from the drug den of Otto Ali, mixing them together into one obscene collage of depravity and evil. Now, driven into his own world of shadows, the ratman's cry had invaded the madman's last refuge. Like any cornered beast, Kempf lashed out.

Johann saw madman and ratkin roll across the floor, their bodies tangled together. When they stopped, both forms were still. Kempf's hands were locked around the ratkin's scrawny neck, pressed together, the furry neck snapped like the stem of a weed. The madman was equally dead, the ratman's rusty blade thrust through his belly with such force that its point erupted from the man's back, the monster's bestial jaws mired in the gory wreckage that had been the dust-fiend's throat.

A low growl of fury finally snapped Johann from his morbid fascination with Kempf's death. He lunged for his knife as the last ratman sprang for him. His shoulder exploded with pain as he sprawled beneath the monster's attack, catching the edge of the skaven's blade. His fingers closed about the grip of his fat-bladed knife, rolling onto his back to meet the creature's next charge.

The attack never came. The ratman stood transfixed, staring vacantly at the wall above Johann's head. Slowly the creature's limbs began to droop, the sword clattering from its claws. It was like watching a pig bladder deflate, as though all the air inside the ratkin was slowly draining away. At last its head slumped against its breast. For the first time, Johann was aware of a little sliver of blackness piercing the ratman. While he watched, the shard of night sank back into the furry chest and the verminous corpse toppled to the floor. Beyond it was a dark shape of shadow and menace.

The wizard's veil of gathered shadow billowed about him as he stepped forwards, sheathing his sword. The magister's stormy eyes regarded Johann coldly and the smuggler felt himself wither beneath the terrible judgement in their grey, misty depths.

'Above,' the wizard's hissing voice intoned, pointing a finger shrouded in black at the stairway. Johann did not question the man's authority, did not even think to protest his right to command. Like a little boy scolded by his father, he hastened to obey, taking the stairs two at a time. Dimly he was aware of a presence following after him, though his ears could detect no sound upon the creaky wooden steps.

The taproom of the *Orc and Axe* was strangely deserted for this hour. Johann could see only a handful of what he took to be grim-faced patrons scattered about the room. They were a disparate group, such that Johann would have sensed no thread of common unity were it not for the identical expressions they wore, each face being a mask of worry and concern. He thought perhaps that the reasons for their concern were the dead men stacked like cordwood in one corner of the hall, but a single glance at the bodies gave him doubts. No one would hang for killing men belonging to Gustav Volk. The mystery of why the thugs had not investigated the violence in the cellar was answered.

'You and your filthy mob brought this on me!' roared Ulgrin Shatterhand when the old dwarf's eyes spotted Johann entering the room. He tried to shake off the restraining hand of a younger, yellow-bearded dwarf standing beside the bar. 'Couldn't leave well enough alone! Had to use my tavern for your idiot manling intrigues!' Ulgrin's bluster died a sudden death when he saw the apparition stalking behind the smuggler. The dwarf muttered some half-audible oath into his beard and decided to busy himself with tending a rack of cracked clay steins.

The other dwarf came forwards, bowing deeply as Johann stepped further into the room. The head of every other man in the room made a similar nod of respect and fealty. Johann realised the gesture was not for him, but for the strange being who had rescued him from the underfolk.

'Report,' the wizard's hissing voice commanded, his smoky gaze resting on the figure of the bowing dwarf.

'All of Volk's men have been dealt with,' the dwarf replied, patting the heft of the broad-bladed axe lashed across his back. 'No prisoners.'

The wizard turned, pointing a finger at one of the men. Johann was shocked to find himself staring at the scarred face of Theodor Baer, the watch sergeant. The watchman was treating an ugly gash in his leg with a bottle of pungent-smelling Reikland hock, gritting his teeth against the pain.

'Report,' the grey-cloaked spectre hissed.

Like a well-trained dog, Theodor set down the bottle, seemingly oblivious to his still bleeding wound, and answered the command of his master. 'No casualties. We took Volk's gang by complete surprise. Only a few minor injuries.'

'Select three unimpaired operatives,' the wizard's voice spoke in a steel whisper. 'They will descend to the cellar. Dispatch any wounded ratkin.'

Theodor nodded. Forcing himself back to his feet, grinding his teeth against the pain from his leg, he began shouting orders at the other men in the tavern. A motley group composed of a villainous-looking Tilean, a pock-marked stevedore wearing the colours of a Fish, and a hulking Kislevite with a thick red moustache, drew daggers and hurried to their butcher's work.

A wiry little man came across the barroom, bowing before the wizard. For the second time, Johann was surprised to see a face he recognised amongst the wizard's crew. Ludwig Rothfels, the street-corner agitator, was another of this mysterious master's thralls.

'Master,' the agitator reported, 'Gustav Volk and five of his men left the *Orc and Axe* shortly before your operatives were in position.'

'Volk is inconsequential,' the wizard replied. 'His mob will wait. The matter of the underfolk cannot.'

Ludwig nodded in servile agreement, but did not excuse himself from the magister's imposing presence. 'Master, an unscrupulous apothecary was with Volk when he left, one Sergei Kawolski.' Ludwig darted an accusing look at Johann. Before the agitator could elaborate further, Johann seized upon the importance of what he had said.

'Sergei with Volk!' The smuggler's eyes were wide with alarm. He felt sick at the ghastly purpose that alone could unite those two names. Ludwig was right to accuse him. He should have waited for the priestess. Now, the quack he had brought to treat his brother was selling out Hans to his enemies!

Johann fell to his knees, clutching at the wizard's hand. It felt cold and unreal beneath his fingers, as though what he touched had no more substance than a fistful of river fog. He stared up at the wizard's face, hidden within the shadow of his hood and the thick folds of his scarf. 'He is taking Volk to my brother! Please, they will murder Hans! You must stop them!'

The wizard's eyes were an icy storm of steely grey as his voice spoke in a soft, hissing whisper. 'This will be a second debt you will owe to me,' he stated, each word laden with menace rather than hope. 'I do not forgive my debtors easily.'

Before Johann could reply, could even explain where his brother was, the hand he held became even less real, less solid beneath his fingers. While he watched, awestruck, the wizard's body vanished, fading into nothingness like fog burned away by the sun. Almost before he could register what was happening, the wizard was gone, only a lingering chill in the air remaining behind.

Somehow, Johann knew he did not need to tell the sinister being about the *Crown and Two Chairmen*. He felt that the wizard already knew where his brother was. There was no secret, Johann felt, that could endure those eyes of mist and fog. Nothing could be hidden from that penetrating gaze, the gaze of the being Johann knew he too must call 'master'.

THANQUOL GROUND HIS fangs together as he followed the treacherous scent of Kratch, his duplicitous apprentice. The grey seer had decided to strangle the adept with his own entrails while allowing pain-pain snails to dissolve Kratch's nethers with their acidic slime. Or perhaps he would have a Clan Moulder flesh-shaper open up the traitor's belly and sew a live bonechewer inside. Watching Kratch squirm and writhe as the terrified mole clawed its way free would be deliciously entertaining.

Changes in the scent brought Thanquol to a halt. The fug of the sewer was oozing into the tunnel now, but mixed with it were the smells of battle: blood, fear-musk, the stench of burned fur and the noxious reek of warpfire. Thanquol cast a nervous glance at Boneripper, the immense monster lumbering beside him, forced into an awkward half-crouch by the low ceiling of the tunnel. It was on the tip of his tongue to order the brute back into the cellar, to dig out the other side of the cave-in and take their chances against the man-thing sorcerer. Whatever had befallen his cowardly underlings and their despicable new leader, the grey seer wanted no part of it.

Then new smells registered in Thanquol's nose, one of which set the grey seer's tail twitching in excitement. The Wormstone! There could be no mistaking that cold, evil smell. Kratch had recovered it! All that was left was for Thanquol to seize the weapon from his slinking apprentice while he was beset by his own enemies! It would be unfortunate not to take his time killing Kratch, but possessing the Wormstone would go far in the way of compensation.

He was just turning to growl new orders to Boneripper when Thanquol detected a strengthening in the scent of both Kratch and the Wormstone. He abandoned his idea of using the rat ogre as a distraction, bursting into the midst of the fray in the sewer while he slipped in and stole, no, recovered, the Wormstone before anyone was aware of him. The Horned Rat had once again smiled upon his chosen prophet. He would not need to go into the sewer to seize the Wormstone or kill Kratch; both of them were coming to him.

Thanquol motioned Boneripper to flatten himself against the side of the wall. The way Kratch's scent was growing, the apprentice was in full flight. He wouldn't be aware of the lurking grey seer and his bodyguard until it was far too late to arrest his headlong, craven retreat. Thanquol drew the ratskull snuff box from his robe, inhaling a pinch of the warpdust powder. Perhaps he would take his time with Kratch. Anything less might be insulting to the Horned Rat for presenting him with such an unexpected gift.

Scurrying skaven appeared suddenly in the gloom of the tunnel. As Thanquol had surmised, their pace was so hurried that they were unaware of his scent until they were almost on top of him. Most of the fleeing vermin were first made aware of their presence when Boneripper exploded upon them in an avalanche of blood and screams. A Clan Skryre skirmisher shrieked into his gas-mask as Boneripper impaled him on the rusty metal fist-spike of his mutant arm. A pair of Clan Skab warriors crumpled into a pile of twitching wreckage as a sweep of Boneripper's claw eviscerated them. A weedy Clan Skaul sneak howled in terror as Boneripper lifted him to his immense mouth. The rat ogre's fangs bit down, severing the screaming ratman just beneath the rib cage. Boneripper crunched noisily on the fore section while the rest of the mutilated skaven flopped to the floor in an obscene display.

Once certain that his enemies were fully engaged by and focused on the terror of the rat ogre, Thanquol sprang from the other wall of the tunnel. His claws locked around the throat of his chosen prey, unholy fire glowing in his eyes. There were so many spells, so many unspeakable secrets of the eldritch and the arcane he had learned over the years. Choosing the right one to send Kratch's wretched soul snivelling from his shrivelled flesh was something it was hard for Thanquol to resolve.

'Great and wise m... master!' Kratch wheezed, gasping for breath. 'Glory-glory that your eminence live-live! We fear-sad that you die-die!'

'I won't be able to say the same,' Thanquol hissed through clenched fangs. 'Die, snivelling traitor!'

'Mercy-pity, kind tyrant!' Kratch pleaded. 'This humble one has saved the Wormstone for you! Saved it from the real traitors!' The apprentice waved a frantic paw at Viskitt Burnfang and a pair of surviving warlock engineers. Between them, the heavy iron box rested on the floor. The Clan Skryre skaven were looking anxiously between Boneripper and the tunnel behind them, trying to decide whether to brave the mutant rat ogre or the battle they had fled.

Thanquol's eyes narrowed, his grip tightened. 'What "real traitors"? Speak-squeak flea-maggot! Who attacks you and your miserable entourage?'

'Skrattch Skarpaw!' whined Kratch. 'He set upon your loyal servants as we entered the man-thing scat-stream! Mighty Thanquol, he seeks the Wormstone!'

'Obviously, you dung-brained swine!' Thanquol cursed, dropping Kratch onto the floor. He looked past the grovelling apprentice to the hulking Boneripper. Thanquol snapped a quick command and the rat ogre relented in his savage persecution of the other cowards who had followed Kratch in retreat. The grey seer's fiery gaze swept over the cowering ratmen, resting at last on Viskitt Burnfang. 'Swear loyalty to me or die, maggot-feeding trash!'

Burnfang held his head so low that his whiskers brushed the ground. 'Of course, mighty voice of the Horned One! Burnfang has ever been your loyal-honoured servant!' The warlock engineer glared at Kratch. 'I follow this slag-scat only because he claims his master is lost-dead!'

Thanquol decided now was not the time to remind Burnfang that he had abandoned the cellar – and the grey seer – before Kratch had made his own escape. As soon as Burnfang spoke, the other refuges began stumbling over one another in their hurry to echo his oath of servitude and devotion. Thanquol waved their assurances aside, recognising them for the empty breath they were. The skaven of Under-Altdorf were absolutely without honour or scruple, they'd do anything to benefit themselves, whoever they had to betray for such advancement. He would use the scum, for now, then dispose of them when they were no longer useful.

'Gracious and merciful despot,' Kratch whined from where he had fallen to the floor. 'You must hurry to save those loyal-true skaven who fight even now against your enemies!' The apprentice pointed a crooked finger down the tunnel towards the continuing sounds of conflict. 'Wretched Kratch will stay behind and protect the Wormstone.'

Thanquol swatted the unctuous adept in the snout with his staff, sprawling him across the floor of the tunnel. He was tempted to unleash the full malignity of his magic against the ratman, but he knew he would need the full might of his sorcery if he would make good his escape... and do so with the Wormstone.

'We will face Skarpaw together,' Thanquol growled. He felt a delicious surge of satisfaction at the fear that flickered through Kratch's eyes as he said the words. Having just quit the battle, the adept was of no mind to return to it.

The grey seer saw otherwise. The fierce snarls of battle echoing up the tunnel had given him an idea, an idea as callous as it was cunning. And Kratch had a part to play... a very important part. More satisfying than slowly torturing the traitor to death would be to use Kratch's destruction to ensure his own survival.

'Back to the man-thing scat-stream!' Thanquol snarled. When the other skaven appeared to share Kratch's opinion of returning to battle, Thanquol snapped a quick command to Boneripper. The rat ogre's paw closed around the closest skaven, crushing every bone in his body with a single tightening of his fist.

After that, the skaven would follow Thanquol straight into the jungle hell of Daemon-Sotek if he ordered them to. At least so long as Boneripper was close enough to enforce the grey seer's commands.

SKRATTCH SKARPAW WATCHED as his little army continued to destroy the ambushed skaven of that preening Skavenblight upstart Thanquol. It had taken every favour bought by bribe or threat to assemble such a force, but Skarpaw did not grumble too much about squandering the resources of Under-Altdorf's branch of Clan Eshin. If he did not capture the Wormstone for Lord Skrolk, his life would end in horror and pain. Even if he failed, a chilling thought, Skarpaw was not about to leave his carefully cultivated resources for whatever upstart succeeded him as clanleader. Better to squander them now when there was a chance they could do him some good!

The assassin looked over his force with pride. Warp-fire throwers from Clan Skryre, black-furred stormvermin from Clan Mors. From Clan Moulder had come a pair of rat ogres and nearly a hundred oversized and extremely ferocious rats. Clan Sleekit spear-rats and Clan Skaul slingers scurried at the periphery of the conflict alongside his own clan's gutter runners and clanrats. They closed the noose tighter about Thanquol's hapless underlings with every passing breath, choking the petty-tyranny of the grey seer with each traitor they cut down.

So far Skarpaw had not seen the grey seer, nor picked up his scent. He had seen the grey seer's apprentice, however, and more importantly, he had seen what could only be the box they thought to convey the Wormstone in. The scent of Thanquol's workshops was familiar to Skarpaw; the assassin had prowled them many nights looking for an opportunity to finish the grey seer. The smell rising from the box was stronger, telling him that what he needed was indeed inside.

Everything depended on the Wormstone. With it, he could force Lord Skrolk to give him the antidote to the corruption the plague priest had infected him with. He could feel the corruption even now eating away at him, sapping his strength, dulling his reflexes, clouding his mind with decay.

Skarpaw would have his revenge upon the diseased Lord Skrolk. Once free of Skrolk's threat, he would find a way to take the Wormstone back from Clan Pestilens. The weapon would be safer in the paws of Clan Eshin, and if he was the instrument of that transfer of ownership, Skarpaw's status within the clan would be second only to the Nightlord and the Deathmasters. A greedy glint entered the assassin's eyes. Why should he set a limit to his ambition?

A chittering cry of agony betokened the brutal demise of some of Thanquol's minions, incinerated in an instant by a blast of warpfire from one of the Clan Skryre weapon teams. Their bodies were little more than charred skeletons even before they crashed to the floor, the sickly sweet scent of burnt meat and fur billowing across the brick-walled confluence of human tunnels that formed the scene of Skarpaw's triumph. The master assassin twirled his whiskers, imagining the moment when he would be free.

Suddenly a new scent drew Skarpaw's attention, a smell that was far from unfamiliar to him. The apprentice Kratch had fled up the skaven tunnel when the ambush had sprung. Now the wretched creature reappeared, leading the less than eager cowards who had fled with him. Skarpaw was pleased to see that the iron box was still with them. He was less thrilled to see that Kratch's master had finally seen fit to enter the fray. Grey Seer Thanquol marched behind his apprentice, always pushing the miserable adept before him. Beside the grey seer lurched his enormous rat ogre, the mutant Boneripper. As the beast emerged fully from the tunnel and straightened his bulk in the higher ceiling of the sewer, even Skarpaw felt a thrill of fear rush through him. The brute was gigantic, dwarfing even the immense rat ogres he had procured from the beastmasters!

Eager to enter the battle a moment before, Skarpaw found himself hanging back, snapping orders to his underlings. Let them take the risks, he would keep himself apart from the fray, the better to adjust to changing tactical situations. Once Boneripper was brought down, then Skarpaw might take a more direct role in the combat. Unless of course it looked like Thanquol still had some magic left.

THANQUOL CURSED THROUGH clenched fangs. The craven idiot Kratch hadn't told him the half of it! This was more than simply an ambush by Skarpaw and the cloaked killers of Clan Eshin, more than some diseased union between Eshin and Moulder! He saw warriors from all of Under-Altdorf's major clans converging on the last hapless clusters of loyal skaven guarding the mouth of the tunnel. He smelled conspiracy! An obscene collusion between all of the clans of Under-Altdorf to destroy him and capture the Wormstone for themselves! Thanquol's eyes narrowed with hate. There was only one skaven capable of forging such an alliance! Skarpaw was just a figurehead – the real villain was that senile scum Thratquee! Well, if Thratquee thought he was going to build his heretical 'New Skavenblight' on the bones of Thanquol, the corrupt old rat was stupider than a sack of goblins!

'We must flee-flee!' Kratch whined as Thanquol pushed him forwards, toward the battle line. The adept vented his glands as Skarpaw's rat ogres made particularly gruesome work of some surviving Clan Skab warriors.

The grey seer snarled at his underling. 'Grow a spleen, coward-meat!' he snapped, pushing the frantic apprentice a few steps further. Thanquol glanced over his shoulder to make certain that Boneripper was still beside him. 'We must fight-conquer or die-die!' Thanquol spat, stamping the butt of his staff against the floor for emphasis. As he did so, a warplock jezzail roared from somewhere in the darkness, its warpstone bullet exploding the skull of a Clan Skaul sneak only a few feet behind Thanquol. Instinctively, the grey seer dropped into a crouch, shielding himself with his apprentice's body. Kratch struggled to free himself from his mentor's fierce grip.

'It is hopeless!' Kratch whined.

Thanquol struggled to raise the ratskull snuff box to his nose, somehow maintaining the box and his staff in the same paw. The intoxicating burn of the powder sent iron flowing through his veins, subduing the fear flooding his system. The fiery sensation calmed the grey seer's instincts. His eyes were smouldering pools of blood flecked with gold when he glared into Kratch's face.

'I will use your power, apprentice-pupil,' Thanquol said, his voice a sinister murmur. 'Your power joined with my own,' he added with a malicious chitter.

'Used to fuel horror.' Thanquol's staff began to glow with a green light. More warplock bullets sped for the grey seer but they were knocked aside by the unseen power of his magic.

'Used to feed carnage.' Thanquol's staff was now a blazing sliver of green fire, its talismans and charms dancing in a dank wind that snapped and crackled through the fur of every skaven it touched.

'Used to call hunger into the bellies and brains of the traitor and the heretic!' Now Kratch could feel the grey seer's power devouring his own, pulling strength from his very soul to feed its own ravenous need. The apprentice felt himself wilting, as though his spirit were being torn from his flesh. Around him, the fighting had ceased. Every skaven, both friend and foe, was drawing away from the two grey seers, their fur standing on end, their glands venting as their every sense recoiled from the malign power of Thanquol's sorcery.

Thanquol's eyes gleamed with an insane light. Bloody froth spilled from his mouth. When he spoke, his words were black with his own stagnant blood. 'Power to summon-call the Black Hunger!'

With the grey seer's maddened shriek, grisly ribbons of power burst from the head of his staff, stabbing into all who stood before it. The eyes of each creature the green vapours struck glazed over, blackening as they filled with blood, as all intelligence shrivelled. Skaven, rat ogre or giant rat, one and all were struck down, their senses and minds drowned beneath one overwhelming urge, one all-consuming need. The verminous throng burned with a terrible hunger, a hunger that could only be sated with warm, dripping flesh!

Skarpaw's army disintegrated into a snarling mob of frenzied beasts, biting and clawing at their own, casting aside weapons and intelligence in the grip of their primal, cannibalistic hunger. Clan Moulder packmasters leapt onto the back of their rat ogres, ripping and tearing at their leathery flesh with fang and claw. Clanrats worried at the throats of gutter runners while Clan Skryre skirmishers cast aside their complex, fantastic weapons to gnaw the entrails of their own fallen.

Kratch could only dimly see the gory display, his senses fading as Thanquol's spell consumed more and more of his essence. It became an effort of concentration to make his heart beat, to bring air down into his lungs. The adept's limbs trembled, his bones feeling impossibly heavy beneath his flesh. He imagined he could feel his eyes slithering back into the pits of his skull. In his ears, he thought he could hear the sardonic laughter of the Horned Rat.

Suddenly, Kratch could feel an incredible surge of strength flow into him. His failing spirit swelled, filled almost to bursting. The adept fought to control the sheer force rushing into him, trying to prevent it from burning out his mind and soul. He could feel the reins of control and command seeping into his own bones, feel himself become connected to each and every creature whose brain Thanquol had filled with the Black Hunger. He struggled to keep the same frenzy from flowing back into himself, even as he understood the dire consequences should he try to banish the spell. Every one of the survivors would descend on him in a vengeful mob.

From the corner of his eye, Kratch could see Thanquol's grin of triumph.

'Quick-quick!' the grey seer snarled at his followers. 'We must flee-scurry!'

Awed by the hideous brutality of Thanquol's magic, the depleted members of his entourage needed little encouragement to obey. Carefully skirting the orgy of feral cannibalism the grey seer's spell had unleashed, the few dozen ratmen scampered down the brick-lined tunnels. Thanquol hurried after them, Boneripper's ever present bulk loping beside him. The grey seer caught the scarred stump of Skrim Gnawtail's tail, pulling the Clan Skaul spy back towards him.

'Not back to Under-Altdorf,' Thanquol warned Skrim. 'They are our enemies! All of them! It was the council that set that ambush!'

'Where-where, mighty one?' Skrim asked, quivering with fear and anxiety.

'Somewhere away from the traitors!' snapped Thanquol. He stabbed a clawed finger at the arched ceiling overhead. 'Somewhere up there, where they can't find us.'

Thanquol gnashed his fangs together in a fit of vindictive fury. 'I will announce myself to Under-Altdorf when I am ready. In my own way.'

KRATCH STRUGGLED TO control the force of Thanquol's spell, as much a victim of its power as any of the maddened wretches tearing and chewing their way through the skaven army. The adept's mind seethed with his mentor's treachery. Transferring the focus of his spell from himself to Kratch, Thanquol had doomed his apprentice to a slow and creeping death. The arcane forces Kratch was trying to control would rip through him, twisting his flesh and mutating his soul into something spawned in the blackest pits of nightmare. Kratch railed against such an ignoble end, yet every sight of the ripping, gnawing mob swirling around him made him only more determined not to break the grey seer's magic. So long as the spell remained, that long did Kratch remain at the eye of the storm. As soon as he broke the spell, he would become part of the storm, defenceless against the clawing, biting, mindless swarm.

A warplock fired from somewhere beyond the melee. Kratch crumpled to the ground, his head bloody. As he fell, he could feel the magic evaporate. Kratch ground his teeth together, waiting for the swarm to descend upon him. It was almost a minute before he dared to open his eyes.

He blinked in disbelief. Nothing had descended upon him with tooth and claw because there was nothing left to do so. Most of Skarpaw's army was just so much gnawed meat choking the canal of the sewer. Those that still drew breath were curled into little trembling balls, panting and wheezing as their bodies struggled to recover from their frenzied madness. It would be many days before they recovered from the Black Hunger, if they ever did.

Dimly, Kratch heard voices raised in argument, sharp, snarling skaven voices. He could see four ratmen garbed in the black cloaks and leather wrappings of Clan Eshin arguing among themselves. One of the ratmen held a smoking jezzail in his paws and he was gesturing furiously at the unspeakable carnage that had consumed Skarpaw's army.

Another skaven, this one larger and bulkier than the jezzail bearer, snarled and snapped at the excited sniper. With abrupt suddenness, the large skaven, who Kratch judged to be no less than Skarpaw himself, plunged a fist-spike into the eye of his rebellious underling. The sniper pawed at Skarpaw's chest for an instant, provoking the assassin to plunge the fist-spike into his underling's body in a blur of vicious violence.

The draconian discipline excited the other two Clan Eshin ratmen. One scrambled into a narrow pipe, his body squirming like an eel down the slender metal shaft. The other dived into the putrid stream of the canal, plunging beneath its filthy water and vanishing from sight.

Rising from the butchered sniper, Skarpaw glared first at the pipe, then at the filthy sewer canal. Kratch could guess the thoughts that slithered through the assassin's crooked mind. He might be able to catch one of his escaped minions, but never could he catch both of them before they returned to Under-Altdorf and reported his defeat to his enemies and rivals. By the time Skarpaw returned to the city, if he was only stripped of his position as clanleader, he could consider himself blessed by the Horned One.

Skarpaw seemed to reach the same conclusion. Sullenly, the assassin turned and scurried down a sewer tunnel that would take him away from the direction of the skaven city.

Kratch waited until the assassin was gone before daring to move. He lifted his paws to his bloody head. The shot from the jezzail had miraculously been deflected by one of his small horns, a certain sign of favour from his god. The Horned Rat had spared him, spared him to pursue righteous vengeance against the traitorous Thanquol. Kratch ground his teeth together. His former master thought him dead, did he? Well, Kratch would show him the error of his arrogance before allowing death to crush the grey seer's corrupt flesh.

Yes, Kratch thought, he would have his vengeance against Thanquol. His murderous grin spread as he turned his eyes back to the tunnel down which Skarpaw had escaped. He also knew of someone who had every reason to hate Thanquol even more than he did. Someone who would help him claim his revenge!

HOPFOOT THE MAUS awoke with a start. He smacked one of his tiny fists against his head, trying to pound the last of his hangover from his skull. It was an effort that was far from successful, made all the worse because he still couldn't shake the ringing from his ears.

No, not ringing. Scratching. A weird, grating sound, like a beaver gnawing at the roots of an old oak.

Hopfoot roused himself, almost banging his head against the top of the table above him. His shop filled to the gunwales with merchandise, the halfling had set his little mattress of fur and straw beneath one of the curio tables. It was an arrangement he preferred to separate sleeping quarters. This way he could keep an eye on his wares and be ready with his trusty blunderbuss should any thieves be brazen enough to challenge his resolve.

The fence rolled over, a surly grumble rolling off his lips as his bare feet encountered the chill metal barrel of his gun. Hopfoot's fat little fingers curled around the stock. There was a definite pattern to the scratching, something more purposeful than the scampering of rats or the nocturnal wandering of cats. Thieves were an ever-present danger on the waterfront, even for a fence. Crawling out from under the table, Hopfoot let the funnel-shaped mouth of his blunderbuss swing around. He hoped he left enough to sell the physicians at the university. Even Hopfoot felt a twinge of shame selling dead thieves to the swineherds.

The persistent sound came from the back door of the shop, and Hopfoot carefully made his way through the gloom of his darkened store towards the source. He cursed as he stubbed his toe against the claw of a stuffed panther. Whoever was working at the back door must have heard him, for the scratching noise fell silent. It was only a momentary lull, however. A few moments, then it returned with renewed violence and vigour.

Hopfoot chose a position behind the wooden counter, cocking the hammer of his gun, aiming its wide mouth at the door. The instant it opened, he would fire and turn the face of the strange thief into so much shredded meat.

How strange the intruder was, Hopfoot discovered an instant later when the weakened door gave inwards, nearly gnawed clean through at its base. Gnawed was indeed the right word, for neither pick nor axe had done such terrible work. Squeezing itself through the hole, its bulk causing the frame to bulge and snap, was a vision of ghastly, verminous nightmare that froze the halfling solid with terror.

It was like a rat, only bigger. Much bigger. Enormous in a way only travellers' tales from the Mountains of Mourn could match. To call it a rat was to call a griffon a sparrow. It crept through the darkened shop on its hand-like paws, dragging its scaly tail after it. Its nearly hairless body oozed with sores and blackened scabs of burned flesh, its face scalded into a skull-like mask.

The blunderbuss fell from Hopfoot's frozen fingers, clattering across the floor. The rat-beast turned its head, its beady eyes focusing on the halfling. It sniffed at the air, raising its body after the fashion of its smaller kin. It chittered, displaying its gruesomely oversized fangs. Hopfoot thought his heart would turn to stone as it dropped back to all fours. If the thing should come one step closer, he should die of fright.

Instead the rat-beast turned away, loping through the clutter of shelves and tables. It tipped over a nest of old shirts and moth-eaten blouses to expose the fence's iron strongbox. Again the monster chittered, a vocalisation of its hunger.

Hopfoot did not even dare to curse as he watched the monster start to chew its way through the strongbox. The iron chest contained all of his wealth, all the gold and silver he had accumulated from his thieving patrons, all the gems and jewels he had bought over the years, even those weird green-black rocks Kempf claimed were wyrdstone.

There was something even more valuable, however, that Hopfoot had not locked away in his strongbox. As he heard the rat-beast's fangs gnaw into the metal box,

Hopfoot decided to save his smooth plump skin and edge out the smashed door. He waited until his hairy feet had carried him a full block from his shop before he started to scream.

By the time he could convince anyone that he was not drunk and that he was not insane, by the time enough people stopped laughing at him long enough to follow him back to his shop, the monster was gone. It had finished its gruesome effort to chew its way into the strongbox. Strangely, all the gold and silver, gems and jewels, were scattered across the floor of the shop.

The only thing that was missing were the wyrdstone shards.

CHAPTER TEN
Shadows of Altdorf

'WHERE IS HANS Dietrich?'

The question was punctuated by a sharp scream, a blood-curdling sound that raised the rafters of the *Crown and Two Chairmen*. The interrogator was a very angry Gustav Volk. The wailing subject of his attention was Mueller. The smuggler's eye patch had been torn away and Volk's gloved finger was probing the scarred cavity with a none-too gentle touch. His face split in an evil grin as blood spurted from the empty socket and Mueller's scream rose still higher in pitch.

'Where's your boss?' Volk repeated, his voice a low snarl. He pressed his finger still deeper.

The employees and patrons of the tavern and its attendant brothel were clustered about the main hall, just beneath the carpeted stairway that rose to the sleeping rooms above. The mobsmen had scoured the entire building of occupants, herding them into a single mass of anxiety and fear at the base of the stairs. Several of

Volk's men, steel-barrelled handguns at the ready, kept even the most frantic from making a break for it. The gory spectacle of what happened to the few who refused to accept an invitation to Volk's gathering kept the hot-heads from getting any bold ideas. No man wanted to risk his life showing off for an audience of barflies and doxies.

'I... I don't... Nooooo!' Mueller shrieked, another spurt of red bursting from the socket. Blood dripped from Volk's leather tunic.

'Wrong answer!' growled Volk, pressing still harder and dragging more screams from the smuggler.

'He's telling the truth!' a shrill voice shouted at the racketeer.

Volk turned his head slowly, his finger still deep in Mueller's empty eye socket. The mob leader glanced across the frightened mass of prisoners, then glared at the nearest of his henchmen. 'Which whore spoke?' he asked the thug.

The brutish thug snarled an answer, then shoved his way into the crowd, pulling Argula from the cluster of cowering harlots. He pushed the woman forwards, spilling her at the feet of his boss. Still maintaining his grip on Mueller's face, Volk glared down at the woman.

'Alright, bitch, you say he doesn't know, then I'll go ahead and believe you.' Volk stabbed his finger savagely into Mueller's socket, then yanked his hand away. The maimed, shrieking man collapsed into a trembling heap on the floor, blood pouring from his ruined face. While Argula was still gawking in horror at the savage spectacle, Volk's bloody fingers coiled in her hair and pulled her from the floor. 'Start talking, or I start cutting,' the racketeer warned, drawing his dagger. His smile became a sneer as he stared into her eyes. 'I won't start with your face, whore. I'll start with the bits the lads are paying for first.'

Argula cast a desperate look at the crowd of patrons, employees and friends, imploring any of them for help. The only one with nerve enough to meet her eye was Gustaf Schlecht, the sometime house surgeon. The piggish man didn't have the same helpless look as the others, but rather had the leering smile of a sadistic child watching an older sibling pull wings off a fly. His lack of empathy sent even more fear pounding through her heart. No one would help her and, given half a chance, grinning Gustaf might just join in!

'He was here,' Argula groaned while Volk continued to wrap the woman's hair ever tighter in his fingers, forcing her ever higher onto her toes to stop the pain. 'That one,' she said, pointing to Mueller's moaning body, 'and the man you killed upstairs brought him, but someone else came and moved him elsewhere later.'

'You see, Herr Volk, I told you true.' The words came from the apothecary Sergei Kawolski, his speech partially muffled by the bloody rag he pressed against the corner of his mouth.

'Shut your face, quack,' growled Volk without looking at Sergei. 'Or maybe you'd like to choke on some more teeth?'

Sergei shook his head, recoiling from the brutal racketeer. The apothecary had thought to turn a quick coin by informing Volk's gang of the hideout of Dietrich and his smugglers. Instead, he was quickly realising he would be lucky to walk away from the fiasco with his life. If Volk's men hadn't found Mueller and Wilhelm, Sergei knew he would already be dead. If they failed to find the sickly Hans, Volk still might kill him.

Gustav Volk's smile was almost reptilian in its merciless inhumanity as he pressed his face into that of Argula, his murderous eyes boring into her own. 'Now, strumpet, who moved that bastard Hans and where did they take him?' He twisted his hand, forcing her to crook her head at an awkward angle, the better to watch Volk's dagger slide slowly down her body, slicing a little ribbon of lace from her bodice and dress as it worked its way down her side. 'Talk or scream, I'll find out and nobody's going to stop me.'

A sudden chill swept through the tavern, bringing shivers to racketeers and prisoners alike. Beads of frost formed upon the bottles behind the bar, wood creaked as the air about it became icy. The darkness of the hall seemed to grow steadily thicker, every shadow attaining a sinister aura of lurking menace.

'Keep a watch on those prisoners!' Volk snapped. Like his men, he was turning about, watching the eerie, supernatural display unfolding all around them. The racketeer pulled Argula close to him, wrapping his arm across her generous chest, using the madam as a living shield against whatever unseen danger had descended upon the *Crown and Two Chairmen*.

Suddenly one of Volk's thugs cried out, followed quickly by a second. Both men fell, their heads split by what looked like knives of solid shadow. Before the horrified gaze of the other mobsmen, the arcane blades began to wither, seeping into the wounds they had dealt even as blood dribbled out.

'Over there!' roared a black-toothed rogue, pointing at the stairway and firing his gun. The shot rushed past a grim apparition cloaked in grey robes, the bullet shattering against the ceiling. Every eye turned to the landing, drawn to the mysterious figure. Gleaming eyes, their colourless depths swirling like the cloudy heart of a tempest, impressed themselves upon all who looked upon the wizard, however far away. Cruel judgement, merciless justice, these were the threat carried in those eyes, a promise of death to all who defied the iron will dwelling behind their steely gaze.

'Kill him!' Volk shouted, breaking the spell of awed silence that gripped his men. The thug who had fired dropped his gun and scrambled to draw his sword. Two other rogues joined him on the stairs, firing their own guns before resorting to their blades. Like the first, the other marksmen failed to strike their target, the ghostly shape seeming to bend and distort around their speeding bullets. Two more missiles smashed harmlessly into the ceiling above the top of the stairs.

A mocking hiss rose from shrouded lips, and the cloaked shape became indistinct as the shadows on the stairway seemed to rush in and converge upon the wizard, wrapping and blurring his form in a mantle of darkness. The thugs on the steps trembled, their vicious courage wilting before the fearsome display of arcane power.

'It is just a conjurer's trick!' roared Volk, making no move to join his men or abandon his living shield. 'Kill him!'

The encouragement of their brutal boss sent steel back into the spines of the thugs. They forced defiant snarls onto their pale faces, glaring at the inky cloud of blackness that now filled the top of the stairway. One of the racketeers began to climb the steps, his fingers white around the grip of his sword.

No sooner had the villain taken his third step than the shadowy mass was billowing down the stairs, rushing towards him like some malevolent fog. The thug cried out, slashing his sword through the formless wall of night. An instant later and the man was enveloped by the shadows, an instant after that and his body was crashing through the wooden balustrade. The thug was already dead when he hit the floor, his neck sliced open and a look of abject terror frozen upon his cold features.

The dead man's comrades on the stairs had no chance to recover from the shock of their fellow's swift destruction. Before they could either move forwards or back, the wizard's concealing darkness swept down, enveloping them as completely as the first racketeer. Briefly, the sounds of swords clashing carried itself from the blackness. A loathsome gurgle, a piteous groan, and all was silence again. One of the thugs emerged from the black fog. He swayed on the stairs for a moment, then toppled and fell, his body rolling brokenly down the steps.

As though struck by a sudden gale, the shadowy mantle was swept aside, streamers of darkness writhing and twisting as they slithered back into the shadows. The grey-cloaked magister stood revealed once more, a bloody sword in his hand, the dead body of a racketeer crumpled at his feet. From either side of his hawklike nose, the wizard's fierce eyes cast judgement upon the men below.

Such cringing valour as remained among Volk's crew withered beneath the renewed attention of that merciless gaze. With a cry of fear, the last two racketeers threw down their guns and ran towards the door. The wizard did not move, merely raised one of his darkened hands. Slivers of shadow erupted from the oily skin of darkness that coated his fingers, flashing across the hall to strike down the fleeing mobsmen. The thugs tottered and fell as the wizard's sorcerous knives slashed through their backs. There was no honour among thieves, and no chivalry to be shown to murderers.

Gustav Volk's body shivered, the first time the mob leader had known abject terror since becoming old enough to call himself a man. His eyes roved the hall, hunting for some avenue of escape, some place of refuge. Argula moaned in his twisting grip. A rat-like smile spread across Volk's lips. He pulled the woman to the tips of her toes, using her shapely figure to completely cover himself from the silent figure standing upon the stairs. He pressed his dagger to her throat, bringing a tiny bead of blood running down the steel.

'Stay back, warlock!' Volk shouted, his voice filled more with panic than menace. 'One step closer, and I'll gut this whore like a pig!'

The cloaked wizard remained unmoving upon the stairs, his eyes still trained upon the mob leader. Volk's face formed itself into a twisted grin. He began to back slowly across the hall, dragging Argula with him.

Volk's slow retreat ended in a cold, icy pain that shivered through his back and belly. The racketeer's dagger fell from his numbed hand, all the strength and vitality withering in his veins. Argula slipped from his slackened grip, shivering as she recoiled from the thug. Volk stared in disbelief at a sluggish crimson stain slowly spreading across his tunic, his incredulous gaze returning to the still unmoving figure on the stairs.

The illusion gradually faded, as the real wizard stepped around from behind the stricken racketeer, the tip of his sword wet with Volk's blood. The pitiless eyes of the magister bored into those of Gustav Volk as his dying frame crumpled to its knees.

'When you sit before Morr, tell him others are coming,' the wizard hissed to the expiring mobsman. A gasped gargle rose from Volk's throat, then the racketeer slumped onto the floor.

The wizard turned from the last of the racketeers, turning his steely gaze across those who had been Volk's prisoners. If the crowd had cowered before the racketeers, they trembled before the grey-cloaked magister. He lifted a hand, his long fingers no longer coated in a dark skin of arcane shadows. He pointed at Argula.

'The smuggler, where was he taken?' the wizard demanded.

Before the violence and brutality of Gustav Volk, Argula had been prepared to remain stalwart and defiant, sacrificing her own life if need be to keep her beau safe. Faced with the eldritch menace of the wizard's hissed words, her courage wilted.

'Upstairs,' she said, her voice quivering with fear and guilt. 'Hans is inside the old priest hole.'

'Show me,' the wizard commanded, gesturing to the stairs.

Reluctantly, Argula stepped around the sprawled bodies of the dead racketeers, trying to keep her eyes from looking at their ugly, blackened wounds. She could sense rather than hear the cloaked magister following her, his very presence exuding an aura of wrongness, of offence against everything natural and pure.

A sharp cry from the hall below caused Argula to turn about. The apothecary, Sergei, was crumpled on the floor, gripping a bleeding leg and moaning. Gustaf Schlecht stood over him, a grisly-looking surgical hook gripped in his grimy fist. He looked up at Argula with the same sadistic smile he had displayed when she was being threatened by Volk.

'The toff's fallen down and hurt hisself,' Schlecht croaked, his voice dripping with brutish humour.

'Figured maybe I should look to him. I'm something of a doctor, after all.' He laughed at his own crude humour. Surgery, even the simple stitches Schlecht was called upon to minister to injured bouncers and bar patrons, wasn't a matter of healing to the man, but rather an excuse for indulging his own sadism.

Argula glanced back at the wizard, expecting that grim figure to intercede, to spare Sergei the cruel attentions of Schlecht. Instead she found the same grim countenance watching her from beneath the shadow of his grey hood. Remorseless, implacable, the wizard continued to follow Argula, utterly unmoved by the plight of Volk's informant. By casting his lot in with racketeers, Sergei had earned his fate.

The priest hole was a tiny alcove hidden behind the closet of one of the bedrooms. Argula pulled aside the rack of dresses that filled the space, exposing the little iron-banded door. A relic from the days of the Ulrican schism, when the cult of Ulric had sought to scour Altdorf of its Sigmarite faith, there were many priest holes to be found in the older structures of the city. They were places of refuge and concealment for the hunted priests, places from which the cult of Sigmar could continue to minister to the masses of Altdorf and maintain a presence and influence in the city.

Now the tiny room hid a different sort of cleric. Leni Kleifoth, the demure priestess of Shallya, huddled against the doorway, her face flush with a resigned defiance. Utterly committed to non-violence, there was little a member of her order could do to oppose brutal men such as Volk's mob, but at the same time, striking down a priestess was one of the few villainies that gave even the basest outlaw qualms of conscience.

When she saw the grey figure standing behind Argula, Leni's expression changed, becoming dour and uncertain. She looked sadly at Argula and allowed the woman to slip past her into the little room. Argula threw herself beside a little heap of blankets upon which Hans's pallid body was strewn like a sickly scarecrow. Filthy brown liquid dribbled from his body, ugly green worms crawled visibly beneath his skin. The groans of pain rising from Hans were quickly drowned out by the weeping of his woman.

'Report,' the cold voice of the wizard rasped, tearing Leni's eyes from the piteous scene.

'I have tended the man to the best of my skills,' Leni said. 'I have made prayers to the goddess and burned incense in the victim's name. I have...' her voice grew weak with guilt. 'I have allowed him to drink the sacred tears, and have administered the other treatments dictated by my orders.'

'Results.'

Leni shook her head, stifling her own tears. 'The victim remains unresponsive, the infection continues to grow and spread. There is nothing more to do except pray to the goddess.'

'This is poison, not true disease,' the wizard said, gesturing to the broken shape of the smuggler. 'It attacks what is inside the man, not the man himself. Your failure to heal him proves the nature of this evil.'

The priestess threw back her shoulders, glaring at the cloaked wizard. 'Even if I fail, I must still try to help this man!'

A dark chuckle hissed from the wizard's concealed lips, amused by the boldness of the priestess and her fealty to her vows. 'Admirable, but useless.' His stormy gaze returned to the stricken Hans. 'The only help you can render him is the only help your vows forbid you to bestow.' His fingers spread, forming a splayed claw.

In response to the wizard's gesture, ribbons of shadow slithered from the gloomy room, enveloping Hans's head. The smuggler gasped as the ribbons wrapped about him. His body thrashed against the blankets while Argula fought helplessly to pull the smothering darkness from his face. A minute, no more, and Hans was still. Argula held his hand, sobbing as she felt life pass from it. At the same time, the ribbons of shadow dissipated, exposing Hans's lifeless features.

'Release from agony,' the wizard told Leni. As he gazed upon the priestess, for the first time there was a hint of sympathy in the magister's grey eyes. 'The tranquil peace of death.' The sympathy drained away, once more the steely gaze was a thing of fire and judgement.

'Check the woman for any sign of infection,' he ordered the priestess. 'Baer will arrive to burn the carcass of the man. My familiar will collect your written record at the usual time.'

'I obey,' Leni said, her tone subservient, laced with equal measures of respect and fear.

There was nothing more. Like a patch of lingering night burned away by the dawn, the wizard's body faded away, leaving only the empty doorway and the narrow walls of the closet.

AFTER THE THIRD attempt, Skrim Gnawtail was finally able to suggest a hideout that was not utterly beneath the dignity and position of Grey Seer Thanquol. The skaven priest-sorcerer's new lair was an old townhouse house on Altdorf's prosperous Reikhoch Prachstrasse. The structure had sat alone and abandoned for years, shunned by the humans who dwelt around it. Ugly rumours had circulated about Contessa Eleanora Daria di Argentisso, the last tenant of the townhouse. Stories of vampirism and even more unspeakable acts of evil.

Thanquol cared for the superstitious fright of humans only so far as it lent itself to his own purposes. If stories of vampires and ghosts kept the foolish animals from intruding upon his solitude, so much the better. He had enough flesh-and fur enemies to occupy his thoughts without adding phantoms and spectres to his worries.

The grey seer prowled through the dusty halls of the townhouse, dead leaves crunching under his feet. He wrinkled his nose as he nearly stepped into the wispy net of an immense cobweb stretching across the hallway. Angrily, he swatted the obstruction down with the head of his staff and smashed a fat-bellied spider beneath its iron-capped butt. The incident in the Maze of Merciless Penance had left Thanquol in no mood to abide the presence of insects, arachnids and all their crawling kind. If he had the underlings to spare, he would have the townhouse scoured from attic to cellar and all its creeping denizens exterminated.

Unfortunately, Thanquol didn't have the minions to spare. Barely two dozen of them had escaped the ambush laid by Skrattch Skarpaw and the treacherous clan lords of Under-Altdorf. Most of the survivors were Skrim's slippery sneaks and Viskitt Burnfang's warlock engineers. It was just as well – they were the most useful to him, far more valuable under the present circumstances than a battalion of stormvermin. Even their small numbers were preferable; too many and they might think to earn their way back into the graces of Under-Altdorf by betraying Thanquol to their old masters. Fortunately, he judged their numbers too insignificant to dare any mischief against a sorcerer of his maleficent might.

Even if they were, there was Boneripper to consider. Since escaping from the sewers, Thanquol had been careful to keep his clever, cunning bodyguard as close to him as possible. It was a situation that had played havoc with the townhouse's doorways and ceilings, but the humans had abandoned the dwelling anyway. More important than Skrim's paranoia about leaving evidence of their brief occupancy was keeping Boneripper where the rat ogre could savage his master's enemies before they could endanger Thanquol's valuable hide.

There had been a few others who had escaped the sewers with the Clan Skaul sneaks and the Clan Skryre warlock engineers. Thanquol saw little value in keeping a motley clawful of clanrat warriors and beastmasters around, especially when their added strength might just give Skrim or Burnfang ugly ambitions. There was another purpose they could be put to that would help him far more than their ability to catch rats or bear arms. All of his slave subjects were back in Under-Altdorf, a place he didn't dare show his scent. It was more important than ever that his experiments with the Wormstone proceed on schedule. Lacking either numbers or leadership, the ragged survivors of the other clan delegations were perfect proxies for Thanquol's absent supply of slave-subjects. Of course, the treacherous cowards didn't see it that way, but Thanquol had ways to enforce his will.

Viskitt Burnfang built a crude laboratory in the spacious old kitchens of the townhouse, even cobbling together a complex array of pipes to divert the smoke from his improvised furnace down into the townhouse's cellar. It wouldn't do, after all, to have smoke rising from a supposedly vacant house. That was the sort of thing the man-things just might take it in mind to investigate.

Burnfang attacked the experiments with his usual scheming and eye for sinister innovation. Using the townhouse's larder as a make-do slave pen, he had found a new way to administer the Wormstone by tainting the drinking water of the unlucky wretches. The liquid somehow diluted the poisonous infection, but if it lacked some of its former swiftness, it retained its grisly potency. Thanquol was pleased with the results, and the new means of introducing the infection to the enemies of skavendom. Indeed, it set the grey seer's mind considering new potential for this weapon, potential that would set him among the greatest skaven to ever live – or at least even higher in those august ranks since no ratman could claim such a legacy of success, brilliance, and valour as himself.

Thanquol paused beside one of the slave-subjects, a moaning warrior whose fur was already starting to fall out as ugly worm-like growths burst from beneath his skin. He watched every flicker of pain and suffering on the captive's face, picturing the faces of Thratquee and Skarpaw and all the other scum who had betrayed him gripped by such pain! His enemies would not be allowed the leisure to regret baring their fangs to Grey Seer Thanquol!

'Skrim!' Thanquol snarled. The little Clan Skaul spy came creeping into the kitchen, his feet slipping on the smooth marble tiles. His head bobbed up and down in frightened subservience to his tyrannical master. 'Get your best sniffers! Somewhere in this filthy human-warren there will be a place of records. The man-things do nothing without writing it down. I want to know where they take their water from!'

'Their water?' asked Skrim, not understanding.

The question drew a look of disgust from Burnfang, but the warlock engineer simply shook his head and returned to his experiments. Thanquol bristled more at Burnfang's manlike gesture than Skrim's idiotic lack of vision.

'Yes-yes, their water, fool-meat!' Thanquol snarled. If the spy had been close enough, he would have cracked his snout with his staff. As it was, he made do with a threatening display of fangs. 'They will have maps, charts of their city. Bring the ones that show their canals and aqueducts!'

Skrim muttered a string of obsequious assurances that he would follow Thanquol's commands and scurried from the makeshift laboratory with indecent haste.

Thanquol looked over at Burnfang, his lip curling in loathing. He would kill two fleas with one scratch. The degenerates of Under-Altdorf were so dependent upon the humans for their way of life, stealing not merely food and supplies, but even customs and mannerisms. He was certain they were also dependent upon the same source of water as the man-things. By poisoning the human city, he would at the same time be poisoning Under-Altdorf and all of his enemies there! It was a grand stroke only a skaven of his genius would have conceived! The capitol of the humans devastated and at the same time the rebellious degenerates of Under-Altdorf annihilated.

Besides, Thanquol thought, if the Lords of Decay did complain, he could always shift the blame to Skrim Gnawtail for bringing him incomplete maps.

ALONE, WET, TIRED, the wound on his head still dripping blood and trying his best to follow the trail of one of Clan Eshin's elite killers, Kratch was far from happy. Only the apprentice's lust for revenge against Grey Seer Thanquol silenced the fear that hammered through his heart, driving him onward. He knew he was too weak to confront Thanquol alone. The trick would lie in convincing Skarpaw that the assassin needed *him* if he was to succeed in eliminating their mutual enemy.

Kratch followed the assassin for what seemed hours, sloshing through the reeking sewers of the humans and old, seldom used rat-runs whose ceilings creaked and whose walls displayed generations of neglect as they crumbled beneath Kratch's whiskers. Skarpaw, like all of the assassins of Clan Eshin, did not have an individual scent, his glands having been removed in one of the clan's mysterious eastern rituals. However, if Kratch could not pick out Skarpaw from any other skaven by his scent, the assassin could not hide the fact that he still had the distinctive smell of all ratmen. So long as no other skaven crossed Skarpaw's trail, Kratch's nose would be able to track him without confusion.

The trail led Kratch into a particularly ramshackle section of sewer. A long-ago collapse had filled the tunnel with rubble from the street above. The wreckage had simply been bricked over by the humans, who had diverted their waste around the compromised section of tunnel. The shoddy excavation that Skarpaw crawled into to reach the forgotten channel was so poor, Kratch doubted it was the work of either man or skaven, more likely the labour of mutants or scrawny, slinking sewer goblins.

Crawling after Skarpaw through the cramped, debris-strewn passage, Kratch was struck by the putrid stink of the place. It was a smell of death and decay, of rot and ruin, of sickness and corruption. No skaven who had once encountered such a smell could ever forget it; the smell of the plague monks, the diseased fanatics of Clan Pestilens.

Kratch's hackles rose and he fought the urge to squirt the musk of fear. He could pick out the individual scents of other skaven from the air, not simply one or two, but dozens. Some were alive with loathsomeness, others were the foul smells of the dead. Kratch recoiled from the horror of realising how little difference there was between the two.

Kratch pressed his body flat in the narrow tunnel, trying to work up the nerve to continue. The faint sound of voices gave him something to concentrate upon besides his own fear. One voice was the whispered snarl of Skarpaw, the other was a gurgling croak thick with evil. The adept strained to make out words, but the distance was too great. Gingerly, with as much care as he had ever shown in his entire life of scheming and spying, Kratch crept closer, clenching his teeth as the sickening smell of the plague monks grew more intense.

Now Kratch could put words to voices. Skarpaw was explaining his recent failure to the plague monk leader. The assassin's tone was strangely servile, lacking the authority and threat of an Under-Altdorf clan leader. There was actually a trace of fear running through Skarpaw's words, a desperate, almost pleading anxiety Kratch had never thought to hear come from the mouth of an assassin. Hearing Skarpaw's fear fanned the flames of his own, and Kratch began to slowly crawl back through the narrow opening. A sudden shift in the conversation arrested his retreat, however, and the adept crooked his ears as he heard the filthy croak of the plague monk mention Thanquol and the Wormstone. He started to creep forwards again, ignoring the stink of death and corruption all around him.

'...certain you have been followed?' the croaking plague monk asked.

'Yes-yes, rotten one!' Skarpaw's anxious voice replied. 'Long-long has his scent been in my nose!'

A tremor of terror sizzled through Kratch's brain. Fool-fool to think he could follow one of Clan Eshin's killers without the assassin knowing it!

Panicked, Kratch started to crawl away. As he did so, the smell of dead ratman swelled around him. He felt scrawny paws close tight about his ankles, holding him firm as he lashed about to free himself. Threshing his body about, Kratch was able to see the dead-smelling things that held him. They were skaven, once, but now they had more kinship to corpses than living ratmen. Their fur hung from their bodies in wet strips, peeling away from skin that looked as lifeless as boiled meat. Tatters that might once have been robes clung to their near-skeletal frames, while blemished eyes gleamed rabidly from the sunken sockets of withered skulls. The things glistened with a sheen of pus that seemed to exude from every pore.

Kratch shrieked and flailed all the harder in the grip of the diseased ratmen, his lips stumbling over the syllables of a spell. Firm paws gripped him about head and shoulder, strong claws clamping his mouth closed before he could work his magic. Beset from before and behind, Kratch flailed helplessly in the grip of his captors.

The oozing ratmen carried their quarry out of the tunnel and into a large vault. Scummy water sloshed beneath the feet of the skaven as they stalked through the chamber. Ahead, on an island of broken bricks and mud, a cluster of ratmen watched the procession with malicious amusement. Robes, pelts and bodies were in better condition than the wretched specimens that had captured Kratch, but not one of them was without the stamp of disease. Even Skarpaw's black-cloaked figure seemed pallid and infirm, his limbs trembling as with an ague.

'See-look!' the assassin crowed, pointing a claw at Kratch. 'The traitor-priest's apprentice! All-all is as I have true-told!'

The creature Skarpaw addressed was such a ghastly-looking specimen that he made even the wretched ratmen carrying Kratch seem the picture of health. Bloated with corruption, his face lost beneath a mass of boils, his fur limited to green-tinged patches, the plague lord peered evilly from beneath the grimy folds of his hood.

'Yessss,' the plague lord's voice bubbled through a mouth almost barren of fangs. 'You have true-told. This time.' One of the creature's wasted hands pulled a little vial from a ratskin bag hanging from the rope that circled his waist. Almost absently, the plague lord dropped it at his feet. Skarpaw pounced after the vial, chasing after it as it bounced down the bricks towards the filthy water. Bloated plague rats, of the four-legged kind, scattered before his frantic pursuit. The plague monks laughed at the assassin's terror, their voices sounding like a chorus of maggots. Skarpaw caught the vial just as it struck the water, his hand coated in green scum as he pressed the vessel to his lips and guzzled its contents with abandon.

Lord Skrolk chortled at the pathetic spectacle. 'Have no fear-fright, Skarpaw-slave. Lord Skrolk keep-honours his promise-squeak. You may wait ten bells before you must earn-beg more medicine.' The plague lord made the last word sound as though it held all the evil in the world within it. The other plague monks wrinkled their muzzles at the sound, muttering a wheezing chant that sounded like nothing so much as the buzzing of flies.

Lord Skrolk pushed his way through his green-robed disciples, his rheumy eyes focused on Kratch. A flick of the plague lord's scabby claw and the wretched creatures holding the adept set him down. They glared sullenly at Lord Skrolk, like so many abused curs fearing their master's cruel whims. Another flick of the plague lord's claw and the sickly ratmen retreated back through the scummy water, keeping just near enough to pounce on Kratch should the apprentice seer try to escape.

'Thanquol's lick-spit,' Skrolk said, fixing Kratch with his putrid gaze. The plague lord's breath was like an over-ripe midden, making the adept gag. 'You are fool-meat to spy-sneak for your master.' Skrolk's lips pulled back, exposing the few blackened fangs still clinging to his gums. 'Tell-speak, where is your master and what he has stolen?'

Kratch found enough desperate courage to force words up his throat. 'I-I serve not-not Thanquol thief-traitor! I-I am brother-under-the-fur to your most obscene eminence, father of decay and despair! Death to the traitor-meat! Death-suffer for Thanquol!' For emphasis, Kratch spat after pronouncing the name of his old mentor.

Lord Skrolk simply stared at the snivelling apprentice, the snarl never leaving his diseased face. 'I... Clan Pestilens desires the Wormstone,' Skrolk growled. 'Arrogant Thanquol is no-no interest. Your revenge is no-no interest.'

Skrolk waved his paw. One of the plague monks drew a rusty dagger from beneath his robes and started to descend the slope of the island. Kratch dropped to his knees, quivering in the cold filth of the flooded vault.

'Mercy-pity, great doom-breeder, sire of a thousand poxes!' Kratch's whines became even more rapid when he saw that flattery had done nothing to arrest the descent of his executioner. 'Kratch can take mighty Lord Skrolk to what his former traitor-teacher has stolen!'

Lord Skrolk's face narrowed with suspicion, but he raised a paw, stopping the executioner's descent. Kratch hurried to explain his meaning to the plague lord. 'When I tried to save-protect the Wormstone from thieving Thanquol, I placed upon it my seer-sign.' Kratch gestured with his claws, giving some hint of the sorcerous symbol he had scratched into the rock. 'I can see-scent my seer-sign wherever Thanquol-thief takes it.' The adept tapped the side of his head, indicating that his sense of the magical mark was something he sensed in his mind rather than a thing some skaven with better eyes or nose could hope to find.

Skrolk's snarl lessened by a fraction. He waved his scabby claw and the sickly ratmen came swarming forwards, seizing Kratch. Savagely they tore at him, ripping away his grey robes and leaving him naked and shivering before the island of plague monks. Skrolk waved his paw again and three plague monks climbed down the mass of bricks and mud, carrying with them the body of a fourth. Callously, they stripped the diseased carcass of its tattered green robe and threw it to Kratch. Instinctively, the adept caught the flung garment. He stifled the impulse to cast it aside, trying not to look too closely at it, or pay attention to the way the flea-ridden cloth seemed to crawl beneath his fingers.

'Brother-under-the-fur,' Skrolk laughed. 'Now you are brother-true. Reject false-words of seers and embrace true face of the Horned One! Bring Skrolk to the Wormstone, and you will be plague priest. Betray,' the word was nothing but a bestial snarl at the back of Skrolk's throat, 'and you become pus-bag.'

Kratch followed Skrolk's extended finger, cringing when he saw that the plague lord was pointing at the rotting, pseudo-dead things that had captured him. Hurriedly, Kratch started to don the filthy green robe, trying to give an impression of enthusiasm.

Skarpaw crept forwards as the adept was dressing himself. 'Thanquol will not give up the Wormstone without a fight. His magic is powerful-strong, and his rat ogre is worth any fifty of your plague monks!'

Lord Skrolk glared at the assassin. 'I will deal with the seer's corrupt sorcery,' his bubbling voice declared. Again, the plague lord made a gesture with his scabby paw. This time it was not the ratmen on the island who reacted to his command, but another group of plague monks gathered at a brick-lined archway across from the little tunnel Kratch had crawled through. At his gesture, the ratmen began pulling on heavy bronze chains, fighting to pull something into the dim light of the vault. Kratch froze and turned his head as he heard something huge sloshing through the water of a flooded sewer and into the vault. Skarpaw drew his wicked swords and dropped into a crouch of tense muscles and pounding heart. Skrolk simply grinned his black-toothed smile.

'Pox and Nox will deal with Boneripper.'

Grey Seer Thanquol inhaled a pinch of warpstone snuff and snickered as he studied the diagrams Skrim's agents had stolen from one of Altdorf's civic buildings. The skaven had stolen dozens of plans for everything from sewers to the Imperial Menagerie, and hundreds of worthless documents even the most addle-witted ratman should have been able to recognise as being useless, but it was this set of mouldy old parchment maps that best suited Thanquol's grand vision.

They were old, hundreds of generations old by the standards of the short-lived skaven. They had been drawn up by dwarf artisans in the distant times when the squabbling humans had warred amongst themselves and laid siege to one another each spring. The men of Altdorf had feared for their security, seeking to establish lines of supply that would withstand any attacker, no matter how large his army. The dwarf diagrams represented a solution to the city's most pressing concern: a reliable supply of water independent of the River Reik. The burrowing beard-things had found an underground lake beneath the oldest part of the human city. Through a clever network of subterranean channels and pipes, the dwarfs had made the lake into a reservoir that could supply the entire city for an indefinite period. Fed by still deeper streams and rivers, the lake was an almost bottomless well to sate the thirst of the humans.

It was also, Skrim reluctantly confirmed, the main source of fresh water for the skaven city of Under-Altdorf as well.

Thanquol lashed his tail in amusement and rolled up the diagrams, stuffing them into his belt. The reservoir would be the perfect place to strike! In one fell swoop, he would poison the largest human settlement in the Empire and destroy the treacherous heretics of Under-Altdorf! Even the Lords of Decay would be forced to bow before the genius of such a masterful stroke. Thanquol rubbed his paws together, imagining the honours and rewards they would heap upon him.

The grey seer rose from the claw-footed chair, some of its decaying velvet clinging to his robes as he stood. Thanquol padded across the dusty wreckage of what had once been the townhouse's study, Boneripper's immense bulk plodding a respectful three paces behind him. He wrinkled his nose, sniffing the air, catching the faint odour of Wormstone. Following the sounds of activity, he descended to the ground floor of the townhouse, creeping into what had been the front parlour.

The room no longer bore even the echo of its former function. Under Burnfang's frantic direction, it had been transformed into a workshop, every table in the abandoned townhouse pressed into service to support stone pestles and mortars. The warlock engineer's minions worked at a frenzied pace, their snouts lost behind masks of rat-gut and leather, their hands covered in what looked like oversized mittens. The workers laboured at their pestles, grinding slivers of Wormstone down into a fine grit of poison. The grit, in turn, was poured into wine bottles looted from the cellar of the townhouse. Fabulously rare and priceless vintages had been callously spilled across the floor as the ratmen emptied the bottles in preparation for receiving far more sinister contents.

Thanquol grinned as he watched his underlings work. Soon they would pulverise the last of the Wormstone. Soon they would be ready to strike! Then none would dare defy the might and power of Grey Seer Thanquol! From the spires of Skavenblight to the lowest rat-burrow, all the Under-Empire would grovel before the fury of Thanquol!

Watching his minions work but taking small notice of their actual labours, Thanquol didn't notice Viskitt Burnfang quietly pour a small measure of crushed

Wormstone into a little glass sphere, nor observe the warlock engineer carefully set the sphere inside one of his many belt pouches.

Burnfang glanced up at the grey seer and struggled to hide his snarl of contempt. The time would soon come to disabuse Thanquol of his arrogance.

DEEP BENEATH THE streets of Altdorf, something stirred in the darkness. Powerful nostrils flared, sniffing at the air. Thousands of scents and smells raced through the tiny brain of the beast, each quickly dismissed and discarded. From all the myriad odours of the city, from the countless stenches of its sewers to the innumerable smells of its markets and thoroughfares, the sensitive nose picked out the one scent that had aroused its interest, the scent that had twice drawn it up from the black underworld and into the city above.

The rat-beast rose from its haunches, filthy sewer water dripping from its scalded hide. The clammy chill of the noxious canal soothed its oozing wounds, the muck of the brick-lined channel cooling its burnt flesh. The monster was loath to abandon its refuge, but the intoxicating scent of the Wormstone pulled at its primitive senses, drawing it like a moth to a flame. It chattered angrily to itself, despising this impulse it could neither understand nor control.

Slowly, the rat-beast began to lope through the dank tunnels of Altdorf's sewers, its keen nose trained on the guiding scent of its poisonous quarry, following the scent with the unerring precision of a lodestone.

CHAPTER ELEVEN
Gone to Ground

'WHAT HAPPENS NOW?'

The question lingered in the little back room of the *Black Bat,* almost as though by being spoken, it had assumed life and substance of its own. The echoes seemed to seep into the soot-stained plaster walls, to crawl into the scarred timber benches and heavy oak table. The uncertain tone recoiled from the stone-lined fireplace, repulsed by the cold breeze whistling down the chimney.

Johann Dietrich's companions shared a grim, forbidding look. It had taken three of them to keep him from rushing to the *Crown and Two Chairmen* to save his brother from Gustav Volk's doubtful mercy. He was uncertain which of the three had struck him with a leather sap, though there was a sinister aspect about the sharp, leathery features of the swarthy Tilean leaning against the room's only door that made him Johann's first choice. The Tilean gave him a sour look in turn, making it clear he didn't care a groat for what Johann thought of him.

The other two were seated at the table with Johann. One was a burly, wild-haired man wearing a heavy leather slicker and an almost shapeless felt hat. If pressed, Johann would have guessed his vocation as coachman or perhaps barge captain. He had a cunning glint to his eye that reminded him of merchants and other swindlers, but was weathered enough to look like he was no stranger to real work.

The second man at the table was less formidable in build, but a good deal more sinister in aspect. He was dressed better than the Tilean and the coachman, his clothes sporting a finery only racketeers and ship captains dared display on the waterfront; the little designs on his eelskin boots were picked out in gold leaf, the buckle of his belt was a monstrous assemblage of amethyst and jade, the pearl hilts of his matched daggers were shaped like snarling sharks and each eye was picked out with a tiny ruby. Seeing the daggers, Johann came to the cold realisation that he knew this man, even if he had never set eyes upon him before. No one on the waterfront had failed to hear of Simo Valkoinen. Next to the 'Murder Prince' Dieter Neff, he was the most infamous assassin-for-hire in Altdorf. How many of the bloated bodies found floating in the Reik could be credited to Valkoinen and his 'Fangs of Stromfels', no one could say for certain. It was certain that Valkoinen, the 'Cold Death' as the criminals of the waterfront had named him, was not offering any official tally of his work.

Valkoinen! Johann's mind reeled under the implication, the certainty that this formidable hired killer was actually one of the helpers, the servants of the mysterious wizard who had saved his life. What sort of man could command the loyalty of a killer like Valkoinen? What sort of man would want to?

'What happens next largely depends on you.'

Johann's answer came from a fifth occupant of the little room. When he had regained consciousness, Johann hadn't noticed the little political agitator Ludwig Rothfels. He took a seat on the bench beside Valkoinen and the coachman. The pleasant-faced agitator looked almost ridiculous sitting between the brawny coachman and the sinister assassin, like a cook's ladle set between a pair of swords.

'You will be given a choice,' Ludwig continued, staring intently into Johann's face. 'The same choice all of us were called upon to make. You will be given the opportunity to serve the master and help him in his work.'

Johann shook his head, snorting with ill humour. 'The master and his work,' he repeated. 'You make it sound very mysterious.'

'Because it is,' growled the Tilean from his place against the wall.

The smuggler growled back at the scowling foreigner. 'Just the same, I'd like to know what noose you want me to put my neck in.' He returned his attention to Ludwig. 'Just who is this "master" of yours and what is this work he asks you to help him with?'

Ludwig seemed to consider the question for a long time, and when he finally answered, there was a note of uncertainty in his voice. 'We know him by the name of Jeremias Scrivner and he is a wizard of terrible power. There are many who serve him, far more than you saw at the *Orc and Axe*. The master has eyes and ears throughout the city, perhaps even beyond. How many may number themselves among his servants, only he could say.' Ludwig paused and sighed deeply as though remembering some past guilt. 'As for his "work", Scrivner is devoted to the defence of Altdorf against all those who would bring evil upon the city.'

Johann stood, shaking his head. 'It seems to me he has a strange way of fighting evil.' He swung his pointing finger around the room. 'A rabble-rouser, a hired killer, a smuggler, a Tilean alley rat...'

The Tilean pushed himself from the wall, one hand dropping to the slender rapier he wore. 'You watch who you call "rat" or I make nice red grin in your neck!'

'Amando, please,' Ludwig called out. 'He did not understand what he said.'

The Tilean sneered at Johann. 'He doesn' understand? They never understand! They bring their dirty rock into the city. Then ratkin, they come to take the rock, and whatever else they wanta take!' Amando's face became livid as he saw the incredulous expression on Johann's face. 'You think maybe I no know what I talk about, hey little thief?' He tapped himself on the chest. 'I'm from Miragliano. I see with my own eyes what ratkin do when they take it into their heads to stop slinking in their tunnels!'

'If the problem is so serious, then why are you sitting around here?' demanded Johann. He trembled as he remembered the ghastly creatures he had fought in the cellar and the hate-filled gaze of their horned leader. 'Why doesn't your master notify the authorities, bring the Reiksguard and the witch hunters and the whole of the Imperial army down upon them?'

'Because the underfolk are a myth.' The hissing words came from the darkened corner of the little room, a space so small that Johann was certain no one could have hidden there. Even the other men in the room betrayed uneasy wonder as a grey-cloaked figure stepped from the shadows, the darkness swirling about his lean form like little fingers of black fog. The stormy grey eyes of Jeremias Scrivner met each of his minions in turn, subduing even Amando's anger with the imperious power of his gaze. The wizard's attention lingered on Johann and the smuggler stumbled back, dropping down onto the timber bench.

'They must remain a myth,' Scrivner continued. 'Ignorance is the best shield the Empire has, the ratkin themselves our best allies against the threat of the skaven. While man remains ignorant of their world, the skaven feel safe to war amongst themselves, pursuing their petty intrigues and vendettas. Given a common foe, given a common purpose, their entire race would unite into a single horde and smother the world of men beneath their numbers. For the survival of the Empire, the underfolk must remain a fable told to children.'

'But you can't just let such monsters go free!' protested Johann. He gestured to Ludwig and the other men in the room. 'They tell me that you are some manner of champion, a fighter against evil. What could be more evil than these ratmen! You must fight them!'

A flicker of approval seemed to pass through Scrivner's colourless eyes. The wizard lifted a long-fingered hand, halting Johann's impassioned words. 'I will fight them. You and your friends brought a terrible thing into this city. In doing so, you have placed Altdorf in great peril. At the same time, you may have saved all who dwell between its walls.'

Every eye was on the wizard as he swept across the dimly lit room. His hands were beneath his cloak, and when they emerged there was a little lead box gripped between his fingers. Carefully he set the box down and stepped back. A muffled incantation hissed from Scrivner's hidden lips and an invisible hand opened the catch on the box. The lid sprang back, exposing a little shard of greenish-black rock that glowed evilly in the darkness.

'Wyrdstone,' gasped Johann.

'So book-foolish men would say,' Scrivner said. He pointed at the box. 'What is in there is more dangerous than warpstone – what ignorant scholars once named wyrdstone to deceive themselves and cloak their own fears. This is poison and pestilence cast into stone by the foulest of magics. To touch this is to touch death.'

'Kleiner! And my... my brother!'

Scrivner nodded grimly. 'They handled the stone and its evil seeped into their veins. Even the grace of Shallya could not stave off the taint which ravaged Hans Dietrich.'

Johann's face became pale, his entire body seeming to wilt as he heard the wizard pronounce his brother's doom. Hans was dead then? Taken by the horrible disease that had ravaged him. No, not a disease, but some kind of abominable poison created by the ratmen!

'I will not accept this!' Johann snarled. 'Kempf handled the rock more than my brother, you saw him in the cellar chipping pieces from it to steal for himself! If it was poisonous, he would have fallen ill long before Hans!'

'Kempf was an addict of a substance called black dust, a foul derivative of warpstone sold to human distributors by opportunistic skaven,' Scrivner said. 'Use of the drug caused the thief's body to build a greater tolerance to the poison, though he too would have succumbed in time. Your brother, lacking Kempf's vice, was more susceptible to even a slight exposure to the stone.'

Johann slumped against the table, holding his head in his hands, his last desperate defiance of Scrivner's words crushed by the wizard's cold logic. Accepting his explanation, Johann was also forced to accept the news that his brother was dead.

'The stone works upon a simple principle,' Scrivner continued, this time his words intended for all within the room. 'It could be likened to a lodestone, only drawn to warpstone instead of metal and operating in far more horrible fashion. It feeds upon warpstone residue trapped within living bodies, drawing it together into tubular, worm-like growths. Warpstone dust is everywhere and in everything, but seldom in concentrations pronounced enough to do harm. This stone,' the wizard pointed again at the box. With his gesture, the lid snapped closed once more. 'This stone draws those harmless traces of warpstone dust into deadly knots of corruption and mutation. I suspect that the stone is even more deadly to the ratkin, whose entire metabolism is saturated with warp-stone.'

'Then why would the ratkin create such a thing?' asked Ludwig.

'Because they do not value the lives of their own,' the wizard said. 'To the skaven there is nothing so cheap as the life of a ratman. If they must lose ten of their own to kill a single enemy, then they count it a bargain so long as they are not one of the ten.'

'We cannot let the ratkin get away with plot! They make of Altdorf what they do to Miragliano!' Amando raged.

'There are agents and powers already seeking the stone,' Scrivner said. 'If the skaven have taken it any-where in the city, I shall learn of it.'

Johann lifted his head from the table, hate smouldering in his eyes. 'They have to be destroyed,' he growled, his voice cold as a winter grave. 'Every last one of them.'

The wizard nodded his hooded head, his grey eyes burning in the darkness. 'You will get your opportunity, Johann Dietrich,' he said.

Scrivner reached to the table, collecting the little lead box. As he removed it, Johann was surprised to see that something had been left in its place. It was a small, flat rectangle of strangely-hued gold like nothing he had ever seen before. The surface of the token was richly engraved with writhing serpents and crawling lizards, a stylised sun peering from between two eclipsing moons forming the centrepiece of the engraving.

'My talisman,' the wizard said, motioning for Johann to collect the token. 'All who serve me bear such a coin,' he continued, watching as the smuggler's fingers lifted the gold rectangle to his face that he might inspect it more closely. 'By accepting it, you become one of my servants. You agree to follow my orders without question or hesitation. You agree to place no loyalty above that which you shall render to me, not that of family, gods or Empire.'

'If I refuse?' Johann asked, his eyes never leaving the strange coin.

'Then you will forget about avenging your brother's death.' The wizard's cold words cut through the air like a knife.

Johann looked again at the grey-shrouded apparition, trying to fathom the mind that regarded him from behind those sinister, colourless eyes. At last he nodded and slipped the coin into his pocket. It did not matter to him any more what Scrivner's motives were, what the wizard's intentions were. It was enough that he promised Johann revenge. For that, Johann would follow the magister into the Mouth of Chaos if he demanded it.

Suddenly there was a sound from the chimney, a rustling, scratching noise that set every man in the room on edge. Valkoinen's hands whisked daggers from his belt in a blinding flash, the coachman had an ugly-looking mace in his hand almost before Johann was aware the man had started to move. Amando drew pistol and rapier while Ludwig backed away, a knife clenched in his fist. Every man stood ready for action, their morbid imaginations fired by talk of ratkin and underfolk.

Only Scrivner remained as he had been, unperturbed by the sounds descending the chimney. The wizard turned slowly as the noise reached the bottom of the shaft, one hand gesturing at the hearth. Johann saw something dark slip from the opening, dropping onto the hearth with a wet flop. The dark shape shook itself, then, to the smuggler's alarm, it seemed to expand, growing in size and distorting its shape. Scrivner swung his pointing hand around, gesturing to the table. The thing in the hearth hissed at him, a low serpentine noise that made Johann's skin crawl. The dark shape launched itself into the air, gliding across the room to land atop the table.

Johann recoiled from the gruesome thing. It was coated from beak to talon in soot, so he could make no guess as to its true colour, but its shape and nature were far too apparent. What was under the soot was not feathers but reptilian scales, the long beak was filled with sharp little teeth, the wings were leathery and bat-like. A long tail stretched behind the thing, lending it even greater resemblance to some nightmarish union of snake and falcon.

The flying lizard's yellow eyes stared at Johann and it took a shuffling hop towards him. Then, suddenly, Scrivner's voice drew its attention away from the smuggler. Johann could not understand the slithering, hideous noises that rose from the magister's muffled face; if they were words then they were such words as did not belong on the tongues of men. His horror increased when he observed the ghastly lizard-hawk bobbing its head and fluttering its wings seemingly in response to Scrivner's hissing speech, as though the hideous thing were conversing with him!

Scrivner turned away from the lizard-hawk, again sweeping his gaze across the room. 'The stone has been found,' he said. He stared at the coachman, fixing the burly man with his stormy gaze. 'Take word to all who participated in operations at the *Orc and Axe*. Bring Grimbold Silverbeard; his knowledge is vital if the foe goes to ground. All operatives are to await me at the old di Argentisso house in the Reikhoch Prachstrasse.'

The coachman sketched a deep bow and hurried to carry out his orders. Scrivner watched him go, then considered his remaining minions. 'The rest of you will accompany me,' he said. His grey eyes drifted back to Johann, this time with a terrible scrutiny that made the smuggler even more uncomfortable than the renewed interest the lizard-hawk had displayed in him.

'Perhaps we will even be in time for Herr Dietrich to have his revenge,' Scrivner said, a trace of heaviness in his tone.

GREY SEER THANQUOL watched as the last of the subjects twitched and writhed on the floor of their cage. It turned out that Burnfang hadn't needed as many subjects as the pool of Thanquol's less useful minions had provided. He was pragmatic about the situation. Even if there was nothing worthwhile to be learned by exposing the ratmen to the Wormstone, it made for a most effective method for exterminating individuals who would certainly be looking for some chance at revenge if Thanquol allowed them to live. No, it was better not to risk their petty and vindictive treachery and simply get rid of them along with the others.

Burnfang and his warlock engineers were scurrying about the kitchen-laboratory, grinding down the last of the Wormstone and pouring the contents into the wine bottles. Thanquol remembered the way the thieving humans had used vinegar to mask the smell of the Wormstone from the skaven. He thought the sour wine from the cellar might do the same, though whether it could deceive something like the warp bats of Clan Moulder or some of Skrattch Skarpaw's slinking backstabbers, Thanquol was uncertain. The less consideration he gave to Grey Seer Thratquee using magic to find the Wormstone – and himself – the more comfortable he was. The sooner he eliminated the threat of that corrupt old rat and the entire treasonous council of Under-Altdorf, the better.

Thinking of Under-Altdorf, and the doom that would soon descend upon it, Thanquol abandoned his morbid observation of the corroding captives. He strode across the kitchen to the small parlour beyond, Boneripper trudging after him like a faithful hound. He had made the parlour into his command nest, filling it with such opulence as the mouldering furnishings of the abandoned townhouse could provide. A small entryway beyond the parlour opened upon the street. One of Skrim's sneaks was posted there, watching through the grimy windows, waiting to give warning should any human invaders descend upon Thanquol's refuge.

Similar lurkers were posted in the cellar and basement of the townhouse. These were separate rooms beneath the structure, the cellar connected to the kitchen, the basement reached only by a hidden door in what had been the study. Tunnels connected both of the subterranean rooms to the underworld of the skaven. If attackers came from beneath the townhouse rather than from outside, then Thanquol would use whichever tunnel his ratkin enemies didn't to make his escape. And if they somehow discovered both entrances...

Thanquol patted the remaining ratskin scroll tied to his belt. He'd inspected the document very carefully, assuring himself that the magic it professed to evoke was no forgery. To use such magic would mean abandoning his minions, but that was a sacrifice that didn't cause a second of doubt. It was, after all, the duty of the common ratman to give his life that the brilliance and fortitude of their betters should endure. Why, if they had the intelligence to see it, creatures like Skrim Gnawtail and Viskitt Burnfang could not fail to understand that the greatest accomplishment they could hope for in their dreary, scrabbling little lives would be to die for the glory of Grey Seer Thanquol!

Sadly, the wretches did not have such vision. As he entered the parlour, Thanquol found Skrim leaning over the teakwood chest upon which the grey seer had set the stolen maps and diagrams. There was a furtive, suspicious quality about the spy's manner that made Thanquol's lip curl. Boneripper sensed his master's disquiet and a threatening growl rumbled through the rat ogre's barrel chest.

Skrim scrambled away from the chest, claws clutching the badly-chewed stump of his tail. Age had dulled the spy's senses, allowing even something of Boneripper's size to steal upon him unawares. Any skaven in such a state was near the end of his race, the ravages of time leaving him easy prey to younger, faster upstarts.

'Find-smell anything interesting?' Thanquol challenged as he stepped to the chest and peered down at the maps. Boneripper lurched around the parlour, placing his bulk between the cowering spy and the doorways leading into the hallway proper and the old study. The grey seer chuckled at his monster's initiative. With himself between Skrim and the kitchen and the rat ogre placed where he was, the only path of retreat left open to the spy was a quick dash into the street outside. Allowing of course that the lurker at the threshold chose helping Skrim over incurring the wrath of the grey seer.

'No-no, mighty one!' Skrim insisted, dipping his head in deference to Thanquol. 'I was merely...'

'Spying?' Thanquol growled. Skrim was so taken aback by the fury with which the grey seer spoke the word that he actually started to nod his head. Thanquol glared at Skrim, taking a menacing step closer, flickers of power burning in his eyes. 'And what did we see-find, crook-backed sneak?'

'Nothing! Nothing most baleful holiness!' Skrim insisted, wringing his hands together. 'Skrim not-not read dwarf letters!'

Thanquol's fangs gleamed in the dingy light of the parlour. Skrim shivered as Boneripper's colossal shadow fell across him.

'Then how did you know they were dwarf runes if you could not read them?' Thanquol's paw rose, a nimbus of green energy gathering about his claws like a nest of swirling fireflies.

Skrim collapsed to the floor, fear-musk spurting from his glands, his mind trying to find some combination of falsehood and flattery that would appease the grey seer's rage. More realistically, he prayed to the Horned Rat for mercy.

Sharp squeals of terror and pain sounded from the kitchen. The glow faded from Thanquol's paw as the grey seer spun about, his body a confusion of anger and alarm. Wet, ripping sounds and bestial snarls thundered from the makeshift laboratory as Burnfang and his attendants burst through the door and spilled into the parlour. The Clan Skryre ratmen scrambled through the command nest, spilling furnishings and tearing tapestries in their headlong flight. One warlock engineer crashed into Thanquol, then careened onwards to upset the teakwood chest and spill the stolen maps across the floor. Before Thanquol could hurl a curse against the skaven who had knocked him over, Boneripper's fist closed about the coward's head, crushing both his iron helm and the skull inside it like an egg.

A familiar scent snapped Thanquol's attention from his bodyguard's gruesome work. It was a smell the grey seer had hoped to never encounter again, the stench of a beast that should be lying cooked, charred and very dead somewhere in the man-thing scat-streams. Instead, the burnt, ravaged, skull-like head of the rat-beast glared at him from the doorway of the kitchen, the badly chewed torso of the Clan Skaul sneak delegated to watch the cellar tunnel lodged in its exposed cheek-pouch. The monster chittered hungrily, its eyes more like pools of blood than things capable of vision. Thanquol scuttled away from the thing's approach, keeping on all fours so as not to arouse its interest by rising from the floor.

The grey seer needn't have bothered. The rat-beast lifted its mangled snout and sniffed at the air. It snarled, then with a savage leap it propelled its immense body into the nearest warlock engineer. The skaven shrieked as half the bones in his body were shattered by the rat-beast's bulk. It perched above him like a lion with its prey and its dripping jaws began ripping at the ratman's leather smock and man-gut harness.

Fresh screams from the skaven beneath the rat-beast's paws brought Thanquol leaping to his feet. The other skaven were watching the gory spectacle with terrified fascination. Thanquol snarled at them, trying to snap the fools back to their senses. While the monster was eating the clumsy fool the rest of them could escape! They could use the basement tunnel – there was no need to fight past the brute to reach the cellar tunnel. Before the creature was half-finished with its meal, they could all of them be many rest-stops away!

It was a sound plan until Thanquol glanced back at the monster savaging Burnfang's minion. The beast was not eating the ratman, it was tearing open the leather bag he carried. Wine bottles rolled free and the monster lost interest in the crushed skaven. It scurried after the bottles. With a shriek of horror, Thanquol and the other skaven watched as it raised one immense paw and brought it smashing down into one of the bottles, exposing the syrupy mix of Wormstone dust and wine. Almost before the suicidal madness of such action could register with the onlookers, the rat-beast brought its muzzle close to the foul mixture. A scabby tongue flicked from its snout, lapping up the poisonous concoction.

Where a moment before Thanquol had been eager for escape, now his blood boiled with outrage! The dumb animal was eating the Wormstone! It was actually eating the grey seer's chance for glory and revenge!

Thanquol spun about on his heels, his staff raised over his head. He glared at Boneripper. The rat ogre still stood between the hall and study archways, the dead warlock engineer dangling from his hand. The dull-witted monster was fully occupied batting the dead ratman with his other hands, fascinated by the way the broken body swayed back and forth when he hit it.

'Lumbering, witless flea-food!' Thanquol snarled, slamming his staff against Boneripper's thigh. The huge rat ogre cringed from the blow, fear clouding his beady little eyes. Thanquol ignored the brute's reaction, instead pointing a claw at the feeding rat-beast. 'Kill that filthy beast, you brainless oaf-thing! Kill-kill! Kill-kill!'

Each command enflamed Boneripper's aggression, each snarl from Thanquol's voice brought the fur on the rat ogre's neck bristling. Drool dripped from Boneripper's jaws as the monster let loose with an ear-shattering roar. The rat-beast looked up from its frantic feeding just in time to be bowled over as Boneripper flung the carcass of the warlock engineer into its face.

The rat-beast was knocked back by the morbid missile, toppling head over tail until it smashed into the wall of the parlour. Plaster rained down upon it from the battered wall. It hissed savagely as it lifted itself and shook its mangy pelt free of plaster. It spun about to challenge Boneripper, but the rat ogre was already upon it.

The townhouse shook as Boneripper launched himself at the staggered rat-beast. The huge brute charged across the parlour, slamming into the rat-beast with the impact of a battering ram, the huge spike on his shoulder guard impaling the creature through the chest as he drove his body into it. The force of the impact drove both monsters onwards, and nothing so humble as timber and brick and stone was going to stop them.

The wall collapsed in a shower of rubble as Boneripper smashed the rat-beast through the parlour wall and back into the kitchen. A table vanished in a cloud of splinters as both of the huge brutes hurtled onto the kitchen floor. Boneripper was the first to rise, tearing his gory shoulder spike free of the rat-beast's mangled body.

The fresh surge of pain inflicted by the withdrawal of the spike brought a shriek of agony from the rat-beast. In a frenzy of pain, the creature flung itself from the rubble, latching onto Boneripper. Even the rat ogre's prodigious strength was not enough to overwhelm the bulk of the rat-beast. Like its smaller kind, the rat-beast scrabbled at Boneripper with all four of its clawed paws, tearing deep furrows in the rat ogre's leathery hide. The ratlike jaws of the beast snapped and slashed at Boneripper's head, trying to work around or through the armour of his helmet to reach the soft skin of his throat.

Boneripper staggered, trying to stay upright with the weight of the rat-beast pulling at him and threatening his balance. Even his brutish mind understood that if he fell, he would be finished, his foe free to tear out his throat. With two of his arms, he tried to grapple the beast. His mutant third arm, its hand fitted with steel and spike, struck again and again into the beast's side until it was coated in blood.

The rat-beast chittered its feral ferocity at Boneripper, each blow only serving to excite its terrible vitality even more. Rather than fading beneath the force of the punishment the rat ogre was delivering, the beast seemed to be empowered by it. Snapping jaws closed against the side of Boneripper's face, tearing away an ear and part of his cheek armour. Boneripper responded with a savage grip, his mighty arms straining as they bent the rat-beast's body upward and back. With a wet pop, the beast's hind legs fell limp, flopping uselessly against the rat ogre's waist.

The beast vomited black blood from its jaws, spattering Boneripper's armour, but refused to abandon its efforts to reach its foe's throat. Boneripper felt incisors scrape against the side of his neck, drawing a thin trickle of blood.

With another thunderous roar, Boneripper threw the rat-beast from him. It crashed in a broken heap against the old larder, crushing the last of Burnfang's test subjects beneath it. Boneripper was not satisfied, however. The rat ogre stomped after the quivering wreckage of the beast, pounding its prone form mercilessly with his huge fists. The wet smacks of fist into dripping meat were a fitting applause to such a primitive, bestial spectacle.

Hearing Boneripper's triumphant bellow, Thanquol decided it was safe enough to creep into the kitchen. A few of his followers crept after him, not willing to risk upsetting the grey seer if his bodyguard had indeed vanquished the terrible rat-beast. Thanquol sneered at their cowardice. Boldly, he stepped to Boneripper, swatting the rat ogre's flank with the butt of his staff.

'Fool-meat!' Thanquol snarled. 'Leave dead-thing. There is work to do!' The grey seer turned and glowered at his shivering underlings. 'Recover the spilled Wormstone,' he snapped at Burnfang. 'Hide your dead as well. My enemies must find-smell no sign that I was here.'

'What of the monster?' Burnfang growled back. 'It is too big to move or hide!'

Thanquol glared at the warlock engineer. 'Then leave it, dung-breath toad! Do not pester my brilliance with your stupidity, tinker-rat!' The grey seer lifted his gaze to the other surviving skaven, both of Clan Skryre and Clan Skaul. 'We waste no more time!' he declared. 'We take the Wormstone to the reservoir! Then the man-things will suffer for defying the will of the Horned Rat!'

The grey seer looked past the throng to see Skrim skulking in the shadows. He pointed a clawed talon at the slinking spy. 'Gnawtail will lead you through the tunnels,' he said. His eyes became as cold as those of a snake and Skrim felt his insides shrivel as Thanquol snarled words he knew were meant for him alone.

'Gnawtail knows the way.'

As the skaven began to scurry from the gory ruin of the old kitchen, none of them gave a second glance to the dripping mass of meat and fur splashed against the larder, nor to the hate-filled eye that sullenly watched them go.

CHAPTER TWELVE
The Triumph of Thanquol

The abandoned townhouse on the Reikhoch Prachstrasse was as still as a crypt when twenty armed men and dwarfs burst through its doors. From front and back, the men rushed through the dusty rooms, swords and pistols at the ready. Each man's brow dripped with a sweat of fear, knowing too well the hideous enemy they expected to find. As they surged into each empty room, their fear only increased. If the ratkin had not confronted them already it could only be because they were waiting for the intruders to stumble into some devious trap.

Theodor Baer led the group that had smashed its way through the entranceway at the front of the townhouse. Baer could feel the hairs standing on the back of his neck as he crept through the silent rooms. He had heard the stories about the townhouse and its last tenant, tales of vampirism and worse horrors. The watch sergeant allowed himself a grim chuckle. Beside his fear of the restless dead, confronting a mob of verminous underfolk would almost seem tame by comparison.

Almost.

Theodor kept his pistol aimed, turning it with the lantern in his free hand. The instant his light showed something monstrous, it would get a bullet through its skull. He only hoped the men with him were as ready for action. Most of them he knew only casually, some of them not at all. Being a vassal of Jeremias Scrivner was not the sort of thing that drew men together for socialising in their off hours. Of course, the very fact that they did serve the wizard spoke of their capability. Scrivner was not one to make time for charity cases. Those who bore his token were men with something to offer him, some skill useful to the wizard's interests.

Entering the parlour, Theodor's lantern revealed a shambles of piled furniture and torn tapestries. The sickly stink of spilled perfume assailed the watchman's senses. He heard Amando, the Tilean duellist, cough violently behind him, clenching a rag to his face against the smell. Theodor controlled his own repugnance, sweeping the lantern across the room. A grey shape appeared in front of him. Before he could tug the trigger of his pistol, a steely grip knocked his hand aside.

'They have gone,' the chill voice of Jeremias Scrivner told him. The wizard reached to Theodor's lantern, throwing open the metal shutters on its sides. The sudden light threw the parlour into sharp relief. Theodor's initial impression of cluster and ruin was justified. Someone had ransacked the entire townhouse to create a gaudy impression of a throne-room, like a child playing king.

Sounds from the hallway beyond the parlour brought Theodor and the men with him turning from their cursory inspection of the room. Certain that the ratkin had sprung their trap, each man tensed, weapons at the ready. Sighs of relief spread across the parlour. The sounds had come from the men who had come from the back of the house. Theodor gave a grudging nod of respect to Simo Valkoinen.

'Report,' the hissed whisper of Scrivner commanded the professional killer.

'Nothing,' Valkoinen answered. 'Nothing alive, at least. There are rooms that look like an orc warband slept in them. Most of those smell like a whore's boudoir. But no trace of what did the damage. No trash, no fur, no scat.'

'They cleaned up after themselves,' observed one of the fighters with Theodor. The speaker was a squat, broad-shouldered dwarf, his frosty beard tied into elaborate braids that fell almost to his knees. His dark eyes twinkled like chips of ore from his wrinkled face, almost matching the mailshirt and steel helm he wore. Grimbold Silverbeard did not speak only of Valkoinen's report. He pointed a stubby finger at the floor. Amid the debris of tattered finery, patches of the dusty floor had been scrubbed so fiercely that the tiles were little more than layers of scratches. 'Skaven blood isn't easy to get up. Back in Zhufbar, if it got on anything that wasn't metal, we usually burned it. Damn bad choice to make between carrying that stink around and cutting your beard!'

'Trying to hide the fact they were here?' Theodor wondered. 'But why drench the place in perfume? You can smell it from the next street.'

'Because it isn't men they are afraid will find their trail,' Scrivner said. 'The ratmen are their own worst enemies. This was done to hide their scent from their own kind. The skaven who possess the stone are afraid they will be discovered by enemies from their own ranks. Perhaps that fear has gripped them enough, that they will not be expecting other enemies to come after them.'

'Magister!' It was Grimbold who called out, his voice betraying an excitement his people seldom allowed themselves to display. Scrivner swung around at the dwarf's call, staring over his shoulder as the dwarf displayed what he had found. It was a scrap of torn parchment, hoary with age.

'I found it poking out from under that chest,' Grimbold explained. 'It's a chart, one of the blueprints of the Grey Dwarfs who helped construct the city's infrastructure. This one,' his thick thumb tapped a set of Khazalid runes drawn at the top of the parchment, 'is for something called the "Dunkelwa…". That's all that's left.'

'The Dunkelwasserkleinmere,' Scrivner finished for the dwarf. 'An old name. Now it is known as the Kaiserschwalbe.'

Grimbold's eyes went wide with horror. 'The reservoir! The filthy ratkin mean to poison the reservoir!'

'We can't let them!' Johann swore, pushing his way through the other men in Valkoinen's group. 'They'll poison hundreds, thousands if they put that filth into the water!' The smuggler clenched his fists in fury, imagining the magnitude of suffering, entire households stricken with the same slow corruption that had beset his brother. Men, women and children, it would be wholesale slaughter such as even a Kurgan warlord would balk at.

Scrivner gave Johann a grim nod, then looked to Grimbold once more. 'You will lead us to the reservoir.'

'I maintained the Imperial sewers long enough to know every way into the place,' Grimbold said. 'But the ratkin are fair diggers. They might have made their own way. We'll reach the reservoir, but without knowing what route they are using I can't say if we'll beat them or simply meet them.'

'Then the surest course is to follow their trail,' the wizard stated. He removed a vial from the folds of his cloak. Johann had never seen such a vibrant purple elixir as that which sloshed against the clouded glass of the vial, but he recognised the dove of the Shallyan temple on the wax seal that closed its top. 'Stay here,' Scrivner commanded, 'and do not move, whatever you see.' His cloak swept around him as he stalked from the parlour and through the broken wall that led into the kitchen.

Tense moments passed, then the men in the parlour heard a grisly sound of laboured breathing and grinding bone. Despite the wizard's warning, the watchers drew back from the grotesque shape that crawled through the wreckage. It was an immense, rat-like thing, not an inch of its body unmarked by violence. Broken bones ground together as the beast pulled itself across the floor, dragging its useless hind limbs after it. The thing gave them no notice as it crossed the parlour leaving a bloody trail after it. The drooling, slobbering horror vanished into the gloom of the study. The men in the parlour could hear wood splintering as the monster attacked the wall with its fangs, gnawing at the concealed entrance to the basement.

'The map was not the only thing the skaven left behind.' The wizard's whispered words startled men who had been fixated upon the rat-beast. Once more, their cloaked master stood among them. Johann noticed that the vial in Scrivner's hand was now empty. 'The tears of Shallya allow the abomination a few more hours. We must trust that they are enough. The skaven learned well from our smuggler friends,' Scrivner added, gesturing to the black paste none of Thanquol's minions had dared clean from the parlour. 'They have mixed their vile poison with wine to hide its smell. Well enough to hide from their own kind and my familiars.'

There was a loud snapping noise as the rat-beast gnawed its way past the secret panel. Scrivner's eyes burned in the darkness as the sound carried into the parlour.

'But there's one nose they can't trick anymore,' he said, stalking after the rat-beast as it disappeared through the hole it had made. Scrivner's servants fought down their own fears and followed after their mysterious master.

'Right now I bet you wish Volk had settled your mob down in the sewers,' Theodor told Johann as they waited their turn to descend into the basement.

Johann shook his head. 'I may die in a sewer yet,' he told the watchman. 'But this time at least I'll do it for more than a few barrels of contraband.'

SKRATTCH SKARPAW SCRAMBLED up the slime-slick sewer wall, clinging to the dripping surface of an archway. As one of the skilled assassins of Clan Eshin, Lord Skrolk had sent him ahead to scout the way for the plague lord's retinue. Despite Kratch's assurances and oaths of loyalty and service, Skrolk was being wary of treachery from Thanquol's former apprentice. Among the skaven there was no such concept as being over-cautious. Skarpaw, being near the end of his usefulness to Skrolk, was not only the most capable of spotting any traps the grey seer might have set, but also the most expendable if he fell afoul of one.

The assassin's claws found tiny gaps between the bricks to maintain his hold. His scaly tail coiled about one of his cruelly serrated swords. Skarpaw's eyes glittered in the darkness, his nose twitching as he sniffed the air. Beneath the fug of human waste, he smelled a familiar scent. The odour of fresh blood was strong as he heard something large sloshing through the muck. Skarpaw tensed as a new scent reached him, the reek of the rat-beast that had routed Thanquol's minions during their expedition into the forgotten burrows of Clan Mawrl.

He held his breath as the huge monster dragged itself through the scum of the canal, its mangled body little more than an open wound. Any moment might see the beast's finish. Scavenging instincts reared up from the depths of Skarpaw's psyche, urging him to leap upon the dying monster, but reason subdued the impulse. There were other sounds now, sounds of many feet trudging through the sludge and scum. Skarpaw pressed himself even closer to the wall, vanishing into the shadow of the vaulted ceiling. He stifled his breathing, willed his heartbeat to an infrequent murmur. Like a verminous gargoyle, he became as lifeless as the stone around him, only his glittering eyes betraying his presence.

Men emerged from the darkness. Skarpaw knew enough of the ways of men to recognise that these presented a motley gang, finery mixed with the rags of the slums, the soft scents of refinement mixed with the hard smells of the lower classes. At their fore, Skarpaw saw a grey-bearded dwarf leading the way, a light glowing from the peak of his helm as he followed the dying rat-beast. Just behind the dwarf, however, was a figure that sent a thrill of fear racing through Skarpaw's pulse.

A hooded man cloaked in grey and with the chill of sorcery about his smell. It could only be the wizard-thing that had fought Thanquol for possession of the Wormstone. He had survived his battle with the grey seer and was once more on the trail of his adversary and his prize. Somehow, in some way, the wizard-thing was letting the rat-beast lead him to Thanquol!

Skarpaw lingered in the shadow of the archway for many minutes, allowing the steps and scent of the men to fade into the distance. After what Kratch had told Skrolk about the wizard-thing, the assassin wanted to take no chance of the human discovering his presence. Even his killer's heart preferred not to pit itself against magic and sorcery. The memory of Thanquol's spell of madness was still too fresh.

Certain he was undiscovered, Skarpaw dropped down from his sanctuary, sliding along the slimy brickwork to the putrid surface of the canal. At first with caution, then with speed, the assassin raced down the black maze of sewers, darting down side-passages and around cross-tunnels. The ratman's winding route seemed a confusion of turns, but he was not relying upon memory to bring him back to his gruesome master. Skarpaw used the rotten smell of the plague monks to lead him through the sewer, a smell even the dull senses of a human would find hard to mistake.

Soon, the assassin stood in the tunnel where Lord Skrolk's festering followers were gathered, impatiently awaiting their scout's report. The plague lord himself shuffled forward as Skarpaw came upon the clustered vermin. Skrolk's boil-strewn face scowled at the assassin, the fumes rising from his censer-staff matching the smouldering temper in his blemished eyes.

'There will be no more medicine until you clear the path,' Skrolk warned the assassin, his voice bubbling with menace. 'If the Wormstone escapes me, you will wish I had let the pox do its work!'

Skarpaw prostrated himself before the ghastly plague lord, taking the decayed hem of his filthy robe and rubbing it across his nose in a show of abasement. 'Horrific one!' he whimpered. 'Others seek the traitor!' He pointed to where Kratch stood among the plague monks, the adept now garbed in the same rotten green robes. 'The wizard-thing still seeks Thanquol! I have seen it and its underlings walking through the scat-stream. They were following the great rat-beast from Clan Mawrl! They were hunting the Wormstone!'

Kratch scrambled from the mass of plague monks, grovelling at the feet of Lord Skrolk. He kissed the plague lord's decaying tail, rubbed his forehead against the monk's leprous foot, anything to make his show of abasement and devotion more convincing than that of the assassin. 'Terrible bringer of suffering!' Kratch wheezed. 'Your humble servant did not know the wizard-thing still lived! I did not know...'

Lord Skrolk's laugh was an obscene gurgle, like heart-blood slopping from a wound. 'We will follow the wizard-thing,' he croaked.

'But if the wizard-thing finds Thanquol first...' Kratch started to protest. Skrolk seized the cringing adept in his paw.

'Do you think Thanquol will simply hand the Wormstone to the human?' the plague lord growled. Kratch's tongue lolled from his mouth as he felt the claw around his throat tighten. 'We will let the human find the traitor first. They will fight over the Wormstone. Then Clan

Pestilens will destroy the exhausted victor and recover what belongs to us!'

Lord Skrolk tossed Kratch aside like a piece of refuse. The adept rubbed his injured throat, sickened to find that one of Skrolk's decayed claws had broken off in his skin.

'The Wormstone will be mine!' Skrolk chittered. 'Then shall all the Under-Empire tremble once more before the might of Clan Pestilens and the true face of the Horned One!'

Grey Seer Thanquol lashed his tail in annoyance as he stepped onto the stone ledge overlooking the enormous Kaiserschwalbe. Once, many centuries ago, it had been a natural cavern, an underground lake fed by springs and subterranean streams. Under the patronage of Altdorf's princes and emperors, however, dwarf artisans and engineers had transformed the cavern into a mammoth edifice of marble and granite. Huge pillars rose from the depths of the lake, their fluted columns reaching up like the fingers of drowned giants until they merged with the tiled ceiling of the cavern, the elaborate frescos shimmering with the reflection of the water beneath them. Massive pumps of steel and bronze hugged the columns. Operating upon an ingenious system of pressure valves, the pumps employed the volume of the reservoir itself to send water up into the city above. Everywhere, from the dam-like restraining wall of the reservoir to the stone walkways that criss-crossed over the aquifer, elegant sculptures and magnificent bas-reliefs lent the place a majesty that made the grey seer's heart seethe with contemptuous envy. That men would squander such time and effort into something they could hardly expect many of their kind to ever see was beyond Thanquol's ability to understand. Of what use was grandeur if it was not used to inspire fear and awe in subordinates?

The grey seer was still chewing over that quandary when his sharp eyes noticed movement on the cavern floor. Restrained by the dam, there was a section of the old cavern that had been left relatively dry except for a deep channel that allowed the reservoir's excess to escape back into the dark of the underworld. It was this stream that provided much of Under-Altdorf's water, the decadent council of the city far too miserly to pay tolls to Clan Sleekit for use of regular river water. Sight of the stream made a fierce smile grow on Thanquol's face, final confirmation that his plot to poison the man-things of Altdorf would also spell doom for his enemies in Under-Altdorf.

Thanquol shook his head, his eyes narrowing as he again focused upon the creatures moving around the reservoir. A work crew of humans, performing some manner of maintenance upon the dam, scrambling up wooden scaffolds with what a skaven could describe as only the most wretched clumsiness. One of the humans gave a shout, a trembling hand pointing up at Thanquol. The other humans turned, tools dropping from their hands, jaws dropping open in shocked silence.

The grey seer's tail lashed in annoyance again, glaring at the stupid animals, awestruck by his magnificence and their own superstitious terror. It was almost insulting that these pathetic dregs should be the final obstacle between himself and ultimate glory.

'Skrim,' Thanquol snarled. 'Have your slinking thief-rats kill those animals!' It would be an abuse of his powers and far beneath his dignity to partake in the slaughter of such a sorry mob. Thanquol would leave that to base creatures like Skrim and his sneaks. Besides, even the most wretched enemy sometimes got lucky.

Thanquol watched the Clan Skaul ratmen scamper down from the ledge, leaping onto the scaffolds and gantries with apelike agility. The men closest to the ledge were already dead before their comrades started to run. Thanquol laughed as he watched Skrim's sneaks do their bloody work. Laughter turned to a snarl of anger as he heard the sharp crack of a warplock pistol. A worker pitched and fell, smashing against the side of the dam before bouncing to the cavern floor hundreds of feet below. Another pistol barked in the darkness, this time blasting a worker off a stone causeway and into the reservoir itself. The wounded man thrashed in the water, desperately trying to keep his mangled frame afloat. The warlock engineer who had shot him rushed to the edge of the causeway directly above him and hurriedly reloaded his pistol, snickering at his flailing victim all the while.

Thanquol stamped his feet, his fur bristling, his fangs grinding together. What were the fools doing! He hadn't sent Burnfang's pack into the fray! He wasn't about to risk what they carried by fighting a miserable lot of defenceless humans!

Grey Seer Thanquol rounded on Viskitt Burnfang. He wanted to crack his staff against the idiot's snout, but he was too far away. Instead, Thanquol contented himself with a very vicious string of obscenities and staff-rattling. 'Fool-meat! Flea-brained mouse-fondler! Did I squeak-say send your tinker-rats into battle! If they lose one bottle of Wormstone...'

Burnfang grinned at Thanquol, a savage, fang-ridden smile that spread from cheek-pouch to cheek-pouch.

'They won't lose the Wormstone,' Burnfang snapped. 'But you will, priest-dolt!' Before Thanquol could even blink, Burnfang whipped his own pistol from his belt, aiming the muzzle between the grey seer's eyes. A deep growl and a heavy footfall told of Boneripper's reaction to this sudden threat against his master. Burnfang didn't even glance at the rat ogre. 'Call him off, Thanquol,' he snarled. 'He couldn't reach me before I pulled this trigger and exploded your skull like an egg.'

Thanquol turned his head, noticing for the first time that he was alone upon the ledge with Burnfang. That was why he had sent his minions down to help Skrim. The warlock engineer wanted no witnesses to his treachery. That thought puzzled Thanquol and occupied his thoughts even as he snapped commands to Boneripper.

The rat ogre sullenly sank to his haunches, head lowered like that of a scolded child. Boneripper could not understand why his master had called him back, his simple mind unable to reconcile the contradiction between the threat in Burnfang's scent and Thanquol's command to sit and stay away from the warlock engineer. The confusion made him rock from side to side, his instinct to obey the grey seer warring with his instinct to tear apart his master's enemies.

'What is your scheme, Burnfang?' Thanquol snarled. 'If you think the council in Under-Altdorf will reward you for bringing me to them, I can promise-swear the Lords of Decay will reward you much-much more.'

'I know that they will,' Burnfang hissed through his fang-ridden grin. He slapped his chest with his paw. 'Skavenblight does not care about you, grey seer. It is the Wormstone they want. They shall have it, but it will be Warp-Master Viskitt Burnfang who presents it to the Council of Thirteen, not Grey Seer Thanquol!'

Burnfang's paw reached to his belt, removing a glass orb from a leather bag. It resembled the gas bombs employed by Clan Skryre, but its contents were a murky liquid. Thanquol instinctively took a step back as he saw Burnfang's bomb and caught the scent of its contents. He flailed at the lip of the ledge, nearly pitching to the floor below. Instead, Thanquol threw himself forwards, landing in a sprawl before Burnfang's feet.

The warlock engineer started to laugh at the grey seer's antics, but the roar of Boneripper stifled any amusement Burnfang felt. The warlock engineer fired his pistol into the charging brute, blasting a fist-sized chunk of flesh from his side. The rat ogre gave a snarl of pain, but kept coming, storming after Burnfang like a hate-maddened juggernaut. Burnfang flung the spent weapon full into the charging rat ogre's face, but succeeded only in cracking one of the monster's fangs. The warlock engineer leapt away as Boneripper's thick arms reached for him, shrieking in fright. Narrowly, he missed hurtling to the floor hundreds of feet below, landing instead on a scaffold. The wooden structure swayed and groaned beneath the abrupt addition of Burnfang's weight.

Boneripper started after the warlock engineer, several ropes snapping as he took a step onto the scaffold. A shrill command from Thanquol called his bodyguard back. Still glaring at Burnfang, the rat ogre lurched back onto the ledge. The grey seer joined him, watching as the treacherous warlock engineer scrambled to the next scaffold, putting a further twenty feet between himself and his enemies.

'An impasse, grey-fool!' Burnfang snarled. 'I don't dare come after you while you have your monster, you don't dare come for me while I hold this!' Again, the warlock engineer brandished the dusky globe of glass. Even in the extremes of his terrified retreat, he had had sense enough to keep a firm grip on the deadly object.

Thanquol did not respond to Burnfang's baiting. Too late did the warlock engineer observe the green glow in the depths of the grey seer's eyes. Too late did he see Thanquol's paw stretch out, his fingers splayed wide apart. With a savage gesture, Thanquol closed his fingers into a fist. In sympathy with the grey seer's motion, without any conscious thought from their owner, Burnfang's fingers did likewise.

Viskitt Burnfang screamed as the glass globe shattered beneath the tightening pressure of his rebellious hand. Howls of terror became shrieks of agony as the lethal contents of the orb saturated his flesh and seeped into his fur. The warlock engineer pawed wildly at his poisoned body, trying to claw the sorcerous venom away. Almost instantly, fur began to drip off his skin, fat green worms began to erupt from his flesh. When, at last, in a fit of panic and suffering, Burnfang threw himself into the cavern, his decaying body was little more than a mass of squirming filth.

'So suffer all who defy the destiny of Thanquol,' the grey seer snarled as he watched Burnfang's writhing carcass burst upon the cavern floor. Thanquol looked up to find the eyes of Skaul sneaks and the remaining warlock engineers fixed upon him. Burnfang's treachery had drawn an audience after all. He glowered back at the frightened skaven, straightening into his most imperious posture. 'So end all traitors!' he growled, slamming the butt of his staff against the ledge. The watching skaven bowed and grovelled, spurting the musk of fear. Thanquol snickered, relishing their terrified devotion.

Boneripper's low growl drew the grey seer away from the adulation of his minions. It was on Thanquol's tongue to chastise the rat ogre, but movement at the mouth of the tunnel that opened onto the ledge made him hesitate. The grey seer's eyes narrowed as he saw something big crawl into the fitful light of the reservoir cavern. He recoiled as he saw the rat-beast pull itself into the chamber, the monster's mangled body leaving a bloody slick behind it.

That anything should survive the punishment the rat-beast had suffered was incredible to the grey seer. Disturbing memories of the necromancer Vorghun of Praag and his lifeless creations sent a pulse of terror rushing through Thanquol's glands.

'Boneripper!' he shouted at his hulking bodyguard. 'Kill-kill! Kill-kill!' Thanquol gestured frantically at the rat-beast with his staff.

Boneripper smacked one meaty fist into another and rushed towards the rat-beast. The monster caught the rat ogre's scent, pushing itself awkwardly from the floor with its forepaws. It snarled at the charging rat ogre, its own blood slobbering from its broken jaw. Boneripper swung at the creature with his armoured third arm, but the rat-beast dropped beneath the blow, crashing lifelessly at the rat ogre's feet.

Thanquol stared incredulously as Boneripper stubbornly poked and prodded the dead hulk, vainly trying to get the lifeless beast to fight him. Whatever monstrous strength had allowed the rat-beast to chase after him, it had abandoned the thing at the very moment when it at last gained upon its quarry. Thanquol's chittering laughter echoed across the reservoir as he considered the cruel irony of the dumb brute's fate.

Cold, mocking laughter, like the whisper of an enormous serpent, stifled Thanquol's own. The grey seer drew a pinch of warp-snuff from the ratskull box as he backed away, retreating onto the stone causeway. He knew that laughter.

A dark figure slowly manifested upon the ledge, seemingly bleeding into substance from thin air. Shadows swirled and crawled about the cloaked wizard, his grey eyes boring into the beady orbs of Thanquol. The grey seer trembled with outrage more than fear. The reservoir was here, beneath his very feet! All he had to do was pour the Wormstone into the water and all his enemies, human and skaven, were doomed to die in excruciating pain! Skavenblight would herald him the greatest grey seer since Gnawdoom recovered the Black Ark!

Thanquol snarled at the sinister wizard. One claw closed about a protective talisman, he thrust his staff towards Jeremias Scrivner. Thanquol snickered as he saw clouds of darkness leap from Scrivner's pointing hands. He felt the talisman in his paw crumble into powder as it absorbed the wizard's spell, drawing the baleful energies into itself to protect its wearer.

The head of his staff erupted into a scintillating sphere of phosphorescence, like some diseased echo of an aurora. Thanquol roared as he flung the dazzling light at the shadowmancer. A blanket of green luminance engulfed the ledge as Thanquol's spell struck. Thanquol had seen how capably Scrivner could protect himself; this time the grey seer chose to attack not the man, but everything around him. What power, he wondered, could a shadowmancer wield if there were no shadows to command!

The grey seer snickered as he saw Scrivner staggering in the spectral glow. Again, Thanquol's shrill voice cried out, his clawed finger stabbing at the reeling wizard.

'Boneripper!' the grey seer cried. 'Kill-kill! Kill-kill!'

CHAPTER THIRTEEN
War of the Rats

BELLOWING LIKE A blood-mad bull, Boneripper thundered towards the staggering wizard, his shoulder lowered to impale Scrivner upon his spiked armour. Still stunned by Thanquol's blinding sorcery, the magister was oblivious to his peril.

Others were not. From the mouth of the tunnel, a voice cried out a hasty command. It was Boneripper who staggered as a volley of shots rang out and his leathery hide tore beneath the impact of bullets. The rat ogre howled in pain, dropping onto all five paws and scrambling away from the fusillade, blood streaming from his wounds. A cheer went up from Scrivner's men as they saw the monster flee.

'Press the attack!' Theodor Baer cried out. 'Keep the ratmen from the reservoir!'

Thanquol heard the watchman's shout, grinding his fangs as he saw the men rush across the ledge. Lightning crackled about the metal head of his staff. Snarling, the grey seer sent a bolt of withering energy to strike down the would-be hero. Sizzling warp energy crackled through the air, like a thin finger of glowing death. Thanquol's beady eyes gleamed as he watched the corrupt power crash down upon the human.

Even as the warp lightning struck at the man, however, Theodor's body was engulfed in darkness, fading, blinking into the shadows. When the grey seer's attack landed, all its fury accomplished was to sear the stones where the man had stood.

Thanquol growled in frustration, glaring at the cloaked wizard. Jeremias Scrivner glared back at him. Recovered from the grey seer's blinding spell, now it was the wizard's turn to frustrate the rat-mage's sorcery. Thanquol squealed, diving behind the nearest of the marble columns as Scrivner gestured at the skaven with his black-coated hand. Knives of shadow given substance slashed through the cavern, slicing into the column and tearing through the ancient dwarf-built pump bolted to its side. Streams of water erupted from the pitted metal, spraying in every direction.

Thanquol snarled from behind his refuge, glaring at his cowering minions. 'Skrim!' the grey seer raged. 'You and your thief-rats! Kill the man-things!'

The Clan Skaul spy hesitated, but a second glance at Thanquol's glowing eyes and snarling face decided him. The crook-backed old skaven snapped orders to his sneaks. The ratmen surged forwards, scrambling along the sides and bottoms of the scaffolds and gantries to frustrate the fire of the humans rushing to oppose them. One skaven lost his grip, scrabbling desperately at the carved face of the dam before plummeting into the cavern. The rest kept scurrying onwards, swiftly closing the distance between themselves and the men rushing onto the causeways.

'Not you! Idiot-meat!' Thanquol howled in disgust. He watched in dismay as the surviving warlock engineers scurried forward to support Skrim's sneaks once more. One of the Clan Skryre engineers heard the grey seer's roar, giving Thanquol a puzzled look. 'Are you carrying Wormstone!' the grey seer shrieked. The ratman gave an embarrassed nod. Thanquol's blood was already boiling, and the human gesture made him lose all control. He sent a bolt of warp-lightning scorching through the warlock engineer, turning him into a tiny torch as he bounced down the layers of scaffolding and into the cavern.

Thanquol slapped his forehead at his own stupid loss of control, grinding his teeth at yet another human gesture. He'd been among the man-rats of Under-Altdorf too long, he was picking up their decadent habits. Certainly he had been infected by their stupidity. If he had to make an example of someone, an underling carrying Wormstone was not the one to choose!

There was at least one benefit from his tantrum, however; he'd gained the attention of the other warlock engineers. Thanquol glowered at the masked ratmen.

'Any of you fool-meat carrying Wormstone!' he growled, lashing his tail angrily as he was answered with more nods. 'Forget the humans!' he snarled. 'Move-scurry your tails up to me!' He pointed at the far end of the dam where another set of scaffolding would allow the skaven to climb up to the level of the causeway and the reservoir. Three warlock engineers started off, scrambling and leaping from platform to platform. The few survivors from the work crew fled at their approach, offering the skaven not even the slightest opposition.

Thanquol peered from behind the column, grinning as he saw Skrim Gnawtail's sneaks pounce upon the wizard's allies. Men might be stronger than skaven, but they were laughably slow. With their terror of Thanquol's power to goad them onwards, Skrim's vermin would make short work of the humans.

Just as Thanquol was deciding the fight was over before it began, he saw one of the sneaks swatted from the scaffolding by a wave of shadow that billowed and clung to him like fog. The grey seer didn't give any thought to the wretch's shriek as he fell, instead concentrating upon the real problem. The wizard was the flea in the fur of his plan, his magic could tip the balance against him. Unfortunately, he wasn't sure there was any way to remove his threat without risking his own hide in the process.

The sound of water lapping against the column drew Thanquol's attention. He grinned evilly as he saw Boneripper trying to climb up from the lake and join his master on the causeway. His beady eyes turned back to the cloaked wizard. Scrivner was on one of the other causeways, supporting his underlings with his shadow magic. The grey seer hissed a command to Boneripper, then pointed at the column closest to the magister. Boneripper dropped back into the reservoir with a loud splash and began to swim towards the other causeway.

Thanquol lashed his tail, amused by his own brilliance. He would wait for Boneripper to attack the wizard. While Scrivner was busy trying to stave off the rat ogre, Thanquol would be able to bring the full fury of his sorcery against the meddling magister. The grey seer teased a nugget of warpstone from the hidden pocket of his robe. He stared at its black, shining depths. There was danger in using warpstone, even the most carefully refined warpstone, to fuel spells, but in this case Thanquol decided the risk was worth it. With the wizard gone, there could be no question of his plan's success. Two cities would die and with their deaths the glory of Thanquol would be like an ocean of magma blazing through the caverns of the Under-Empire!

Thanquol popped the piece of warpstone into his mouth, feeling its burn against his tongue. Soon, soon the moment would come. He would unleash such havoc upon the wizard that all that would be left of him was a greasy smear! No! That was the warpstone talking! He had to be careful, only use enough power to get the job done. Dead was dead, he didn't need to make a spectacle of the wizard's destruction.

Then, with Scrivner gone, Thanquol could savour his triumph. There would be none to oppose him then!

Fresh sounds and scents from the tunnel caused Thanquol to spin around. The grey seer nearly choked upon his warpstone as he saw a horde of chittering, green-clad skaven pour onto the ledge. Plague monks! The vile heretics of Clan Pestilens! Thanquol was under no delusion about their purpose here and what they had come for. He lifted his amulet, the richly jewelled medallion engraved with the sacred symbol of the Horned Rat. Thanquol scowled at the image, thinking of this fresh batch of adversaries come to stand between himself and his triumph.

'Are you testing me, Horned One?' Thanquol demanded.

JOHANN DROPPED DOWN onto the scaffolding and fired the pistol he had been given by Theodor Baer full into the face of a ratman climbing up to meet him. The monster squealed and hurtled into the abyss below the reservoir wall. Other shots sounded and Johann risked a quick turn of his neck to see Grimbold standing on the ledge wall above him. The dwarf's leather apron was hanging open now, its surface fitted with loops through which had been secured an array of fat-muzzled pistols. Thongs secured the weapons to the loops in the apron, and as the dwarf began his fusillade, he let each gun drop from his hand, slapping against his belly as the thong prevented it from falling. The dwarf quickly filled his hands with fresh pistols and continued to persecute the cringing, slinking beasts.

'If you don't want to catch your death from plague, manling,' Grimbold chuckled, meeting Johann's stare, 'kill the ratkin before their stink gets in your nose!'

The smuggler nodded his understanding and fumblingly tried to reload his weapon. The punishment the dwarf had delivered with his barrage had not quite been enough to drive the skaven into retreat. Valkoinen's deadly throwing knives picked ratmen from the scaffolding as they tried to swarm the men, pitching still more of the monsters into the darkness, yet still they came, encouraged by the feral snarls of their leader, a crook-backed old ratman with a stumpy tail.

Sight of the defiant ratkin enraged Amando. The Tilean hurled an epithet that would have shocked the ears of the Lord of Murder and threw his empty pistol after it. Shrieking furiously in his native tongue, Amando rushed across the scaffold to break the skaven attack in the surest way he knew: by killing their leader.

'Someone stop that fool!' Theodor barked.

Before he knew what was happening, Johann found himself running after Amando. The smuggler leapt over the blade of a ratman crawling up from the underside of the scaffold, punctuating the manoeuvre by kicking the monster's teeth down its throat. He didn't linger to see if the blow caused the ratkin to lose his grip, but pressed on in his rush to save Amando from the suicidal frenzy that had seized him.

The crook-backed ratman was snarling and spitting at the others now, calling them back to protect it from the Tilean. The ratman drew its own pistol from the filthy rags that served it as clothes and raised it to fire at Amando. Johann heard a shot sound from behind him. The crook-backed rat jumped in pain as a bullet smashed into it, its own pistol falling from its paw as pain from its wound seized it.

Amando gave a cry of triumph, leaping down to the last platform between himself and his prey. A ratman reared up before him, slashing at him with its notched blade. The Tilean screamed as the sword clove into his leg, then brought his own sword smashing down into the ratkin's head, scraping against its skull and ripping an ear and most of its scalp free from the bone beneath.

Johann dropped down to drag Amando away, but the Tilean shook him off, pointing at the cowering rat-leader.

'I kill that pig, then you take me back!' Amando growled.

Johann had no chance to argue. At that instant the seemingly dead ratman at Amando's feet found some measure of strength in its dying body. With a hiss, the skaven buried its fangs in the Tilean's foot. Amando shrieked in shock and pain, then brought the edge of his blade slashing across the monster's throat, banishing its filthy life for good.

Foul black blood sprayed as Amando opened the ratman's neck, splashing across Johann's body. The smuggler felt disgust at contact with the loathsome ichor, but quickly this was forgotten as tearing, crawling pain wracked his body. It felt like his body was ripping itself apart from within, like his veins were trying to slither free from his flesh. Johann clawed at his skin, trying to combat the itching sensation. He slumped to the shaking floor of the platform, horrified by what he was doing.

Amando, stunned by the strange agony that had seized Johann, was torn from his blind rage and turned to help his comrade in arms. A shot sounded and most of the Tilean's face vanished in a spray of blood and bone. On the higher platform, Johann could see the crook-backed ratman fling aside a second pistol. The monster glared at him for a moment, then threw itself at the causeway edge above it. No man could have made such a leap, nor found purchase for his grasping fingers, but the wiry ratman managed the impossible. An instant its stumpy tail swung from the lip of the causeway, then Johann heard a splash as the rat-leader threw himself into the reservoir.

The reason for the ratman's flight was revealed as Johann heard men rushing across the platforms.

'More ratmen have swarmed into the cavern,' Theodor shouted at Johann. 'We need to find a defensible position on the other side to fend them off!'

Johann only dimly heard the exchange. He was too busy staring at his arm, at the disgusting suggestion of movement beneath his skin where the black blood of the skaven had stained it. He reached a hand towards Amando's body, to see if the Tilean's flesh was also affected, trying desperately to deny the hideous truth fighting to dominate his brain. He recoiled, biting down on his lip to keep from screaming. Not only was

Amando's skin unmarked, but as his hand reached towards his head, where the sickly glowing warpstone bullet the ratman had fired was lodged in his skull, Johann saw a filthy green wormlike growth push itself free from his wrist.

Poisoned! Poisoned by that damnable stone from the sewer! Poisoned like his brother Dietrich! He saw in his mind the ghastly scene of his brother's deathbed, the filth and horror of that lingering sickness.

The wizard had known! Johann realised the fact with a sickening horror. Scrivner's terrible familiar had smelled it on him. Perhaps the wizard had known even before that. He had known, and he had said nothing! Johann rose to his feet, glaring at the causeway where the wizard stood before the oncoming horde.

'It's suicide to go back,' Valkoinen snarled at him.

Johann nodded stiffly to Valkoinen.

'Sounds like exactly what the doctor ordered,' Johann said, then turned and hurried to fit words to deeds.

THE FESTERING RANKS of the plague monks came scuttling out of the tunnel like so many rotting corpses, their fur hanging from their emaciated limbs in mangy strips, their frayed robes crusty with filth from their decaying bodies, and in each rheumy eye the ecstatic madness of the true fanatic. The plague monks did not see horror in their abominable condition; they saw power.

Instinctively, Thanquol looked past the mouldering mob of common plague monks, over the cowls and hoods of the frenzied wretches swinging obscene incense censers over their heads, past the diseased dregs carrying profane fly-strewn icons of crumbling bone and rusting iron, beyond the shrieking zealots with prayer scrolls clenched in their scrawny fists. He looked beyond the tide of madness, seeking the master of this deranged throng. He found him, perched upon the backs of four bulky ratmen who had somehow managed to retain some semblance of strength despite the ravages of their many ills.

Thanquol hissed an oath through his fangs. He knew that filthy rat, the insane, gibbering heretic who stood at the position of command behind his miserable congregation. Lord Skrolk, perhaps second only to Nurglitch himself in the loathsome ranks of Clan Pestilens and the foul plague priests!

Skrolk caught Thanquol's eye. The plague lord's lips peeled back, displaying his rotten smile. There was a look of unspeakable triumph in Skrolk's expression, as though all the hate and malice in his entire clan had been boiled down into a single display of emotion. Thanquol knew Nurglitch wanted the Wormstone for himself and Clan Pestilens alone. Accepting the will of the Council had been a ruse. His true plan had been to send Lord Skrolk to steal the Wormstone once Thanquol found it. And if, in the process, the grey seer was eliminated, so much the better for Skrolk and Nurglitch. Thanquol's killing of Plague Lord Skratsquik would be avenged. With the Wormstone in their possession, Clan Pestilens would need fear no retaliation for striking down one of the Horned Rat's sacred priests!

Thanquol bit down on the warpstone in his mouth, feeling its fiery power blaze through him. His vision became a brilliance of golden light, his arms felt as though they swelled with power. He could see the swirling threads of magic all around him; the grey darkness surrounding the human wizard, the green putrescence that billowed about Skrolk. They were as nothing to Thanquol's enhanced sight, petty tricks drawing upon but a few of the sorcerous strands that writhed all around them! The grey seer would show them real power! He would show them true magic!

Chittering wildly, Thanquol opened himself to the aetheric forces surrounding him, drawing all the many strands of magic into his body and into his mind. He formed the power into a thought, forced the thought to become purpose, forced the purpose to become action. Forced action to become words, gestures, binding the power with the secret knowledge handed down to the grey seers by the Horned Rat himself. Skrolk, the pathetic heathen, would suffer for his impiety! The Horned Rat would gnaw the heretic's bones!

As he started to point the blazing head of his staff towards the corrupt plague lord, Thanquol's sorcery-soaked vision noticed another figure drawing arcane energies into itself. The efforts of this one were even more laughable than those of Scrivner and Skrolk, like a whelp trying to raise a rat ogre's maul. Yet there was something naggingly familiar, insufferably annoying about the pathetic aura of the wretch. Thanquol's fangs snapped together, grinding against each other as he realised who the little scum-mage was!

Adept Kratch! The treacherous little bastard-flea was still alive! He was there, at the fore of the plague monks, his grey robes cast aside for the green decay of his new friends. The riddle of how Skrolk had found him was solved. The plague monks were here courtesy of some trick of his deceitful former apprentice!

Kratch vanished in a blaze of green-gold fire, the fur stripped from his bones as he was engulfed by the full fury of Thanquol's magic. Plague monks near him pitched and fell, their hearts burst by the magnitude of the sorcery that had smashed into the adept. Other plague monks whimpered and howled as the refuse of Kratch's sorry carcass splashed across them, greasy black drops that sizzled and burned whatever they touched.

Thanquol felt every eye in the cavern drawn to him as shocked silence drowned out the roar of battle. Man, dwarf and skaven, every face was pinched with horror at the unfathomable power the grey seer had unleashed. Fur and hair stood on end, patches of ice bobbed upon the surface of the reservoir. The air itself seemed charged, flickering with a weird afterglow along the course the grey seer's annihilating blast had taken. Even Lord Skrolk's blemished face was filled with astonished terror. If the decayed villain still had functioning glands, Thanquol knew they must be spurting the musk of fear like a runt in a snake pit.

The grey seer straightened, holding himself high as he felt the terrified appreciation of his enemies. Then his pride wilted, along with the tremendous strength he had imagined flowing through his limbs only moments before. Thanquol struggled to keep standing, succeeding only in sliding down the length of his staff, wilting into a weary pile upon the stones of the causeway. Bile rose through his throat, burning as he vomited a mix of warpstone and blood. Quivering like a leaf, Thanquol tried to focus his vision. It was a horrible effort, his brain swimming with pulses of pain and throbbing against the inside of his skull as though trying to batter its way out of his head.

Across the stone ledge, Skrolk's eyes were not having the same problem holding the image of his enemy. Gone was the terror, and in its place a snickering scorn.

Thanquol had drawn such incredible power, unleashed such unspeakable havoc, and to what purpose? Skrolk lived, as did more than enough of his vile disciples to slaughter both Thanquol's miserable servitors and the meddling human wizard's agents.

Skrolk's bubbling laughter oozed through the cavern, echoing from the walls. It would be some time before Thanquol could muster the concentration for even the most minor cantrip. Before that happened, he intended to be wearing the grey seer's entrails for a belt.

Thanquol groaned as his vision finally steadied. He saw Skrolk clap his paws together, saw two mammoth shapes emerge from the tunnel. Horror clawed at the grey seer's heart. The things that lurched out onto the ledge were rat ogres, brutes nearly the equal of Boner-ipper in size. Where his bodyguard had prodigious strength and savagery, however, these had the same dis-eased viciousness of the plague monks. Their emaciated bodies were nests of boils and sores, their flesh betray-ing a leprous tint, rabid foam dripping from their black-toothed maws. He didn't need Skrolk's pointing finger to tell him what victim the plague lord had cho-sen for his monsters.

Thanquol tried to lift himself, but his wobbly legs just crumpled beneath his weight. He ripped the escape scroll from his belt, but his pounding head and bleary vision would not cooperate enough to read the com-plex spell.

The grey seer groaned again, smacking his horned head against the cold stone beneath him. It had been a fit of temperamental stupidity, an outburst of tempo-rary madness! Satisfying as obliterating Kratch might have been, it was a woeful blunder tactically.

* * *

JEREMIAS SCRIVNER STRUGGLED to maintain the bonds of shadow wrapped about the gigantic hulk of Boneripper. The rat ogre refused to submit, forcing his huge body onwards, regardless of how much power the wizard put into his spell. Inch by inch, the monster was breaking free, his tiny brain too dull to submit to Scrivner's magic. More formidable even than the grotesque rat-beast had been in Dr Loew's workshop, Boneripper had enough of a mind to focus upon the commands of his master. The rat ogre had been told to attack the wizard, and whatever Scrivner did, he was determined to obey that command.

Scrivner glanced at the gloating grey seer. He knew the fiend's intention. Callous as all his breed, the rat-mage would wait until the wizard was completely and hopelessly occupied by Boneripper, then Thanquol would leap to the attack. Scrivner knew there was no hope that the grey seer would stay his magical assault out of concern for his bodyguard. For any skaven, there was only one life that was not expendable: his own.

The wizard began to slowly fall back along the causeway. If he could put enough distance between himself and Boneripper, he might be able to strike Thanquol before his bodyguard could reach him. He struggled to tighten the wispy fetters wrapped about Boneripper's legs, but the monster stubbornly pressed on, slogging through the arcane chains like a behemoth trudging through a quagmire. Scrivner could not gain enough ground on the brute. If he ended his spell, Boneripper would be upon him before he could even wag a finger at the gloating Thanquol.

'Master!' The harsh bellow sounded from behind Scrivner. The wizard recognised the voice as that of Grimbold Silverbeard. The dwarf had extricated himself from the fight on the scaffold. His pistols spent, his hands instead were filled with black metal objects, round at the base then tapering to a point from which a hemp fuse protruded.

'Back!' Scrivner ordered his minion. The wizard could read the concern in Grimbold's voice, but the dwarf had a much more important role to play in the drama unfolding around the reservoir. If he could not stop the skaven, it would be left to Grimbold to cheat them of their victory. 'Do not interfere,' the wizard snarled when he saw the dwarf set down the bombs and start to reload one of his pistols. A shot at the rat ogre would only enrage him further, allowing the brute to completely break free of Scrivner's tenuous hold. A shot at the grey seer might only wound the fiend, and make Grimbold the new target of Thanquol's wrath. As things stood, Scrivner himself was more expendable than the dwarf.

The magister restored his attention to Boneripper, struggling to push the hulk back. Boneripper growled, snapping his fangs and flexing his claws in a primitive display of his ghastly strength. Scrivner was not intimidated by the brute's bestial boasting; it was enough to tax his mind just keeping the monster enmeshed in his coils.

Scrivner's fixation upon the task at hand bore tragic fruit. Too late was he aware of a new menace, lurking close by. He twisted his body around, shouting a warning, but word came too late.

With skill to match that of the wizard, made all the more impressive because it did not depend upon magic and illusion to accomplish, a black-clad shape emerged from the shadows. Snarling, the shape pounced on Grimbold, knocking the pistol from the dwarf's hands.

Grimbold staggered, his beard darkening as blood seeped into it from a ragged wound in his chest. Stabbed in the back, the dwarf's armour had folded like cheesecloth before the unnatural venom of an assassin's blade. The dwarf had time to stare into the face of his killer before slumping to the ground.

Skrattch Skarpaw sneered at the dying dwarf, raising his poisoned blade for another thrust. The blow never fell. Black blood exploded from Skarpaw's mouth as his body was bisected by a lance of darkness made solid. The assassin's confusion and disbelief was a mirror of the expression that had filled Grimbold's face. He looked from the magic spear that had ripped through him to the causeway. He shook his head, refusing to accept what he saw. The wizard had attacked him, voluntarily abandoning his spell against Boneripper to strike down the dwarf's killer! Madness, Skarpaw's brain screamed, to the last unable to understand the peculiarly human concepts of loyalty and sacrifice.

Skarpaw's body crashed to the causeway, then rolled over the edge, sinking slowly into the cold waters of the reservoir. Only his dropped blade and Grimbold's bleeding body gave silent testimony that he had ever been at all.

Scrivner hastily began to cast a new spell. He knew it was hopeless, and his knowledge was proven as a fierce, vice-like grip closed around him. The wizard was wrenched from the floor, the hot breath of Boneripper washing over him. He felt ribs cracking beneath the cruel pressure of the beast's paws. Boneripper's mutant third arm drew back, the blood-crusted length of its fist-spike poised for the killing blow. The magister spent his last moment invoking a death curse that would take his killer with him. He only hoped that the grey seer was petty enough to still use magic to finish his foe rather than allowing Boneripper's brawn to settle the score.

Neither spell nor fist fell. Confusion showed on Boneripper's dull features, the brute staring in perplexity at the ledge. Scrivner could tell that something unexpected had happened. Diseased cries and a stagnant stench told him what had happened without the need to look. More skaven had arrived, but these were no allies of Boneripper or his master. Easily distracted by the unexpected, the rat ogre had lost his focus.

Where a moment before, Scrivner had braced himself for certain death, now he seized opportunity. Instead of finishing his death curse, he instead wove a new spell from the grey wind of magic. The rat ogre was oblivious to his incantation, Boneripper's dull mind instead watching his master work himself into a fit of anger. The first Boneripper was aware something was amiss was when the physical substance that had been Jeremias Scrivner seeped through his thick fingers in long streamers of darkness. The rat ogre stared stupidly at his empty paws, scratching his horn with his mutant hand.

The darkness that had become the wizard reformed into a human shape only a few feet from the immense monster. Dangerous magic, changing the corporeal into the incorporeal; Scrivner had trusted his spell only as far as he needed to escape Boneripper's clutch. Now the wizard stood between the monster and Grimbold's body. The dwarf had served him faithfully for many years. Scrivner would not abandon him while there was still the flicker of life in him. Not while Grimbold still might have a role to play saving the capital of the entire Empire from a hideous fate.

Boneripper must have smelled Scrivner as he took shape once more. The rat ogre stopped staring at his empty hands and instead glared at the magister. Drool glistened as the monster roared his rage.

The rat ogre started to rush towards Scrivner, but then his roar was drowned out by an even more monstrous sound. The entire cavern shook, the air burst into golden light. The wizard shielded himself with his cloak as ice erupted from the reservoir in bursts. Impossibly powerful magic had been unleashed, sorcery both awesome and reckless, the wild raw malevolence of absolute destruction. He knew he was fortunate that such a spell had not been unleashed upon himself, for there was no curse or charm or protective talisman known to mortals that could have withstood it. It was like the fist of an angry god smiting down from the heavens or up from the hells.

When the aftershock of the arcane blast had dissipated enough for Scrivner to focus his thoughts again, he saw Thanquol staggered on the next causeway. He saw the newly arrived skaven; green-robed plague monks, rushing forwards at the command of their putrescent leader. At the head of the chittering host were a pair of hulking rat ogres, festering kin of Boneripper's breed. True to Scrivner's prediction, these were no allies of the grey seer. Indeed, they seemed oblivious to the wizard in their haste to settle with Thanquol.

Scrivner lifted Grimbold from the ground, moving him just in time to prevent the dwarf from being crushed underfoot by Boneripper as the monster thundered past. With a brain too small to hold Scrivner's illusions, he was intelligent enough to recognise the peril threatening his master. Like a loyal dog, Boneripper was rushing to protect Thanquol from his enemies.

It was not fear for Thanquol that caused Scrivner to shout orders to his men, commanding them to attack the plague monks. It was a matter of choosing the lesser of two evils. Thanquol would use the Wormstone if given the chance. The plague monks, however, might do much worse. Scrivner knew about their fiendish ability to create new diseases and ways of distributing them. Given a chance, they might not only use the Wormstone, they might be capable of replicating the spells that had created it. They might be able to make more!

BONERIPPER PLOUGHED THROUGH the swarming mass of plague monks, smashing and crushing them with his monstrous claws. The diseased ratmen refused to break, chittering and snarling as they leapt upon their hulking attacker. Rusty daggers sank into the rat ogre's leather hide, staves of worm-eaten wood splintered against his bones, yellow fangs ripped at his flesh. The monster's charge floundered as plague monks threw themselves at him with lunatic abandon. Before he had taken more than a dozen steps onto the stone shelf, Boneripper's shape vanished beneath a clinging, clawing mass of ragged green robes and leprous flesh. Even the mutant's prodigious strength faltered before the onslaught. He stumbled, dropping to one knee. A plague monk shrieked as he was crushed by Boneripper's shifting weight, but the wretch's maniacal brethren gave his fate passing notice. Chanting their obscene prayers to their vile god, the plague monks struggled all the harder to bring their prey down.

Rescue came from an unexpected source. Shots rang out, blasting clinging ratmen from Boneripper's body. Scrivner's minions had heard their master's command and rushed to attack their new and horrific foes. Plague monks turned to meet the renewed assault by the humans, snarling their vile shrieks as they surged towards the scaffold. Crazed skaven wielding smouldering censers of rusted iron led the charge, the pestilential fumes spewing from the foul incense almost visibly corrupting their wasted bodies as they scurried to the attack.

Theodor Baer held the survivors of Scrivner's band together, ordering them into a rough skirmish line. Those few who still bore loaded pistols fired into the diseased throng, spilling another pair of ratmen onto the ground. The filthy stink of incense and disease reached out to the men, threatening to engulf them in a fog of plague and decay.

Suddenly, the charging ratmen were lost beneath a shroud of darkness, a cloak of shadow that descended upon them like a falling curtain. The diseased ratmen howled and whined, shrieking and chittering in confusion and frustrated rage. Some, confused by the supernatural darkness, rushed too far forwards, choking as they entered the cloud of noxious fumes spewing from the heavy flail-like censers. Less inured to the smoky filth than the censer bearers, these ratmen writhed on the ground, coughing and bleeding as the fumes overwhelmed their disease-ravaged bodies.

The spell of darkness did no more than delay the charge of the plague monks, however. Lost in a frenzy of bloodlust and hate, the acolytes of Clan Pestilens were not so easily provoked into fright as the hapless minions of Thanquol had been in the basement of the *Orc and Axe*. They used their keen sense of smell to pursue their prey through the murk, emerging on the other side of the wizard's spell in a snarling mass.

Scrivner's agents had not been idle while the plague monks were blinded, however. Instead of holding their skirmish line, as soon as the wizard's spell had struck, the men turned and fled back onto the scaffold. With as much haste as their weary bodies could summon, the men ran, retreating before the vengeful mob of ratmen chittering for their blood.

Such was the maddened bloodlust of the plague monks, they scarcely paused as they scrambled onto the wooden scaffolding to give chase. Ratmen were knocked from the rickety wooden platforms by the reckless haste of their comrades and the press of the frenzied mob behind them. Their shrieks as they fell into the cavern were all but lost beneath the obscene chanting and hungry chittering of those who swarmed across the scaffolding, hot on the heels of their enemies.

Another sound was also lost to the ears of the snarling pack. Designed to support the weight of a few men at a time, the scaffolds groaned and sagged beneath the scrabbling mass of plague monks. Ropes snapped, boards splintered. Too late, some of the plague monks sensed their peril. Fear swept through the swarm of green-cloaked fanatics, transforming into panic as the less desiccated skaven began to vent their glands. No longer did they pursue the tiny band of humans who were climbing onto the stone ledge at the far side of the reservoir. Instead they fought and clawed and pushed to reach the safety of the near ledge, to find refuge from the wooden platforms that creaked and buckled beneath their paws.

Few of the plague monks reached the security of the ledge before, with a titanic groan, the first section of scaffolding broke and tumbled into the chasm. The dissolution of one section aggravated the distress of the others. The plague monks wailed and screamed as the entire scaffold broke away, carrying the swarming fanatics with it as it toppled hundreds of feet to the rocky slope below.

Upon the shelf, Boneripper tore the last stubborn plague monks from his body, smashing them into gory paste upon the floor. The rat ogre, blood dripping from hundreds of cuts and bites, pounded his paws against his throbbing chest, creating a drum-like report. He wiped blood from his jaws, his beady eyes squinting at the ragged survivors from his assault and the ill-fated chase onto the scaffold. The plague monks shivered, frozen with fear. Only their blister-faced chieftain seemed unfazed by the menace of the rat ogre. Calmly, Lord Skrolk clapped his leprous hands together and pointed a shrivelled claw at Boneripper.

Two gigantic shapes turned at the plague lord's summons, their rheumy eyes fixing upon Boneripper's mangled bulk. Nox and Pox lumbered away from the causeway, leaving Thanquol to the plague monks who had already crawled out ahead of them. Like roaming wolves, the two diseased rat ogres circled their prey, their blackened teeth grinning from behind their crusty lips. They were not so far gone to the ravages of pestilence and plague that their tiny brains had forgotten the pleasures of life; such as an enemy wounded and outnumbered, just waiting for their fangs to close about his throat.

Nox growled, a sound like the wheeze of a dying mammoth. The rat ogre's snarl drew Boneripper's attention, the mutant brute roaring his own defiance at the decayed abomination. Nox, however, made no move to close with Boneripper. A vile cunning lingered in the disease-ravaged minds of the plague-ogres.

As Boneripper turned towards Nox, Pox charged the mutant's back. The plague-ogre's thick arms wrapped about Boneripper's body, crushing him in a bear hug that pinned his limbs against his sides. Pox's slobbering mouth worried at Boneripper's neck, shredding his flesh and soaking the abomination's muzzle in the mutant's dark blood. Boneripper shrieked in pain as the plague-ogre's fangs gnawed into him. He tried to twist his head around, to slash Pox with his horn. The plague-ogre ducked the clumsy attack, shifting his grip and sinking his fangs into Boneripper's shoulder.

Seeing Pox launch his attack, Nox rushed the besieged Boneripper, rabid froth bubbling from his diseased jaws. The plague-ogre raised a clawed hand to slash open Boneripper's belly, but the blow never fell. Boneripper slashed at the monster with his tail, driving the spiked steel ball Thanquol had nailed to the tip of the rat ogre's scaly tail against the knee of the plague-ogre. Nox gibbered in pain as his knee exploded beneath the strike, the bones of his lower leg shattering as the plague-ogre's full weight pressed down upon them. Nox smashed against the floor, fangs snapping from rotten gums as his face smacked into stone.

Startled by his fellow's alarming distress, Pox failed to remember his earlier evasions of Boneripper's horn. The steel-capped sliver of bone scraped across the plague-ogre's face, bringing treacly blood spurting from a deep gash that ran from forehead to chin. Pox reared back, instinctively recoiling from the source of his wound. Boneripper's mutant arm, unrestrained by Pox's crushing hug, stabbed at the plague-ogre's head. The monster released Boneripper and staggered away, clutching at his blood-soaked face.

Boneripper sniffed at the putrid eye impaled upon his fist-spike, then growled his own challenge to the plague-ogres. Slowly, the mangled monsters lurched after their foe, snarling their own savage defiance. Beast against beast against beast, there could be no quarter in such a struggle; the only measure of victory would be the cold still bodies of the vanquished.

JEREMIAS SCRIVNER STARED down into the bloody face of Grimbold Silverbeard. There was more shame than pain in the dwarf's eyes as he stared back. That changed as the wizard's palm slapped against his grisly wound. The dwarf gritted his teeth as he felt the magister's magic pour into his body.

'I am no healer,' Scrivner warned him. 'Against the poison of the skaven, even a healer might be of no use. But my magic will slow the ratkin's venom.'

Grimbold nodded, fumbling at the straps of his apron. Tearing it loose, he exposed a set of bandoliers that criss-crossed his chest. More of the curious metal bombs were secured to the loops of the belts. 'Th… the fuses… will burn… even in … the water.' The dwarf grinned, an effect ruined by the blood staining his teeth. 'No time… to set them… proper. But I know… where they will do the job!' A grim laugh rumbled from the dwarf's throat.

Wizard and dwarf looked up as they were joined upon the causeway. Johann Dietrich had not followed Theodor Baer across the scaffold. Something more terrible than skaven and monsters had seized the smuggler's mind. He pointed at his torn shirt, at the crawling things he could see just beneath the surface of his skin.

'Why didn't you tell me!' Johann demanded.

'Would knowing have made any difference?' Scrivner answered coldly. 'There is nothing that can be done.'

'But I should have known!' growled Johann. 'You should have told me!'

'Count it a blessing, manling,' coughed Grimbold. 'It's not every one learns the hour of his death. It's not every one can make his last minutes such to make his ancestors proud.'

Scrivner pointed at Johann. 'Crawl into a hole and die, or stay and help avenge your brother. The choice is yours, but choose quickly.'

Before Johann could even think about the wizard's words, the shadows seemed to reach out and surround the magister. Scrivner's figure darkened until it was indistinguishable from the blackness around him. Then, as man and shadow merged into one, both slowly faded into nothingness.

Grimbold shook his head sadly and started to drag himself across the causeway, leaving Johann alone with his thoughts and his decision.

GREY SEER THANQUOL watched with horror as Skrolk's abominable minions charged the causeway. Even the onset of Boneripper's valiant attack had not been enough to break their diseased determination. Worse, the stupid rat ogre had allowed himself to become embroiled in a scuffle with Skrolk's disgusting beasts, leaving Thanquol alone against the plague monks.

Thanquol managed to rise to his feet, leaning heavily on his staff for support. His head was spinning, swimming with colours and sounds only he could sense. His guts felt on fire, his limbs still shook as muscles twitched and shivered. Too much power used unwisely had left the grey seer as helpless as a whelp.

It was fortunate, then, that the last of his own underlings did not appreciate just how helpless their tyrannical leader was. If they had, they would certainly have abandoned him, or perhaps even tried to gain some favour with Clan Pestilens by delivering Thanquol to Lord Skrolk. However, the grey seer's awful displays of sorcery had impressed upon his minions the magnitude of his power, filling their hearts and minds with a lingering fear.

Instead of fleeing, the warlock engineers who had circled the entire reservoir to avoid Scrivner and join Thanquol pulled pistols and fired into the oncoming plague monks. The foremost of the fanatics shrieked and fell into the icy waters; those behind hesitated, unwilling to be the next to die from a sudden barrage.

Thanquol snarled at the two warlock engineers. Killing the plague monks was all fine and good, but the vermin had more important work to do. He pointed a talon at one masked ratman, gesturing at the leather bag slung from his left shoulder. 'Leave the Wormstone,' Thanquol snapped through clenched fangs. He pointed to an almost identical leather bag hanging from the engineer's other shoulder. 'Keep-keep the heretic-maggots back-away while I do what needs to be done!'

The warlock engineer nodded his head in almost eager fashion and dropped the heavy leather bag down beside his comrade. His gloved paws rummaged in the other bag, producing a globe of smoky glass. Tightening valves on the sides of his mask, the skaven scurried forwards and hurled the globe at the lurking plague monks. The glass grenade shattered on the stone of the causeway, spewing an acidic fog that corroded the flesh from the plague monks caught in the mephitic cloud. Shrieking in agony, the wounded skaven leapt into the reservoir, but the cold waters did nothing to stifle their burning flesh. Other plague monks, killed outright, lay sprawled upon the causeway, foul steam rising from their smouldering carcasses.

The warlock engineer chittered madly as he saw the terror on the faces of the other plague monks and pulled a second poison wind globe from his bag.

Grey Seer Thanquol turned his attention away from the globadier, fixing his gaze instead upon the engineer beside him. He gestured at the bag the globadier had discarded and at the similar one the warlock engineer held. 'You, dump-pour Wormstone into pool-pool, quick-quick!' The grey seer put a growl into his voice to spur the hesitant engineer onwards. Thanquol had no intention of getting any closer to the Wormstone than he already was, that risk he was perfectly content to leave to his underling. Once the reservoir was safely contaminated, he'd then be free to use the escape scroll, secure in knowing that his victory was complete.

The warlock engineer drew heavy gloves of chain and copper from his belt before opening either of the bags. Gingerly, he started to lift one of the wine bottles from the bag. Thanquol glanced away for only an instant, checking that the globadier was still holding the plague monks back. When he looked again at the engineer, he found the skaven sprawled across the causeway, his throat slashed from ear to ear. Standing over him, dripping wet from his swim in the reservoir, was old Skrim Gnawtail. The Clan Skaul spy glared at Thanquol, fangs bared in a contemptuous snarl.

'Thanquol-meat is finished!' Skrim snapped. The spy's grin broadened as his claws closed around the strap of the leather bag holding the bottles of Wormstone. 'I scent-see your treachery, grey-flea! I shall be hero of Under-Altdorf when they learn I saved them from your poison!'

The old ratman grunted with effort as he lifted the heavy burden. His crooked back trembled as he tried to straighten. For an instant, his attention was away from Thanquol. It was a mistake Skrim would never have made in his younger days, but those days were long past. Crippled by age, instincts dulled by time, the spy could not concentrate upon both the grey seer and the heavy bag.

Thanquol sprang at the spy, smashing the metal head of his staff into Skrim's grey head. The spy uttered a shrill gasp, then crumpled to the floor, blood spurting from his cracked skull. Thanquol scrambled to grab the bag of Wormstone, but the satchel was already slipping from Skrim's dead clutch. The grey seer gave voice to a furious wail as he watched the leather bag drop from Skrim's fingers and sink into the black depths of the reservoir, its lethal contents harmless and inert inside their bottles.

Scowling, Thanquol kicked Skrim's lifeless body, the ferocity of his vindictive rage snapping the spy's neck as his foot smashed against the side of his head. Still not content, Thanquol swatted the twitching corpse with his staff, sending it rolling into the icy reservoir.

Turning, the grey seer smiled as he saw the second bag of Wormstone bottles. There would still be enough to poison the reservoir and kill his enemies! Thanquol reached his paw towards the leather bag. Suddenly, he cringed away from his objective. Standing just beyond the grey seer, between himself and the lone globadier holding back the crazed hordes of Clan Pestilens, was a figure draped in a charcoal-grey cloak and hood. Once more, Thanquol felt the wizard's intense gaze bore down upon him.

Thanquol fought down the fear Scrivner's abrupt appearance provoked. The grey seer fingered his protective talismans, wondering if any of them would be potent enough to dispel the magister's magic. He did not display his fear, however. Instead he screwed his body up into his most imperious posture.

'Leave-go,' Thanquol pronounced. 'You may warn-tell the humans not to drink-taste the water. It is the traitor-rats of Under-Altdorf I will destroy! You go tell-warn the Emperor, be good hero for all man-things! This does generous Thanquol offer his worthy enemy!'

Mocking laughter rewarded the grey seer's proposal. Slowly, his stormy eyes still fixed upon Thanquol's beady orbs, Scrivner drew his sword from its sheath. 'Your sorcery has fled-betrayed you,' the wizard's chilling hiss sounded, forming the words in perfect Queekish. 'Draw-take your blade, Grey Seer, and meet-find your death with spleen!'

Thanquol backed away from the wizard's challenge. His paw fell to his belt, but it was not his sword he fingered but rather the escape scroll. Would he have enough time, he wondered, to invoke the spell before Scrivner could run him through with his sword. Suddenly, Thanquol found himself with more pressing concerns.

Peering past the wizard, Thanquol could see the globadier engulfed by a stream of burning green filth. The warlock engineer's leather garments dissolved in the vile spray, his fur and flesh dripping off his bones as the corrosive consumed him utterly. His dripping skeleton made a loathsomely squishy sound as it collapsed to the floor.

Beyond the globadier's steaming wreckage, Thanquol could see the ratman's killer. Lord Skrolk wiped a paw across his dripping jaws, wiping away little burning bits of residue from his mouth. Like the fabled plague dragon Bubos, Skrolk had used his magic to spit searing death at the warlock engineer. The plague lord chuckled grotesquely as he plodded forwards, pestilential vapours rising from the bowl of his censer-staff. The fanatic's decayed paw caressed the ratskin binding of the massive book that swung from a chain on his belt. Thanquol's fur bristled with horrified recognition: the book was the *Liber Bubonicus*, an abominable artefact stolen from the disciples of the horrific Dark God Nurgle by Clan Pestilens long ago. Thanquol, and indeed all the grey seers, had thought the abomination long since destroyed. Knowing that Skrolk had studied the book's spells of plague and destruction, the grey seer found himself more eager than ever to evoke his escape spell.

Scrivner saw the horror in Thanquol's eyes. The wizard knew that, for now at least, the grey seer could not draw upon his own magic, his body still recovering from the rampant excess of the spell that had obliterated Kratch. If he was still confident in his own powers, he would hardly have tried to wheedle a deal from the wizard. Scrivner had sensed the discharge of Skrolk's black magic, knew that there was another foe who was not so drained as the grey seer. For Thanquol to find terror rather than rescue in such magecraft, Scrivner knew the perpetrator could only be one of the plague priests, creatures he had already determined were an even greater threat than the grey seer.

The grey-cloaked wizard spun about, glaring at Skrolk just as the plague lord opened his rotten mouth once more. A spew of maggot-ridden broth exploded from the decayed skaven's jaws, a burning stream of noxious putrescence that glowed with the filthy light of unclean gods. Such a breath of rotting disease had destroyed the globadier, now Lord Skrolk evoked the same magic to settle with the meddling wizard and the cringing Thanquol.

Talons of shadow swept down from the ceiling and up from beneath the causeway, intercepting the stream of plague-magic, swirling about the filth in a complex pattern that echoed the motions of Scrivner's wildly gesturing hands. Thanquol blinked in disbelief as he saw Skrolk's ghastly sorcery scattered by the magister's arcane powers. Skrolk, however, was far from finished. Snarling, the plague lord reached to his rotten face, tearing one of his blemished eyes from his decayed skull. Thanquol realised with horror that Skrolk's staring eyes were not real, simply cleverly painted chips of warpstone!

The plague lord uttered another croak of laughter as he popped his false eye into his mouth. Skrolk seemed to swell with power as the weird energies of the warpstone rushed through him.

Scrivner's voice came in a low hiss, forming slithering words that seemed to charge the very air. He was drawing upon the last reserves of his own power to ward off what was coming, tapping spells and energies that would drive most men mad. He invoked cold gods, ancient and strange, called to the slithering forces of lost worlds. Secret words, forbidden before the first man crawled from the slime, rasped past the magister's hidden lips. His fingers cracked as he forced them into gestures nearly impossible for human anatomy to mimic. He only prayed it would be enough to stop the surging malignity of Skrolk's arcane might.

Thanquol was less hopeful. He opened the escape scroll, his mouth started to form the first words of the incantation. Then his eyes darted to the bottles of Wormstone lying on the causeway. He looked up, grinning as he saw Skrolk and Scrivner locked in their wizard's duel. Focused upon each other, there was nothing either of his enemies could do to stop him now!

Thanquol the mighty reached into the leather bag, snickering contentedly as he pulled the first bottle into the dim light.

JEREMIAS SCRIVNER STRUGGLED to maintain his sorcerous shield against the noxious spellcraft of Lord Skrolk. Foul spell after foul spell smashed against the arcane defences he had erected, splattering against the shadowy folds of his magic like waves battering a shore. Skrolk did not throw his warpstone-fuelled power into a single burst of havoc. Instead the plague lord used it to craft a barrage of deathly magic that taxed Scrivner's powers to their limit. Beads of blood dripped from the wizard's pores as he struggled to maintain his focus and his strength. Inch by ghastly inch, he could feel Skrolk's malignity prevailing.

The plague lord could smell the weakness of his foe, and croaked with bubbling laughter. Skrolk's false eye saw the world in waves of purple and green; it had been many years since he had clawed his natural eyes from his face after beholding the wondrous putrescence of Arch-Plaguelord Nurglitch. Sorcery gave him sight, the same sorcery that now allowed him to crush the grey wizard and the grey seer like a pair of gnats. Slow and persistent as the holy poxes of the Horned Rat, Skrolk brought his insidious magic of corruption and decay gnawing at Scrivner's defences.

A bellow snapped Skrolk's attention from the wizard. Scrivner wilted to the floor of the causeway as the plague lord's barrage of spells abruptly ceased, completely drained by his desperate efforts to hold back the monster's power.

It was a different sort of monster and a different sort of power that threatened Lord Skrolk. Towering over the plague lord, his body torn and gashed, Boneripper glowered at this festering toad of a rat who thought to kill his master. The severed head of Nox hung from one of the rat ogre's claws, the better part of Pox's belly was skewered on the brute's horn.

'Boneripper! Kill-kill!' came a frantic shout from further along the causeway. The rat ogre, only a moment before looking as though he might pass out from fatigue and injury, abruptly rallied at the sound of Thanquol's shriek. Snarling, he slapped his chest with Nox's mangled head.

Lord Skrolk glared back at the beast with his last eye. The plague lord did not need spells to deal with such a brute. He tightened his hold on his staff, flicking a pinch of yellow powder into the smouldering bowl of the censer. 'Boneripper, die-die!' Skrolk snarled, lunging at the hulking brute before he could attack.

Boneripper swatted at the plague lord with his claw. Skrolk ducked beneath the wounded rat ogre's swipe, striking at him in turn with his sinister staff. The rod of corruption sank through the meat of Boneripper's arm as though it were butter, blisters and maggots spreading from the grisly, gangrenous wound. Boneripper howled in pain, lifting his injured arm to his face, sucking at the putrid wound in a futile effort to ease the pain.

'No-no! Stupid brute! Kill Skrolk! Kill-kill!'

But it was already too late for Thanquol to command his bodyguard. Boneripper had drawn a lungful of the foul fumes spilling from Skrolk's censer into his body when he voiced his painful howl. Coupled with the vileness he drew into his belly when he sucked at his wound, the rat ogre's body was beset by the supernatural poxes of Clan Pestilens and their most abominable plague priest. Boneripper slumped to his knees as his flesh became pallid. His eyes rolled back in his skull as pus began dripping from his ears. The rat ogre's horns and claws became brittle, crumbling like clay. Boneripper opened his mouth to snap at the gloating plague lord, but his fangs fell out of his bleeding gums.

Whining like a whipped cur, Boneripper crashed onto his face, his skull bursting like a crushed egg as he struck.

Skrolk licked the rat ogre's blood from his face as he turned back to his other foes. 'Where-where were we?' the plague lord snarled. 'Oh yes-yes! First the wizard, then the fool!'

Lord Skrolk lifted his paw, the claws glowing with foul energies. Scrivner could only watch as the plague lord began to work his magic. Thanquol fingered his protective charms, but knew that they would be useless. He could still smell the warpstone fuelling Skrolk's malignant sorcery.

Before Skrolk could unleash his death spell, he was again beset by an enemy from behind. The plague lord's followers, faced with Boneripper's rage and the dire magics being unleashed by their own prophet, had abandoned Skrolk, diving into the reservoir in their bid to find safety. In deserting their master, they had left the path open for Boneripper. In destroying Boneripper, Skrolk had left the path open for a different kind of adversary.

Johann did not shout or roar challenge to the decayed monster, he did not announce himself in some honourable call to battle. What he did was climb onto

Boneripper's lifeless mass and leap down upon Skrolk, locking one arm about the skaven's waist, another about his throat.

Skrolk flailed in Johann's grasp, slithering and squirming like an eel in that clutch. Then the plague lord's diseased sight focused upon the state of the arm that was wrapped about his neck. He saw the ugly green-black worm growths squirming up from the man's skin. Johann Dietrich – last victim of the Wormstone!

Even the decayed face of Lord Skrolk was capable of expressing the horror the sight of those writhing worms evoked. He knew what sort of death the worms would bring, and knew they were erupting from the man's body, being drawn into his own by the scent of warpstone in his blood! Skrolk redoubled his efforts to break free, clawing at the face of his captor, but Johann would not relent.

Johann met the silent gaze of Scrivner's grey eyes. He saw a respect in those eyes, something approaching admiration beneath the swirling storm of shadow and fog. The wizard gave the slightest nod of his head. The smuggler tightened his hold upon the struggling Skrolk and launched himself into the icy waters of the reservoir, dragging the squealing monster with him into the dark depths.

Scrivner looked back at the last of the skaven. Thanquol was perched at the edge of the causeway, upended wine bottles in each paw. More bottles lay empty all around the grey seer's feet.

The wizard glared coldly at the laughing skaven. His own icy smile was hidden beneath the folds of his scarf. He turned his head and shouted across the reservoir to a little shape lying upon the causeway nearest the restraining wall. His words were thick and harsh, the stony tones of Khazalid, the ancient tongue of the dwarfs.

'Honour your ancestors, Grimbold Silverbeard, and tell the gods the way of your death!'

The shape on the causeway shifted slightly, then plunged into the black embrace of the reservoir. An instant later, the entire cavern shook with such a roar as made even Thanquol's rage-filled spell seem the babble of a child. The shaking tremor spread, the roar intensified and the entire restraining wall seemed to lift up, then come crashing down again!

GREY SEER THANQUOL stared in mute horror as the reservoir rushed from the ruptured wall, hurtling down into the chasm, rushing into the darkness. The cataract of water bore with it the Wormstone powder, speeding its poisonous taint far from where it would wreak havoc upon the people of Altdorf. Even the traitors of Under-Altdorf would be spared; such a torrent would hardly stop at the pools and streams the skaven used, it would rage onwards until it reached the sunken ocean beneath the world, far beyond the reach of men or dwarfs or goblins or even skaven.

It was not fair! Just as he had accomplished his victory, Thanquol had been cheated of his triumph! The glory and power, the authority and riches that the Lords of Decay would have showered upon him! All of it lost, lost because of that heretic Skrolk and those traitors Burnfang and Gnawtail, Skarpaw and Kratch! Stolen from him by that damn meddling human mage-thing!

Thanquol saw the cloaked wizard rise weakly to his feet. Now it was Scrivner who was the weak one! The grey seer drew his sword, the foul rune engraved upon the black blade glowing evilly in the shadows. He wanted to test Thanquol's blade, did he? Well, the grey seer was going to show him how much courage there was in his spleen!

Scrivner stared back at Thanquol as the grey seer stalked towards him. This time it was the wizard's turn to look at something just beyond his enemy. A hiss of laughter rasped from the magister's muffled face.

Thanquol spun about, his eyes narrowing with outrage as he saw the wizard's men rushing at him from the far side of the causeway. Having escaped across the now destroyed scaffold, they were returning, rushing to their master's aid.

'Strike, coward-meat,' Scrivner jeered. 'Or does Grey Seer Thanquol fear-shiver because my warriors will avenge their master!'

Thanquol snarled at Scrivner, but refused to rise to the wizard's bait. The magister was trying to delay him, keep him lingering about this place long enough for his man-things to get him. Thanquol had lost enough already, there was nothing to be gained risking his pelt further.

The grey seer opened his scroll, his lips moving in a rapid stream of spits and squeaks. Abruptly there was a crack like lightning and a stench of brimstone. A black cloud of smoke lazily swirled about the place where Thanquol had stood.

SCRIVNER'S MEN STARED in amazement at the deathly cloud, stunned by the grey seer's sorcerous disappearance. The wizard himself simply shook his head sadly, wondering if perhaps the world might have been made safer trading a Jeremias Scrivner to remove a Grey Seer Thanquol.

'We failed you, master,' Theodor apologised, taking Scrivner's arm and supporting the weakened magister as he started back along the causeway.

The wizard shook his head, pointing to the ruptured wall of the reservoir. Grimbold had worked on the Kaiserschwalbe. The dwarf had known the exact spot where a little explosive would do a lot of damage. The entire reservoir was draining away, taking with it the vile poison of the skaven. There would be much hardship and suffering in Altdorf in the weeks and months to come. It might take years before the Kaiserschwalbe could be repaired and in that time, the city would be forced to find other ways to satisfy its thirst. Water-barons would grow rich carting potable water into the capital, the poor would be reduced to boiling the polluted waters of the Reik. Unrest and disorder would follow hard upon such a crisis, politicians and nobles exploiting it towards their own ends, growing fat off the suffering of the masses. The authorities would be busy trying to maintain the peace, and with their attention diverted, many terrible things would be free to slink into Altdorf's dark streets and forgotten corners.

Scrivner would have spared Altdorf its suffering, but Thanquol had left him no choice. To save the city from the horrible fate the grey seer had planned for it, the reservoir had to be broken.

'Failed?' Scrivner asked Theodor. He pointed at the one section of reservoir wall that had resisted Grimbold's demolition. Like the outer surface, the inside of the wall had born a fresco. Despite the build-up of algae and the ravages of time, the subject of the fresco was still intact, almost whole despite the destruction all around it. Theodor's mouth dropped as he recognised whose image it was depicted on the tiles.

'Magnus the Pious!' the watchman gasped.

Scrivner nodded his hooded head. 'Saviour of the Empire,' he said. 'But to save it, he first had to destroy the corruption within it. That is the way of saviours, if they would succeed, they must know when they must play the part of the destroyer.'

Black smoke and green lightning swirled about Grey Seer Thanquol as his body was thrust through the daemon world of Chaos. Every hair on the ratman's pelt stood on end as he became a thing of substance and shape once more. Thanquol hated those terrifying retreats into the maddening realm beyond the spheres of order. Even though it passed almost quicker than a single heartbeat, he could not shake the horror of even so brief a glimpse at planes of existence alien and hostile to creatures of flesh and bone. It was a door that was opened only in moments of the most dire duress, and shut again as swiftly. Yet he could not help but feel the malevolent gaze of hungry eyes watching him as he blinked between worlds, daemon things that might, with the least effort, close the door before he had passed through it!

The thought was horrible enough to make the grey seer's empty glands clench. He shivered at the idea of being trapped in that horrible void between the physical and the astral, his very soul nothing but a plaything for monsters of the aethyr, his only companions those ever watching eyes of malice and hate.

Thanquol fell into a wary crouch, his staff held before him to ward off lurking foes. Eyes glittered at him from the darkness, bright yellow eyes wide with the most rapt attention. For an instant, he thought that some of those daemon things had passed through the doorway with him when he used his spell to shatter the harmony of the spheres. His paws scrambled beneath the folds of his robe for even the smallest pebble of warpstone he might have forgotten, anything that might give him the power to fend off, or at least run away from, such ghastly foes.

A familiar smell made Thanquol's terrified expression tighten into a sneer of annoyance and contempt. He knew that smell, the stink of the mangy felines man-things kept as pets. There must be dozens of the vile beasts all around him, filling the air with their reek.

Now that the grey seer's eyes were completely adjusted to physical colours and a world where light and darkness existed as separate and disparate things, Thanquol could see that he was in some man-thing's cellar, a dingy little brick-walled room filled to bursting with clutter. Old chairs, empty barrels, mouldy portraits of long-dead birth-kin, the accumulated rubbish of several generations of garbage collecting humans. Beneath, around, and on top of the clutter, a riotous array of cats were curled into little frightened balls of fur and eyes.

Thanquol hissed at the closest of the beasts, sending the flat-eared tabby scurrying backwards beneath a three-legged table, its frightened eyes never leaving the grey seer. It started yowling, a quivering sound quickly picked up by other cats scattered about the cellar. The grey seer scratched at his ears, deciding he'd never heard quite so abominable a sound.

A voice called down from the room above the cellar, the soft shrill sort of voice Thanquol knew commonly indicated an older breeder among the humans, what the man-things called a woman. 'Karl! Franz! Beatrice! My little babies! What is going on down there?'

Thanquol's eyes darted from side to side, scanning the rubbish for some new sign of foes. It took several breaths before he realised that the human was calling down to the menagerie of shabby cats. The grey seer ground his teeth together. After all he had suffered, all he had lost today, this was the final indignity – jumping at a bunch of snivelling cats!

'What is all that racket, babies?' the woman called down again. Thanquol could hear a door open, a little sliver of light shining down into the cellar. He could hear a step creak as someone started to descend. 'What are you dong? Do you have a rat cornered down here?'

Thanquol's lips pulled back, exposing his sharp fangs. He'd worked up quite the appetite, what with all the fighting and leading and run–tactical withdrawals. Eating the stringy meat of a cat was one of the few things a skaven found too revolting to contemplate, but an old human breeder…

'Don't get too close to that old rat, babies,' the woman cooed, her steps now rapid as she descended the stairway. 'He might bite you and make you sick, darlings!'

Grey Seer Thanquol rolled his eyes. He hoped she was fat, at least. It was going to be a long trip back to Skavenblight and he'd need something to nibble on along the way.

'I have a broom, sweeties!' the old woman called as she stepped down onto the floor. 'I'll swat that old rat…'

Her words faded into a horrified gargle, her eyes rolling into the back of her head as she fainted dead away at sight of the ghastly creature standing at the foot of the stairs.

Thanquol watched impassively as the old woman's body crashed to the ground. He let a pleased hiss rasp through his fangs as he bent over her. She was one of the fattest, plumpest specimens he's seen in quite some time.

In the long catalogue of things that had gone wrong today, Thanquol was happy to steal any crumb from the Horned Rat's larder. At least he'd have a full belly when he made the trip to Skavenblight. Perhaps by the time he got there, he'd have concocted a lie to tell the Lords of Decay.

Perhaps he'd even think of one good enough to keep Seerlord Kritislik from blasting him into a greasy paste...

ABOUT THE AUTHOR

C. L. Werner was a diseased servant of the Horned Rat long before his first story in *Inferno!* magazine. His Black Library credits include the Chaos Wastes books *Palace of the Plague Lord* and *Blood for the Blood God*, *Mathias Thulmann: Witch Hunter*, *Runefang* and the *Brunner the Bounty Hunter* trilogy. Currently living in the American south-west, he continues to write stories of mayhem and madness set in the Warhammer World.

Visit the author's website at www.clwerner.wordpress.com

WARHAMMER

PALACE OF THE PLAGUE LORD

C•L•WERNER

ISBN 978-1-84416-491-2

ISBN 978-1-84416-417-2